Praise for the novels of
Louise Candlish

'A brilliantly told, emotionally charged tale'
Dorothy Koomson

'Heartbreaking and heartwarming all at once.
We couldn't read it fast enough'
Cosmopolitan

'Moving and thought-provoking'
Daily Mail

'An emotional page-turner'
Marie Claire

'Will have you racing to get to the final chapter'
**** *She*

'Page-turning, thought-provoking'
Glamour

The Day You Saved My Life

My Life

Louise Candlish

sphere

SPHERE

First published in Great Britain as a paperback original in 2012 by Sphere

Copyright © Louise Candlish 2012

The moral right of the author has been asserted.

A CIP catalogue record for this book
is available from the British Library.

ISBN 978-0-7515-4355-1

Typeset in Sabon by M Rules
Printed and bound in Great Britain by
Clays Ltd, St Ives plc

Papers used by Sphere are from well-managed forests
and other responsible sources.

MIX
Paper from
responsible sources
FSC® C104740

Sphere
An imprint of
Little, Brown Book Group
100 Victoria Embankment
London EC4Y 0DY

An Hachette UK Company
www.hachette.co.uk

www.littlebrown.co.uk

For Chuck Wills, RIP, and Heather McCarry

Acknowledgements

Thank you to Emma Beswetherick, Dan Mallory, David Shelley, Lucy Icke, Charlie King, Emma Graves, Tamsin Kitson, Madeleine Feeny, and the rest of the brilliant team at Little, Brown who have brought this book to life. Also to Jo Dickinson for her earlier, invaluable part in its shaping and to Emma Stonex for a super-sharp edit.

Many thanks to Claire Paterson at Janklow & Nesbit; also to Rebecca Folland, Tim Glister, Kirsty Gordon and Jessie Botterill in the London office.

Thank you to Julia Harris-Voss for patient help with French and for her library of Paris books. Two I recommend are *Paris, Paris: Journey into the City of Light* by David Downie and *Chic Shopping Paris* by Rebecca Magniant and Alison Harris.

The photograph Alexa gives James in the story is inspired by Robert Doisneau's 'Swimmers on the Pont d'Iéna during the Occupation', c. 1944, featured in *Paris Pictured* by Julian Stallabrass.

The line of poetry mentioned by Joanna is from 'When You Are Old' by William Butler Yeats.

Finally, my heartfelt gratitude to Nips, Greta, Jane, Michael, John, Heather, June, Joanna, Karen, Lucy, Monique, Jo, Bernie, Sara-Jade, Kate, Mandy, Nigel, Sharon, Gerry, Elissa, Pat, Mark, Mats 'n' Jo, Julia (again) and all other friends and family who may have suffered earache during the production of this book. I know I've gone on a bit.

Part One

'Il y a une personne à l'eau en Seine'

Chapter 1

Paris

There was nothing about the riverboat itself that foretold of a terrible accident.

Quite different from the Seine's famous *bateaux mouches*, the ones you saw with tourists and schoolchildren straining over the rails to call to pedestrians on the bank below, it was small and quaint, with wooden decks, a shaded roof and open sides. On the lower deck there were steamer chairs for sunbathers and a little bar that served wine in proper glasses and coffee in old-fashioned china cups. Staff, who wore spotless naval white, were delightfully quick to smile at the passengers.

Very nice, Joanna Walsh thought. Just how I remember Paris.

'Comfortable?' she asked her daughter, turning optimistically towards her. But Holly just murmured something unintelligible and gazed blindly at the water.

Please enjoy this, Joanna pleaded silently; for Mikey's sake, if not your own.

This was, however, a moot point since the boy was asleep in his pushchair, which was wedged fast against the rails. They'd boarded late and got two of the last seats on the upper deck, commandeering just enough legroom to avoid having to extract Mikey from the buggy and fold it away. Once he lost consciousness, Holly liked him to stay that way for as long as possible. If it was down to Joanna, she'd have woken him, for he had not been on a boat before and would surely enjoy the sensation of sailing, all children did: that lovely slippery illusion that it was the buildings that were in motion and not you, making you want to reach out and hold them still.

'Really packed, isn't it?' Holly said, starting, almost as if she'd forgotten where she was.

'You'd expect that,' Joanna said. 'It's Paris in June, the honeymoon season. Everyone wants to take a river trip, don't they? It's the romantic thing to do.'

But Holly had used up her words and the only reply Joanna got to this was a sniff, followed by a blink, followed by a yawn. She was used to the rhythm by now – sniff blink yawn, sniff blink yawn. There was nothing sullen about it, nothing disrespectful, but it served its purpose in repelling further attempts at conversation.

No matter: with piano jazz dripping gently from its public address system, the boat was setting off from its pier at Pont d'Iéna, and Joanna wanted to concentrate. Soon, the music gave way to the tour commentary. They were about to share all the treasures of historic Paris, it said (in English, thankfully), treasures she had last shared with her sister and parents over twenty years ago. One of the first, a bridge with golden statues standing ablaze in the sun, made many of the tourists gasp and raise their cameras to their faces; some even sprang to their feet. Joanna had decided not to take any pictures herself but to buy the souvenir brochure at the end: that way she'd miss nothing and the photos would be ten times better. She didn't want to spend this whole trip working out the best angles by which to remember it later.

The curve towards the Pont des Invalides was gentle, the pace of the engines brisk, and she felt her excitement grow. 'Look,' she said, half to herself, 'that must be the Tuileries up ahead. We're almost at the Louvre already.' They'd been to the gallery

4

yesterday and the memory gave her a disquieting feeling, made her listen more closely on the words of the commentary: Louis XVI . . . the storming of the Bastille . . . the guillotine's merciless blade . . . the Seine running red with blood. This last prompted Joanna – and several others – to peer down at the water in fear of some sinister transformation, but from the upper deck, even on a hot, thin day like today, the river was green-black, sucking the sunlight as if into the kind of depths found far out to sea. Were they travelling upstream or down? She had no idea, but you could see the infamous currents tussling below the surface, fast and evasive as eels. In a way, it *was* sinister.

'Shall I get us something from the bar downstairs?' she asked Holly, coming up for air again. 'An ice-cream, maybe?'

Holly shrugged. 'I'm not hungry.'

'Then what about a cold drink?' She allowed a smidgen of impatience to rise. 'Come on, Holls, perk up a bit! We'll be back home the day after tomorrow and you'll have missed all the fun.'

At last Holly's eyes connected with hers and Joanna read the message in them as plainly as if in print: *What's the point?* It was not Holly speaking, she knew, it was the depression, but for once she wanted to defy the professionals' advice and let her tongue work unbitten: 'Mikey's the point, you silly girl! Your son is the point, just as you were mine, and still *are* mine, even if I hardly recognise you any more!'

But she couldn't do that, of course she couldn't. 'Right,' she said, brightly, 'I'll choose you something. Back in a minute . . .' As she left, she touched Holly's shoulder, hoping to communicate something positive by the gesture, to effect some miraculous reconnection.

It was oddly pleasurable, standing in the queue for the kiosk. The boat felt steady and powerful beneath her feet, easing them closer to the left bank and into the narrower waters of the Ile de la Cité. Then, just as she was about to be served, there was the sombre facade of Notre-Dame itself – so soon! – heralded by a rise in enthusiasm in the tone of the commentator and a story of a bell that rang in F-sharp only on the most significant of occasions. Joanna wondered what those occasions might be, and then she fancied the bell sounding out right at that very moment, jolting Holly from her daze, exorcising her of her demons like something from a fairytale.

More and more she was thinking in terms of fairytales, of miracles, as if ready now to give up on the possibility of human salvation for her daughter.

Reaching its optimum vantage point of the great cathedral, the boat slowed and the photography became even more frenzied, only one or two of those on the lower deck remaining in their seats. Now Joanna pictured Holly as she almost certainly was, the only passenger aboard who was unmoved by the sight, perhaps not even glancing up at it, and she allowed herself, very briefly, to feel a little sad.

'*Qu'est-ce que vous voulez . . . ? Madame?*'

'Oh, yes, *pardon . . .*' She realised she was being asked for her order, decided she'd get a biscuit for Mikey and dithered for a moment as she tried to remember how to pronounce the word in French. She thought again what a shame it was that he should miss this experience: it was proving briefer than she'd expected, Paris more compact than she remembered. When she'd come before, as a teenager, the city had seemed immense to her, a place that glittered day and night, both its monuments and its people designed to catch the light.

How they'd hoped, she and her sister Melissa, that they did it justice, that they caught the light too.

It was as the hot water was being poured into her cup and the selection of teas offered that she became aware of the screaming. It was a continuous and unsettling sound, from a source somewhere on the same side of the boat as Notre-Dame. At first she made no personal connection with it or even associated it with their tour group, not until she picked out the single human word that arose from it – '*Mu-um!*' – and realised with a breathless slam inside her ribcage that it was Holly. Holly was screaming, she was screaming above her, around her, through her, *for* her.

'I'm sorry . . . I need to . . .' Abandoning her order, she dashed to the stairs, emerging on the upper deck with a sensation of pure disorientation – had she come to the wrong place? Was there another set of steps up to this deck? – for there was not a single passenger sitting in the spot he or she had occupied five minutes ago. Chaos reigned, everyone crowding at or moving towards the island side (it crossed her mind that the boat might even capsize), whole blocks of seats left empty or strewn with belongings. Such was the crush that it was not possible at first to see Holly, or even to hear her any longer, for her cry had either stopped or been lost in the roar about her: everyone was speaking at once, in a variety of languages, asking, answering, shrieking, gasping, panicking. Only the tour commentary continued as if nothing were amiss: '*We are now at the point where the two famous islands almost kiss . . .*'

'Let me through!' Joanna called out in desperation. 'I think something's happened to my daughter! Please, let me through!'

Holly's cry came again then, no longer the ghostly wail but short, shrill outbursts, quickly obliterated by a half-hysterical English voice right in Joanna's ear: 'Why aren't the crew doing anything? What do they say for "man overboard" here? Do they not have a distress signal in France?'

'Don't know,' a companion replied, not quite so excitable but plainly concerned, 'but they must be on the case because we're slowing – can you feel it? Whoa!'

Sure enough the boat was dragging heavily to a halt, nosing slightly towards the island as it did. The manoeuvre prompted a collective readjustment at the rail and Joanna was at last able to find a crack through which she could see Holly. The girl was pressed against the side, doubled over it as if about to vomit, barely an inch from tumbling right over. Two women close to her were reaching out with urgent gestures of restraint, causing Joanna to make her first stab at understanding this scene: Holly was the cause of all this hysteria; she had tried to jump overboard but had been pulled back; someone had alerted the crew to the emergency and now the boat was stopping. Holly was . . . she was attempting suicide.

Oh God, no.

She pushed forwards more forcefully, only half registering a graze to her leg as she caught the edge of a seat, and managed to seize her daughter's right shoulder. 'Holly, get back from there! What are you doing?'

Holly straightened and turned with wild, rough movements. 'Oh, Mum . . . oh, Mum . . .' Her face was a shocking sight, swollen with high colour, her eyes feverish, almost deranged.

'Come and sit down,' Joanna urged her, 'you'll fall in if you lean over like that!' She motioned to their seats, noticing as she did Mikey's pushchair, still fixed in its original position by the rails, the straps now unbuckled and the seat empty.

Her insides clotted. 'Holly? Where's Mikey?'

There was no answer, just that same twisting, feral expression on the girl's face.

'Where is he, Holly, tell me? *Holly?*'

Man overboard . . . Only then did she hear those words properly, only then did she understand: not Holly, Mikey. Turning from Holly she crushed herself against the rail, needing the grip of another passenger to stop her from overbalancing, but all she could see of the water was the wake of churned yellow-white around their boat, that horrible sucking brown beyond.

'He's fallen in,' Holly managed to say at her shoulder, speaking in the most ghastly, choking syllables, 'he went over the side . . .'

'How, Holly? When? *When?*' But Holly was sobbing violently as a new surge of hysteria overpowered her and Joanna renounced any hope of getting useful answers to the demands that now besieged her: How far had they come since she first heard the screams? Ten metres? Twenty? More? How far was the drop to the water? Could it be survived by a child – an infant not yet two years old? Why couldn't she see him, where were his splashes? Then: Should she go in after him? Was that what Holly had been trying to do, leaning over the side like that? One of them had to rescue him, didn't they?

The questions, the connections, had a dizzying downward trajectory of their own, drawing her over the rail once more and closer to the water, closer to the point of having the dilemma decided for her, until, behind the suffocating panic, came a tiny flare of oxygen: the crew knew, they had known before she did – 'They're on the case,' that man had said – and they had stopped the boat. Any second now they were going to turn back or reverse, fish Mikey out and bring him to safety. It couldn't have been more than a few seconds since it happened: trained professionals would save him.

Wouldn't they?

She hauled herself upright, evading the curious gazes and urgent questions of those around her, and returned her attention to Holly. Sensing that the girl was losing the last of her strength, she lunged to steady her body, pressing it close to her own. At once Holly monopolised her energies entirely, becoming a groaning, clutching thing in her arms. The sound came from her mouth like water from a hose, the pressure of it at such close range painful, unbearable. The feat of reaching their seats was beyond Joanna; she could only stand, supply enough power to stop Holly from falling to the deck and herself from looking once more at that terrible empty pushchair with its straps hanging loose over the sides.

Then, all at once, beyond the desperate clutch of her daughter and that terrible groaning, she felt a change in pitch, a swarm to the rear, a new clamour of voices:

9

'Oh my, oh my . . .' An American voice rose above the others: 'He's in as well now, look, Jeff! When did that happen?'

'He jumped from the lower deck, did he?'

'All his clothes still on, look at that!'

'He must be totally crazy!'

Then a third person spoke, obviously tearful, a British woman: 'Oh, I hope he gets to the little boy in time, this is absolutely awful. What's the official procedure here? Where's the lifeboat?'

Straining on tiptoe, Joanna could just see past Holly to the water, catching the frantic movements of a man swimming fast in the direction from which they'd come; he seemed to be bypassing a rigid orange-red ring that was attached to thick rope and, presumably, the boat. She was aware now of a gathering of spectators on the quayside of the Ile Saint-Louis, and on the footbridge that joined the two islands.

'Listen, someone's gone in after him,' she said to Holly through the noise, enunciating distinctly and directly into her ear, as if to a blind person. 'It must be one of the crew. He'll know what to do. Mikey will be fine, don't worry, sweetheart.' She had no idea if either of these last statements were true, but kept repeating, 'He'll know what to do,' as if that was enough to make it so.

In her arms Holly began suddenly to shake, the convulsions gripping the length and breadth of her. Involuntarily, uselessly, Joanna remembered how her daughter had shaken after Mikey's birth, for almost half an hour, rocking the hospital trolley bed as she was pushed back to her ward, Joanna walking alongside with the baby resting in the crook of her left arm. She began speaking to Joanna again now, in a despairing, choking voice that cracked Joanna's heart. 'It's too late, Mum . . . it's too late . . . he's gone under, he can't swim . . . it's too late . . .' As the words went on, Joanna felt herself accept them as fact. Holly knows, she thought, a mother knows, that's why she's shaking. We've lost him. Then: She won't recover from this. It's not just Mikey who's gone, it's both of them.

There followed an unfamiliar sensation of release, of hovering in pure white desolation, like how she imagined dying to feel.

This was the bad end they always said would come, the true punishment she was owed.

It made no difference now how hard she had tried, because she had lost.

Chapter 2

Before the accident, Joanna had had no instinct whatsoever that something *this* extraordinary was going to take place during their weekend in Paris.

Actually, this was unusual in itself, for over the course of her adult years she had come to pride herself on the accuracy of her instincts. She'd had a sense, for instance, when she'd sent off her competition entry to the magazine that this was one she might win. Entering competitions had become something of a passion lately, as had reading romantic novels set in exotic other worlds, though she didn't like to consider why. As well as travel, hotel and spending money, included in the winnings were tickets for the Eiffel Tower, the Louvre and seats on a luxury river cruise. The perfect weekend in Paris: just what the doctor ordered (his other prescriptions didn't seem to be working, after all).

It was a prize intended for a couple, that was obvious from its inclusion in the Valentine's issue of the magazine, and it was true that she had imagined how it might be if circumstances were different and she was able to invite her former partner Adrian instead of her daughter, to make a reconciliation of it worthy of one of those romantic novels. As it was, she'd known of course that it would be Holly she would bring. Holly had not been on holiday since Mikey was born, at least not abroad, a known deprivation for a girl of twenty-two. Her working friends, the few who had remained since she'd dropped out of college to have a baby, seemed to tear off constantly to Ibiza or God knew which other party island, treating the months in between – real life – as prison stretches to be endured before it was time to check in for the next flight. Joanna thought it was a generational thing, this attitude of entitlement: expect not respect, as her friend Suze put it every time another Saturday girl let her down.

But not Holly. She expected nothing. She'd been claimed by a force outside her – or anyone else's – control.

Postnatal depression, it had been diagnosed as, an extreme form of the baby blues that received an awful lot of attention, Joanna had come to realise, for Holly was constantly being told she was not alone in her affliction. Quite why knowing that thousands of others suffered similarly should make you feel any better was beyond Joanna, but that was by the by. Over the past year there had been a deluge of professional aid, including three types of antidepressant medication, a specialist counsellor, leaflets and books to read and support groups to attend, but nothing had come close to reversing the original slump.

Paris will succeed where the rest of us have failed, Joanna decided; it will bring back Holly's interest in life, her sense of fun, her desire to succeed. Even when she heard she'd won the competition, it felt less like a lucky break than a simple necessity; a life saver, if that wasn't too dramatic.

It was a lot of pressure to put on a city, but if anywhere could do it, Paris could.

Of course they'd hardly been there five minutes when Joanna realised the fundamental flaw to her plan: *she* was not the one who needed to believe in the power of Paris, it was Holly herself.

'No one's speaking French,' the girl said, as they joined the queue at the Louvre on their arrival in the city on Friday afternoon. 'It's all tourists.' This was not a complaint, but more a statement of deep sorrow. She gripped the handlebars of Mikey's pushchair as if she expected to be knocked to the ground at any moment by a charging mob of non-Frenchmen.

'Yes, isn't it?' Joanna's tone was one of happy agreement with a positive statement. Over the last year or so she had found this was the best way to counter the pessimistic world view caused by Holly's condition. Contradiction, challenge, criticism: all seemed to have an effect similar to that of physical injury. Even mild sarcasm could cause an instant collapse.

'Bit hot,' was the next mournful comment.

'Yes, it's a perfect day,' Joanna said. She had grown expert in concealing her impatience and, at times, especially when she looked at her daughter's face, her heartbreak: how easy it was to forget what a pretty girl Holly was! In spite of the heat her skin was so deathly pale you'd think her breaths too shallow for oxygen to reach the surface of her, her freckles like those flowers that could grow on the arid banks of volcanoes; and her dark, almond-shaped eyes were vacant, seeming never to focus properly on anything, even Mikey. She was walking proof that beauty was more than an accident of bone structure, but an emotion expressed through shining eyes and glowing cheeks, through engagement with *life*.

Unable to bear it, Joanna removed her gaze and scanned instead the triangular segments of the glass pyramid in front of them. When she was last here, almost twenty-five years ago in the 1980s, the structure was a work-in-progress and the subject of controversy, even scandal. Her parents were against its construction, she remembered, and for that reason alone she had considered it vital for the very future of mankind. Today it looked settled in, even classical, a reminder – along with every queuing tourist's casual acceptance of it – of just how much time had passed since.

'I'm tired,' Holly sighed, her eyelids half closed, 'really, really tired.'

'That might be a side effect of the new pills, do you think? You'll feel better when your system's adjusted.'

How many times had she said *that*? Enough for Holly to no longer dignify it with a response.

Joanna felt a sudden swell of passion, longed with all her heart to be able to cry out, 'Isn't this wonderful? I *knew* you'd love Paris!' and to get an excited exclamation in return, a request to hear all about that first visit, how she had fallen for the city on sight. But she did not, allowing instead the old doubt to lurch forward and replace the joy, allowing herself to think how different her own childhood had been from the one she'd given Holly, the one that had brought the girl to this point.

The point at which she could stand in one of the world's most beautiful cities and hate every moment of it.

Did she, Joanna, bear some of the responsibility for that? She *had* to be guilty on some level, surely?

Now the doubts had broken ranks, she was unable to stop them advancing, as if she'd been planted in the queue to the Louvre expressly to confront her own ghosts. Is this my life? Is this how I expected it to turn out when I came here all those years ago? Am I really a grandmother at forty-two, an age when many women are just starting their families? Have I failed my daughter, failed myself?

One thing she *did* know: you were supposed to do a better job than your own parents had, not worse. You were supposed to give your children the things you'd missed, not conceal from them the more enviable details of what you had once had but that they never would.

A father, for instance.

Admitted more quickly than expected, they stood in the vast entrance space of the museum and faced a choice that was over-whelming even for those of sound mind: thirty-five thousand works of art, but which was the one that might speak to Holly?

'Is there anything in particular you'd like to see?' Joanna asked, knowing as she spoke that the question was probably redundant.

Holly, however, was still sentient enough to detect a dip in Joanna's own spirits and to summon the smallest of enthusiasms of her own. 'The *Mona Lisa*?' she said, in the voice of a quiz contestant making an embarrassingly wild guess and already anticipating the direst humiliations for her blunder.

Joanna nodded encouragingly. 'It's as good a place to start as any. If we head in that direction we can always wander off if something catches our eye along the way.'

They did not wander off, though, but were swept along the fast-moving current as if on dinghies. Well, it *was* the most famous painting in the world, she thought; they were hardly going to get a private view, were they.

'Exciting,' she whispered to Holly, when after a short wait they were released into the Salle des Etats and the company of the hallowed lady herself. They took their places at the back of the throng, among those holding cameras high above the heads of the people in front, as if at a stadium concert, no hope of seeing the stars on stage with their own eyes.

Holly made a half-hearted bounce on to the balls of her feet to catch a quick glimpse, before remarking, with signature dis-appointment, 'It's smaller than I thought.' A little ahead of them, a toddler of Mikey's age was screaming in delight at the dazzle of a camera flash and Joanna watched Holly wince at the sound, as might someone who had no experience of small children, no understanding of their high spirits. She was indifferent to the cries of her own son, who was straining to be released from his buggy.

Joanna bent to unbuckle him. 'Look, Mikey, it's the most famous painting in the world! Come and see.' She held him in her arms, partly to stop him from darting off, partly in the hope that he might accidentally focus on the fabled picture and

16

remember this cultural highlight in years to come. Maybe he'd be a painter or an artist himself one day! But he only wriggled and bucked and faced the wrong direction and her lower back soon ached with the weight of him on her hip, her forearms with the effort of keeping him still.

'Hey, Mikey,' she told him, 'let's be a good boy for Mummy and Grandma.'

Holly's helplessness, Mikey's lack of cooperation, these she realised she had expected. What she had not bargained for was her own reaction to the portrait. For there was one glorious moment when the crush of bodies between them parted freakishly in her favour, offering her a clear view of that pale oval face with its famously unknowable gaze. Except Joanna thought she *did* know it, actually, now that she was faced with it. It was the picture of tenderness, she decided; not the extravagant tenderness of a new lover or the playful kind of an old friend, but the quiet, private kind, like that of a mother on seeing her child sleeping. It was how Joanna herself had felt as she checked on Holly at night when she was younger, and it was what she feared to be fatally absent when Holly checked on Mikey (if she ever did).

It gave her the chills to turn from that serene, glowing face on the wall to the young woman behind her, to the downturned eyes, the shoulders rolled forward, the relentlessly negative aura. Mikey might have dashed out of the room and been trampled underfoot by sculptures come to life and Holly would not have noticed.

'Want to try and get a bit closer?' she suggested.

'No, it's OK,' Holly said. 'I've seen it.'

After that she scarcely said another word. When they stopped for a cup of coffee and Mikey became fractious, the decisions that needed to be made – sweets that would pacify him initially but send him frantic afterwards, or the more difficult sell of a piece of fruit? – were left to Joanna. Holly sat as if

17

in a party of her own and sharing their table out of necessity alone, her fingers listlessly cupping her café au lait. What went on in that head of hers? Joanna wondered. Did she fill it with dreams or did she close down her thoughts in a form of meditation? It was impossible to know.

'Anything else you fancy seeing?' She pressed the museum plan on the table under Holly's nose and Holly looked as terrified by it as if she'd been presented with a warrant for her arrest. 'Or do you want to just head off back to the hotel?' This, in fact, was Joanna's own preference, for they'd been up early to catch their train from St Pancras and it was obvious that Mikey was overtired, but she was determined to force at least a small share of the decision-making on her daughter.

'Sorry, Mum, I'm not that into museums,' Holly said in a tiny, tragic voice.

There was no point reminding her of the many she'd enjoyed as a child in London.

'OK. Well, tomorrow will be more your thing, maybe.'

Holly glanced up with a small show of willing. 'What's happening then?' She'd obviously not absorbed the basics of their itinerary, announced several times before departure and outlined once again, in more detail, on the train. It was official then: Joanna had been talking to herself all along.

'We've got the Eiffel Tower in the morning and then the river trip in the afternoon, haven't we?'

'Oh,' Holly said. And she looked at Joanna as if she'd been hoping for the light of the moon and been given instead the dog-end of a matchstick.

For as long as she lived Joanna would not allow herself to imagine what might have happened if Holly had decided to skip the boat trip and go up the Eiffel Tower instead. For she had not the energy for both, it transpired the next morning.

'Would it be OK if you just took Mikey up the tower on your

own?' As was often the case, hers was a last-minute withdrawal. They'd made it as far as the lobby of the hotel when she shuffled to a halt and asked the question – the question that was never *really* one.

'You don't want to see the view?' Joanna exclaimed. 'Oh, it's something special, Holls. And we've got pre-booked tickets, we won't have to queue for long.'

Holly looked at her with the eyes of a lost infant. 'I'll come on the boat trip later. I just . . . I just feel exhausted, like I haven't slept.'

'You slept like a log, darling.'

'Did I?' The girl shrugged in surprise. Joanna wondered if her new pills prevented her from appreciating the benefits of sleep. She supposed it was the depression itself that did that: if you hated waking up, then no sleep was too deep or too long.

'Fine.' She knew from experience that attempts at persuasion could make Holly distressed. 'The boat leaves at one, so we'll meet you at the pier at twelve-thirty. It's walking distance from here. I've marked it on this map, OK?'

Holly took the map from her.

'I'll pick up some lunch for Mikey, so don't worry about that.'

It was unlikely that Holly *had* been going to worry but Joanna made a point of saying these things for such a time that her daughter got better and took over the practical aspects of Mikey's care. It provided a kind of subliminal training, she hoped.

'Come on, Mikey, we're going into the sky!'

'Sky, sky, sky!' He was so easily, joyously stimulated; sometimes she couldn't decide if his joy helped compensate for Holly's depression or made it more painful to witness.

The guidebook called the great structure a true Tower of Babel and, sure enough, every nationality appeared to be represented in the first elevator. Though she hadn't said so to Holly yesterday, Joanna, too, wished more of the people they were seeing were not tourists but locals; she liked seeing the real Parisians. The women her age were so different from her they were almost a different gender altogether. They were better dressed, of course, their faces better preserved, but it wasn't that that fascinated her, it was their composure, their self-assurance. They stood at the windows of their apartments looking out, or at the windows of shops looking in, with an expression of resolution, as if they'd brook no nonsense from the world. Poise, she supposed it was. Dignity.

Did you get those things because you lived in Paris or did you only get to live in Paris if you had those things?

Whatever the answer, you certainly could not recreate it while a crushed elevator bore you upwards through a tapering brown cage, a toddler preventing you from breathing thanks to his marsupial clutch.

'They use three different shades of paint to make the tower look all the same colour from the ground,' she told him. 'And when we get to the top you can see a view in all directions. The word for that is a panorama.'

'Paromana,' Mikey mimicked, making some of their fellow passengers chuckle.

'Almost, good try!' She tried not to notice the Lowry-like figures among the latticework of the lower frame: those who'd chosen to take the steps rather than wait for the elevator. When she'd visited the tower as a teenager all those years ago, her father had suggested going up that way, quick to dismiss Joanna's protests that she was scared of heights. But then Melissa had been consulted and she'd refused too, much to Joanna's relief; she'd said she was wearing the wrong shoes for climbing, and that was that. Melissa *always* got her own way.

Joanna couldn't remember her sister's footwear that day but she felt sure she could picture her clothing: a full-skirted cotton black sundress patterned with white stars, a green woollen beret that was too hot for the weather but who cared when it was angled with such insouciance, and shocking red lipstick that would be considered crude and theatrical now but was, at the time, an everyday sight. Joanna could not recall what she herself had worn, only that Melissa looked better. Of the two sisters, Melissa alone was mistaken for the native Parisienne they both longed to be, and chatted up by the local boys.

That was right, Joanna remembered, it was the day of the Eiffel Tower trip that Melissa had fallen into that self-pitying reverie over the handbag. The two girls had had their allowance paid that month in French francs and spent it mostly on cheap clothes and jewellery from markets, but the bag, vivid blue and encrusted with shells, was ten times Melissa's budget. 'This will be perfect for college,' she said, as if that settled it. 'No one else will have this bag.' As her father's golden girl, she might have expected him to make up the difference, but on this one occasion he did not.

'I hate Dad,' she muttered to Joanna as they left the shop, causing in Joanna that rare thrill of hope that the status quo might at last be about to collapse.

'Yeah, he's such a Scrooge,' she agreed eagerly.

Melissa nodded in approval. 'Old miser, what's a few francs to *him*?' And she'd hooked her elbow through Joanna's to seal their temporary alliance, drawn her into the exalted realm where she was so rarely granted access.

Joanna could still feel the sensation of those linked arms, the bony angularity of Melissa's against the rounded fleshiness of her own.

Now, when people asked, she said her family were so scattered it made regular get-togethers difficult. Some knew the full story: her oldest friend Suze, for instance, with whom Joanna and Holly often spent Christmas and birthdays; and Adrian, who she'd been with for four years and from whom she'd parted soon after Mikey was born – she could trust him not to tell anyone whose business it was not; and Holly knew the bones of it, of course.

'You've given us no choice,' her father had said, though what he had really meant was that Melissa had given them a choice – and they had gone ahead and made it. 'You have to leave,' he said. 'Go now, Joanna, before you do any more damage.' It was hard to believe that was just two years after the Paris holiday, when she'd felt so adult and yet been still a child.

You've given us no choice . . . She remembered the words, but she could no longer bring to mind the expression on her father's face, or recall whether her mother and sister had been present to witness her reaction.

'Fine!' she'd huffed. 'If that's how you feel, then I'll go! And don't expect me to come running back when you change your mind!'

The clichés of break-up were all there, complete with multiple exclamation marks and tear-stained eyes. She had left home with all the naïve bluster of a young woman who thought she didn't need her family, didn't need anyone in the world, but who at the same time fully trusted they'd be there waiting for her should it ever turn out that she did.

That, in the end, had been the mistake that hurt the most.

Chapter 3

Alexa could smell the foreignness of the hotel room even before she opened her eyes: the fragrance of professionally laundered bed linen, of polished wood and fresh flowers – there were no fewer than four vasefuls in the little top-floor suite – and, seeping through the window frames, the city air itself, with whatever exotica that contained. Traffic fumes, she supposed, though she tried to allow only vintage Citroëns into her imaginings; the steamy aromas of the neighbourhood's *boulangeries*; and hot, hot human breath, all those gasps and sighs and kisses. The way people reacted to Paris, the way they behaved in its streets and squares, that became a part of the city too.

Not that she and James had contributed a great deal to the gasping and sighing and kissing – not yet. But she remained hopeful.

Oh, she thought, remembering: it's Sunday, our wedding anniversary. Five years they'd been married, far too soon to be worried, and yet . . . Well, the truth was she had gone to inordinate trouble and expense to arrange this trip in the belief that something was unravelling between them. Maybe not *unravelling*, but there was a dropped stitch or two, a distinct loosening of their togetherness that James appeared not to have noticed and that Alexa had not remarked upon for fear that he had.

She sat up in bed, wriggling against the pillows to get comfortable, and surveyed their chamber, the honeymoon suite, no less. Every detail was correct according to her original brief: the decor was glamorous in a traditional French way, with silk-lined walls for fingertips to trail across and deep carpeting for bare feet to sink into, with big silvery mirrors multiplying artfully the soft spheres of lamplight, the room's only illumination. Across the little entrance hall there was a black and white marbled bathroom, with a tub big enough for two and an antique chaise longue set within hand-holding range (the whole suite was designed with the understanding that its two occupants would not want to be parted for long). Most important of all, from the row of four windows there was a view of Paris: old Paris, seventeenth-century Place des Vosges Paris. Here, high above ground in the steep slate roof, they had a pigeon's outlook on the famous arcaded square itself, on the fountains and sandboxes, the shaded corners and gravelled pathways, the proud central statue of Louis XIII. It was enchanting, just as she'd longed for it to be. If they didn't fall in love again here, they wouldn't fall in love again anywhere.

There was, however, a flaw to this romantic certainty: she was waking up in the honeymoon suite alone. Where was James?

Oh, she thought, remembering again. That awful thing on the boat trip yesterday . . .

It was still shocking enough for her to suspect she might only have dreamt it – after one glass too many at dinner the night before, perhaps – but no, it really had happened: in the middle of their sightseeing cruise down the Seine, her husband had jumped overboard and saved a child from drowning. He honestly had! One minute the two of them were sinking into their recliners in the early afternoon sun, Paris breezing by as Alexa's chin nodded pleasantly towards her collarbone, the next there was a terrific eruption of yelling, a rush of energy of the kind she had come to dread more than anything – crowd panic – and then, abruptly, unimaginably, James was on his feet and vaulting the rail, plunging out of sight. At first she'd thought there must be another deck below, a balcony of some kind, though what could have possessed him to leap down on to it, she had no idea, and she was still scrambling to her feet, trying to make sense of it, when she caught sight of him quite a distance away in the middle of the river. In the middle of the river!

'James!' she screamed, though there was no question of him being able to hear her, and then, 'What's going on?' to no one, to anyone, to herself.

'There's a little boy in the water,' an English voice called from beyond the wall of backs and shoulders that had formed between her and the rail, 'and it looks like someone's gone in to get him.'

Alexa was grateful for the simple definition of what her senses had failed to grasp independently. 'It's my husband, he just jumped in. I don't understand wh—'

But someone else was interrupting, his news the newest, voice raised above the clamour: 'He's got him, look, he's got the kid! He seems like he knows what he's doing as well!'

'What, what?' Alexa clawed desperately at the man's shoulder, but he held firm, not giving her a millimetre of a glimpse. 'Are they all right? Oh, God, this is a nightmare!'

'The boy's all right, I think. Looks alive, at least. They're drifting a bit. Aren't the crew going to pull them in?'

'No,' came the reply. Alexa was having trouble matching voices to backs of heads. 'It looks like he's making for the island, worried about the engines maybe . . .'

'Why don't they turn them off?' Alexa asked, her voice shriller with every utterance. 'What if they get sucked under the boat?' She was becoming aware of a tremor in her body, an imminent collapse of all emotional control.

'River laws, I guess. It's just as close, anyway, maybe closer. We've come out quite a way from the bank.'

'But what about the other boats?'

'There's nothing coming that I can see—'

Alexa screamed out again: 'Please, I need to see, he's my husband!'

At last her claim was acknowledged, the bodies parting to give her a spot at the rail and a clear view of the action in the water: a good twenty metres from where she'd first glimpsed James, there were two distinct faces above the surface, white skin spotlit by the sun. James's was turned upwards to the sky, disfigured with physical effort, the other was smaller and straining from side to side, not still enough to focus on; what looked like James's forearm, an elbow, was hooked close to the neck. As her neighbour had reported, the linked pair were moving away from both the boat and a red ring that must have been thrown out to them by the crew, and towards the near quayside of the Ile Saint-Louis. There, where the river wall sloped and a run of steps was cut into the stone, a group had gathered, one figure already down at water level on the lowest visible step, arm outstretched towards the approaching swimmers.

And then, miraculous and surreal as it was, they were there – they'd made it to the quayside, back to land! Amid the knot of helpers, James could just be identified, on his hands and knees, clothes and hair soaked black, and then the small child too, passed from person to person, lain on the cobbles, moving and kicking, his legs white and bare. The initial clamour of horror and disbelief was replaced wholesale with cheers of excitement, both on the boat and from the banks of spectators: there were hundreds now, on every quay, on the bridge that crossed from the Ile de la Cité; it was the scene, almost, of a regatta.

As others rejoiced, many returning to their seats to discuss the drama as they awaited instructions regarding the cruise, Alexa lost the last of her nerve and began to sob. 'I have to get to him,' she repeated through her tears, once more to no one in particular, simply to anyone who might take pity on her. 'Please, someone, get me off this thing!'

Now, with convulsions threatening afresh, Alexa heard a knock at the door and flew to it, thinking it might be James, though she knew he had a key card and would let himself in. It was silly, but she needed to confirm for herself that he was still alive, that her memory of his having been pulled to safety was real.

'*Bonjour, madame.*' It was one of the hotel staff, bearing a pair of satin-covered coat hangers that held dry-cleaned clothes: the jeans and shirt James had been wearing yesterday. His shoes and socks had come off in the water, lost now and never again to be paired.

'Thank you.' They'd done a good job, the hotel laundry. You'd never know the items had been in that . . . well, cesspool was a bit strong, but the Seine was hardly made of Evian and rosewater, was it? Like the Thames, it contained innumerable harmful bacteria and it was a miracle James hadn't contracted something terrible during the minutes he'd been submerged. As it was, they had been briefed by the medical team to prepare for stomach upsets and fever.

'I don't suppose you've seen my husband?' she asked, hiding her anxiety behind a hopeful smile.

The young man displayed no surprise as he pointed out what she at once realised she should have known on her own: 'He is with the newspaper journalists in the Salle Royale.'

'Oh, of course. Thank you.' Closing the door, Alexa recalled how the hotel manager, Laurent, had suggested a press inter-view in one of the function rooms downstairs. He'd said the media enquiries about the accident were becoming too persist-ent to ignore and that one short press conference should satisfy curiosity.

Certainly, coverage of their river drama had so far been very limited: no interview with any of the parties involved had been included in the item she and James had watched on the local TV news last night before going to bed. Instead there had been footage taken from the upper deck of their boat of a blurred, submerged figure completely unrecognisable as James, as well as shots from the riverbank of ambulances, fire and other vehicles and their grave-faced personnel. She had not been able to follow the fast-talking French voiceover, but it had been excitable enough for her to agree with Laurent that the media was not going to let it pass with an initial report. People would want to know more about the British hero who'd jumped into the Seine to save a drowning child, how they'd both emerged uninjured.

According to Laurent, if James agreed to the interview then interest would fade within a day or two, particularly when it was established that neither rescuer nor rescued was a French national and therefore of far less interest domestically.

'Thank God for that,' Alexa had said. Not that she wasn't overjoyed that a child's life had been saved, as relieved as everyone else to learn that the poor mite – a boy called Mikey, only twenty-one months old, apparently – had been discharged from hospital and returned to his family after only a short period of observation. It was just that the whole thing was . . . well, it was as if her carefully orchestrated holiday had been ambushed midway by some kind of alternative reality.

Was it inappropriate to celebrate their anniversary so soon after a terrible tragedy had been averted or was it more important than ever to do so?

The thought was interrupted by a second delivery to the room: breakfast *pour une personne*. James must have ordered it for her, or perhaps Laurent, knowing she'd be alone this morning. Separate breakfasts on our anniversary, she thought, lifting the big silver dome from a plate of eggs; before we know it it'll be twin beds and slippers . . .

But that only brought to mind the conversation she'd had

with her closest friends Lucie and Shona just last week, the subject that had consumed her before and until the events of yesterday:

'You can't take him to Paris to get things back on track and not tell him that's your purpose,' Shona said.

'Back on track' was a phrase that came up uncomfortably frequently in her discussions about James lately, often uttered soon after, 'It's just not the same any more,' and once, hopelessly, horribly, 'Do you think he might have changed his mind about marrying me?' (She would not forget their faces at that: the cold shock of a broken taboo, the shudder of there-but-for-the-grace-of-God deliverance.)

'Surely he'll guess?' Alexa said, optimistically.

'Men don't guess,' Lucie told her. 'Not unless you've told them there's something to guess. They don't guess spontaneously.'

'But it's our anniversary. He'll know it's a romantic exercise.'

In retrospect, 'exercise' seemed like the wrong sort of word, though none of them had questioned it at the time.

In any case, once in Paris she had quickly come to see that her friends were right: James, who had had a hectic first half of the year at work, wanted nothing more than to spend his time catching up on sleep. He most certainly had not guessed that the aim of the trip was to stay awake and pay her something close to the levels of interest she remembered – and missed – from the earlier years of their relationship. When they'd met, she had been, at twenty-seven, the older woman, a fully formed object of desire rarely available to his eager new graduate. How his friends had professed their envy of him! So convinced were they all that a woman with an extra five years under her belt should be privy to mysterious erotic secrets, she had almost come to believe it herself.

'Women can be very self-defeating,' Lucie said. 'They're hardwired to think that they shouldn't want someone who

29

doesn't want them. They know, in evolutionary terms, that it's a waste of time and they should cut their losses and find a more sexually aggressive mate.'

Sometimes Lucie spoke as if she were not a woman herself and susceptible to such contradictory forces.

'I don't want another mate,' Alexa said. 'I want the one I've got.'

'All marriages have their troughs,' Shona said, kindly.

Considering such advice while taking in the classic lovers' sights on Friday, Alexa had decided that she was not going to be self-defeating, and nor was she going to allow her marriage to languish in a trough. Saturday was going to be the day her husband's passion for her was reignited, just in time for the anniversary itself – and what could be more mood-enhancing than a cruise down the Seine? The irony was that it had been working, she was sure of it: when they'd pulled away from the riverbank, the sun hoisted high above, James had turned to her and murmured, 'This is really nice, Al. Just us. Thank you.' And he'd looked at her in the private, rapturous way he used to, giving her a toppling sensation in her abdomen, bringing to her lips the first spontaneous smile of the weekend.

Just us.

And then the rescue.

Now, less than a day later, here she was, just her, feeling as vulnerable to the currents as the poor little boy James had saved. Whatever was coming next she did not know, only that she was entirely at its mercy.

It wasn't going to be breakfast, at any rate. With great reluctance she put the lid back on the plate, taking only the coffee. She hadn't eaten anything as rich as Eggs Benedict in years; who knew what greed would be unleashed if she succumbed now.

James had been peculiarly casual about his heroics; he would, if it had been down to him, simply have strolled off afterwards, dripping. But the Parisian authorities had taken it all extremely seriously and the whole of the afternoon and most of the evening had been given over to medical and police ministrations. Alexa lost count of the variety of uniforms she saw at the scene, the number of different organisations represented – who had known, for instance, there was such a thing as the *Brigade Fluviale*, a dedicated river patrol? Did they have one of those on the Thames? Every time she suggested they bring the questioning to a close and let her take James back to the hotel for a hot shower and some rest, one more uniformed figure would appear with his own set of enquiries and her plea would be disregarded.

Such was the thoroughness of official procedure, and of the hotel staff's aftercare, that Alexa and James hardly had a chance to discuss the incident between themselves. Finally, alone in their room last night, after they'd watched the news report and before both had passed out from exhaustion, they'd sat quietly for ten minutes on the little sofa under the window and she'd had the chance to add to the marathon interrogation he'd just endured:

'What made you do it? Jump in like that?' Though she spoke calmly, she was still very shaken, unsure of her emotions.

James looked surprised. 'Someone had to, Al. Toddlers can't swim. They can't grab hold of a lifebelt.'

'I know that, but why you? Surely one of the crew should have done it?'

'They didn't though, did they? Not in time. He would have drowned if it had been left any longer.'

'You might both have drowned,' she pointed out. 'The currents in the Seine are infamous.'

'Are they?'

'Yes. Not to mention the risk of catching every water-borne disease known to man – you heard what the paramedics said.'

He grinned. 'What, you're worried about cholera? You sound like my mother.'

'Well, I'm sorry if I care about you!' she cried, as surprised as he was by the sudden eruption of anguish. She supposed it must be tiredness, tiredness and relief.

'Come on,' James said, mildly, 'I knew I'd be fine.'

She gazed at him, uncomprehending. She wanted very much to take him into her arms or have him take her into his, but instead they remained side by side, shoulders turned only fractionally inward. 'I was terrified,' she said. 'When I saw you in the water, before I saw the boy, I thought you were trying to commit suicide or something.'

James only carried on grinning. There was an evasive glitter to his eyes she'd never seen before. 'You can't possibly have thought that.' Once, as a teenager, he and three friends had swum across the Thames near their school, and he reminded her of this escapade now. 'That was a suicide mission,' he added. 'This was just, I don't know, reflex or something.'

A reflex she'd not been aware he owned; a sharper one than any she possessed. She was suddenly overwhelmed by the instinct that this was more than a plan waylaid, an interruption to her hopes for marital rejuvenation, but something incendiary, the force of its explosion yet to be felt.

'And it's not like you've been to the gym recently,' she said, anxiously. 'You could have had a heart attack just from the exercise.'

'I'm not *that* unfit,' he said, still smiling freely, as if this were all some great lark. True, his fitness was a little joke between them. The zeal with which she had set about remoulding her body in the last two years – a fear of forty, a quest to recapture that desirability of a decade ago – had been matched only by the eagerness with which he rejected all notions of self-preservation. And yet somehow, without lifting a finger, he had become more attractive than ever.

Noticing her failure to join in his laughter, he reached for her hand and gripped it, rare enough a gesture these days for it to bring colour to her face. 'I'm sorry I gave you a fright, but it all turned out OK, didn't it? Maybe it was a bit of a risk, but it was the right thing to do, wasn't it? You must agree with that?'

She hesitated, making a tremendous effort to think positively and by doing so banish that awful sense of premonition she'd had. 'Of course I do. You were brilliant. And it's just as well you did do it, since no one else did. Not just the crew, but the parents. I'm surprised they didn't go in after him, aren't you?'

'There was only the mother,' James told her. 'Didn't you say you saw her getting off the boat? Apparently, she's only a young girl herself.'

Alexa struggled to put faces to the other people involved in the drama. She'd been so distraught on the boat she hadn't paid close attention to anyone else, and then once they were all over the bridge the ambulance containing the boy and his family had left immediately for the hospital. There'd been no time for introductions. But it had been impossible to forget the animal sounds of distress she had heard as she waited to disembark, the accompanying attempts to comfort and subdue. 'There were two women,' she remembered. 'But I thought the older one was the boy's mother? I assumed the girl was his sister or something?'

'No, the girl is the mother, the police said. The other one's the grandmother. I don't think there's a father in the picture.'

For the first time since the rescue, James yawned, lifting his eyebrows in self-parody, as if he had no right to be as tired as he was. He seemed genuinely oblivious to the reality of the risk he had taken, and utterly without need of congratulation. It was not at all how she would have expected a hero to behave, but then she had never seen him do anything heroic before. On the contrary, he was famously laid back, immune to emergency rather than alert to it, content to let others step in and take the chance.

Then again, what have I ever done? Alexa asked herself,

studying the bones of James's face, as if she had missed something fundamental these last ten years. Yes, she was one of the busiest, most driven people she knew, but what had she ever done that had determined, as James had, whether another person lived or died? And the inevitable blank her mind offered in reply felt, just for a moment, like a line of separation between them.

It was almost twelve o'clock and he still hadn't come back upstairs. Finding her way to the larger of the two function rooms on the ground floor, Alexa saw that a dozen or so chairs had been arranged in rows in front of a raised table set with two chairs. Who had taken the seat at James's side? Laurent? An interpreter? Should she have insisted it be she? In any case, all who'd attended had now departed and so she headed for the bar just off the lobby, the natural gathering point in the small hotel.

She was attracted at once by a woman at the window bobbing on her heels and waving an arm to catch her attention. It was Frances, whose husband, Andrew, James knew from university. When the two men had spotted each other in the bar on Friday night Alexa had felt a little dismayed to encounter someone they knew in their lovers' hideaway, but now she felt only gratitude for a familiar face.

'Over here!'

Before she could lift her own arm in response Frances was by her side, Andrew scuttling in her wake. Both were shorter than Alexa, Frances birdlike and expensively coiffured, Andrew balding and less well-maintained generally, but each had an air of worldly entitlement that Alexa found alluring and intimidating in equal measure.

'Were you sleeping in?' Frances demanded. 'You've missed all the action.'

Alexa nodded, feeling foolish. Clearly she *should* have been at the conference.

'James is such a star! And so modest. The way he tells it you'd think he'd done nothing at all.'

'It's true,' Andrew agreed. 'He's not milking it at all. I would be, I can tell you that.'

'God help us,' Frances said. 'The moment you saw yourself on TV you'd be trying your luck with that skinny girl on reception and then where would we be?'

'I know where *I'd* be,' Andrew said and the pair smirked wolfishly at one another, extremely pleased with themselves.

Alexa remained speechless, mortified by the thought of the spousal faux pas she may have committed, and prompting Frances to supply a line for her: 'You must be really proud of him, Alexa.'

'Yes,' she said, recovering. 'I am, of course I am. He was absolutely amazing. It's just hard to take it all in.'

'I bet it puts him in a completely new light, doesn't it?' Frances let her hand flutter theatrically in front of her face. 'I have to admit that when I saw him just now I felt quite overcome with hero worship. *Le culte des héros!*'

'Oh, me too.' Andrew grinned. 'We're all susceptible to a bit of that now and again.'

Frances's eyes became so wide that Alexa could see an unbroken thread of white around each iris. 'You know what, if that's how *we* feel, then imagine what the parents of the child must be feeling! They must think he's God! Did you meet them yesterday, Alexa?'

'No, they were rushed straight off to the hospital. James says there's only a mother, actually, a young girl.'

'That must have been her we saw on the news this morning,' Frances said. 'They showed her leaving the hospital carrying the child, but you couldn't see their faces properly. Oh my God, did you see that footage of James in the water? We hardly recognised him at first, it was so blurry. I'm surprised they couldn't get anything clearer, there must have been so many cameras at the ready.'

as pretty chaotic,' Alexa told her. 'Only a few people at the rail would have had a good view and they were probably too shocked to do anything. And the tour was cancelled after that, so everyone must have wandered off before any reporters even got wind of it.'

'Something will come out of the woodwork and you'll have a better souvenir of it,' Andrew said.

'Yes.' But Alexa was not sure she wanted a souvenir of something that had frightened her almost to death.

'So did he jump or dive?' Frances asked. 'I'm trying to picture it.'

'He jumped.'

'Did you know he was going to do it? What did he say before he went in?'

'Nothing, really.' Of all their questions, this was the one that caught Alexa short, made her see what it was she had been getting at in her conversation with James last night – 'But why you?' – because normally she *did* know what James was going to do. After ten years, if it wasn't something she had directly suggested herself then it would certainly be something she could have predicted.

'He's a very strong swimmer,' she told them. 'He used to compete at regional level when he was at school.'

'That's right, he swam at college, as well,' Andrew agreed.

'Oh, well, that explains it,' Frances said, pleased. 'Any normal mortal would have been dragged under by the currents. All his old techniques must have come back to him.'

'Yes, he told me they did proper life-saving training,' Alexa said. 'And once he and a few others from the squad swam across the Thames for a bet. They almost got expelled.'

'Wow!'

'Did you know they pull fifty corpses out of the Seine every year?' Andrew confided, not without relish. 'The barman just told us that.'

'Andrew!' Frances exclaimed, poking his arm rather sharply with her elbow. 'That's a bit morbid, don't you think?'

'Not as morbid as it is for the fifty bodies. And at least three times as many fall in but are saved.'

'So this kind of thing must happen a few times a week,' Alexa said, working it out. 'Why are the press so interested in this one?'

'Because it's so spectacular, with a child and a proper hero,' Andrew said. 'Normally it's probably just drunks falling from the quays. Drunks and tourists.' He said this as if he himself did not belong to either of these categories, though he was an Englishman in a foreign hotel bar at noon with a large vodka in his hand.

It was at this juncture that James made his entrance, escorted by Laurent and a second member of staff, both of whom slipped discreetly from his side once they'd seen him safely delivered to Alexa. Sensing the attention of everyone in the lobby – there was even an outbreak of light applause – and seeing Frances's instant deference, Andrew's outstretched hand, Alexa couldn't help eyeing her husband with a certain new caution. She felt as if she were welcoming home a man of war, not knowing whether all that he'd experienced since they'd parted had rendered old lives, old loves, obsolete.

'How did it go with the press?'

'Oh, fine.' He was flushed, his gaze distracted. 'Laurent says it will definitely all blow over after today. It's not like anyone's on life support or anything. People fall in the river all the time.'

'Andrew was just saying.'

'Drink?' Andrew offered, holding up his own glass as an enticement.

'Why not?' James said. 'Aren't you having one, Al?'

'I don't think there's time,' she said. She knew he would have liked one; deserved it, too, after his morning's questioning, but she felt the overwhelming impulse to get him away from the other couple and all the other well-wishers who hovered beyond them. Selfishly, unforgivably, she wanted to reinstate the true nature of this anniversary trip before . . . before it was too late. What did *that* mean? she wondered. And what if Laurent was wrong, what if this was a story that did continue to interest people, to turn James into some sort of folk hero? Was she about to lose him on the very weekend she'd set out to reclaim him?

She banished the thought, telling herself it was irrational, needy. 'Maybe this evening,' she said, glancing apologetically from Andrew to Frances, 'but we've got a lunch reservation in half an hour.'

As she named the restaurant, one she'd booked six weeks ago, James turned to her in surprise. 'We're still going for lunch?'

'I suppose we could cancel if you want to,' she said, but, ridiculously, the idea made her want to put her face in her hands and sob.

Frances came to her rescue. 'Oh, you can't cancel. The food is amazing there and you won't get another reservation before you go back. We went on Friday, didn't we, Andy?'

'It's good chow,' Andrew confirmed. 'You shouldn't miss it.'

Whether it was this endorsement or her own crestfallen expression, she couldn't tell, but James fell in with the plan happily enough. They said their goodbyes and made for the doors.

Alexa waited until they'd emerged into the square before announcing, 'Happy anniversary!' in an unnaturally delighted tone, as if her voice had been dubbed.

James just blinked at her, his eyes adjusting to the sunlight – or his brain to the new information. 'Oh yes,' he said, at last. 'Of course! Happy anniversary!'

And Alexa concealed her disappointment well enough. Given all the drama, it was understandable that he'd forgotten.

Chapter 4

Joanna did not wish to give the wrong impression: life with her incapacitated daughter and infant grandson had not been, until this point, *entirely* miserable; some days *were* better than others.

She'd found she could judge fairly swiftly each one's place in the spectrum by the tableau that greeted her when she arrived home from work. A good day involved Mikey playing with toys on the rug, Holly staring over the top of his head at the TV screen. If one of them was dressed in clean clothes, Joanna upgraded affairs a notch. An unprompted greeting from her daughter or a few words of news occasioned a second upward swing.

Once or twice there might even be a smile.

The problem was the bad days were the ones that caught everyone's attention. Often she'd get word of it before she'd even turned her key in the lock, like the evening the elderly lady in the flat across the hall opened her door at the sound of Joanna's footsteps, clearly having been listening out for them. 'Is everything all right with the little boy?' she asked, her worried face at odds with the casual enquiry.

'I think so,' Joanna said, politely.

'It's just he's been crying all day. Is he not well?'

Joanna felt familiar prickles of anxiety. 'He was fine this

morning. Oh dear, I hope he hasn't picked up a bug or something.' (From whom? Mikey mixed little with other babies.)

'I wondered . . .' The neighbour faltered, but honest concern gave her the courage to persist. 'I wondered if there was actually anyone at home with him?'

'Of course there is. Holly's there, she's there right now.' Of this Joanna was quite certain. Leaving the flat and occupying herself in the outside world was considerably more than Holly could manage. 'Leave it with me,' she told the neighbour, tempering her tone of authority with a certain lightness, a downgrading of significance. 'I really appreciate your coming to check.'

She closed the door behind her and stepped through the hallway and into the living room. There Holly was, flat on her back on the sofa, eyes open but catatonic with exhaustion or hopelessness or both. As promised, she *was* present – but only bodily. There was no sign of Mikey.

'Holly, sit up, love!' Daytime sleeping was common, even in spite of the continuous stimulants of instant coffee and cigarettes, for Holly simply had no impulse to stay awake, no energy to undertake even the lightest of daily tasks. The truth was that if you were hiring a childminder she would be the last person you'd choose, and yet here she was, for nine hours a day in sole charge of Mikey; precious, innocent Mikey.

'Where's Mikey, Holly?'

Not waiting for an answer, Joanna hurried to Holly's and Mikey's bedroom. The blind was down and Mikey was asleep in his cot. His nappy was heavy, the smell acute enough for her to know that it should have been changed hours ago; the sheet had shrunk from the mattress and there were stains where he'd regurgitated milk. It was hardly the kind of squalor you read about in the papers, but, still, she wondered if he'd seen daylight since she'd left this morning or been held in his mother's arms. He'd been fed, yes, there was evidence of that, and he'd cried, as the neighbour had testified. She guessed that he'd cried and cried until eventually he'd given up and slept. It meant he'd be awake most of the evening, in Joanna's care; he was learning to sleep during the day and get his entertainment in the evening.

She ran a bath, assembling fresh clothes, baby shampoo, the thick white cream for his nappy rash. She sang, too, allowing the sound of her merriment to wake him naturally. Her body ached from having been on her feet in the shop all day, but she ignored that. Soon, if she was lucky, he'd play at her feet as she rested.

'Hello, gorgeous!'

He smiled at her, his interest immediate and intense, just as Holly's had been at this age.

'Shall we get you nice and clean? Play with the bubbles? Then we can do your animal puzzle together.'

After the bath, his skin looked like a different fabric, shiny and pink. His eyes blazed with curiosity as he grabbed for the toys she offered.

Phoning Suze on her mobile, she asked if there was any way she might take the following day off. Suze owned the gift shop where Joanna had worked for most of her adult life, at first part-time and then increasing her hours to full-time as the teenage Holly's independence had grown.

'Is it Holly?'

'She's like the living dead, Suze. I'm going to try to get her to the doctor's, ask them for different medication. She can't be left in charge of Mikey like this.'

Suze clucked in sympathy. 'I'll sort something out. You just get things straight there.'

In the living room Holly was almost halfway to sitting upright, like a patient who'd been propped with pillows against her will and was relying on gravity to return her to her preferred position.

'We need to focus on Mikey,' Joanna told her gently. 'If you're feeling like you can't cope on your own, put him in the buggy and push him along to the shop to see me. It'll break up the day a bit for you, stop it stretching out in front of you so much.'

There was no reply.

'We need to think about what *he* needs,' she repeated, 'and I think he needs a bit more of you.'

At last Holly spoke, her voice powerless, the tone bleak. 'He'd be better off without me.'

'That's not true.' Joanna sat beside her with Mikey on her lap, twisting and squirming. It was as if all Holly's vigour had been rerouted to him; he had hours of play in him. 'What would help, Holly? Can you think of anything that would make things better for you? What would be your dream situation?'

It was unusual for Joanna to urge her like this for she had been advised that such methods did not succeed, but on this occasion the pressure did seem to stir Holly from the depths of her despondency and a glimmer of emotion could be detected: it was pure yearning. 'I want Sean,' she said.

'Sean,' Joanna said, blandly, suppressing all criticism and distaste. She'd had three years' practice by now, after all. Three years in which she had watched her daughter's undesirable boyfriend become something far more troubling: an undesirable ex-boyfriend and co-parent. Sean was present now in their lives, in one form or another, *forever*, and yet never there when anyone actually needed him.

'That's all I want,' Holly said, 'just Sean.' And Joanna did not dare correct her by adding 'and Mikey' for fear that Holly would contradict her and make plain once and for all what Joanna most dreaded, that the girl did not love her child, not as she should.

Holly repeated her son's father's name one last time before

dropping her gaze and sinking into the sofa, lowering herself once more below the surface of her solitary world.

The morning after the accident, they all woke up late, Joanna first by a few minutes. She waited until she'd heard Mikey stir in the cot between the twin beds before scooping him up and kissing his face. *You're still here,* she marvelled, *you are still alive. You were saved by a man called James Maitland and I will never forget his name as long as I live.* What the next disaster might be in his young life she couldn't begin to guess, but for now she was content just to bury her nose in his soft, sleep-dampened hair and relish the living warmth of him.

Presently, from the pillows of the other bed, came Holly's voice: 'I feel different.'

Since she said the words almost to herself – using a soft, lilting kind of voice entirely unlike her customary monotone – Joanna wasn't sure if she was expected to respond. Her immediate instinct was to soothe: 'You had a terrible scare yesterday, love. We all did.' She couldn't quite elude the shudder that claimed her upper body at the word 'scare' and caused Mikey to look at her face in surprise. She beamed at him, saying in a bright voice, 'A quieter day today, eh?' Then, across to Holly: 'I wouldn't wish yesterday on my worst enemy.'

'Worse emeny,' Mikey mispronounced, keen to join in.

At this, Holly slipped out of bed with unexpected agility and came to sit on the edge of Joanna's, reaching at once for her son. Reluctantly, Joanna passed him to her, watched her daughter repeat her own grateful embrace of him.

'I feel like . . . I feel like this was meant to happen,' Holly said, then exclaimed, 'Yes, that's it! That's it!'

Startled by her sudden passion, Joanna asked, 'What do you mean, Holls, what was "meant to happen"?'

Holly turned to look at her. Her eyes were fully open and

peculiarly alight. 'Coming here, the accident, the way he was rescued – by a total stranger, Mum!'

'Well, yes, I was just thinking about him,' Joanna said. 'What an amazing man!'

Holly nodded eagerly. 'It's like some kind of second chance.'

Joanna wasn't sure she fully understood what her daughter was saying, but she summoned her tone of agreement as easily as she always did. 'Something like this certainly makes you appreciate what you've already got.' She gestured to their hotel room and added, chuckling, 'Who needs The Ritz now?'

'I know. The room's actually really nice, isn't it?'

This was a reference to their disappointment with the hotel on arrival. A charmless, utilitarian 1970s structure, it was more reminiscent of an under-funded night school than the elegant mansion house Joanna had envisaged. Their room – evidently not the one pictured in the magazine spread – managed to be both sparsely furnished and uncomfortably crammed, especially once Mikey's bulky travel cot had been constructed, and the bathroom was hardly more luxurious than their own at home, which was saying something. There was heavy traffic noise, too, and, no matter how athletically you craned, you had no view whatsoever of the tower or the river.

'Come on, Mikes,' Holly said, animatedly, 'let's sort out this nappy, shall we?'

Joanna watched with curiosity as Holly set about changing and dressing her son with the vim of a woman beginning a spring clean she'd long been itching to get underway, speaking to him playfully as she did and finishing by sliding him safely to the floor to explore. Next, she dressed herself, before standing at the mirror with a hairbrush, still seeking Mikey's eye in the glass and talking to his little reflection. It was a baffling spectacle when you considered that most days in the last two years she had not brushed her hair or washed her face or even changed out of her pyjamas. Some days she'd not eaten; on occasional ones, she'd not spoken. She'd certainly not spoken like this, in the excitable falsetto of a besotted new parent.

'You're probably in shock,' Joanna told her. 'What's happened is the equivalent of an earthquake or a car crash. It's no wonder you feel different.' She echoed her daughter's choice of adjective, thinking it kinder and safer than her own, which was 'strange'.

'But in a good way,' Holly told her, nodding.

'Right.' Joanna simply could not remember the last time her daughter had uttered the phrase 'in a good way' – it was like hearing her speak a foreign language learned in secret. 'I thought you might be in shock last night, as well. It was all so overwhelming, wasn't it?'

She cast her mind back uneasily to the period after the rescue: if Holly's initial hysterical collapse had been anything to go by, she was on course to being hospitalised alongside Mikey, leaving Joanna to handle both his recovery and the procedural interviews. Instead, from the moment they were told by the emergency paediatrician that Mikey had survived his ordeal unharmed, that he would be able to return home with them that night, Holly had dried her tears, straightened her shoulders and become a capable, focused adult.

During her interview with the police – just a formality, for the authorities seemed relieved by the outcome of the accident, especially when Holly agreed that she would be making no complaint regarding the safety fixtures of the boat – she'd hardly been in need of Joanna's support at all. Afterwards, she'd held Mikey close as they returned to the hotel, whispering reassurances to him in exactly the right way and not once complaining of tiredness; she'd put him to bed, watching as he nodded off before whispering good night to Joanna and surrendering to sleep of her own.

It was Joanna who felt as if her nerves had been shredded, never again to mend. It was Joanna who had been up in the night on the hotel computer, Googling accidents on the Seine, needing to know in black and white what Holly accepted as dumb luck – that infants did not often fall into the river and come out alive. Mikey's rescue was extraordinary.

Three times she had watched the BBC footage of a boat that had sunk further upstream a year ago, a young boy among the fatalities; that accident had been at night. Would Mikey have perished if theirs had been an evening cruise? Would the water have been colder, the light more dangerous, the hero less inclined to jump? Less reliable sources offered statistics that even allowing for exaggeration made the blood run cold. The fact was that, on paper, Mikey should be dead. She'd thought he *was* dead: she would never forget that ghastly moment of acceptance on the boat, the gigantic and silent nausea of it.

Returning to their room in the dark and weaving on tiptoe through the awkward maze of available space, she had peered at the little boy in his travel cot, hardly able to believe he was here and not in the hospital morgue. He'd kicked off his blanket, the dark-blue outline of his pyjama-ed arms and legs stark against the white sheet. He looked whole and unscathed, with colour in his cheeks and healthy breath in his chest, a little Moses unaware of his watery adventure.

At lunch in the café next door to the hotel Joanna suggested to Holly that they look up Mikey's rescuer later that day; deliver him a present, perhaps.

'Should we, though?' she wondered aloud. 'Disturb him on his wedding anniversary trip?'

The police officer with the excellent English had told them this detail. Might they do better to keep a discreet distance? To say they'd already bothered him enough was an understatement. On the other hand, a news item on television earlier had shown the hero being interviewed at his hotel that morning, his manner friendly and cooperative, which implied he might be open to callers. In a way, it was odd for them all *not* to meet.

'It's only an anniversary,' Holly said. 'It's not like it's his honeymoon.'

Having never been married herself, Joanna could only concede the distinction. 'James Maitland,' she said. 'That's what he's called.' She thought he sounded like the hero of a novel or a cartoon strip; a mortal who turned superhero after dark and, thankfully, in this case in broad daylight too. 'I didn't see him properly yesterday, did you?'

'No,' Holly said. 'Only on TV today.'

Joanna had hardly been able to glance at him after the rescue: once transported over the bridge, she and Holly had been escorted to the one of two ambulances that contained Mikey and had left for the hospital at once. Though Mikey was breathing well, the paramedics insisted on giving him oxygen and taking him in for tests and observation just the same. In any case, with Holly still inconsolable at this point, Joanna would have had little attention left over for the life saver even if he had directly approached them. As it was, she had heard from one of the hospital staff that he had received his medical treatment at the scene and been permitted to return to his hotel to rest.

'I'll go to his hotel,' Holly said, decisively. She had devoured her omelette and fries, the first time in months Joanna had seen a cleared plate in front of her.

Joanna was surprised. 'On your own? Why don't we all go? I'd love to say thank you and, anyway, he might like to see Mikey again, don't you think? See that he's really all right?'

Holly lowered her mouth to plant a light kiss on the top of Mikey's head; he sat contentedly on her lap, reaching for fries from Joanna's plate. 'It might be too much for him, Mum. For Mikey, I mean. He might get some sort of scary flashback. It's only been twenty-four hours.' She cupped a protective palm over the back of the boy's head and gently stroked his hair. 'When we're home I'll get some advice about it. Maybe he should even see a child psychologist or something? We don't want him to develop a fear of water. It would be awful if he never learned to swim.'

Joanna struggled to conceal her amazement. Holly sounded so sensible, so maternal, entirely unlike the parent she'd been at any but the rarest of occasions during her first twenty-one months on the job. And normally when they were in a café that did not provide a high chair, Mikey sat in *her* lap, not Holly's.

'If that's all right with you,' Holly added. 'If you would be OK to stay with him while I'm out?' And it was a request, not an assumption, another first. It made Joanna feel almost indignant that Holly felt she needed now to ask what she never had before, as if the arrangement they had had was ad hoc and not a long-term commitment on Joanna's part.

'Of course I'm OK,' she said, good-naturedly. 'We'll go to the park, won't we, Mikes? They've got a cl— sandpit, I noticed.' She was about to say climbing frame, but stopped herself. Mikey's passion for climbing had got them into enough trouble for one holiday.

'Great,' Holly said. 'The doctor said he could do normal activities today, so long as he's kept warm and dry.'

She looked completely sure of herself. The word that kept coming to Joanna's mind was serene. Watching her play with Mikey, making rattles of the little sachets of sugar, Joanna had a memory of a film she'd seen in which a man had survived a plane crash and believed himself to be immortal. Was that what Holly was experiencing, then? The same feeling, but by proxy? Was it simply a standard manifestation of post-traumatic shock? And yet this perfect composure, this erasure of her previous state of mind, it was more like something you'd expect after a hard drive had been replaced. It was as if she'd been rebooted, turned off and restarted.

It was the very opposite of how she, Joanna, felt. She was exhausted, overwhelmed, liable to burst into tears; her head –

every sinew of her – was still too full of the near-tragedy of yesterday to make room for anything else. It was a relief, in a way, to not be going to meet James Maitland. The encounter might give *her* a scary flashback.

'I thought I'd take some flowers,' Holly said, 'if I can find some on the way that aren't too expensive.'

Joanna nodded. 'You need some euros, love?'

'No, thank you, I'm fine. I've got enough.'

Back in their hotel room, before she left them, Holly squeezed Mikey to her, crooning goodbye into his chest and making him giggle with the tickle of the vibrations of her voice against his skin. The joy on the little boy's face was a gift in itself.

Incredible, Joanna thought, truly incredible.

Unable to halt it, she allowed a forbidden image to rise closer towards the light: a spirited teenager always in motion; a smart, vibrant girl who'd been on course to avoid all of the mistakes her mother had made – not repeat them. The original Holly, the *real* one. Could this really be possible? Was she going to get her daughter back, as well as her grandson? Or must she do with the thought what she'd learned to do with all her fantasies? Like the one about Adrian, the only man she had loved in twenty years, of going to him and saying, 'I got it wrong, you *were* important, you *are* important . . .' Countless times she'd rehearsed the lines in the deep of night, only in the morning to dismiss them as foolish, false, out of reach. And in the name of self-preservation, all of it.

As she watched Holly open the door and cast a final look Mikey's way before leaving, Joanna remembered again the character in the film. He had not been immortal, as it turned out; he had not been made invincible.

He had been only lucky.

Holly had left her phone and cigarettes behind. Cigarettes, she could buy on the way if she had to – come to think of it, she had not smoked one today, which was revolutionary in itself – but Joanna half expected her to return for the phone, so unwilling was she normally to be parted from it, so painful the separation if ever she was. Even though she'd lost everyday touch with her friends, she kept it close for the sporadic messages she received from Sean.

It rang almost straight away, of course, set at top volume, startling Joanna with whatever ringtone Holly favoured this week. Mikey looked up at once, toddled over to her and made a grab for it.

'Mama phone,' he said.

'Yes. Shall we answer?'

The name 'Sean' had appeared on the display.

He was with another girl now, of course, one unburdened by motherhood – or a brain. For all her blindness to Sean's faults, Holly *was* intelligent. But at least Letitia wasn't someone Holly had known from before, an old schoolmate, one of the ones who had drifted off since their friend gave up college to have a baby. As if babies carried a contagious disease.

She picked up the call, swallowing an anxious sigh before she spoke. 'Hello, Sean, this is Joanna. Holly's not here, I'm afraid.'

'Mmm, hi.' Sean spoke in a mumble at the best of times, properly problematic on the phone when you could not see his mouth or glean clues from his body language. Without those accidental good looks of his to deceive you, he was, in her opinion, more imbecile than object of desire. 'How's Paris? All right?'

'Fine. A bit tiring. There's such a lot to see.' Feeling sure Holly had not spoken to him during the weekend, Joanna thought it best not to mention his son's near-fatal accident. Did they have a responsibility to do so? Holly did, surely, but the question of contacting him had not come up last night amid the battery of medical tests and succession of visits from officials. Still, however hopeless he was, he remained the boy's father. She made a mental note to discuss the matter with Holly when she returned.

'Mikey with you?'

'Yes, he's just here, right as rain. I'll pass you over if you like?' But after half a minute of bemused listening (was Sean actually saying anything to him?), Mikey dropped the phone to the floor without uttering a syllable, his eye caught by one of his toys at the foot of the nearest bed.

Joanna returned the phone to her ear. 'You still there, Sean?'

'Yeah.' There was an awkward pause. 'So, did Holls tell you what I said earlier?'

Earlier? So they *had* spoken, then. But he couldn't possibly already know about the accident or he surely would have raised the subject right away, asked after Mikey's recovery. 'No, I don't think so,' she said, cautiously. 'I didn't realise you'd been in touch while we've been here.'

'This morning I rang.' The way he spoke, it often sounded as if he had the words in the wrong order, translated from another language, perhaps. 'Said I wouldn't mind hooking up for real again.'

Joanna didn't speak, couldn't, not if he'd just mumbled what she thought he'd just mumbled. *Hooking up for real*? Presumably that meant reuniting with Holly with something more than a day-by-day commitment in mind. Why had Holly not told her this? She supposed the conversation must have taken place after breakfast, when Mikey had napped and Joanna had showered. She'd spent some time in there, willing the hot water to rinse her of her emotions, numb her. Was this, then, the reason for Holly's change in attitude: the longed-for return of Sean the wastrel? How disappointing – though not unpredictable – that it should turn out to be he and not Mikey who had inspired it.

But no, the change *had* to be directly linked to the accident because it had been evident last night and again on waking. Unless texts had been exchanged between the two of them at

51

the hospital or during the night, Sean couldn't have had anything to do with it.

'Well, I thought you were with Letitia now, Sean? Is that not the case?'

There was a pause, and she imagined him frowning at the query, scratching the back of his neck, waiting for a mate to help him out as if he were back in the classroom. Joanna knew she was guilty of imagining both Holly and Sean as far younger than they were, still of school age. Was it any wonder, though, the way the two of them had conducted their relationship?

'It's for Mikey's sake,' he offered, eventually, adding, as he often did, 'y'know?'

Again there was no direct mention of the accident; this was, then, a peculiar coincidence. In a more sensitive boy she might have suspected a form of paternal instinct, a sixth sense that his son had fallen in harm's way and was in need of protection, but not Sean. The jury was still out as to his basic *five* senses.

'And what does Holly think about all this?' She spoke with forced cheer, knowing he was not the one she should be asking.

'Don't know. Said she'd think about it. By the sounds, not that keen.'

'I see.' Joanna honestly could not identify which was the dominant of the emotions this second, most casual of revelations caused in her. It was either relief that Holly would not be getting back together with him – the temporal equivalent of throwing good money after bad – or disbelief that she had not bitten his hand off at such an offer. Wasn't this, rightly or wrongly, exactly what Holly wanted? The one thing she claimed would succeed where the counsellors and the antidepressants had failed? (The thought reminded her that, with everything going on, she had not checked if Holly had taken her medication that morning.)

She must be playing with him, Joanna thought, wearily; making him wait a day or two before consenting, biding her time before beginning the necessary process of persuasion that would lead to Sean moving in to the flat with them. Realistically, it was either that or Holly and Mikey move in with Sean's family, and Joanna would agree to anything before she agreed to *that*.

'Well, I'll tell her you called, Sean. I'm sure she'll phone you back soon and talk about it some more.'

'Yeah, I thought that.'

And he hung up without saying goodbye, unaware evidently of the turmoil he had provoked.

There was much for Mikey to do in the park at the foot of the tower, the Champ de Mars, as it was called. There were pigeons to shoo and dogs to chase, teenage girls with long blonde hair to charm as they took photos of each other and then turned the lens on Mikey to surprise him. They looked at the fountains and the trees, the buskers and the dancers. Mikey screamed out in delight at the spectacle, struggling to be allowed to join in. He was exactly his usual self, apparently unscarred in any way.

Even so, Joanna decided to avoid the donkey rides and the pedal cars on the miniature racetrack, either of which might lead to some new unscheduled danger. She distracted Mikey from them by calling out, 'Look at the tower! We were right at the top yesterday, do you remember – isn't it tall?' and turning him towards the huge receding structure. Each time he gazed up at it as if having never seen it before in his life. She loved that about small children, their endless capacity for surprise. Holly had been the same, always gasping, always straining to get at objects in the distance, as if she could touch anything in the world for herself if she only kept on reaching.

She let him toddle on the grass, kick up the dust on the pathways, as he saw other children do, and when she'd grown tired of running after him she took him to the enclosed playground and lowered him into the sandpit. Passing by, one of the teenage girls they'd seen earlier called out to him again and his little cheeks swelled with pleasure at the attention. Something about the girl's smile made Joanna think once more of Melissa on that family holiday years ago, of her winning heart-shaped face with its strong jaw and wide-set eyes, that high-value blonde hair combed smooth beneath the beret.

Perhaps it was her agitated state of mind after yesterday – her emotions tumbled and oscillated, quicksilver creatures with wills of their own – that allowed a memory to break to the surface that must have been buried for decades. She'd certainly had no sense of it when she'd been thinking previously of Melissa and the coveted bag, the petulance that had followed its denial, how Melissa had refused to speak to either parent for two whole days, communicating only through Joanna. But all of a sudden Joanna knew how the stalemate had been resolved. On the last day of the trip, as they waited to check in at the airport, their parents gave the two of them souvenirs, a family tradition at the end of every holiday. For Joanna there was a book of Impressionist paintings, for Melissa the bag.

At the sight of it Melissa squealed with joy, her feet leaving the ground. After hugging her father and modelling the item over her shoulder, she called triumphantly to Joanna: 'See, he's not such a Scrooge after all, you were wrong!' Which caused their mother to frown unhappily at Joanna and say, 'Well, if that's how you feel about your father, Jo, we'll take that book back, shall we?'

Joanna began to defend herself – 'That's not what I meant, that's not what we . . . !' – before quickly giving up. There was no point in putting the record straight, no more point than in mourning her sister's betrayal. She should never have believed in their accord in the first place; sixteen years of experience should have told her that.

But something had begun to sprout by the time of that Paris trip, she knew, some embryonic shoot deep inside that moved a

54

cell at a time towards the light – what was it? *Of course*, it was to do with Melissa going off to university. Contrary to their parents' pronouncements that Joanna would miss her sister as terribly as they would, she was in fact looking forward to Melissa leaving home that autumn, for it stood to reason that the golden girl would be taking her shadow with her, finally freeing Joanna from it. Perhaps, at last, Joanna would be able to keep her parents' eyes on her for longer than a few seconds.

Instead . . . Well, if someone had told Joanna that day at the airport that little more than two years later she would be cast out, lost forever to her parents and her sister, she'd have dismissed it as impossible, unnatural. Now, of course, it was their having been together in the first place that seemed impossible, not only Paris and other family holidays but also her whole childhood, like something she'd read in a story and chosen to superimpose over the real history of her early life.

'Gama,' Mikey said, by her legs, using the whine that meant he was tired and would be difficult to extract if she didn't do it quickly. His clothes were coated in sand and he held a bucket that belonged to another child. There was sand in his hair, too. She needed to get back and wash him, start his evening routine. He twisted defiantly when she tried to strap him into his pushchair, rejecting the biscuit she hoped would ease the process of returning the bucket to its owner and screaming noisily.

'Calm down, sweetheart, we'll soon be back at the hotel . . .'

Walking through the park gates, the light fading to dusk, she had again that feeling she'd had at the Louvre on Friday: is this how I expected my life to be?

Is it?

For it was no longer a case of restarting, rebooting, as Holly may or may not have been in the process of doing. No, *her* life was well underway, halfway through, at least, the best in all probability behind her.

Maybe it was the effects of anticlimax or relief, a draining of adrenalin from her nervous system, but as she pushed the buggy in the direction of the hotel entrance she was struck by an emotion she had not felt in years, not since Holly was born and rendered secondary the whole horrible mess of what had gone before.

She felt shame.

Chapter 5

A week ago – no, even two days ago! – Holly would have been too intimidated by the Hôtel des Vosges to go in. Had she had any cause to, that was, which she had not, for such places – elegant, modish, obviously costly – might as well have been in a different solar system for all their relevance to her.

It took longer to get there than she'd estimated and, by the time she arrived, swollen with heat and the skin on her heels beginning to break, it was late afternoon and the entrance was quiet.

'*Bonjour, mademoiselle . . .*' In spite of the correctness of his greeting, the doorman appeared reluctant to let her through the glass doors, stepping aside only at the very last moment (even in south London she had never been physically barred entry to a place!). She supposed it was because she looked like a street person or something, sweaty and dishevelled and with bleeding blisters, but she didn't care. Let him judge her. She felt she knew exactly where she belonged, or at least someone knew on her behalf, her guardian angel or whoever it was who had chosen this weekend to intervene in her life and give her this second chance, and right at this moment where she belonged was wherever James Maitland was.

In the lobby there was silence, the expensive kind, all sound absorbed by layers of luxurious fabric – wool rugs on the polished floors, silk on the walls, velvet on the sofas and chairs – and the few guests in evidence were speaking so discreetly they looked as if they might not actually be talking at all but only mouthing words to one another; miming. It seemed to Holly that the whole place had been designed as a puzzle or a test: no piece of furniture had the right number of arms or legs, the lighting was low to the point of hazardous, and there were none of the helpful signs you usually saw in a public place.

Naturally, the front desk was not at the front at all but at the rear, out of sight of the main doors and stumbled upon only after two false starts. The receptionist had likely been hired as much for her beauty as for her receiving skills and she treated Holly to the kind of cool inspection that a week ago – no, even two days ago! – would have reduced her to tears. But not now. She smiled warmly and asked for James Maitland, giving her own name quietly and without explanation.

'Holly Walsh?' The girl's accent made it sound like Holy Walsh. However she said it, she put the names together quickly enough and, thawing noticeably, made a phone call to convey the message. With new attention, she told Holly that *Monsieur* Maitland would come down directly if she would like to take a seat.

'*Merci*,' Holly replied, though the exchange until that last word had been in English, and she was rewarded for her belated effort with an actual smile.

She perched on the edge of a three-legged velvet stool, longing to take off her sandals and sink her sore feet into the deep grass of the carpet. She had not planned what she was going to say to James Maitland, trusting that the guardian angel would supply the words, just as he or she now did the confidence needed to spring up, beaming, at the sound of lift doors opening, at the sight of a man striding into the lobby towards her. He was in his early thirties, not especially tall or athletically built but moving with attractive litheness; even from several paces away she could see he was as handsome and kind-eyed as he'd looked on television.

'Are you Mr Maitland?' she asked as he came to a halt in front of her. 'I'm Holly Walsh.'

There was a faint quizzical cast to his eyes as they settled on her. Perhaps he couldn't relate her to the figure he'd glimpsed yesterday at the scene. She understood this: even allowing for her hysterical weeping, the girl she'd been twenty-four hours ago was not the one she was now.

'I'm Mikey's mum. I hope you don't mind me dropping by without warning?'

'Of course not, I'm glad. And call me James, please.' He smiled back at her, meaning his words. His voice was low and confident, with the kind of well-educated accent that seemed to make agreement a foregone conclusion. 'I was hoping to meet you before we left.'

He reached out and shook her hand. His skin felt dry and warm; hers, she knew, was still clammy from the trek, but she gripped eagerly, savouring the contact. Her eye moved from their joined hands to his wrist and forearm and up to the outline of his shoulders, hard and broad within his white shirt. These were the same arms and shoulders that had propelled him through the currents of the Seine, allowed him to reach her son with superhuman speed. They seemed to her to radiate pure male strength.

For a few moments they stood facing each other, neither speaking. She would have liked to have taken a step closer to him, the better to examine his handsomeness, the very thick brown hair, the square white teeth, the well-defined jaw. He looked more American than British, she decided. Once, she would have thought this type too bland, too safe, the very opposite of the love of her life, Sean, who was boyishly pretty and edgy and cool, but not now. Now, James Maitland represented the adult to Sean's adolescent, the future to the past.

'So how's the little man?' he asked, at last. 'Has he recovered from his ordeal?'

'He seems all right, thank you. Quite perky, actually.'

'Well, I'm not a doctor but I'd say that's a good thing.' As he dipped his gaze, he grimaced a little: he'd noticed the blood on one of her ankles. 'What's this?'

'Oh, it's nothing,' Holly said, hooking the sorer of the two ankles around the other. 'Just a blister. I walked from my hotel and it was further than I thought.'

'It's bleeding quite badly. Wait here a second . . .' To her dismay James was moving away from her, out of sight towards the reception desk, and she could hear him asking for something in French – a first aid box, she realised as he came back a minute later with a handful of plasters. Her delight returned, redoubled, as he ushered her through a nearby archway to a big lavender-coloured sofa and told her, 'Sit here. Much better for the walking wounded than those ridiculous tripods. '

The deep corner of the sofa cupped her body more firmly than she'd expected, making her sigh out loud with the relief of being supported. This drew another smile from James. Seated in the opposite corner, he patted his lap, and she saw he was proposing to take her foot into it and apply the plaster himself. Her desire to feel the touch of his dry hands again outweighed her embarrassment at the condition of her foot. In fact, she felt only his fingertips, a small pressure from his thumb, and once the plaster was in place, she drew her foot towards her and lifted a smear of dried blood with a quick rub of her own saliva.

'Done like a true mother,' he said, which she thought a lovely remark. *A true mother*, no one had ever called her that before. 'That looks painful,' he added. 'How far have you walked?'

'From . . .' She wasn't sure how to pronounce the name of the street their hotel was on and so said, vaguely, 'Near the Eiffel Tower, right by the park there.'

He looked even more concerned now. 'That's miles away!

You should have jumped on the Metro. But I guess it makes sense you might be a bit wary of the city's transport system after what happened yesterday.'

That was kind of him. The accident had been no fault of the tour operator, of the city itself; if it had, children would be falling overboard at the rate of several an hour, littering the Seine like buoys.

'Are you all right?' he asked, and she didn't know if he meant the ankle or the fact that she was staring so frankly at him, and, worse, seemed to have no way of making herself stop. She was like Mikey when the TV was switched on, magnetically drawn to the music and light, impossible to distract from it. 'You must be exhausted, and no wonder. Let me get you a cup of tea or a glass of wine or something. What would you like?'

'Oh, just water, please. I'm thirsty.'

'No problem.' Though they weren't seated in the bar – that, she saw, was through an arch on the other side of the lobby – it seemed as if a member of staff sprang from thin air at the first turn of James's chin, ready to do his bidding as a matter of highest priority. Was this superior service or just the effect he had on people? she wondered. Conscious of her ankle throbbing, she sank deeper into her seat, stretching her legs in front of her as she watched the waiter retreat.

'This is a lovely hotel.' She nodded to a painting above James's head. 'What's that a picture of?'

He glanced up at the large rectangle of curdled grey. 'God only knows. The French view of the English, perhaps? Dim and murky.'

They both laughed. Holly marvelled in the sheer unfamiliarity of happiness – or absence of unhappiness; it was so pleasurable a feeling, so liberating. She felt she could say or do anything she pleased and it would be utterly right. 'They didn't want to let me in here, actually,' she said, without complaint. 'I'm way too scruffy, I suppose.'

James looked insulted on her behalf. 'They were probably just being a bit overzealous because of the press. They didn't know who you were.'

He made it sound as if she was special, someone worth knowing about, and she liked that. She'd file it in her memory of the meeting alongside 'a true mother'.

'That's why they've got a doorman today,' he told her. 'They don't normally have one, this is only a small place, but there were a whole load of media people here this morning. The manager told them that was it, just the one interview, but a few came back to take some pictures this afternoon when we were out and they decided to camp out until we got back. Alexa's getting pretty sick of it.'

This was the first time Holly had heard his wife's name. There was a subtle note of longsuffering to it that didn't sound right for a man celebrating his wedding anniversary and she did not like to examine the hopeful feeling that gave her.

'We heard it's your anniversary this weekend,' she said.

'Today, actually.'

'Oh. I'm really sorry if it's been ruined.'

'No need to be sorry. It's not your fault.' But he didn't deny that the weekend had been ruined and she didn't like to dwell on the feeling *that* gave her, either.

The water arrived just then and she gulped half at once.

'Have you had the same?' he asked her. 'Reporters hanging around your hotel, phoning and begging for quotes, that kind of thing?'

'At the hospital there was a TV crew waiting outside when we left, but we didn't speak to anyone. We just wanted to get Mikey back to the hotel.'

'Oh, yes, I think we saw a shot of you leaving on the local news.'

'And we saw a clip of you too today, it must have been a bit from the interview you mentioned, but someone was talking over you in French so I couldn't work out what you were saying.'

'Nothing worth listening to, I'm sure,' James said, grinning. 'Anyway, I think it is all over now. They've got bigger fish to fry.'

She wondered if he was thinking what she was: how different this would have been if Mikey had not survived the accident, if James's rescue had failed; how different this meeting would be, if it were to take place at all. She couldn't stop the shudder the thought caused, or the grimace, a brief bodily denial of this exciting new self-composure of hers, this condition that allowed laughter, and he must have seen it because the atmosphere between them changed in that instant and when he spoke next it was with a voice that came from low in his throat, an intensity that seized his whole face: 'What happened on the boat, Holly? How did he fall?'

She realised then that everything she had said to those who'd come before him, to the police and the doctors and the dozens of other emergency personnel who'd tended Mikey and her, even Joanna, had been no more than a prelude to this, the real conversation.

'He was standing against the rail,' she said, her strained tone echoing his. 'He wanted to climb it like a ladder . . . I turned away from him for a second, I was just getting his beaker from the bottom of the buggy, but I still had my hand on him, on one of his legs, I think. I felt it pull a couple of times as he tried to climb again, and then suddenly much harder, and he slipped out of my grip.' As she spoke, the flow of concentration between James and her felt unyielding, a mutual thrall. 'I turned back, reaching for him, but he was gone. It happened like lightning, I didn't even see it. When I looked up he just wasn't there. I knew he must have fallen.' She paused to fill her lungs, her eyes still gripped by his. He remained utterly still. 'I thought he'd gone under the boat: that was my first thought. I thought he must have been sucked under. I imagined those wheel things, you know, like you get on a paddle steamer or something. I can't really remember much after that, I lost my mind.' For the first time in this meeting her voice eluded her control, rising with emotion. 'It was worse than any nightmare, it was horrific, but it wasn't real either. I don't know the right word to describe it.'

'I don't either,' James said, very gently. 'Horrific will do.'

At the first intimation of that gentleness it was already too late: her eyes were filling. 'Did you . . . did you not see him fall, then?' she whispered. James, she'd been told, had been on the rear lower deck with his wife, and she had pictured them gasping as Mikey's tiny body – arms and legs outstretched or curled into a protective foetal ball? – streaked vertically in front of their faces before it hit the water.

'No,' James said. 'I was lying back in my seat, not really looking at the buildings, or just out of the corner of my eye, anyway. But other people saw him go in, obviously, because everyone was screaming out, calling for the crew. I remember jumping up and looking to where everyone was pointing. I saw him straight away; the boat was still moving, of course, away from him, but I could see him bobbing. He must have just resurfaced.'

Holly waited, rapt.

'So I climbed over the side and dropped into the water after him.'

'Just like that, without thinking?'

'I reacted on instinct, I can't remember what I was thinking, and Alexa says I didn't say a word to her. I just knew I had to be quick because he was going to be pulled under at any second, and I realised he was very young and might have been injured by the fall as well. Obviously he wouldn't be able to swim.' He paused, frowning to himself a little. 'At least I think I must have been thinking those things, but I might have added them afterwards, you know?'

'Yes, I know,' Holly said, 'it's hard to know what was real. I don't remember it like a normal memory.' Her voice had grown so faint she'd become one of the hotel lobby's mouths that murmured inaudible words.

James went on: 'I do know that the boat was slowing down by then, but I could hear the engines were still on and I was worried about propellers, so when I got to Mikey I decided not to swim back towards the boat just in case. I wasn't sure whether it was going to turn or come back towards us, I didn't know how well the crew could see us.'

'There was no distress signal,' Holly remembered. Other than her own, she thought.

'They don't have an alarm or anything like that here. They'd definitely contacted the authorities, though, by then. They told us the procedure afterwards; the crew calls the river police radio and says: *Il y a une personne à l'eau en Seine.* That's the official message.'

Holly repeated the words to herself.

'I thought that if they held the boat where it was then the island was almost as close anyway and so I might as well aim for that. I could see steps built into the quay – there aren't that many along the Seine and so I just went for it.'

'Mikey didn't drag you down?' Holly asked.

'He was too light for that. He was like a puppy or a kitten.'

Holly felt tears roll towards her chin, dropping in turn from each eye.

'If I hadn't gone in, someone else would have, you know,' James said, with conviction. 'One of the crew, probably, some-one trained in life-saving. Just as soon as they realised what was going on. He was always going to be reached in time.'

Holly shook her head. What he was saying opposed her every instinct – that this had been a freak survival, a one in a million lucky chance; any other combination of elements and Mikey *would* have drowned.

Meeting his eye once more, it seemed to her that he was look-ing at her as if she were the one he'd rescued.

And I am, she thought.

'It's true,' he said, and she heard the words not as an addition to his previous statement but in answer to her own thoughts.

'Was his . . . When you got to him was his head still above the surface or did you have to dive under and look for him?'

'I think his head was above water. It's hard to remember exactly, I was just aiming for the splashing and the current was bringing him towards me, which helped. But when he fell in he must have gone under for a second or two at least, mustn't he? He went in from quite a height. What did the hospital say? He can't have swallowed too much water if they were happy to dis-charge him so quickly?'

'They tested him for everything,' Holly said. 'They said it was incredible he even survived the fall without any broken bones, let alone all that time in the water. The temperature, all the pollutants . . . They kept saying it was a miracle. Everyone who examined him said that. I don't speak much French but the word is the same.' To her great consternation, tears were now teeming from her eyes and her nose running. 'I'm sorry, I didn't mean to get upset . . .'

He moved closer, reaching for her free hand. 'Hey, it's OK. It must have been terrible for you, of course you're upset. Far easier to be in the water *doing* something.' His hand squeezed hers, stayed in place. She could feel the bones of his fingers. 'But the great thing is there's a happy ending. The miracle went your way.'

She looked up, blinking through the wet. The way he said it, with a faint emphasis on 'your', made it sound as if there was also someone whom it had gone *against*. For everyone who gained there was someone who lost: a child in a river on the other side of the world, without the hero on board ready to leap as if to a starter pistol, without the current going 'the right way'.

She sniffed, took her hand from his and wiped her running nostrils with her fingers, tried not to think how dreadful this must look.

'My mum says dozens of people drown in the Seine every year, and even more in the Thames. Some of them die because they're trying to rescue someone else. They don't realise when they jump in they're just going to double the body count.'

James blinked. 'I suppose because I used to swim competitively it didn't feel such a crazy thing to do. I wasn't in the Olympics or anything, but I was in the regional squad for a while. I was always quite fast and so I knew I had a pretty good chance of getting to him.'

Holly's heart rate quickened. 'Do you still train?'

He pulled a face. 'No, I hardly ever go near a pool now. But it's like riding a bike: your body knows what to do.'

'Thank God it did.'

There was a silence. She swabbed again at her nose and eyes. 'Anyway, I know you must be busy, I won't ask you any more questions.'

'You can ask me as many as you like,' James said, smiling.

Her tears stemmed, she watched his face come back into focus, handsome and caring and good. He looked so good he seemed almost *holy*. Perhaps that was what made her remember her little offering. 'Oh, these are for you.' She passed him the small packet of yellow tulips she'd bought on her way and he took them with unexpected ceremony, laid them across his knees like something irreplaceably precious.

'Thank you.'

'We go home tomorrow morning,' she said.

'You're just here for the weekend?'

'Yes. My mum won the trip in a competition.' She paused. 'It was supposed to cheer me up, actually, because I haven't been very happy recently.'

He raised his eyebrows. 'Well, I'm sorry that hasn't happened.'

'No, it's all right. I *do* feel better, that's the weird thing. *Much* better. I know that must sound funny, I don't know how to explain it, but it's like I've had that electric shock thing they give people when they've lost their heartbeat. You know, to get it started again?'

'I *do* know, yes.' And there was a flare in his face, something caught between curiosity and gratitude, as if she'd given him the solution to a calculation that had been tormenting him. Never, ever, had Sean looked at her in this way.

'I just want you to know . . .' Though she breathed in a normal lungful of air she felt as if she'd just inhaled twenty balloons' worth. She had reached the crucial moment, the part she realised she had come for. 'I just want you to know that I owe you my life. I mean mine as well as Mikey's. If he'd died, I couldn't have gone on. I'll do anything to repay you, anything.'

She could see he was taken aback by this declaration because he looked for the first time at a loss for words; his smile lost some of its assurance. 'You don't need to repay me. It's not that kind of situation.'

'*Anything*,' she repeated. 'I really mean it.' Feeling wet on her leg, she saw that the hand that held the glass was shaking, making the water spill.

'Let me take that,' James said. He leaned forward and took the glass, held it steady in his own hand.

She knew they had reached the natural end of this conversation, that he would soon need to go back upstairs to his wife. It might be the last time she saw him, she thought. What could she say to keep him here, just for a few minutes longer?

'Where is Mikey's father?' he asked, suddenly. 'Do you mind my asking? He's obviously not in Paris with you?'

'No, we're not together any more.'

'Ah.'

For a moment she felt the weight of her old inferiority, the shame of broken families in her history, but just as quickly the brand new truth of her situation reasserted itself, her sense that salvation that weekend was hers as well as Mikey's. Just now she'd described it as having been brought back to life by electric shock, but that wasn't quite right. What was the word when people on death row were let off at the last minute? *Reprieved.*

'It's better without him,' she said. 'I mean, he loves Mikey, he really does, but he's not much use. He's a bit of a moron, actually.'

James laughed, a gruff sound like a dog's first bark. 'Well, we'll just have to hope Mikey takes after you instead then.'

She accepted the teasing with good grace. 'I'm sorry. You don't want to know about Sean.' And nor do I, she thought, not now.

'You didn't want to bring him with you?' James asked. 'Mikey, I mean?'

'No, he's back at the hotel with my mum. I wasn't sure if he'd get upset if he saw you again so soon.'

'I hadn't thought of that. A shame, though, it would have been nice to see him again on dry land.' The grin reappeared, along with steady eye contact, thrilling her. 'Well, maybe we can organise a reunion back home some time.'

Holly's heart bounced.

'Do you live in London?'

'Yes, in Crystal Palace.'

'We're Chiswick,' he said. 'Right near Bedford Corner.'

She imagined his house, something smart, posh, with an interior like the one of this hotel, perhaps, everything soft and low and clever, with paintings of unidentifiable emotions above sofas. The front door would be glossy black like Downing Street, or the shiny red of Mikey's toy fire engine.

When it was discovered that neither had their phones with them, James scribbled her number on notepaper supplied by the receptionist. 'Can I get a taxi for you?' he asked. 'I can't let you limp all the way back to the Eiffel Tower.'

'No, no, thank you. I'm fine. I'll get one outside, or find a bus or something.'

'Well, if you're sure.' He looked at her a final time. 'Safe trip home.' And then he laughed. 'I really mean that. Get yourself home safely, Holly, for me.'

It was blissful, like something from a favourite dream, to hear him say her name, the words 'for me'. She wished it was the first of a thousand times he'd say those words together; she couldn't bear it to be the last; she already knew this wasn't going to be enough.

As she walked through the dusk of the square, cutting through its centre, surer now of her route, she remembered above all one phrase from the conversation: Maybe back home.

Definitely back home.

She was disappointed that Mikey was already asleep by the time she reached the hotel.

'We stayed in the park for almost three hours,' her mother said. 'He couldn't keep his eyes open when I was changing him for bed. He was shattered. What a weekend!'

The word 'shattered' made Holly linger a fraction longer at the foot of Mikey's cot, watching his chest inflate and deflate. Her mother had dimmed the lights and adjusted the air conditioning to the most comfortable temperature for him. They would not eat out that evening, as they had the first night and had intended to each of the three, using the spending money Joanna had won. Instead, one of them would go out and pick up some takeaway food and then they'd sit on their twin beds and watch television, the volume so low it would be a strain to hear it. Joanna would probably get out her book; Holly would lie awake and just *marvel*.

'How did it go?' Joanna asked, her voice hushed. 'What was he like?'

'It was great. He was nice, really nice. We talked about the accident.'

Joanna looked anxious. 'Oh yes? What did he say?'

As Holly repeated the new details James had supplied about the rescue, her mother closed her eyes in resistance, as if to picture it again was to alter the outcome. 'He said he just reacted without thinking.'

Joanna shook her head in wonder. 'How many people would do that, Holly? And a competitive swimmer when he was younger? We were very, very lucky he was on the same boat as us.'

'*He* said someone else would have gone in if he hadn't, like one of the crew,' Holly told her. But she knew her mother shared her view – and, for that matter, that of the officials who had spoken of miracles – that no one else would have reacted 'without thinking', and the seconds they would have taken to do that thinking would have counted.

'Sounds like he's modest on top of everything else,' Joanna said.

'He is. He's lovely.'

There was a pause. 'Sean phoned. You left your mobile behind.'

'I realised,' Holly said. 'I wanted to phone you and let you know I was on my way back. I'm sorry I took so long.'

'Don't be silly, we were fine here.'

Holly could see her mother thought she had missed the point of her original comment, but wasn't certain what that point was.

'Sean spoke to Mikey a bit,' Joanna continued. 'I didn't say anything about what happened, I hope that was right? I wasn't sure if you'd told him or not.'

'No, I didn't think that would be a good idea.'

Joanna looked unconvinced, but said only, 'No need to get everyone worried, I suppose.'

'I mean on the phone,' Holly said. 'I want to tell him about it in person, when he can see for himself that Mikey's alive and well. I don't want to upset Geraldine.' Geraldine, Sean's mother, was as apt to dramatise as Sean was indifferent.

Her mother was relieved by this judgement. 'Yes, that's the right thing to do. There's not much he can do now anyway, but he ought to know.' She paused, meaningfully. 'He said he asked you to get back together with him?'

Ah. *Now* they'd reached the point. Though Holly didn't particularly wish to discuss it, wanting nothing but to be allowed to lie on her bed in silence and replay her conversation with James, she knew it must seem strange to her mother that she'd withheld news that a week ago would have gushed from her in a fountain. The truth was that she'd dismissed Sean from her mind almost as soon as the call ended, thinking of him again only when asked by James. By the time Joanna had come out of the shower Holly had begun thinking about something else.

'He did, yes, I meant to tell you.'

'And?'

'He says he's split up with Letitia. They had a big row.' It was quite clear to her now that Sean had got in touch with her because he'd argued with Letitia and not that he'd argued with Letitia because he wanted to get back with her. Her mother's expression told her she had seen the distinction straight away.

'And I said no.' She tried to sound more interested than she was in order to do justice to her mother's incredulity, which was almost comical to watch.

'He said as much himself, but I wasn't sure if I heard him right. Do you really mean it, Holly?'

'Yes. I don't need him. I want him to keep in touch with Mikey but I don't want anything to do with him beyond that.'

Joanna's eyes were wide with hope. 'Well, you've always got me, you know that, don't you?'

'Yes.'

'I'll always be here to help, no matter what.'

'I know.' And for the first time since her son's birth Holly had an inkling of what it might feel like to not need *that*, either, to not need to rely on her mother's support every day as she had in the past.

To look only to the future.

Chapter 6

'So, Mrs Maitland . . .' James eyed Alexa with mischief as they awaited the arrival of the hotel's only elevator. 'What's on the agenda for our last day?'

It was a joke, that 'Mrs Maitland', a well-worn one, for Alexa had kept her own name, of course, when they'd married. It had never struck her until now that it should be significant, the relegation of a centuries-old tradition to the realm of ironic nicknames, and she felt momentarily just a little regretful of her original stand. After all, wasn't the name she defended only a man's, too: her father's?

'We said we'd have lunch in Montmartre, didn't we? And then shopping in Saint-Germain in the afternoon.'

'Oh, yes, that's right. Toulouse-Lautrec followed by Sartre: the beaten path.'

'There's a reason why paths are beaten,' Alexa pointed out with a playful lift of her brows. 'It's because there's something worth seeing at the end of them.'

'You're no fun,' he sighed.

'Well, that depends on your definition of the word, doesn't it?'

The lift doors slid apart and they stepped into the mirrored box towards their reflections. The lighting was even more flattering in here than it was in their room, widening her eyes, filling her lips, blurring her frown lines. She was not as attractive as James, she was the first to admit to it; you couldn't argue with bone structure any more than you could the five-year age difference. For, ten years into their relationship, the exoticism of 'older' had long come to feel like a liability and was, she well knew, the direct cause of her recent weight loss campaign, her ever-intensifying grooming programme. She considered both drives painful but worthwhile, had been gratified that Andrew, who had been at their wedding, had not recognised her when he saw her with James in the hotel bar.

Catching James's eye, she considered initiating a movie-style clinch, pressing him hard against the wall and watching the mirror behind his head mist with her breath, but it was too late: the five storeys had passed by and they were already being deposited on the ground floor.

'No press today, thank God,' she observed as they walked towards the lobby. Her heels clacked briefly on the square of marble by the reception desk, before being silenced by wool. 'Looks like your fifteen minutes of fame must be up, darling.'

'Oh, I didn't do it for the fame,' James joked, on cue. 'I did it for the sex.'

'Pleased to hear it.' She stopped herself from casting the meaningful glance she wanted to because she didn't think she could contain what this exchange represented to her, but, oh, what a wonderful feeling it was to know that she would go back to London and report to her friends that her mission had succeeded. For she and James had made love yesterday evening – on their anniversary itself! What a relief to know her fears had been unfounded: he did still want her, he did still love her.

True, it had not been at all promising when he'd returned upstairs from his meeting with the girl whose child he'd rescued. He'd been gone *ages*, causing Alexa to wonder if this was what

75

house arrest felt like, albeit a luxurious version, for she seemed to be spending so much of the day alone in their room.

'*That* was a long hello,' she remarked from in front of the mirror, where, still in her robe after a bath, she was finishing her make-up.

'What? Hmm.' He was holding a bunch of tulips and began looking about their suite, obviously trying to work out which of the several well-filled vases he could squeeze the new flowers into.

'Flowers?' Alexa was unable to decide if she was cross with him or not. 'Are they from the girl? That's very Eliza Doolittle of her.' The comment sounded snider than she'd intended – she *was* cross, then – and James sent her an unimpressed look.

'If Eliza Doolittle had a son who almost drowned, yes.' He took a bowl of white roses from the mantelpiece and began poking the tulips between the crossed stems. The tulips were shorter and looked silly, but she stopped herself from commenting.

'Was that her, with the red hair and short skirt? I think I saw her out of the window.'

'Must have been.'

'She looked like she was limping?'

'Yes, she had a really bad blister. The skin was completely rubbed away.'

Alexa watched as he returned the vase to its original spot and discarded the wrapping from the tulips. His hands seemed to have unusual control and precision as he balled the paper and aimed it at the waste paper basket. It landed dead centre, not touching the sides. She turned back to the mirror and began to fork her fingers through her hair and touch up her lipstick. It was a colour she hadn't used before, dark, plum-coloured, and in the mirror she could see James's eyes settling for a moment on her mouth before moving restlessly on.

'So what did she say to you? Tell me everything.'

His mouth twisted in reluctance. 'Nothing to tell, she just said thank you. We had a quick drink. She's a really nice girl.'

His mood was quite different from when he'd left. After a long lunch, during which he'd answered Alexa's questions about the press conference and shared its highlights, he'd been relaxed, but now he was jittery, ankles rocking, fingers tapping. She had a feeling he was going to spring up from the armchair and leave the room again, leave her here alone again.

'I was starting to feel a bit cooped up in here,' she remarked.

'It's hardly a coop.' James's tone sharpened. 'It's one of the best hotels in town, Andrew said.'

I know that, Alexa thought, that's why I chose it for our anniversary. This conversation was going wrong and she needed to rescue it. 'You're right,' she agreed, with humility, 'I've got nothing to complain about, not like that poor girl. God, it must be awful, absolutely horrendous, almost losing a child like that.'

At last, James seemed willing to focus. 'Yes, terrible. She said she thought he'd got trapped under the boat, she couldn't see him in the water. She kind of shuddered in front of me, gagged almost. I was worried she was going to be sick.'

'Really? The poor, poor thing.' Alexa felt a sudden surge of real gratitude, gratitude for having her life and not this other woman's, for being able to stay in this lovely suite, be married to a wonderful husband, and with no children to bring drama and destruction to their lives. 'It's a mother's worst nightmare, isn't it? It would haunt you forever.'

James's expression altered to one of amused suspicion. 'Don't tell me you're feeling a maternal twinge all of a sudden?'

Alexa spun to face him, her compassion for Holly Walsh, her patience with him, vanished at a stroke. 'Just because I don't want children yet doesn't mean I'm a monster. No one ever questions *your* paternal twinges, do they?' All at once she felt sick and tired of being the only one to be worrying about their marriage, of wanting to celebrate their anniversary in style – or at all, apparently – while he devoted all his energy to other people, strangers. She knew it was wrong, because these were exceptional circumstances – of course he should meet the mother of the boy he'd saved, of course he should feel moved by that meeting – but she couldn't help it, and now she had begun ranting internally her mouth was quick to take up the baton: 'I hate this perception that only mothers have emotions, like other women haven't been properly activated or something. It's the media that does it, telling us who's allowed to feel and who isn't.' She glanced again out of the window, wishing she'd got a closer look at this Holly girl. 'Well, d'you know what, James? We all hurt. When I get a blister it bleeds just the same as hers, you know.'

Infuriatingly, James just stretched his legs in front of him, no less amused now than before. 'There's no need to get all Shakespearean about it,' he said, mildly. 'I *know* you bleed, I remember when you started running. Your feet were in a real mess until we got you those decent trainers.'

Alexa snorted. That was more like the real James: diffusing conflict with a flip remark. 'Don't change the subject, I'm talking about how women are still manipulated by men in a completely iniquitous way.'

'Oh, come on, Alexa,' he laughed, 'as if you're not proof enough that women have equalled men by now, surpassed us. Possibly begun to scare us!'

She paused, deciding whether or not to take offence at this last remark. Yes, she decided, she would. 'Well, thank you very much. It's always good to hear that you strike fear into your own husband.' Glancing at the time – it and the air temperature were beamed in blue light on to the wall by the door, an avant-garde touch amid all the vintage silk and roses – she added, 'Perhaps we can continue this romantic discussion over dinner? Aren't you going to change? The restaurant's supposed to be quite smart, you know.'

He shrugged. 'In a minute, yeah. There's loads of time. We've just got back from lunch.'

'James, it's already—'

But he held up a palm, as if he couldn't bear another word. 'Oh, stop moaning, Al. I can tell the time all by myself, I'm not a child. And while we're on the subject, why did you book all these restaurants with Michelin stars or whatever they are when you don't want to eat anything when we get there?'

Alexa felt tears rise: why was he being so horrible to her? And why couldn't she think of a better way to defend herself than sarcasm? It *never* worked. 'Well, excuse me for booking a nice restaurant for our anniversary dinner. I'm sorry you're being asked to eat *two* high-quality meals in one day. Next year we'll just stroll down to McDonald's, shall we?'

Now he did leap up, not to leave the room but to pounce straight at her, startling her a second time by pulling her towards him, towards the bed. With his other hand, he undid the sash of her robe and tore the thing off.

'James,' she said again, her lips opening in a gasp, but she couldn't say any more because his mouth was pressing aggressively against hers. Admittedly, this was exactly what she had wanted today, this weekend, but its context seemed unjust and the fingers of her right hand, wrapped around the nearest bedpost, seemed to confirm her ideological resistance. Still kissing her, James prised them free without too much effort and pulled her roughly on top of him on the mattress. Her bare skin tingled against the weave of his jeans, the softness of his shirt.

'OK then,' she said, excited.

'OK then,' he repeated.

'Aren't you going to take *your* clothes off?'

'No, just you.'

Her eyes narrowed, assessing him. 'You're in a very strange mood.'

'Maybe I am.'

It was light, lighter than it usually was when they made love, and so she was able to look down and see her own body properly as she straddled him, gripping him fiercely with thighs that felt lean and rigid against him. Her hips and elbows and collarbones made a lovely symmetry of sharp angles and there was hardly any sensation of wobbling, even from her breasts, which were smaller now and firm from repeated localised toning exercises. It was the best feeling in the world, she thought, to see the kind of proportions on yourself that had for so long belonged to other women, women like Lucie. A couple of years ago she would have wondered if she was crushing him, but now she felt weightless and sexy and flexible.

She noticed James eyeing her body with a slightly pained expression. 'What?'

'Nothing. Don't stop.'

'What?' She halted the motion of her hips. 'I want to know what you were thinking just then.'

'For fuck's sake, Alexa, not now!'

'No, tell me.'

The look he gave her was both exasperated and challenging. 'Just that you've got too skinny. Way too skinny.'

'Too skinny?' Of course, she took this as a compliment, though she knew he hadn't meant it as one. Not so long ago he'd told her she was getting the physique of a long-distance runner; he'd said he wished she'd drop the exercise 'obsession'. The way he'd said it, it was as if he couldn't see how any woman would think this was what a man wanted, other than in the realms of fetish. The memory brought new indignation to her mood, along with an edge of cruelty. 'Stop, then, if you don't like how I look,' she said, moving again, 'if I repulse you.'

James groaned. 'You don't repulse me. And I'm not going to stop.'

'I thought not.'

'That's not what I said, anyway.'

'Yes, it was.'

This was new, this combative quality, they didn't usually argue during sex, and this was real, not playful, but somehow it was necessary if this was going to work.

'Do you like being a hero?' she said, goading, squeezing him hard inside her. 'Do you think it makes you more attractive to women? I bet that girl downstairs would *love* to be in my place right now—'

'Oh, shut up,' he said, glaring at her.

'Eliza Doolittle. She'd love to be fucking you like this, wouldn't she?'

'Alexa . . .'

'You started it, James.'

'Just stop talking,' he pleaded. 'Please, just shut up for once.'

She closed her eyes, enjoying herself. When she came it felt like much more than a simple biological release, more like an expulsion of months of fear and tension. And with it she lowered her defences and allowed herself to soften. She cuddled up to him, purring and saying, 'I love you.'

Lying there together, sensing rather than watching the Paris sky darken, it was probably the closest they'd been to one another in months. Alexa thought they could be a *bit* late for their dinner reservation.

It had been worth it, then, this trip.

'Five years,' James said, suddenly, as if the concept had only just occurred to him.

'Yes. Are you happy you married me?' she asked, meek and baby-voiced.

'Of course I am.'

Something in his tone, the faintest note of obedience, placation, made her glance up to check his eyes, but they were firmly closed.

'Don't fall asleep, James,' she warned him. 'We don't want to be *that* late.'

Her marriage had not been the only thing on her mind recently. First, there was the biggest project she'd worked on to date in her career as a senior marketing executive for a major soft drinks company: their new smoothie was eight weeks from launching. Second, there was the small matter of moving house. The upgrade from low-maintenance two-bedroomed flat to six-bedroomed Behemoth in need of total redecoration had taken place just two months ago.

'The stress might help you lose weight,' Lucie had said, quite seriously, for she and Alexa's other friends had cheered on her shrinkage with the pride and commitment of parents.

'That's what I was hoping,' Alexa agreed, quite seriously.

All in all, she'd lost another ten pounds.

They'd moved into the house – or villa, the agent called it, a rarely available Italianate property on the street just behind the street she really wanted – a month ago and she'd spent every spare moment since getting it into a half-habitable state. She had begun by making a list of all the items of furniture they'd need to buy – in trebling their square footage it followed that they must also treble their number of possessions – and most of the larger items had now been ordered. As for the walls, very few of the abstract prints they'd had in their old flat suited the period-perfect palette of Alexa's vision; they'd need to be relegated to less public areas, leaving blanks at all the key strategic points. Which meant that new ones were required, and where better to buy art than in Paris?

And so it was that they pulled up in Saint-Germain at a chic row of independent dealers.

She knew exactly what she wanted for the spacious new hallway: something bold, witty, something that made a statement to all who entered. She didn't want people coming into their new house and saying, They've got such *subtle* taste, James and Alexa. The way they've done the house is really . . . *understated*, you can't put your finger on it. No, she wanted them to put their finger on it right away, she wanted them to say, Oh my God, is that what I think it is? Only Alexa would dare do that.

What 'it' was and what others might think it was had yet to be discovered, of course – that was the point of shopping.

In only the third gallery they visited she knew she had her painting. It turned out to be a portrait, a huge nude of a woman's back and neck, with lots of green in the flesh tones. The setting was outdoors, you could feel the breeze on the woman's skin. It had the feel of Manet's *Le Déjeuner sur l'Herbe*, which they'd seen a few days ago in the d'Orsay.

'What d'you think?' she asked James, hardly bothering to conceal her excitement from the hovering gallery assistant.

He glanced at it. 'It might be all right in a bedroom, I suppose.'

'But no one would see it in a bedroom, would they?'

'*We* would.'

'Only for about two minutes a day. It would be a waste of money. Come on, it's so beautiful.'

But he failed to look convinced. 'Don't you think it's weird to walk into someone's house and be greeted by a picture of someone with their back to you? I bet that's considered rude or bad luck in some cultures.'

'Who cares, it's not in ours. I don't think it's weird at all. It would be like she's leading you in.' Then, allowing her voice to lower a note, to become slightly more private, she added, 'I really, really like it, James.'

There was a pause. 'I really, really don't,' he said.

And he turned away from it, from her, matter of fact, *bored*, and began eyeing a bronze figurine by the door. Alexa was stunned, so much so that the battle between her natural dismay at being denied and the unpredictable thrill of being overruled by someone who *never* overruled her could not yet be joined.

She remembered how James had torn off her robe yesterday; she remembered how he'd said that women like her were starting to surpass men, scare them, even. Well, if not getting her own way every time they disagreed was the price she had to pay for the return of passion to their relationship, then it was possible it might be worth it.

'OK,' she murmured, finally. 'Let's move on.'

There was more sex that evening, before they went out for their final dinner. Timing was the key, Alexa decided. Waiting till bedtime had been her mistake previously: the quality of the hotel mattress was too fine, their bodies too exhausted. She and James exchanged anniversary gifts then too, having agreed to choose them in Paris and delayed doing so a day, thanks to the accident: his to her was a beautiful beaded bag she'd admired on the first morning and dithered over the price tag, hers to him a framed photograph from the 1940s of a man diving from a bridge into the Seine. She'd found it on their gallery tour, paying for it while James was distracted by a phone call and arranging for it to be delivered later as a surprise. The figure had been captured midair, at an almost horizontal point in his dive; the photographer must have leaned right out over the water to get the shot.

'A memento of your heroics,' Alexa said as he unwrapped it.

James studied it, head tilted. 'I'm not sure I looked quite so graceful.'

'Well, you did have your shoes on. Do you like it?'

'I do, yes. Thank you.'

In the restaurant, she speculated on where the photograph might be hung in their new house, but James's attention soon wandered.

'I wonder how the Walshes are getting on back home,' he said.

'The Walshes?' For a second Alexa couldn't place the name. 'You know.'

'Oh, yes, of course.' He'd mentioned them that morning when they passed a road sign for the Gare du Nord and then a second time, in a café in Saint-Germain, when another customer, an American woman, came up to ask him if he was the one who'd jumped in the river to save that baby. She'd recognised him from the news, she said.

'Holly and Mikey,' James reminded Alexa. 'I don't know what her mother's called, do you?'

'No.' She followed his gaze over her shoulder to a pale girl with cropped auburn hair at the table behind theirs; she was bent over her menu, exposing a dusting of freckles on the nape of her neck. He wasn't usually the kind of man who ogled other women in front of her, but given their recent intimacies she could hardly have claimed to be threatened.

In the end the dinner was subdued. There was a sense that this was one of those holidays where you needed another one to recover from it. It had been momentous, it had – she hoped – eased her mind on a few issues between them, but it had not been restful. It had not been what she'd planned.

'So, do you think you'll be able to handle going back?' she asked him as he ate crème brûlée. She never allowed herself dessert but took perverse pleasure in watching him eat his.

'Handle what? Going back to work? Quite looking forward to it, actually.'

'I don't mean work. I mean all of the hero stuff. The adulation.'

James shrugged. 'I think adulation's overstating it a bit. More a laughing stock, I'd say. A lot of people think I'm a complete lunatic.' This was true: while Andrew and Frances and the foreign tourists in the hotel had been unreservedly admiring of his rescue of Mikey Walsh, the Parisians who'd voiced an opinion were not so much approving as incredulous (the word *fou* had been used).

'Just so long as you don't make a habit of it, whatever you want to call it,' Alexa said, sounding more light-hearted than she felt. 'If the Seine is risky, then the Thames is lethal. You're not sixteen any more, you're not immortal.'

'I've been aware of that for some time,' James said, eyebrows raised. He put down his spoon and reached for his wine glass. There was an unfamiliar tension to his movements.

'Seriously, J, it's great what you did, really, really brave, but I want you to promise me you're not going to do it again.'

'I'm not likely to, am I? It was a freak thing, a one-off.'

She held his gaze, frowning now. On her lap her fingers fussed with the beaded bag. 'Just promise.'

James raised his glass, still looking at her over its rim as he drank. 'What is it you're so worried about, Alexa?'

'What d'you mean?'

He set the glass down again. 'Is it what I did that bothers you or is it the fact that I didn't tell you I was going to do it?'

It was a crucial distinction, not only regarding the rescue but also the dynamic between the two of them generally, and neither had ever cared to make it explicit before. There was an odd, arrhythmic silence, during which Alexa saw the glitter in James's stare and felt all at once as if her fate hung in the balance. For the second time that day she knew she had to be the one to concede.

'Don't be silly,' she said, lightly. 'Let's just forget it.'

Chapter 7

London

When she woke up on the first morning after returning from Paris, Joanna registered Mikey's absence in her bedroom as she might a missing hand: blurry incomprehension followed by abject terror. Then, with relief that came in short, choking surges, she heard his squeals in another part of the flat and understood that he was present, awake, *alive*. Still in her pyjamas, she tracked the sounds along the hallway to the kitchen: there he was in his high chair, clothed, washed and drinking his beaker of milk, a trinity of accomplishments that would once have represented – without her supervision – a minor miracle.

Holly, also dressed, was sitting next to him at the table, helping feed him his Weetabix. Her own bowl was finished. All the clues pointed to the two of them having been up for at least half an hour.

I must have overslept, Joanna thought, disorientated. Though it was a work day, she had not set her alarm clock, just as she had not for the last twenty-one months – there had been no cause to when Mikey could be counted on to wake her long before she needed to get up. If he hadn't already found his way into her bed in the night then he would be sure to at the first hint of daylight, knowing to bypass the less responsive Holly. (Before he was mobile, his crying would have got her up, Holly

87

often having placed a pillow over her own head to plug the noise.)

But this morning Holly must have responded so promptly to his demands that he hadn't yet reached Joanna's bedroom. He hadn't needed to.

'I was just going to come and give you a shake,' Holly said, cheerfully, unwittingly parroting one of Joanna's own most frequently used lines and only deepening her sense of disorientation. 'You're not late for opening up, don't worry.'

'Gama!' Mikey was reaching for her from the chair, trying to pass her his spoon, wanting her to help with his breakfast instead of his mother. After all, she was the one who had done it most mornings in the past.

'Clean teeth!' He was telling her, proudly, that another of her duties had already been taken care of.

'Clever boy, brushing your teeth,' she responded, her first words of the day dry in her throat. She needed tea.

'I made a pot,' Holly pre-empted, casually helpful, as if she made pots of tea all the time and wouldn't dream of leaving single teabags to seep over the worktop, or perhaps on the floor, having aimed for the bin but just missed it. She *meant* well, Joanna used to think as she retrieved it and wiped up the stain.

'It should still be nice and hot,' Holly added.

'Lovely, thank you.' Joanna poured herself a mug and added the milk, blinking as if to activate her vision, though she was fully awake now. It wasn't the first time since Sunday she'd caught herself wondering if she had somehow mistaken how life had been before, even though 'before' represented a period of time that had lasted almost two years and this incarnation mere days. Already it took some effort to picture Holly's face at that café table in the Louvre last Friday: pale, flat, blank; and her posture during those first twenty minutes on the boat trip the next day: listless, helpless, joyless.

She hadn't realised quite how many of the adjectives she was used to applying to her daughter ended in 'less'.

Holly had not repeated those first wonder-filled comments of Sunday morning about feeling 'different'; she had simply continued to *be* different. The girl sitting in front of Joanna now was another creature altogether, not only in energy and conversation but also in colour. It was as if someone had taken a faded pencil drawing of her and applied a wash to it, reviving her with warm rose to her face, a silver glitter to her eyes, a soft gold to the skin on her arms, and some of the wash had spilled over the lines as well, giving her something more: an aura, a charge.

'Do you want a piece of toast?' Holly offered, springing to her feet once more. 'I'm making Mikey some? He's starving this morning, look at his bowl!'

'Er, no, thank you,' Joanna said, 'I'm fine with just this.' If she lit a cigarette to have with her tea the situation would have amounted to a perfect reversal.

As yet, she had not pushed Holly to describe how she was feeling or what this transformation might signify. It was far too early to know whether Holly had reverted to her original self or somehow reinvented herself into a third version; whether this was a temporary state, liable to come and go, or something that might endure. She was anxious about how it might affect Mikey if his mother began some sort of up-and-down behavioural pattern: would that be worse than the known quantity of a permanent down? You were always hearing that children needed constancy above all else.

But that was silly. When she looked at her daughter's and grandson's faces, how could she not wholeheartedly welcome this re-emergence from hell? Let Mikey enjoy his mother as she could be, let Holly be encouraged by that enjoyment, let them be for however long *normal*. Holly, happy again – there was no greater cause for rejoicing that she could think of!

'What are your plans until I get back?' she asked, casually, watching Holly butter toast and pass Mikey a neat set of fingers. He at once crammed two into his mouth. 'Want to come and meet me for lunch?'

The shop where she worked was situated just off Church Road, a ten-minute walk from home, and she often made this suggestion as a way of ensuring that Holly and Mikey left the flat at least once in the day. It also reassured her that the boy was being given a midday meal. Now that summer was here, it was an arrangement that worked especially well, for they could go to the park to eat their sandwiches; the fresh air benefited all three of them and the general merriment of the other park-goers helped camouflage Holly's silent half-presence.

'I don't think we can, sorry.' Holly answered the question at its first asking, another innovation. Joanna was accustomed to having to repeat her suggestions until she was blue in the face. 'I'm going to take Mikey to the One O'Clock Club, and I heard about this class in the park where you can go running with a buggy. I want to get fit again.'

Joanna too had heard of this activity – Pushy Mamas, it was called, or something like that; in fact she had told Holly about it herself soon after Mikey was born, brought her the flyer decorated with illustrations of slim, happy young mothers. She noticed for the first time that Holly was wearing black leggings and a T-shirt, her hair tied in a ponytail. She had dressed for exercising: she really intended doing as she said. 'Want to go fast in the buggy?' she was saying to Mikey in a breathless tone. 'Really, really fast?'

'Fast, fast,' he echoed, spitting soggy toast crumbs in his excitement.

'With lots of other boys and girls? Maybe make some new friends?'

'Mikey, friends!'

Holly giggled and Mikey rewarded her by offering her a

spoon encrusted with dried cereal. 'Thank you, that's very kind.' She pretended to eat from it. 'Yum.'

'That sounds great,' Joanna said, finishing her tea. 'Do you have to pay?'

'It's five pounds a session,' Holly told her.

'Right.' She wanted to offer the money, but it seemed wrong to draw attention to the limited resources of this new, self-starting Holly.

'I'll use my cigarette money,' Holly said, answering the question anyway.

'You're trying to cut down on smoking?'

'I've given up.'

'Really?' Joanna could hear the doubt in her own voice, but Holly did not seem to mind or, indeed, consider the subject worth expanding on.

'I hope I'll be able to keep up with everyone in the class, I'm so out of shape.'

'Oh, you're probably fitter than you think, love.' Holly had played in the school netball and hockey teams years ago and had competed in track events too. She'd been strong and fast, with fantastic hand-eye coordination. Only with the arrival of Sean had she given up sport and taken up smoking and God knew what else. Oh, if this were to be the beginning of lots of outdoor games for Mikey, what a change for the boy!

'I've got a few other things to do as well,' Holly said. 'Just locally, though.' She spoke as if she routinely undertook expeditions to other parts of the city and beyond. Again, Joanna took care not to show her disbelief.

'Well, I should start getting myself ready . . .'

'I'll cook tonight,' was her daughter's parting shot – no less staggering than any that had gone before. 'I think I should from now on, on the days you're at work. It's not fair that you do everything. Not fair on you, I mean.' The clarification told Joanna that Holly was aware that she was blindsiding her with this display of positive energy (any energy at all, frankly); she wasn't asking anyone to forget the previous two years, to pretend it had been any different from how it had been – and for this Joanna was grateful. Accepting history as past was one thing but rewriting it was something she could not do.

'If you're sure,' she said. Before Mikey, while still studying for her degree in catering, Holly had done much of the cooking, and become very good at it.

'I've got the time,' Holly added. 'And Mikey can help me, can't you, sweetie? You could chop some vegetables.'

'Mikey chop. Chop!' He brought down his spoon swiftly, a baby samurai, making Holly giggle once more. Joanna wanted to caution against letting the child touch sharp knives, or any number of other kitchen implements he was invariably attracted to – the pizza wheel sprang to mind – but something told her Holly had the situation covered.

Twenty minutes later, she had showered and dressed uninterrupted and was zipping her handbag, ready to go. 'Well, I'll see you later,' she said to her daughter and grandson, playing now on the rug in the living room.

'Bye bye!' they cried in happy unison, like something from a TV ad.

Glancing at her watch as she headed for the stairs, she did a double take: eight-fifteen. Though she'd got up later than she should have, she was leaving for work earlier! It was a sensation so unnatural, it jolted a memory of departures decades ago, of her schooldays and of Melissa's anger at having always to wait for Joanna to come out to the car in the morning – only for their mother to notice she'd forgotten something and send her back in to get it, making them all late.

'Why are you so useless?' Melissa would ask from the passenger seat, when Joanna finally threw herself into the back, her black schoolbags piled beside her like a litter of pups.

'She's not useless, Mel,' their mother corrected, 'she's just not a morning person like you.'

'She's not an any-time person,' Melissa said.

'Oh, get lost,' Joanna muttered. (Not being a morning person meant that her retaliations were less than brilliantly original.)

'*You* get lost,' Melissa hissed back.

'*You* get lost.'

'I said it first.'

'No, you didn't, *I* did.'

And so on.

It was the 'and so on's that Joanna remembered most clearly – the bit after everyone else had tuned out and before she, frightened by a glimmer in her sister's eye that threatened bodily harm, gave up and let her win.

Melissa always got to sit in the passenger seat. There was no such thing as taking it in turns in the Walsh family. If Joanna were to make a list of all the times her sister's wishes took precedence over hers, it would be long enough for them both to trip over: first go on the garden swing, first choice of ice lolly or yoghurt or television programme, first morning kiss, first bedtime story, first answer from their father if they both asked a homework question at the same time. Later, Melissa won without contest the bigger bedroom with its own en suite bathroom; the automatic priority if there were any conflict in the sisters' demands on their mother's chauffeuring services; the extra allowance for all the things she *had* to have or she would *just die*, Daddy.

Favouritism was the only word for it, for her parents' unrelenting, soul-devouring preference for their eldest daughter. The simple truth was they didn't love one daughter as much as they loved the other. And the moment the chosen one recognised this, she gave every impression of being prepared to defend her supremacy to the death.

It was a little piece of Greek mythology played out in the Midlands, and there was only ever room for one heroine in the family. For a long time Joanna thought all families were like theirs: first come, first served.

It was to do with the length of their parents' wait for their first baby: she absorbed this from an early age, even before she had any understanding of the biological facts of reproduction. 'She was worth the wait, wasn't she?' their father would say to their mother over the top of Melissa's shiny blonde halo, their expressions those of pure romantic accord, and the infant Joanna would imagine them standing at a bus stop or in a queue at the post office, waiting, waiting, waiting for their baby to arrive. Later, she understood that a period like that – almost fifteen years and before the advent of mass IVF – when hope and dread became indistinguishable, could only have intensified the joy when a child finally did arrive. How could it not? When she, Joanna, had followed two years later, it had perhaps felt as though she'd been too easy to come by, Lynn and Gordon Walsh's pleasure in their firstborn not nearly slaked – nor hers in them.

She remembered the moment when she began to suspect that the system might not be quite right. The girls were still young, perhaps nine and seven, and they'd been bought party dresses of the same style but in different colours: Melissa's lilac and Joanna's sky-blue. The blue, with Joanna's toffee-coloured hair, was strikingly pretty and she enjoyed her parents' praise when the dresses were tried on and paraded in front of them.

But afterwards, in her bedroom, Melissa told her: 'You look really ugly in that dress.'

'"Ugly" is a bad word,' Joanna protested.

'Well, you're a bad girl. *Dad* said. If you wear that dress you'll catch the plague and *die*.'

At that, Joanna began to cry, though not for long, her attention span being juvenile. The moment Melissa left the room she rediscovered her pleasure in the swishing sensation of the blue taffeta against her knees and started to play at being a bridesmaid to a famous pop star bride.

Then she heard her mother calling her name from the foot of the stairs. By her mother's side stood Melissa, her eyes luminous with tears. 'Can you take the dress off before you get it too grubby,' her mother commanded. 'It's got to go back to the shop.'

'Why?' Joanna asked, dumbfounded.

'Melissa wants the blue as well, you see.'

'We can't both have blue,' Joanna cried. After a year or two at school she knew all too well that since the sisters were uniformed identically five days a week it was unacceptable to Melissa that they should in any way match at weekends.

'Well, that's the problem,' her mother said, more kindly. 'Obviously, you both want to be different. So we thought you wouldn't mind if we switched yours for the lilac?'

From the sidelines, the tear-stained Melissa watched for Joanna's reaction, her silent willing far more powerful than any of their mothers' verbal persuasions.

'Lilac?' Joanna wavered as her customary wish to oblige met opposition in the form of a hot, tight feeling she had not experienced before but would later know to be instinctive human resistance to injustice. 'But I like the one I've got already,' she said, bravely. She felt an urgent need to remove herself from their sight, close her bedroom door behind her and stand guard over the contentious garment.

Melissa could no longer contain herself. 'Mum, tell her she *has* to swap! I'm the oldest!' With which she erupted into violent tears, tearing her hand from her mother's and falling against the wall. To Joanna's alarm, she began thumping her forehead against the hard wood of the doorframe.

Apparently not noticing this and still addressing Joanna, their mother said, 'Let's see what they've got in your sizes when we get to the shop and we can decide then, OK?'

'OK,' Joanna said, and Melissa stopped beating her head and began instead to smile.

Of course when they got to the store, Melissa was out of her clothes and into the sky-blue faster than Joanna could get her fingers to the buttons on her coat, and the assistants gathered to exclaim at how prettily the colour went with her baby-blonde hair. When the dilemma was explained, a third colour, a navy blue, was offered to Joanna. She shook her head – navy blue was for school, everyone knew that – and so someone brought out a silver-green.

'Do you like this one, sweetie? It's got this extra ruffle here?'

'It's nice,' Joanna admitted.

'Then let's see what it looks like on, shall we? I bet you'll look just like Cinderella!'

At no point in the car afterwards, nor when they'd got back home, nor the first time the dresses were worn, did Melissa acknowledge the concession Joanna had made that afternoon (or, as it felt, sacrifice) and in time its importance faded. The silver-green *did* look pretty and in any case she was years from developing any appetite for rivalry, much less revenge. Even if she *had* had the sort of personality that dwelt on such betrayals, well, this one could hardly have justified what she was later to do in return.

For the sisters were young adults by then and the objects of their desire no longer shop-bought.

Owning and managing a larger branch of Grove Gifts in Beckenham, Suze varied her visits to the Crystal Palace outpost according to how busy the main shop was and how congested the traffic between the two.

'Nothing doing down there,' she told Joanna that afternoon. 'Bloody recession. I might as well drink my tea in an empty shop here as down there. And I want to hear *all* the details about what happened in Paris.'

But an hour into her visit Joanna still couldn't decide whether or not to voice her bewilderment about the effect Mikey's accident had had on Holly's personality. To mention it at all might be to tempt fate and yet . . . . Well, if she couldn't confide in her closest friend then she couldn't confide in anyone and that was no way to live.

Suze had listened to Joanna's account of the rescue with horror, pressing both palms to her heart as she asked, more than once, 'He's all right, though, isn't he? You know that for sure?'

'Yes, he's completely fine. You'd never know he'd been in anything but Johnson's Baby Bath.' Joanna repeated the pronouncements of the Paris doctors, still feeling that tight wringing of disbelief that they could possibly have been as lucky as they were.

'What about Holls? She must have been hysterical, was she?'

'She handled it very well, actually.' Joanna paused. 'I mean, she *was* hysterical when it was happening, when we didn't know if he was alive or not . . .'

'Anyone would be.' Suze, who had short hair and commonly wore low-hanging chandelier earrings, had a habit of shaking her head when in strenuous sympathy. The tinkling of the earrings seemed to emphasise her fellow feeling.

'But afterwards . . . Well, to be honest, Suze, it seems to have had a magical effect on her, spurred her into action.'

'Into action? How d'you mean?' Suze really cared, as well. She was like an aunty to Holly, had known her since she was younger than Mikey was now. She'd been a great support to Joanna these last two years in particular.

'It's only been a couple of days, but she's getting up in the mornings, getting Mikey ready, doing things . . . She's really *cheery*.'

As these last syllables were stressed, Suze, not often at a loss for words, looked winded. If she had not already just had a fresh mug of tea placed in her hands she would have insisted on making one before the story could be continued.

'She says she wants to start exercising.' Again Joanna hesitated, unable to shake the fear that in announcing it like this she was threatening it, jinxing it. 'You know how she used to just . . . lie around.'

This was a euphemism if ever there was one. Suze had been with her that awful afternoon when they'd come into the flat and found Holly passed out on the sofa, an almost empty bottle of vodka rolling on the rug, little Mikey pushing at it as if it were one of his toys, no different from the plastic shapes and oversized jigsaw pieces he threw about the place. At first they'd been unable to wake Holly, then, when they succeeded, she tried and failed to get up for the bathroom and was sick all over the cushions.

She didn't have a drink problem; that sort of solitary binge was mercifully rare and related on that occasion to her having heard the news about Sean and Letitia, if Joanna remembered rightly.

'She's stopped smoking, as well,' she told Suze.

'Wow.' Another jangle of the earrings. 'That *is* good news. That'll be a big saving money-wise, Jo.'

'Yes, if she keeps it up.' Joanna had long disapproved of the proportion of her daughter's benefits income spent on cigarettes. Supporting the household single-handed was one thing – before Mikey, Holly had been in full-time education and so Joanna had always been responsible for paying all the bills – but to stand at the supermarket checkout paying for nappies and wipes and baby food while the child's mother queued at the kiosk for her fags was quite another. It was plain wrong.

'How did she do it?' Suze herself had been unable to stop smoking, though she'd tried countless cures.

'She just woke up and stopped.'

'When?'

'I'm not sure, exactly, she didn't say a word about it till this morning, but I think her last one was on the boat, just before the accident.'

'Maybe she associates the two things? Did she have a fag on the go when he fell in?'

Here, Suze had hit on one of Joanna's private suspicions. If Holly had been smoking at the time of Mikey's fall, lighting up perhaps or opening a new pack . . . well, it stood to reason that if one hand was occupied it put her at a disadvantage when trying to restrain a wilful child.

'I don't know. But I'm not going to make a fuss about it in case it reminds her and she starts up again.'

'Quite right. You don't need people talking about chocolate all the time when you're on a diet.' Weight was another of Suzanne's struggles. She made a hobby of her health campaigns, even a pleasure. In retrospect, Joanna thought that might be what she'd liked about her when they'd first become friends years ago, soon after Suze had offered her a part-time sales assistant's post in Grove Gifts *and* given her the number of a good childminder (two breaks in one conversation: Joanna would never forget that day). She admired that the other woman wore her weaknesses so lightly, that she could forgive herself as quickly as she forgave others. It contrasted powerfully with Joanna's own attempts to keep everything controlled, to forgive herself so grudgingly.

'It was only a matter of time before something brought her to her senses,' Suze remarked. 'We never thought it was only down to hormones, did we? Or heartbreak.' Since she didn't mention Sean specifically, Joanna decided to save that particular subplot for another conversation. Suze shared her disapproval of Holly's old love, though she occasionally and correctly pointed out that around here a girl could do worse. 'She was never going to stay in that gloom forever, was she?'

'Yes, you're right.' And, seeing her friend's willing acceptance, Joanna realised that this was genuinely what Suze had believed, and what others must have too: 'that gloom' had always been going to pass, Holly had always been going to snap out of it. Only she, Joanna, living with it, worrying about it first thing in the morning and last thing at night, only she had let the notion take root that it was going to be neverending. She'd come to believe that Holly would always be a shadow of her childhood self, like someone tragically invalided in a car accident, the family member who would need to be cared for at home for the rest of her life. She'd come to believe that Mikey would always be her responsibility, less a grandson than a son – her second child, to all intents and purposes.

Intents and purposes that seemed to have changed overnight.

The mother-and-son activities continued apace: a trip to the Horniman Museum in Forest Hill – with its free entrance and easy access by bus, this had long been one of Joanna's most persistent suggestions; daily walks in the park, always now including the dinosaur trail that Holly had previously ignored, and to other green spaces within striking distance; games in the small garden of their block with a ball and with skittles; two more of the Pushy Mamas classes. Then, on the second Saturday after Paris, Holly announced she wanted to explore a different part of London and was going to take Mikey on the tube. 'I thought Kew or Chiswick, somewhere where we can walk along the river.'

Joanna and Holly looked at each other then.

'You don't think that would bring it all back?' Joanna said. 'It's only been two weeks.'

'I don't know,' Holly said. 'Maybe I need to do it to find out. Especially if we're going to start swimming lessons, like the doctor said.'

'Yes.' In fact, their GP had simply recommended continuing

normal activities, including any regular trips to the swimming pool. Though Mikey had only been a handful of times in his life, Holly had been inspired to look into subsidised classes at the local pool. These, it turned out, were oversubscribed, and his name was now on a waiting list that typically took six months to clear. Joanna couldn't help feeling grateful for that queue of water babies ahead of them; the doctor's confidence and Holly's solicitude notwithstanding, instinct told her there should be a decent interval between Mikey's last submersion and his next. *She* still felt her hackles rise when he was sitting in the bath!

She wished she could go with them on this river walk, just to be on the safe side, but she worked every third Saturday in the shop and today was her turn. 'He'll be fine, I'm sure,' she said, convincing herself. 'He sees the pond in the park every day, doesn't he? And it's not as if you're taking him on a boat.'

'No, definitely not.' Holly visibly shivered then, one of very few signs of disturbance Joanna had seen in her since she'd turned her corner. (This was how Joanna had taken to phrasing it to herself: Holly had 'turned a corner'. It allowed for optimism while discouraging excessive excitement.) 'Sean's coming over at five,' Holly added, as if that moment of disquiet had naturally reminded her of him, 'and *he* won't want to take him out. So I thought we'd go on a little adventure first.'

It was as if she had appropriated Joanna's own thought processes from their life before: how often Joanna had devised ways to keep Mikey active and stimulated while on her watch, knowing the boy would be back in front of the TV or in his cot when returned to Holly. Sometimes, at work, she thought of him captive at home, a restless foal that never left the stable.

'I haven't ever seen him this happy,' she said, helping Holly assemble the bits and pieces needed for the trip. 'He loves all this activity.'

'Oh, really?' Holly said, pleased. 'I'm so glad you think that.'

'I do.' Joanna decided that, after almost two weeks, a simple enquiry could not hurt. 'You're obviously feeling much better, then, love? You seem to have a lot more energy than before.'

Holly nodded, face glowing. 'I do.'

'Do you think we've finally found the right combination of meds? They've said all along it's trial and error?'

'Oh, I'm not taking the pills any more,' Holly said. 'At least I won't be soon.'

Joanna was taken aback. 'What? Isn't it dangerous to suddenly stop taking prescription drugs?'

'Don't worry, I've been cutting down gradually each day. By next week I won't be taking anything at all.'

Joanna swallowed her cries of protest but could not prevent a frown so deep it almost caused a headache. 'Are you sure about this? Did you talk to someone at the surgery about it?'

'I didn't need to. No antidepressants, no cigarettes. Just me, how I really am.'

There was a pause as Joanna decided how to respond to this. The sight of Holly's radiant expression made the decision for her. 'Well, that's wonderful, really wonderful.' Instantly her eyes began to water and she dropped her gaze, determined not to get carried away, however much she longed to. When she looked back, Holly was watching her, her eyes full of thankfulness.

'I know,' Holly said. 'It's like someone's waved a magic wand and made me better. Sometimes I can't believe it.'

On cue, Joanna had an overwhelming instinct to cry out that it wasn't credible – how could it be when there *were* no magic wands in life? – and to blurt out her fear that their family was being held in a strange and powerful thrall that would, sooner or later, release them again, flinging them back to earth with bruising force.

It was a relief when Holly turned from her to get Mikey into his jacket and shoes, and Joanna, simply by holding her breath and counting backwards from ten, was able to subdue her urge.

Chapter 8

It was ridiculous to pretend she did not remember that James Maitland had told her he lived in Chiswick. It was preposterous to hope – no, stronger than that, to *believe* – that when she arrived in the neighbourhood she would be propelled through the streets and into his path with need neither of address nor map, and yet she did. It crossed her mind that she must be mad to have such blind faith, but if she was then it didn't *feel* mad, not as it had before, before the accident, before James.

Right near Bedford Corner, he'd said.

Whatever his intentions in claiming her phone number in Paris, she had always known the next move would be hers and she was ready for it. Though it was a close, humid day, she felt little discomfort as she piloted Mikey's buggy along the streets of Bedford Park and criss-crossed the common what must have been dozens of times. Every so often she stopped for him to get out and play until, eventually, as she looped once more in the direction of the tube station, he was lulled to sleep with her relentless motion.

That was when she heard her name being called across the traffic from the other side of Turnham Green Terrace: *at last*.

'Holly? Holly, over here!'

She turned eagerly to see James crossing the road between

stationary cars, dodging cyclists and pedestrians to get to her as if nothing would stop him, keeping his eyes on her despite all the distractions. And then he arrived on the pavement beside her, standing close enough to touch, which she longed to do more than anything.

'I *thought* it was you!' He was grinning, slightly breathless from the dash. In his right hand he gripped several bulging shopping bags as easily as if they carried feathers.

'It is me. Hello.' As she smiled she was seized by pure delight, a sensation that deepened to elation when it became clear that he was alone, no wifely figure hurrying in his wake.

'How are you?'

'Really well, thank you. You?' She felt herself blush very faintly as his eyes rested on her nose; he was noticing perhaps the spray of freckles that might not have been visible in the dim light of the hotel. Not everybody thought them pretty; Sean once said she looked as if she'd been smeared with mud.

'I'm good. And is this who I think it is?' James peered under the hood of the pushchair. '*That* looks like a very comfortable arrangement.' The seat had been flattened into a bed and Mikey had thrown a bare arm back over his head, his skin sticky with sleep. 'How *is* Mikey?'

'You remember his name,' Holly said, pleased.

'Of course I remember his name. Is he well?'

'Good as new, thank you. He's just fallen asleep.'

James continued to gaze fondly at the stretched, sleeping form. 'Well, he certainly looks as if he's made a full recovery.'

As if in recognition of being discussed, a faint wince crossed Mikey's face. Noticing a slant of sunlight on his cheek, Holly adjusted the shade and manoeuvred the buggy into shadow.

'So what are you doing in this neck of the woods?' James asked, following her. 'You live in south London, right?'

'Yes . . . I was supposed to be meeting a friend, but she bailed on me.' Though untrue, Holly decided this was easier and less deranged-sounding than the reality ('I was following my destiny by circling the streets in the hope of bumping into you'). 'It seemed a shame to just turn around and go home so I thought we might have a walk by the river.'

She had no idea where the river was.

'Oh, that's a different part of Chiswick,' James said, 'further south from here.'

'Is it far?'

'About fifteen or twenty minutes. But if you plan to go anywhere near open water I might have to insist on chaperoning you . . .' Sweetly, he faltered, as he realised what he'd said, checked her reaction in case the joke had been in too poor taste, and so she continued to smile at him. How could she ever take offence at something he said or did? It wouldn't be possible.

A succession of impatient noises told her they were obstructing the flow of pedestrian traffic. 'Should we get out of everyone's way?'

'We should. If you're not rushing off, why don't we grab a coffee?'

'OK.'

'I know a good place with outside tables. It's a gorgeous day, isn't it?'

'Yes.' It struck her that 'gorgeous' was not a word Sean had ever used, or any man she had met for that matter.

Seated at the café table, Mikey parked in nearby shade, Holly closed her eyes and held her face up to the sun, exhaling with pleasure. It *was* a gorgeous day, the café terrace a peaceful, sheltered suntrap. Lowering her face again she saw that James was staring at her, as if her enjoyment of the sun fascinated him.

'It's nice to relax, I've been walking for ages,' she told him.

'You've *always* been walking for ages,' he replied.

She was utterly at ease in his presence. This didn't feel like only the second time they'd met and nor did there seem any necessity to refer to the first (she'd cried!). No, it felt as if they were already close friends and could bypass politeness because they somehow knew each other intimately already.

'This is a very smart area,' she said. 'I don't think I've ever been here before. I'm not sure I fit in.'

'You said that in Paris as well,' James said, his fascinated eyes not leaving hers.

'Did I?' It was thrilling to think that he remembered their conversation well enough to pick out details she'd forgotten.

'Yes, or something like that. I think you're a perfectly good fit here. You could be an out-of-work actress or something.'

Holly raised her eyebrows. 'Do I look like no one would employ me then?'

He grinned. 'That did sound a bit rude, didn't it? But that's what Alexa said when we first came here, that it was all out-of-work actors. Then when we saw the house prices she said, No, it's all highly paid *in*-work actors. So you must be one of those.'

Holly giggled. 'I don't think so.'

'Well, why not? You're beautiful enough to be an actress, that's for sure.'

They looked at each other, neither blinking. His compliment aside, it was his directness, his instant frank attention that delighted her so much: it reflected so exactly how she responded to him. She knew it was unusual for her to be so self-assured with someone, but she didn't know if it was for him. Rationally, she supposed it was not; her instinct, however, her faith, told her it was just for her.

'I can't act,' she said, at last. 'I used to get all the rubbish parts in the school play. Or they'd ask me to help with the props.'

'OK, then you could be one of the local yummy mummies. We've got them in droves around here.'

That made them both look at Mikey again and Holly experienced the jolt she'd felt sporadically since the accident: a brief but whole glimpse of how it would be if things had gone the other way in Paris. (That was how she termed it, 'gone the other way,' unable to form the specific, brutal words of what it was.) She'd have taken no pleasure in the sunshine today, she'd not have undertaken this expedition, but stayed at home shuttered and grieving. She might, by now, have swallowed all her prescription pills or the entire stock of Joanna's paracetamol in one go or she might have allowed herself to step in front of a bus or a train. And James? What if he had not acted as he had but been witness to an infant's drowning instead of preventer of it? Would he still be thinking about it now? Would his and Holly's paths ever have crossed again?

Everything, *the whole world*, had hinged on the moment he had jumped.

'You suddenly look very solemn,' he said to her.

'I'm sorry. I was just thinking about Mikey, about what happened.'

He nodded. 'Me too. It's not something you can easily forget, is it?'

'No. Never.'

For the first time he looked less than wholly relaxed, abruptly pulling from his pocket a pair of sunglasses, though he had his back to the sun and didn't need them. She wondered if he wanted to hide the emotion in his eyes from her the way Joanna sometimes did, as if she, Holly, could not in her fragile state be expected to withstand it.

With the sunglasses, a scribbled shopping list fell to the table and James gave it a grim look before stuffing it back into his pocket. Alexa must have written it, she guessed.

'Where's your wife today?'

'She had to go into the office.'

'On a Saturday?'

'She works for a big drinks brand and they've got a new product launching next month. Actually, she'd probably still be there even if they didn't, she's very dedicated. Not that she'd touch the new drink with a barge pole.'

'Why not?' Holly asked, puzzled. Not being able to see his eyes – missing seeing them already – she found it harder to decipher his tone.

'It's a smoothie,' James said, 'so too many calories. Natural sugar is evil, apparently. She and her friends prefer the fake kind that doubles as a laxative.'

Holly's lips twitched. 'I'm not sure what to say to that.'

James sighed. 'There are no words. Anyway, we're having some friends for a barbecue tonight so I'm supposed to be buying all the food. Actually, the barbecue's just a cover. The true object of the exercise is to show off our new house.'

'You've just moved?' There was a downward tugging inside her ribcage: dismay. At the same time she devoured the new information, eager to update her mental picture of him at home.

'About a month ago, yep. I've been instructed to buy a new barbecue, as well. Our old one's been declared too scruffy for its new postcode.' He grinned. 'Listen to me, I'm being very rude about my wife. Let's change the subject before I say something that really gets me into trouble.'

Holly didn't think she wanted to talk about Alexa, anyway. 'So *you* don't have to work on weekends then?'

'God, no. I'm far too lazy.' But his physical bearing belied this assertion: he looked as if energy was coursing through him, readying him for anything. Had he been in the same state of alertness in the seconds before he rescued Mikey? she wondered. Just as she had in Paris, she longed to reach and touch his arms, feel the tensed muscle below the skin, try for herself the strength in his wrists and fingers.

Such was the temptation, she would have been forced to sit on her hands had not their coffee and croissants been delivered just then. Holly began chewing hers at once. She was enjoying food immensely these days, both cooking it and eating it. James watched her, smiling.

'What?' she asked. 'Am I really greedy or something?'

'No, no, nothing.'

She wondered if he'd been going to mention Alexa again, asked him, 'Are croissants evil as well?' at which James just continued smiling and she knew she'd read his thoughts correctly. The truth was it wasn't so long since she, too, had been anxious about her shape: Sean was so skinny, she'd feared she might weigh more than him, that they'd look ridiculous together, like Jack Sprat and his wife. And then, after Mikey was born, he'd made her more self-conscious than ever of her extra pounds, dismissive of Joanna's and Suze's theory that she had the luckiest figure they'd seen. They said she was like the old movie stars Sophia Loren and Marilyn Monroe and Jane Russell and had shown her vintage photos of women with conical breasts and mermaid hips in dresses that looked painted on.

'So what do *you* do?' she asked James. 'Do you sell smoothies as well?'

He lifted his coffee cup. 'No. I work in the insurance business.'

Holly halted mid-bite. 'Do you? I *never* imagined you doing that!'

Her exclamation seemed both to please and surprise him. She realised she'd made it sound as if she regularly sat about imagining what he might do for a living, which, in fact, she did.

'What *did* you imagine?' he asked, smirking.

'Well, I don't know exactly, but something that helps people. Like a doctor or a teacher. Maybe a politician.'

'You think politicians help people?'

'Well, they could. They *should*. And you're just like some of the guys I saw on TV during the election.'

James mused on this judgement while beginning his own croissant. 'Maybe. I suppose I must seem like the type: good school, good university, career in the City. All that crap. To be honest, I don't know whether I'm too selfish or not selfish enough.' As he chewed she watched his fingers tear the pastry. She had never before been riveted by someone's hands like this. 'Giving something back, my mother calls it, doing your bit for society. Ethical tourism, voluntary work, fund-raisers for Chinese cities flattened by earthquakes: she's into all that.'

Holly heard this out, puzzled. 'You saved a life,' she said, her voice quiet. 'You've already done something huge for society.'

As in Paris, he dismissed the reference to his heroism with a shrug and she did not comment further; there remained that mutual sense of their not needing to revisit the conversation about the accident. It had all been said and could now only be rephrased. Maybe they would never mention it again, she thought.

'Anyway,' he said, 'the big problem with any kind of public office is you can't have any skeletons in your closet.'

Holly leaned towards him a fraction, intrigued. 'Why, have you got some, then?'

'I don't think so, but that's not to say there might not be one in the future. It seems a shame to rule it out.' The playfulness of this brought a blush to her cheeks. Somehow this conversation was both more than she'd hoped for and exactly what she'd expected at the same time, which produced in her a strange and exhilarating sensation she'd never felt before. Best of all, she seemed to know instinctively when to press for the intimacy and when to pull away from it. It was the very opposite of the floundering she had experienced with Sean.

'Well, I think you'd be brilliant,' she said. 'Giving speeches, organising people, doing interviews. I saw you on TV: you seem like a natural at that kind of thing.' Once more she wished he would take off the glasses; not being able to see his eyes was making her feel as if she'd been blindfolded.

'What about you?' he asked. 'Do you work or do you look after Mikey full-time?'

In his buggy, Mikey swung his head from one side to the other, burrowing into the fabric, reaching deeper into his slumber. It seemed to Holly that he responded whenever James spoke his name.

'I look after him. I was at college before, but I had to leave when I had him.'

'You "had" to?'

'They didn't force me, I don't mean that, but I couldn't cope. Everything was very overwhelming. Now I think maybe I shouldn't have left when I did, it's not like I've been a very good mother so far, anyway.' She admitted this quite freely, knowing it was true.

'Being a parent is obviously a pretty tough job,' he said, delicately.

'It's just, well, it's hard to describe, it's . . .' She chose her words earnestly; it was as if she'd only just become a mother and hadn't had almost two years to consider its demands. 'You have to be selfless all the time, I see that now. Or at least you have to be selfless all the time that they're awake.' Now she smiled; it felt liberating to be able to make a joke about parenthood. Was this what other people did from the start? 'You don't have any children, do you?'

'No, but I have two nieces. I can see what hard work they are. My sister has help and my mother does a huge amount.'

'Mine too. She's been fantastic. She's done everything for Mikey, far more than me, *and* she's worked to support us all. I can't believe I've been so useless. If I saw someone else behaving like I have, I'd think they were pathetic, totally pathetic.' She gave him an unflinching look. 'I've had postnatal depression, you see.'

'Ah, I'm sorry.' She sensed he did not want to pretend knowledge he didn't possess. 'And yet you don't seem unwell?'

'I think it's passing. I think I'm finally all right.' She could hear the wonder in her own tone, as if the 'passing' were taking place as she spoke.

'In that case, you could always go back to college? If you're feeling a bit more on top of things?'

She drew her lips tightly together as she nodded. 'I've been thinking that. I could probably go back to my original course in catering, it's just at a local college.' She smiled a little ruefully. 'It used to be my ambition to run a restaurant, maybe even become a chef. But I don't think that would be practical with a small child.'

'You could do something less full-on? Something part-time? You could finish the course, at least?'

'I suppose I'm put off by having to deal with all the forms and applications again. I'd have to reapply from scratch, get new loans, all of that. And I've been a bit worried I'd feel out of place now.'

'Why?' James asked.

'Well, I'm so much older.'

'How old is older?'

'Twenty-two.'

He smiled. 'Believe me, that's not old.'

'In my case, it feels ancient.' She widened her eyes, feeling herself grow in confidence under his gaze. 'So maybe I should earn some money instead of taking out a whole load of loans. I've let my mum fund me for far too long.'

'You live with her?'

'Yes. There's been no choice, really, not while I've been ill. But now . . . well, plenty of single mothers work out how to go to college or get a job without needing to live at home and use their mother for free childcare.' She meant this without self-pity; having so recently woken up to her situation she was still in the process of defining it, of committing herself to the business of putting things right.

'Sounds like a perfectly sensible set-up to me,' James said. 'You shouldn't be too hard on yourself. You've obviously been through more in the last year than most people go through in twenty. Hence the feeling ancient, I suppose.'

She felt her resolve settle. 'I think I'm going to look for an evening job, just something to get myself going again. I thought waitressing or bar work, there are a couple of new places opening in our area.' She had a vision of herself in a large, noisy café, hurrying from table to table until she came upon James, sitting alone, staring up at her. The image had such brightness and clarity it felt less like a fantasy than a premonition.

To her surprise, James had begun laughing, a disbelieving, helpless kind of laughter.

'What?' she asked. 'Does it sound like a stupid plan?'

'No, no, I wasn't laughing at you.'

'What then?'

'I don't know. This, today, everything . . .' And he took off the sunglasses, his bared eyes riveted, not by her but by the frustration of something he could see but not identify. She watched as he frowned into his coffee, shaking his head faintly as if the blame for this headiness of mood lay in its blend. 'Let's just say I don't feel like my usual lazy self. Something's different at the moment.'

Holly felt her heart rate quicken. Did he mean . . . was it possible that he was undergoing the same strange rejuvenation that she was, the same inexplicable transfusion of life? For *life* really was the only word for it.

'It's not the coffee,' she heard herself say.

He looked up. 'What isn't?'

'How you're feeling. The thing that's different.'

His head tilted a little. 'What is it then?'

'I don't know,' she said, simply. 'Or at least it's nothing I can explain. I just know that it's real and you shouldn't be scared of it. I'm not.'

They looked at each other, kept looking. Their immediate surroundings, the rest of the world, even her sleeping child: it had all ceased to exist for Holly and there was only James in front of her, the true angles of his face, the taut muscles of his neck and shoulders. She didn't regret what she had just said to him, but nor did she want to say anything else. They had reached where they were going to reach, for now.

'OK,' James said, as if reading her thoughts. 'OK.'

Their coffees finished and their table being eyed by a waiting group, they prepared to leave. Holly gave Mikey's shoulder a gentle tug, singing, 'Mikey' in the softest of voices to try to rouse him, but he was not to be disturbed. She smiled at James. 'Sorry he hasn't woken up to say hello.'

'That's all right. It's been nice to have the chance to chat again. Last time . . . Well, it seems a long time ago now.' He paused. 'I lost your number, you know.'

'Really?'

There was no chance to evaluate this news, for he was already pressing ahead.

'Can I take it again? I'd really like to meet Mikey properly, get to know him a bit. It seems right, do you know what I mean?'

'Yes, absolutely.' Holly had an idea, decided to voice it before she could change her mind. 'You could visit us tomorrow if you're free? We've got nothing planned.'

'I would love to.' She watched as he corrected himself, as he was always going to have to: '*We'd* love to. I know Alexa was sorry to miss you when you came to the hotel in Paris.'

'And my mum would love to meet you, too,' Holly said. 'She's as grateful as I am for what you did.'

They exchanged numbers, agreed to confirm when they'd spoken to Alexa and Joanna. Holly said she had decided against the river walk after all and asked him to remind her of the way back to the tube station. She would take Mikey instead to Covent Garden to see the entertainers in the piazza.

It seemed to her that there was a reluctance to their good-byes, a shared resignation. 'What are you doing now?' she asked. 'More shopping?'

115

'Yes. Then I thought I might go for a run.'

'You really aren't lazy, then?'

'No, not any more.' And he gave her a last smile, one that was to Holly both wonderful and full of wonder.

'Me neither,' she said, before finally moving away.

Chapter 9

Alexa was on the phone in the kitchen, her spirits fading as they invariably did these days during conversations with her younger sister Sammy, when she heard the front door open and close, the sound of James's footsteps on the stairs.

'I have to go,' she told Sammy. 'We've got friends coming over for a barbecue. What are you doing tonight?'

'Well, Mum and Dad are babysitting for us and we were going to go out, but we're so tired we thought we'd just stay in with them and watch a DVD.'

Though this was a typical response from Sammy, who was, she was under no illusions, their parents' favourite, Alexa was unable to stop herself from being offended by it afresh. Not that she wanted to cancel her own evening to 'just stay in' with them, but the point was that even if she did they never invited her. Somehow, at some indistinct moment over the years, she had accidentally fragmented from her family, only to watch it reform without her, shoring itself in rejection of her.

At least that was how it *felt*.

She frowned to herself as she hung up the phone. She couldn't share this hurt with James because he would only say she should let her family live the lives *they* wanted to lead and she the one *she* wanted. There was no reason to be upset. And perhaps he was right: she relied on him to keep in check her more histrionic instincts. In any case, what actually chafed, and what was harder to admit to James or even to herself, was the knowledge that her family were not *proud* of the life she led; far from being impressed by the leaps she'd made from the one she'd started with to the one she had now, they were nonplussed by them. 'I don't know how you find the energy,' her mother would tell her when she mentioned her extra hours in the office, or, with regard to the new house, 'A place that size is a lot of work, Alexa. Sooner you than me.'

Sammy used that expression, too, sometimes: *Sooner you than me*. It bewildered Alexa as it hurt her pride.

Reaching the hallway she almost stumbled into a huge cardboard box containing the new grill James had bought, before pausing briefly to admire the extraordinary polished alabaster chandelier overhead; it had been salvaged, according to the dealer, from a Spanish ambassadorial residence and she loved to look at its pale, smooth surfaces. The walls were still bare, but to her credit she'd made only one wistful comment since returning from Paris about the portrait she had wanted so badly.

Proceeding from the hall and up the stairs to the bedrooms was an inevitable exercise in disappointment, for it was her plan to beautify the house in the strict order in which visitors saw it. This meant that while the hall resembled the entrance to a boutique hotel and the adjoining guest cloakroom something from a Balinese spa, their bedroom, right at the top of the house, wouldn't have looked out of place in a squat. Still awaiting the arrival of new wardrobes, they had not yet unpacked most of their clothes and so it was no surprise to find James on his knees, sifting through boxes for something to wear.

'There's no time for that,' she said from the doorway, using the chivvying tone that she'd developed – almost to the day – since they'd taken possession of the house. 'Just wear whatever's come back from the cleaner's.'

James glanced up. 'I didn't realise you were back.'

'Of course I'm back, there's dinner for six to organise! Come on, we need to get the barbecue set up and lit as soon as possible. The guys'll be here in half an hour.'

James shrugged. 'They're sure to be late.'

'They're sure to be on time,' Alexa said. Hosting made her anxious. 'They're dying to see the house again and no one's laid eyes on you since the weekend before Paris.'

'That's only a few weeks ago, Al. You make it sound as if one of us will die if we don't realign.' He spoke the last phrase in the irritating style of a sci-fi movie trailer voiceover. 'I'll be down in a sec. I need to shave.'

She sighed. 'I *mean* it, J. We have to get moving.'

'No,' he said, on his feet. 'We have to *relax*. It's the weekend, remember?'

It was official, she thought, as she took the stairs with a hectic urgency that almost tripped her up; he was behaving completely differently towards her since they'd got back from Paris. Yes, the intimacy issue had been resolved, but in its place had emerged this scarcely less perturbing habit of constant disagreement. It was not confrontational, it was subtler than that, but already it was being done almost as a matter of course.

Which meant more bewilderment, more hurt pride.

Huffing, she lugged the grill to the garden herself and tore the box into pieces for recycling. In the kitchen, having already prepared salads and other dishes, she now began unpacking and assessing James's fish and meat purchases.

'They're definitely sea bass this time,' he said, appearing at her shoulder in a rumpled blue shirt and the same jeans he'd been wearing earlier. He referred to a famous historical blunder in which he had supplied her with unwanted mackerel.

'But they're enormous! We'll never be able to eat one of these each *and* the steaks.'

'Then we'll freeze some.'

'We'll just have to hope everyone's starving. I wonder if they've had lunch? Barbecues are so hard to judge.'

'We never worried about it in the old place,' James pointed out.

This was true. Even Alexa now acknowledged that the new house was drawing from her a level of perfectionism she could not hope to accomplish, not without sacrificing something huge and impossible, like her social life or her career, both of which were crucial if she was to remain sane. Post-purchase, post-Paris, the house struck her as far too big for James and her, a family home with no children in it, a level of accommodation that would only encourage the arrival of more staying guests than either of them could bear to host. She had a vision of the two of them standing at the barbecue every night of their lives; the only thing changing the faces of the guests (and of the sea bass), the conversation suspended forever on the subject of how the house renovations were going.

Sooner you than me.

She felt suddenly like bursting into tears and running away.

'What can I do?' James asked her, in a dutiful tone.

'Please,' she said, wearily, 'just set up the barbecue and light it.'

'Yes, sir!' But he smiled. He was, she realised, in an excellent mood, buoyant and playful, ready to entertain.

Well, at least one of them was.

The guests were on time. Lucie and Graham, eight years married, were the kind of pair who had come over time to reflect each other's glamour to the point of dazzle, ever more stylish of dress, ever more gleaming of skin and hair. If one were to leave the other, the discarded party would cease on the spot to be flesh and blood, Alexa thought, like that Greek nymph who was turned in a stroke to dust.

Shona and Joe (the woman's name always came first, James

once pointed out, regardless of how it scanned), were less well-matched visually, Shona being finer featured and better preserved than her husband, but rarely dissenting in opinion. All four were exactly the people you'd expect James and Alexa to be friends with – unlike her family, they saw nothing baffling about working all the hours God sent or stretching themselves perilously to buy the best house they could – and, in the case of Lucie and Graham, represented what Alexa would ideally like James and her to *become*.

They assembled in the garden, voices raised with *joie de vivre* or sheer entitlement, depending on your perspective. Alexa liked to think that she was still down to earth enough to understand the difference.

'James, look at you!' Shona cried.

'Have you lost weight?' Lucie asked. It was she, the style leader of the group, who had inspired Alexa's short haircut, her own highlighted crop growing out and straying sexily into a pair of flirtatious blue eyes.

'I don't think so,' James said. 'I did go for a run earlier, though.'

'A *run*?' Alexa pretended to stagger in amazement. 'Well, I'm glad someone's had the time to work out today!'

'You're the one always telling me to get back in shape,' he reminded her. 'I thought I might start swimming again, as well.'

'Really? What's brought this on?'

'I don't know, DIY aversion?'

'What, the house? We've hardly scratched the surface, James. Don't lose your nerve already.'

The others listened to this exchange with amusement.

'Well, we heard about your heroic rescue,' Shona said to James. 'What a story, tell us exactly what happened!'

And so James launched into his tale, just as he'd been bidden dozens of times since Paris. It was astonishing to Alexa how it continued to capture people's imagination. His assistant at work had told her the mothers in the company now reserved for him the kind of looks you normally saw at the foot of Michelangelo's *David*. To her, they all said the same: 'You must be *so* proud.' Almost as if . . . as if he were not her husband but her *son*.

'He's making it sound like it was nothing,' she chipped in, embarrassed by the previous show of discord and blaming herself for it, 'but it was amazing. And really, really frightening. Everyone was screaming their heads off and crowding to one side of the boat—'

'Port or starboard?' Graham interrupted, no doubt meaning it as a joke, one that assumed female ignorance on the subject, but he should have known better for Alexa answered him crisply – 'Port' – before continuing: 'I honestly thought it might capsize and we'd *all* drown.'

'How scary!' Lucie exclaimed, fingertips to her lips.

'The poor mother!' Shona said, big-eyed.

'Oh, I know,' Alexa said, '*she* really was distraught.' She did not mention her own loss of control, of which she felt ashamed. 'She turned up at our hotel the next day with a bunch of flowers.'

'How sweet!'

At his stainless steel grill station, James touched the stiff silver skin of the sea bass with one of his shiny new barbecuing implements; he was obviously itching to get started, though the grill was not yet hot enough. 'Actually, I just saw Holly Walsh,' he said, over his shoulder.

Alexa frowned. 'Holly Walsh?'

'Yes, the mother from Paris.'

'What d'you mean, you just saw her? Where?'

He turned to meet her eye. 'She was in Turnham Green earlier. We had a coffee.'

'*Did* you?' Such was her tone, not so much put out as distressed, that the others turned to look at her, their glee in the promised story now shadowed with unease. Checked, Alexa decided there was no need to spell out her objection – a run *and* a coffee, while she'd been at work all day *and* done all the food preparations – but simply communicated it to her husband in a bleak look. She was becoming frightened by her own mood, wondered if she ought to be medicated during this stressful period, or, a voice whispered, better nourished.

Undaunted, James put down the tongs and picked up his beer. 'She had Mikey with her, actually. It was good to see him again, to see with my own eyes he was all right.'

'Is that the kid you saved?' Lucie asked, casting Alexa a quick, questioning look.

'She must *love* you, this Holly woman,' Shona said. '*I* would.'

That made Alexa think of Paris, what she'd said to James when they'd been making love. *That girl would love to be in my place* . . . But the memory of it did nothing to improve her spirits, releasing as it did a flare of naked insecurity.

'What's she like, then?' Joe asked James. 'How come she let her baby fall off a boat?'

There was general tittering at the pejorative tone of this.

'She didn't "let" him fall,' James chuckled, 'he climbed up on the rails and went over. It was an accident.'

'Thank the Lord,' Alexa drawled, recovering. 'If the French police had thought for a second there was foul play involved we'd still be there now answering their bloody questions. Honestly, talk about thorough! Giving statements took up the rest of the day.'

'Well, the whole thing puts me off having children,' Shona exclaimed. '*So* many things can go wrong. I don't know how they all survive to adulthood.'

'Most people take better care of them,' Alexa said, with a flippancy that was only half joking. She couldn't help feeling pleased that Joe had made that joke about the girl's basic incompetence – why had no one else brought attention to it until now?

'I think Holly is a perfectly good parent,' James said, with more of an edge to his tone. 'What happened in Paris was just terrible luck. Anyway, you'll be able to see for yourself, Al, because I said we'd go and visit them tomorrow afternoon.'

Alexa stared, aghast. '*Tomorrow*? Where do they live?'

'Crystal Palace. I checked your calendar: there's nothing booked in.'

Before she could protest, the others had launched a fusillade of mocking comments, comments that glanced easily off the hero as he stood smirking at the group, taking up his tongs again and holding them aloft in surrender; it was a form of display honed over the years, the target interchangeable among them.

Shona: 'Of course she wants to keep in touch with you, you're her knight in shining armour, aren't you, James?'

Lucie: 'Or maybe you're the stallion?'

Graham: 'And you *are* in Superman-blue tonight.'

Joe: 'They'll be inducting you into some superheroes hall of fame if you're not careful.'

Lucie: 'Don't tell Tracey about your rescue or she'll have you standing on the *Cutty Sark* in a pair of Speedos for that awful paper of hers!'

Tracey, a friend of theirs, worked for the features desk of a national tabloid, her speciality being the scandalous true stories of ordinary people, though only the kind of true stories that sounded too made up to have happened to any but the most extraordinary people. Personally Alexa thought James's feat far too tame for Tracey: if he'd accomplished it one-legged she might be interested – or two-headed.

'Right,' James told them, ready to bring the discussion to an end, 'if you're quite finished, I'm going to get the steaks on.'

Only half listening to the others' chatter, Alexa watched as he established a private rhythm of prodding and turning and side-stepping the gusts of smoke. He was absorbed, deep in a world of his own, unreachable. She felt sure that if she spoke his name now he would not look up. She'd noticed other spells like this recently and hardly knew what to make of them; they were just as mysterious as the other changes. She was beginning to wonder, was *rebellion* too strong a word?

She continued to watch until he flipped the first of the steaks, at which point she reminded herself that their guests needed new drinks.

Her mood lingered into the following afternoon as they set off to call on the Walshes; if anything it had darkened somewhat. She knew she should overcome it, salvage what was left of the weekend, but she simply could not.

There's something wrong with me, she thought.

'We should have got the train,' James said, when she complained about the traffic. 'It would have been quicker.' But they both knew that Alexa avoided public transport where possible, complaining of feelings of panic in rush-hour conditions and growing ever more reliant on the taxis and other private services that ensured her separation from crowds.

'Where is this Godforsaken place, anyway?' she grumbled.

'Come on, I think "Godforsaken"'s a bit strong,' he said, settling back against the tan-leather headrest as if in the throes of a joyride and not a five-mile-an-hour crawl. He looked particularly handsome in profile: wrong lane or not, driving suited him. She could imagine him in the 1960s in an E-Type with Christine Keeler at his side; or racing at Le Mans with Steve McQueen.

'I just don't like wasting a Sunday like this.'

'It's not "wasting".' James slowed to let in the dithering driver of an old Fiat, which only encouraged the stream of cars backed up behind it to dart in afterwards. Sometimes he was just too nice. 'We're not fighting the Trojan War – we're allowed a day off now and then.'

'If you call this a day off.' She attempted a more playful tone, but it was too late, he was already irritated by her.

'I do, funnily enough. We're getting out of that bloody house, for one thing. I'd visit the Addams family for that.'

Alexa snorted. 'What? Don't be ridiculous! This is much harder work than painting a couple of skirting boards.'

She was fairly certain that not so long ago she'd have been able to talk James out of a trip like this simply by appealing to his lazier nature. But that nature appeared to be updating itself before her eyes: after his run yesterday, he'd been for another this morning and there was already a charge to him, a sense of his body reconditioning itself.

She compromised by falling into a pleasurable sulk, resurfacing only as they approached Crystal Palace and passed a sign for an antiques market. 'Ooh, we could pop in there on the way back. They might have a pedestal table for the hall?'

James nodded. 'It'd be cheaper down here, as well. It's unbelievable how much furniture costs.'

Alexa gasped in open surprise. 'I have *never* heard you complain about things being expensive before.'

'That's because I've never had to furnish three and a half thousand square feet of house before. It's a money pit.'

She continued to gape. It was a source of secret envy in their circle that the one who earned the most was the one who needed it the least, for James's parents were very well-off and unburdened by any of the inconvenient principles you sometimes found in wealthy families, an insistence that grown-up children fend for themselves, for instance. It would make little difference to James whether the table cost twenty pounds or two thousand pounds.

First the painting, now the table: thank God they'd already bought the house itself!

'This is it, I think,' James said, turning cautiously down a steep drive that led to a trio of 1970s local authority blocks of flats. 'There's parking at the back, apparently.'

The Walshes' was the tallest block, its exterior paintwork in dire need of renewal, and Alexa allowed herself the briefest grimace of distaste.

'It's all right, isn't it?' James said, cheerfully.

'All right? Do you think?' Were they destined *never* to agree on anything again?

'Well, yes. It's quiet, tucked down here off the main road, and there are lots of trees. These flats are mostly privately owned now.' He sounded like an estate agent. 'And, look, there's a little playground around the side for Mikey.'

'Yeah, handy for the drug dealers.' Admittedly, this failed to sound as droll as Alexa had intended, but even so she was unprepared for James's reaction. Pulling up and switching off the engine, he turned to her with dislike: 'Look, Alexa, if you really don't want to be here then don't come in with me, all right? I'd far rather make an excuse for you than have you say something like that to them. They live here. This is their *home*. No one is asking *you* to move in. Have some fucking respect.'

'I was only joking,' she protested, for he'd never sworn at her in anger before. But it was the message in his eyes – not a trace of persuasiveness, just pure, unequivocal dismissal – as much as his words that shocked her. And it worked, jolting her into remembering what this visit was about. How quickly she'd forgotten that a child had almost died!

'James . . .' She watched him get out of the driver's seat and thrust the door shut, scrambling out after him. 'Of course I want to be here,' she told him. 'I'm just in a bad mood, all the stress at work. Ignore me.' Noticing the flowers and gift they'd brought, she retrieved them from the back seat, adding, 'It will be lovely for you to see the little boy again, knowing you saved his life.'

'It's not about that,' James said, impatiently. 'You make it sound like I'm getting off on some saviour trip or something!'

'No, I don't, I just meant—'

'And anyway,' he interrupted her, 'with any luck, Mikey won't remember the accident, so don't say anything to him, will you?'

'Can he even speak, then?' Alexa asked, genuinely puzzled. 'I thought he was only little?' It occurred to her that she had never asked James what the child had said, if anything, during the rescue or immediately afterwards, who he had cried out for, if anyone. She would do so on the return journey, she decided.

'I should think he can speak quite a bit if he's nearly two,' James said. 'He'll certainly be able to understand some of what's being said. Like Isabella.'

One of their nieces had just turned two and Alexa could not remember an occasion when the girl had not brought proceedings to an unscheduled halt with her incessant wailing. Privately, they had often referred to her as Rosemary's Baby, but Alexa couldn't help wondering if she was now alone in that opinion. And the way James was speaking about this Mikey made her fear another sudden conversion, one that might *really* cause problems between them.

The Walshes' flat was on the second floor of the building, the door eagerly opened by a woman half familiar to Alexa from those last fraught minutes on the boat when they'd waited to disembark. 'Hello! You got here all right! Come on in, come on in . . . Oh, what *amazing* flowers, I don't think I've ever seen such a beautiful bunch! I'm Joanna, Mikey's grandmother.'

She was in her forties, with a keen, intelligent face and warm, youthful demeanour. Her pleasure in meeting the two of them was instantly touching. 'Oh, I wish I could have thanked you in Paris,' she told James, 'but it was chaos at the scene, wasn't it?' Having placed the flowers on a nearby table, she hugged him freely. 'We would have written to you, but we didn't have your home address.'

'It's OK,' James said. 'Holly passed on your wishes, and anyway I told her there's absolutely no need to thank me.'

'Oh, there certainly *is*! I was so pleased when she said she'd run into you yesterday and we were going to be able to keep in touch.'

Was this a long-term arrangement, then? Alexa wondered. What was the correct social etiquette in matters of saving lives? Were she and James 'family' now, automatically invited to Mikey's birthday parties, bound to the Walshes forever by pure chance? As one who sometimes planned what her next thought would be, Alexa did not much rate pure chance.

Joanna led them into a small, spruce living room, where a pair of square windows gave surprisingly good light. As well as seating and a coffee table, there was a white shelving unit with some pretty vases and dishes, several candles placed out of child's reach and two neat rows of paperbacks and library books. The place smelled of furniture polish and cheese on toast, comforting domestic smells; there was not the odour of festering nappies and warm milk you usually got in the homes of small children. Oh, but it was tiny! You couldn't walk with your normal stride length for more than a few steps without going smack into a wall.

'Here he is!' Joanna cried, and Alexa wasn't sure who was being announced, James or Mikey. Both she and James turned automatically to the little boy who had toddled up to Joanna, peeking around her legs in a cartoon act of infant shyness. While James crouched to greet him, Alexa waved hello before raising her eyes to the adult figure hovering beyond – the boy's mother – and she was so taken aback by what she saw she didn't quite succeed in suppressing a gasp. Far from being the broken, sobbing figure glimpsed in Paris, Holly Walsh was both enviably composed and – it had to be admitted – very pretty. Yes, she was dressed cheaply, even sluttily, but she had many natural advantages to compensate for that: she was young, for one thing, her complexion smooth, with cute Pippi Longstocking freckles; her eyes were almond-shaped and wide-set and her nose neat, giving an Oriental daintiness to her face; and her body was shapely, with proper hips and a full bust – not Alexa's idea of a dream figure, it was true, but one that she knew very well James liked. Her hair, reddish brown and streaked amateurishly with gold, somehow managed to look both fashionable and well-conditioned.

Unable to wait for Joanna or James to make the introductions, Alexa held out her hand to the younger woman. 'I'm Alexa. You must be Holly?'

'Yes, that's right. Hello.' A second surprise: her voice was not the girlish, breathless sort Alexa had been expecting but low-pitched and sultry and, in the right circumstances, seductive. 'You found us all right?'

'Yes, we used the sat nav.' Alexa felt unnerved by Holly's open-mouthed, unblinking expression, which barely concealed a reciprocal sizing up. Already they'd been looking at each other for far longer than was natural or decent for people who'd just met.

The first to unfasten her eyes, Alexa cast about for a diversion and, seeing the child still clinging to his grandmother's legs, James squatting in front of him, she exclaimed, 'So this is Mikey! Hello, little man! You look a lot happier than the last time we saw you!'

At once she sensed a tensing in the posture of the others, an exchange of glances that did not involve her, and she couldn't work out why. Then, hearing Holly say, 'Do you remember James, bunny?' in a soft, murmuring voice, she recalled what James had said in the car park about there being concern that references to the rescue might spark a distressing memory of the ordeal.

She remembered also that James had said Mikey had been asleep when he'd had that coffee with Holly. What on earth had the two of them found to talk about? A repeat of the details of the accident, she supposed, a comparison of notes; it was perhaps a kind of therapy in these situations.

They couldn't possibly have anything else in common, she told herself.

'James,' Holly repeated to the boy, saying the name several times and glancing up at its owner as she did, her expression doting. Since their exchange of greetings, she had not spared another glance for Alexa.

'Dames,' Mikey said at last with a sweet lisp. Despite the concern, there was no sign whatsoever of post-trauma as he took James's hand and led him to a pile of toy bricks behind the sofa.

James grinned over his shoulder at the others. 'We brought a present for you, Mikey, didn't we, Al?'

Mikey hardly looked at her either as she handed over the gift, nudging it into James's free hand to ask for help in removing the paper. Holly joined the unwrapping ceremony, exclaiming at the toy Mini Cooper as if it were the keys to a real one. James, who had selected the item with some care, looked thrilled. The flowers, of which Alexa had been in charge, remained untouched on the table; if they weren't put in water soon, she would itch to do the job herself.

Clutching the toy, Mikey pulled at James's hand, saying what sounded like, 'Mikey room.'

Holly beamed across the top of the boy's head at James. 'He wants to show you his other toy cars in his bedroom.'

And James beamed back. 'Lead the way.'

'If you're sure you don't mind?'

'I don't if you don't.'

Holly's laugh was deep in her throat. 'Not this time. Luckily we just tidied up before you came, didn't we, Mikey?'

Then Mikey was proudly leading James out of the room, Holly bringing up the rear; the hallway was so narrow they had to walk in single file.

Alexa stared after them, wondering why it was that she felt she had just witnessed a kidnapping.

'A cup of tea?' suggested Joanna, at her side.

'Thank you.' She accepted the invitation to sit. Two of four mugs set out on a wooden tray on the coffee table were efficiently filled with tea, and her attention directed to a mountain of chocolate biscuits that she did not touch for fear of a loss of control that would cause her to devour the whole lot and gain twenty pounds on the spot.

Joanna settled beside her on the sofa and began crunching.

'He hasn't been affected then?' Alexa asked, in a discreet undertone, though Mikey was now well out of earshot. 'Do you think he even remembers what happened?'

'We're not sure,' Joanna said. Her accent was more neutral and less local than Holly's, Alexa noticed. 'The doctors don't know if there'll be any long-term effects. We're just hoping not.'

Hope seemed to Alexa a rather abstract treatment of what had surely been a terrifying episode for the child, but what did *she* know about children?

On cue, Joanna asked, 'You and James don't have kids, then?'

Alexa gave a sharp laugh. 'God, no. We're still getting used to being married. One step at a time.'

'Of course. We felt absolutely terrible that your anniversary was disrupted by the accident.'

'Oh, you mustn't worry about that.' Too late Alexa was realising how inappropriate her previous remark had been, with its implication that you needed to be settled in marriage in order to procreate: how tactless, when Holly was a single mother, and Joanna as well, presumably, for there was no evidence of a man of the house, and no space for him, either.

'Was it your first anniversary, then?' Joanna asked her.

'No, our fifth.'

'Oh.' Joanna looked puzzled. 'I thought you said . . .'

'I was only joking: we're *very* used to being married.' Alexa wondered what the other woman would say if she told her she'd arranged the Paris trip because they'd needed to be reminded of why they'd been attracted to each other in the first place; or that her list of romantic sights and *bonnes adresses* had been drawn up only after obsessive research, the kind of exhaustive preparation normally reserved for a honeymoon. That their trip *had* been disrupted, it had been disrupted at the very moment they'd begun to enjoy themselves. *This is really nice*, James had said, his voice an intimate murmur. *Just us. Thank you . . .*

'We've been together for ten years,' she said, 'but it took us five to decide to take the plunge.'

Another truth she could have blurted: James had not minded either way about getting married – *she* had proposed to *him* – and he probably never would have, not until such a time that Alexa became pregnant and the prospective grandparents started making noises about her being made an honest woman of. She, on the other hand, had become fearful of going to other people's weddings and being identified as the only one left, ever conscious of her extra years as James's male friends appeared with younger and younger women. Honesty had had less to do with it than she was prepared to admit.

'Well, I'm sure it won't be long,' Joanna said. She was just making conversation, saying the sorts of things said to married couples routinely, but it bothered Alexa that she should voice her casual assumptions about two people she hardly knew. Alexa would not ask Joanna about *her* fertility.

'We'll see,' she said. 'Maybe we *won't* have children. I think you can lead a perfectly happy life without them.'

To her credit, Joanna took this in her stride, remarking, above Mikey's excited screeches from the next room, 'Yes, and a quieter one, I should think.'

'There's nothing that says you *have* to have them.'

'No, of course not.'

'Plenty of people don't.'

'That's right.'

The way Joanna kept agreeing with her made Alexa think she might be coming across a little antagonistically. (How could this be? Once, she'd been known for her charm.) She took a sip of tea and softened her tone. 'So how long have you lived in this area?'

Joanna glanced towards the window as if reminding herself of where she was. 'Oh, years and years now. It's changed a lot since we first came here. This used to be a terrible block before the council sold it off.'

Seeing the older woman's expression – it flickered from optimism to defeat to optimism again – Alexa was flooded with remorse for her previous spikiness. 'It's got a really good vibe,' she said, warmly. 'We were saying on the way over how up and coming this area is. I don't know if you own this place but, if you do, I bet it's really increased in value.'

'We've always rented,' Joanna said.

Alexa blinked. That eliminated the one topic that was both a favourite of hers and a speciality. 'You didn't grow up around here, then?'

'No, no, I didn't come to London until I was pregnant with Holly.'

'You must have been very young?'

'I'd just left school.'

This meant she must have had Holly at an earlier age than Holly had had Mikey. What on earth had possessed these women to have children so young? It seemed to Alexa so fundamental a mistake she simply could not understand its having been made.

'Do you have family close by?'

'Mikey's father's side is local. Sean and his mum are just down the road towards Penge. I grew up in the Midlands, in a

134

small town near Peterborough, and we don't see that side so much.'

'Distance can be a good thing,' Alexa said wryly, 'at least it is in my case.' Rather to her own surprise she began to describe her parents to Joanna, their growing preference for Sammy, who they saw almost every day and who was raising her young family in the same neighbourhood, their indifference to Alexa's more metropolitan choices. Thinking she saw a flare of fellow feeling in Joanna's face, she paused to allow her to contribute, but the other woman said only, 'Family can be difficult, there's no doubt about that. The same situation can look completely different to the separate generations.' She had a natural dignity, a discretion that ran deeper than the duties of a polite hostess and impressed Alexa greatly. She was beginning to sense that Joanna had not grown up in so modest an environment. That confirming glance to the window: this was not necessarily where she had expected to find herself.

A sudden outbreak of high spirits on the other side of the wall prompted her to ask Joanna how many bedrooms the flat contained.

'Just two. Holly and Mikey share the bigger one. It's not ideal, but it's OK.'

Alexa wanted to ask how Holly managed with boyfriends; she would have liked to have gone and had a look herself at the bedroom next door, imagined James perched on a low bed heaped with soft toys, an oversized bra draped over the back of a chair near his head.

Before she could fabricate an excuse, the others were tumbling back into the room, faces flushed, voices warm with laughter. James pulled up a child's beanbag to sit on, finally getting to his cup of tea, while Alexa made room for Holly on the sofa. Their thighs were side by side, Holly's bare and splayed, Alexa's slender in skinny jeans and slightly tensed. With Joanna tending eagerly to James, Alexa was able to devote her attention once more to the young mother. Instinct told her to keep their exchange pleasant – the last thing she wanted was James saying she'd been snooty to her.

'When does Mikey turn two, Holly?'

'In early September, quite soon.'

'I bet it feels like time's flown since he was born?'

'A bit.'

'Or maybe the opposite? All those sleepless nights, eh?'

'I suppose. He's a good sleeper, though.'

'Do you know lots of other mothers?'

'Not really. A few, I guess.'

Alexa couldn't help feeling frustrated by the way her questions, though dutifully answered, were not matched by any of Holly's own, and by the way the girl's gaze kept drifting back to James.

'Does he go to a nursery?' she asked, brightly, drawing on a subject that could be counted on to rouse debate from both her own sister and her sister-in-law.

'No,' Holly said. 'I just looked into it this week, actually. The state ones are full and the private ones are too expensive and mostly full anyway. Maybe in the future, though. I think he'd enjoy it.'

'Don't you have to put their names down really early, though?' As a forward planner par excellence, Alexa felt slightly anxious that someone might only have 'just looked into it'.

'It turns out you do, yeah, for some of them. It's mad.'

Again Holly glanced towards James, who was explaining the basics of his job to Joanna in a typically self-deprecating style. It was impossible not to notice the admiring glow in the girl's eyes: there was something almost worshipful about it, something religious. What had Shona said? 'She must *love* you, this Holly woman. *I* would.' But he was nobody's hero, James had insisted earlier. It's not about that, he'd said.

What *was* it about then? Alexa looked again at Holly's face,

136

at that alluring blend of youth and ripeness, the taut young throat that produced that sexy, half-hoarse adult voice, and she thought: *Don't be ridiculous*. Holly was a single parent with no job and no home of her own, a grown woman still dependent on her mother, crammed into a tiny bedroom with her son. She had the sort of build that suggested little, if any, toning work. She probably didn't exercise at all but smoked forty a day and did drugs and rolled out of clubs at three in the morning before staggering home to her poor child. There was no evidence of any of these details, of course, but they fitted the stereotype and Alexa felt safe with stereotypes.

The bottom line was that Holly Walsh lived a life that was the polar opposite of her own well-heeled, well-ordered, well-married one.

Really, there was no comparison.

Chapter 10

Any illusion Joanna had had that Melissa's sun would suffer an eclipse when she left home for university proved to be exactly that, for the diminishment was not even partial. On the contrary, her absence seemed to hold a tantalising new power over their parents, one that Joanna imagined reanimated their anticipation of her birth almost two decades ago.

Now it was weekend visits home that they awaited so ardently, notice of which would inspire pure euphoria in them, not to mention the kind of detailed planning of eating and drinking normally associated with Christmas or a birthday.

Was that when Joanna began finally to resent her sister seriously, terminally? Was it the realisation that even when absent she remained at the centre of everyone's attention, her position utterly unchallengeable? Was that when she began to acknowledge within herself an appetite for revenge?

For so long she'd simply accepted Melissa's supremacy as empirical law. She'd accepted it when those dresses were exchanged in Melissa's favour; when their school invited her to move up an academic year and her parents decided against it because Melissa became hysterical at the prospect; when Melissa subtly sabotaged her friendships or openly commandeered them; she'd even accepted it when, in adolescence,

Melissa's rivalry turned to indifference as she redirected her powers of caprice to boyfriends, boyfriends she could select from echelons inaccessible to the likes of Joanna.

But somehow she could accept it no more. She refused to witness the laps of honour that were Melissa's weekends home, arranging to be out before her sister woke and back only after she'd gone to bed, or even to stay the night with a friend so as to avoid the homecomings entirely. There was a sense, not yet wholly clear to her, that she was biding her time.

And it came. It came in the summer term of Melissa's second year and the closing weeks of her own A-level course, in the form of Melissa's new boyfriend, Dan. Though her sister had often been accompanied home, it had been by a succession of individuals so alike that Joanna sometimes forgot to notice that the name had changed: if not strikingly good looking, then each would certainly be well-educated and self-assured, a boy in training to be his own father.

But not Dan. He was another species entirely, an *actual man*, older than his student lover by several years. The moment Joanna met him she knew she'd been fooling herself by fooling around with local boys, including her current boyfriend and fellow sixth-former Stephen. Dan was not especially tall, but somehow he towered; he was not unusually muscular and yet radiated potency. It was to do with his gaze, she decided, which was bold and challenging, a trait entirely absent in the boys of her age, who often could not clear the first hurdle of eye contact. It was to do with the blue of his irises, too, the French Ultramarine of her Winsor & Newton colour chart, a living blue that could catch your attention like a flag lifted by the breeze or an exotic butterfly fluttering into frame.

Ridiculous to be seduced by pigmentation, by the accidental density of cells, but there it was.

'So . . . you're the sister then.' His first words hammered her firmly where the rest of her family had long ago nailed her:

under the sign 'Nameless Afterthought'. 'I've heard all about you from Melissa.'

With Melissa ensconced between her parents on one sofa, Dan had taken a seat next to Joanna on the other. It was early Saturday evening and they all drank gin and tonics from the family's best glassware; even the selection of nuts was of a superior quality than usual. Her parents had really pushed the boat out, Joanna thought, simultaneously objecting to this and falling helplessly into line. How grateful she was that she'd made an effort with her appearance; her next exam scheduled for Thursday, she was allowing herself a night out with friends.

'Oh, well,' she drawled, 'if *she*'s your only character witness then I'm already on my way to meet the firing squad.'

'Is that what you think? Sounds like there might be some crimes we don't know about yet.' He smirked, and the effect of his half-bared front teeth biting idly into his lower lip, the blue gaze narrowed in amused scrutiny, made Joanna gulp. From across the room, Melissa glanced, interested but not yet drawn to issue any warning.

'There are no crimes,' Joanna said, holding her nerve, refusing to acknowledge her sister's attention. 'How did you and Melissa meet?' What she thought, however, was, Imagine if Melissa weren't here. Imagine if we were on our own. I think I could seduce him. The idea made her blush under her protective layer of pale foundation.

'Oh, we met the usual way: in a pub.' His voice was low-pitched, almost hushed, the words something to luxuriate in, and she could tell that he was fully aware of its effect: it was as if he knew about the blush without being able to see it. He could feel it, perhaps, in her increased body heat.

Sitting on her hands to stop herself fidgeting, she succeeded in dragging the fabric of the scooped neckline of her long black dress lower still, half hoping it might cause his gaze to lower. Yes, her sister had all the conventional attributes of beauty, but

Joanna liked to think she had developed a style of her own. She was a different shape from Melissa – fatter, said Melissa; heavier, said their mother; curvier, said Dan's eyes.

But then – as ever – she was instantaneously outshone: across the room Melissa was stretching her arms above her head and yawning, her cropped pink mohair jumper rising perilously high to unveil skin as cool and pale as chilled cream, the motion of it in any case making it obvious she wasn't wearing a bra (an omission Joanna could never have made without feeling utterly bovine). Dan's eyes swivelled mid-dip, thereafter transfixed. Defeated, Joanna could no longer prevent the arrival of an image of Melissa and him kissing in the car before coming into the house, the backs of his knuckles grazing the pink wool as his fingers explored her skin, Melissa promising, 'Later, you have to wait,' and Dan groaning in frustration.

For the first time in her life she not only thought, It's not fair, but *felt* it too, felt it at the point of impact as a proper trauma, not a background ache to be managed. And instead of defeat she registered something new: a determination to rise to the challenge.

'Joanna?'

She realised he was looking expectantly at her.

'Sorry?'

'I said, you're doing your A-levels next year, right?'

'No, not next year, I've just finished them!' She said this vehemently enough to make him hold up his hands in joking apology. 'Well, two more exams to go,' she conceded.

'Sorry, Melissa said you don't leave for college for another year.'

'I don't.' More calmly, she explained that the art foundation course she needed to complete before taking her degree was only funded by her local college of further education and so she would be remaining an extra year at home.

'Oh, I thought you were younger,' Dan said.

'I'm eighteen, nineteen in October. I want to go to London for my degree. I'm only going to live at home because it doesn't seem worth the expense to move out while I'm studying in the same town.'

'Sure.' She saw to her dismay that the conversation had begun to bore him; he'd preferred her sardonic opening style.

'Jo's expected to do very well in her A-levels,' her mother put in, and Melissa permitted this instance of small acclaim with magnanimous grace. Of course she did, Joanna thought, why wouldn't she? She had *him* now and he was demonstrably a thousand times more covetable than any A grade. Joanna thought she would have traded all her academic qualifications past and future for one (proper) kiss in the present.

When the doorbell rang – her friends arriving to pick her up – she felt close to despair at the casual assumption she'd made that dinner at home would be just another one to avoid.

As she rose, Melissa asked, 'Are you staying over with your boyfriend tonight? Kevin, is it?'

'Stephen,' Joanna corrected her. 'No, I'll be coming back tonight. I never stay over with him.'

'How chaste,' Melissa said, sweetly devilish.

Under his breath Dan uttered something that may or may not have been, 'His loss,' which caused in her a thrilling catch of fear, until she assured herself that if she hadn't quite heard it then Melissa certainly could not have.

'So what do you think of 'ole blue eyes?' Melissa asked her the next morning in the kitchen, before the guest was up. Melissa, dressed in a silky robe, was making a mug of tea to take up to him in bed.

'He's lovely,' Joanna told her, for it would be absurd to deny it. She pictured him upstairs, naked under rumpled bedclothes and reaching out for Melissa as she brought the tea, pulling her down on top of him. She wanted to scream her objection to this

142

intimacy, hurl her own tea at the wall, perhaps. 'Really good looking.'

'I know,' Melissa chuckled. 'When I saw him, I thought, wow, he's like Rob Lowe or something. I didn't think he'd go for me for a second.' But since it had been said that Melissa resembled Michelle Pfeiffer, this could only be false modesty and Joanna couldn't stop her mouth from pulling in annoyance.

'Oh, don't look so *miserable*, Jo. You'll meet more interesting boys when you finally leave home. There's no one worth a second look in *this* town.'

'Hmm.' Joanna was accustomed to the tone Melissa used when advising her about men, the patronising air of the experienced woman to the virgin, the beauty to the plain Jane, and the more she did it the less Joanna felt like sharing her own stories, including the fact that she was not a virgin. (Sadly, the experience of sex with Stephen had proved disappointing enough for her to be familiar early in adulthood with the urge to evade its taking place.) It gave her a sense of satisfaction to withhold information from her sister, to keep secrets. Without realising it, years of being the one who wasn't Melissa, of being second best, had made her expert in subterfuge.

'How long have you been going out?' she asked, not wanting to fuel Melissa's self-satisfaction but nonetheless *needing* to know.

'Three months now. But I'm hoping he'll propose before the end of the year.'

'*Propose*? You mean marriage?'

'Yeah, that's the mission I've set myself – or him! I don't want anyone else getting their hands on him!'

Her envy palpable, Joanna watched Melissa retreat to the stairs, to her bedroom, to him. She was shocked both by her sister's announcement and her own exhilaration in response to it, instantly reactive to this raising of the stakes. 'Mission' was the word Melissa had used, and it took her less than five minutes to realise that it could also be applied to her own intentions.

For intentions they now were.

Of course, it was utterly predictable that now Holly had rejected him, Sean decided he wanted her after all, a dynamic as old as the hills. The less foreseeable part was that Holly seriously meant her rejection of him. She was not playing hard to get, as the magazines of Joanna's adolescence used to put it – and a tactic that would have been, frankly, a little late given the circumstances – but had undergone a genuine curtailment of interest. Her change of heart was absolute.

Whether or not Sean understood this was another matter. Judging by the snippets of conversation Joanna overheard between the two of them during his latest visit to Mikey, he did not.

'How's Letitia?' Holly asked, affably, as if the other girl's arrival in their lives had never driven her into paroxysms of despair and, eventually, derailed her young life catastrophically.

'Told you, we're not together now.' Sean's forehead furrowed in frustration, his black eyebrows joined in a pretty little storm of bewilderment. Joanna was used to his appearance now, of course, and singularly unsold on the offering, but it was not hard to see how effortlessly he might inspire worship in girls his own age or younger, girls like the one Holly had so recently been. Tortured and artistic-looking, with fine features and a slight twist of vulnerability in his smile, he looked as if he ought to be an offbeat actor or cult singer-songwriter. Since he looked nothing like his mother or sisters, Joanna assumed he must resemble his father, who was no longer with the family and whom she and Holly had not met. You might have said this was an unhappy coincidence the two of them had bonded over – absent fathers – if it weren't also true for more than half the other kids they knew.

'Oh, yes, you did say you'd split, but I wasn't sure if you meant it.' Holly addressed him as she might a younger brother, with kindly superiority. Vanished completely was the animal yearning Joanna had found so painful to watch in the past, the open understanding between Sean and her that he was the prize and she the candidate.

'Course I meant it,' Sean said, insulted; if anyone was betraying any yearning it was he.

'Oh, right, sorry,' Holly said, politely.

What was odd, Joanna thought, was how much Holly's indifference diminished him, as if his attractiveness was something his admirers conferred on him rather than something he intrinsically possessed. She supposed that since he was *not* an offbeat actor or cult singer-songwriter but a drugs-smoking man-child and occasional and disastrously unskilled motorcycle messenger, the illusion that he was something special had to be sustained by attitude rather than achievement. If the attitude slipped, so did the illusion.

It was slipping now, as he tussled with the reality of Holly as something other than his love-struck dope. And this couldn't have been the only change he'd noticed, for there was also her altered manner towards their son. Whereas previously neither parent had exhibited any instinct for the task, she as clueless as he, Holly now updated Sean on Mikey's recent development with the authority of a Norland nanny.

For the first time in years, Joanna felt a little sorry for him. He was so crestfallen by the new order. She's grown up, she wanted to explain to him. She's not impressionable any more, she's an adult woman, a proper mother. It had taken a near-tragedy to get them here but here they were.

'Where'd Mikey get this?' Sean asked, noticing the toy Mini Cooper by his feet.

Holly's face lit up at the question, rather as it used to when Sean walked through the door. 'Oh, it was a present from the man who rescued him in Paris. James Maitland. He came over last week to see how Mikey was doing.'

'Oh yeah? It's cool, isn't it?' He played idly at opening and closing the miniature doors before asking Holly if she'd been out anywhere good recently. Joanna thought it incredible that he should display no further interest in the man who had saved his son's life: shouldn't he be eager to meet him in person, to thank him for his extraordinary act of courage? Instead, it was as if James's feat had been little more than the retrieval of a beaker from under the seat on the bus, or the drawing of attention to a dropped sock.

'I haven't been out that much, actually,' Holly said, 'not in the evening, anyway. Mikey's up so early.'

Sean blinked uncomprehendingly at this. Why would an early start be an issue when you had a live-in babysitter?

Pride – or was it habit, the need to speak for Holly because she had so many times in the past been unwilling or unable to speak for herself? – made Joanna chip in. 'Plus you're starting your new job on Friday, aren't you, Holls? You'll need your energy for that.'

'Yes, that's right.'

'Where're you working?' Sean asked, managing to sound both impressed and put out at the same time.

'Butler's, that new restaurant on Westow Hill. Just a bit of waitressing. Nothing major.'

Nothing major, no: something *much* more important than that. As far as Joanna was concerned, the job formalised Holly's return to the land of the living. When Holly had told her the news, she had chosen for her the largest congratulations card in the shop and they and Mikey had had a celebration cake.

Holly rose from her seat, clearly signalling the end of this small talk. 'So, Sean, now you're here, would you like to take Mikey to the park or something? Shall I get him ready to go out?'

146

Sean's face was wary. 'On my own, you mean?'

'Yes, he needs a run around. Could you take him to the swings?' At the word 'swings', Mikey began tearing into their legs, bouncing off them as if his chest – and their legs – were made of rubber. 'Look at all this energy, he needs to get out!'

'Why don't you come with us?' Sean suggested, rubbing his left shin and tilting his face at her with a look of endearing query he might have learned from James Dean.

A year ago – a month ago – this proposal, this facial expression, would have been an instant happy pill for Holly, but now all she said was, 'I can't, sorry. I've got some things I need to do.'

'What things?' It was a Sunday afternoon, a fair enough question.

'Just things.'

Joanna smiled to herself. As she watched Holly strapping on Mikey's little shoes and running a brush through his hair, she felt the unfamiliar sensations of pride and peace. For the first time in years she had even had substantial periods of time – as long as half a day, even twenty-four hours – in which she was not worrying about Holly *at all*. It had reached the point where she could, if she wanted, go back to worrying about herself.

She was not the only one to have had this thought, evidently. Just yesterday, Suze had said something to her that had struck her as significant: 'Now Holly's a bit more settled, maybe you can think about looking again?'

'Looking?' Joanna's immediate thought was of her sister. Was Suze suggesting she try, after all this time, to contact Melissa and make another appeal for clemency?

'For a man, I mean,' Suze said.

Ah, of course, as if life partners were mislaid house keys, found in the end if you only kept hunting, under a cushion, perhaps. Much as Suze adored Holly, she had long viewed her as the single most obstructive element in Joanna's private life. To her, it was no coincidence that Adrian and Joanna had split up when the complications of Holly's pregnancy and single moth-erhood had begun to gather pace. 'Who's having this baby, you or her?' she would ask, and that had been *before* Sean's depar-ture, before the depression, when Holly's youth and naïvety had been the primary source of concern. 'Do you have enough space to have a baby living with you? Won't Sean have to move in as well?'

Adrian, one step on, had said: 'The day that moron dumps her is the day you'll dump me.'

'Don't be crazy,' Joanna had protested, though the inevitability of Holly being dumped was never in dispute.

'He's the problem in all this, you know that, right? When you analyse it, he's the rotten bit at the core. He's probably the one who's told her it's evil to have an abortion, and yet he's not going to stick around to help.'

They had both been right, of course, Suze and Adrian. The flat *was* too small, too small for her to be able to separate Holly's needs from her own; she *might* as well have been having the baby herself. And when Sean deserted Holly, Adrian had not waited to be formally dismissed before fulfilling his own prophecy. In their final conversation he had described himself as having been squeezed into the narrowest of spaces. He said he had to leave before he began to run out of oxygen.

'You're hung up on this whole history repeating thing,' Adrian told her and she'd tried not to let the accusation sting.

'This isn't history repeating itself. It will be completely differ-ent for Holly. For instance, I had no support from my parents, not emotionally, and I'm not going to put her in that position.'

'That's what I mean, you're more interested in stopping the same thing from happening again than you are in getting on with what *you* want from life.'

'Keeping my daughter safe and happy *is* what I want from life,' Joanna said, firmly.

'And that's it?'

She looked him in the eye, answered truthfully: 'It's not "it", but it is the most important thing.'

She had not attacked him for walking away. Having not offered him the encouragement to be a stepfather (or step-grandfather), she could hardly blame him for failing to fulfil the role. The bottom line was that once Mikey was born, while Holly had thought only of Sean, Joanna had needed to think only of Mikey. Someone had to and there was no one else.

Would it have been different if Holly had decided on a termination and left home at the planned time, in the usual way, for a college hall of residence or flat share with friends? Then, would Joanna have agreed to Adrian's suggestion that they live together? Even encouraged his hints about marriage? These were questions she could not answer, however, because she had vowed she would never use the word 'sacrifice' in relation to Holly, not ever. Even when her low-paid shop work exhausted her body and choked her imagination, when thoughts of a different neigh-bourhood, a fresh start, were weighed unfavourably against all that was local and reliable and risk-averse, even then she never used that word.

'You're far too young to resign yourself to being on your own,' Suze said yesterday, not for the first time.

'I'm not resigned,' Joanna said, not for the first time. 'I'm fine like this.'

'Some women are just starting their families at your age, not ending them.'

But Joanna didn't want to believe she was ending anything.

Resistance, however, would only intensify her friend's encouragement. And she could hardly deny that the forecast was suddenly brighter.

'Yes,' she agreed, smiling. 'Maybe I should start looking.'

Every so often Joanna found she connected with someone instinctively, was so convinced by that person's inherent good heart that she was prepared to argue his or her corner from the outset, whatever anyone else said. She was surprised to find that James's wife Alexa stirred such an instinct. Though it was obviously James to whom she and Holly owed a debt of eternal gratitude, it was Alexa of whom she thought as she wrote the couple a thank you note for the flowers and gift. She hoped it wasn't rude to have left over a week before doing so, but she had been awaiting a stock delivery that included a batch of particularly classy thank you cards she wanted to choose from.

Dear James and Alexa, Holly and I just wanted to say how lovely it was to meet you both last Sunday . . .

Actually, she wasn't sure that Holly would have worded it quite that way for she'd been decidedly lukewarm about James's wife after the Maitlands' visit. It was a testament to how used Joanna was becoming to her daughter's new positive energy that the lack of enthusiasm for Alexa was so noticeable.

'She wasn't what I was expecting,' Holly said, and her lower lip protruded slightly as if in resistance to the very notion of Alexa.

'Oh? What were you expecting?'

'Maybe someone a bit more relaxed, more like him. She was really uptight, I thought.'

'I know what you mean,' Joanna said. 'She was quite tense when they arrived, but she warmed up. The visit was probably sprung on her.' This, it stood to reason, was true, considering the short notice she herself had been given. She had recognised in Alexa something she knew she was guilty of herself, a need to control her environment, or, if that was putting it a bit strong, a preference not to be caught unawares by it. Some people relished the sudden brakes and accelerations of taking life as it came, but Alexa, like Joanna herself, had too great a fear of whiplash. And it put a strain on her, anyone could see that. She had been visibly worked up on arrival that day, only relaxing properly when James had left the room. Was it to do with children, perhaps?

She'd been defensive on the subject, which Joanna knew could often conceal real heartache.

There was also her confession about her rivalry with her younger sister; that, too, had struck a chord with Joanna. It was odd, though, how she had offered it up like that, almost as an entertaining story, something she thought might raise a laugh. Was her bitterness so close to the surface that she gave it voice so casually? Or had she somehow intuited that Joanna would sympathise?

'Well, anyway, I liked her,' Joanna said. 'I can see why James is with her. She has something about her.'

Holly could not agree. Nor could she supply an address for the couple.

'I could text James and ask?'

'No, that's a bit intrusive. We'll send it to his office. I remember the name of the company, I'll look up the address.'

I hope we can get together again, Joanna wrote in a PS. Then, after a short pause in which she worried she might be hijacking the couple from her daughter, she added, *I know Holly would really like that too.*

Posting it, she had the warm-blooded, buoyant feeling in her chest of unchallenged optimism: knowing the Maitlands was a sign of good things to come, she was sure of it.

Chapter 11

Later, it would come to seem to Holly that it had happened at full tilt, as hastily as everyone said it did, as recklessly uncaring of the other people involved; but at the time it felt only natural, impossible to influence or avert, like sunrise or the fall of rain.

The first text message from James came when she was in the park with Mikey. They'd been to the swings and looked at the dinosaurs and eaten the picnic she'd brought for lunch; now, resting on a bench, she was telling him that she was about to start a new job, her first since he'd been born.

'I'll be working when you're asleep,' she said, standing him on her thighs and swaying him back and forth, thinking he'd soon grow too big for this game. 'You won't even notice I'm not there. When I come home in the middle of the night, I'll be as quiet as a mouse' – she broke off to squeak (Mikey expected any animal reference to be accompanied by its correct sound) – 'and I'll give you a really soft kiss you won't feel because you'll already be dreaming.' She pecked playfully at his little nose to demonstrate, causing him to giggle.

She talked to him all the time now, almost non-stop; he was becoming her friend and companion as well as her child. Though she regretted deeply the time she'd lost to her depression, she knew her early failure could not be altered. She also knew she shouldn't really think of it as 'failure', any more than you would a broken leg, but she couldn't help it. All she could do now was to make his future as full of her love and attention as it could be; she wanted never again to tell him she was too tired to play with him or that he should go away and leave her alone. She remembered times when she'd felt so lethargic she needed to rest on her way to the kitchen to get his bottle: twelve steps, fifteen, maybe, that was all! The milk would be in the microwave for less than a minute and she would not have the strength to stand while she waited.

Now she was free of the depression she was able to understand better how it had worked on her: she'd been lost in a lightless underwater maze with no instinct whatsoever of where the exit might lie, and, in any case, no energy to tread water. She was able to see that without Joanna, she and Mikey simply would not have made it.

There was something else too, something she had not confided in Joanna and was not sure she could: a secret acknowledgement that her reasons for going ahead with the unplanned pregnancy might not have been the ones she'd professed such faith in at the time. She'd told herself – and Joanna – that keeping the baby was the right thing to do, the natural, moral choice: yes, she was very young, but how would she feel if she had a termination now, only for circumstances or medical health to intervene and rob her of all future chances? Yes, it would be exhausting, limiting in terms of career aspirations, but Joanna had managed it and so could she.

Now she accepted that there had been something less principled at work. She had been deeply in love with Sean and had known almost from their first meeting that his feelings for her were not so true, that they never would be. Keeping his baby meant keeping him; it guaranteed, if not power, then a share of identity: even if he left her she would always have a part of him, almost like having one of his kidneys transplanted into her.

Except a baby was not a kidney, it was a third life all its own. And far from keeping Sean close, it had hastened his departure.

Her phone throbbed in her pocket. She'd deleted all her former ringtones, which reminded her of Sean and which, if she was honest, had been downloaded for his benefit in the first place, so that he might remark on it if her phone happened to ring when they were together and gain her a fraction of a credit in cool.

She let Mikey clamber down from her lap and peered at the display: *1 new message: James.* Christian name only. She knew no other Jameses – there *were* no other Jameses. And there was an immediate thrill, even before opening the message, a sensation that rippled outward from the core of her as she clicked it open, making her fingertips tingle as if from the touch of the keys.

The text read: *Thank you for last Sunday. Great to see you and Mikey looking so well. James*

She texted: *Thank you so much for the present. Mikey really liked it – and you!*

And he responded: *I like him. (And you, of course.)*

That made her smile. She took a moment to savour it, and to compose her reply, but before she could begin there was another from him: *I meant to ask you, how are you getting on with your job hunt?*

Holly's fingers tapped: *I got one! Waitressing in a local restaurant, Fridays and Saturdays. Nothing amazing, but it's a start.*

I think that IS amazing. Congratulations!

Feeling delight even in the grooves between her toes, she hardly paused before replying: *Why don't you come and see me there if you're ever down here again? I'll buy you a drink.*

And then there was nothing.

After a few days she stopped checking. She didn't regret her invitation, for it might just as easily have been read in the plural as the singular (and in noting the distinction she only confirmed to herself that she'd been aware of one in the first place); all she knew was that whatever happened next, it would turn out fine because that was how things were for her now. Always her guardian angel hovered close by, making everything go her way. Perhaps James *was* the guardian angel.

She didn't think much about Alexa. She wasn't sure she thought much *of* Alexa, either. The way the other woman had looked at their flat – and at her – as if the smell bothered her and it was all she could do not to gag. Alexa was exactly the sort of woman Holly used to be intimidated by, the sort for whom everything existed to be judged: how you spoke, what you wore, how much money you earned, whether you were married or not, if and when you had children. Even without a single word being uttered on the subject of age, Holly knew Alexa despised her for having had a baby so young. Nineteen or twenty was no different to her than thirteen.

Then again, as her mother had pointed out, if James had chosen to marry Alexa there had to be something right about her, something good, otherwise it made James flawed and James was not flawed. Holly could not make a villainess of Alexa even if she wanted to: easier, then, to not make anything of her at all.

'Couples are not always the same as each other,' Joanna had said to her after the Maitlands' visit. 'Look at you and Sean.'

Holly made an 'Urgh' face. 'We're not a couple.'

'You *were*.'

'Not any more, thank God.'

Oh, it was a miracle, a liberation, to have felt her longing for Sean evaporate so entirely, not a drop of it remaining. It was another spell broken once and for all, another maze exited. To be able to see him and not feel immediate despair; to stand touching distance from him and not feel desire rise through her airways, choking her as she recognised, every time as if for the first time, that it was a desire no longer returned; for him to leave the flat with that half-mumbled goodbye of his and for her simply to get on with whatever needed to be done next instead of crumpling on to the sofa in a deluge of tears that lasted the rest of the day. To not think of him when she woke in the night, her brain on standby to create an obsessive fantasy in which everything she wanted him to say was said, everything she needed him to do was done.

Now, when she saw him, he was just another cute boy slouching around the place thinking he was going places while never actually going anywhere. He was half-hearted, she saw now, half-hearted about everyone and everything. What he gave was all he *could* give.

She, on the other hand, was wholehearted.

And so, she knew without needing to ask, was James.

It was ten days later, a Thursday evening, when he contacted her again. Mikey had been bathed and put to bed, her work uniform ironed for the following night's shift, and she was settling down to watch television with Joanna.

Are you working tomorrow night? I thought I might take you up on that offer of a drink.

I am, Holly replied. *That would be lovely.*

She added the address of the restaurant and the time her shift ended, flushing at the thought of seeing him again so soon. Joanna noticed her busy with her phone and asked, 'Who was that?'

'Er, James.'

'James Maitland?'

'Yes.' Hearing his full name spoken aloud like that caused a pleasurably possessive tingle in her, not dissimilar to how she felt when she scrolled through her contacts list and saw his name and number.

'What does he say?'

'Nothing in particular.' Not answering truthfully was Holly's first real admission that she had hoped all along that James would want to see her again on his own. Not that she needed to voice her innermost desires, in any case, because her mother seemed quite able to guess them.

'Don't forget he's married, Holly.' Joanna spoke in the same agreeable tone she always used when saying something disagreeable.

'I know.'

'They were in Paris for their wedding anniversary. Five years, Alexa told me.'

'I know,' Holly repeated. As awkward moments went, this was one of the easier ones, for she knew her mother wouldn't say any more than this and was probably fretting about having said this much. Though she had always been careful to let Holly make her own decisions – including, *especially*, the one about keeping Mikey – Holly knew that what she dreaded most was her daughter making the same mistakes she had. She wouldn't say that out loud, though, because it would mean conceding that they *were* mistakes, or if not outright wrong decisions then definitely ones bittersweet enough to have caused her regret.

Even at twenty-two, Holly felt she knew all there was to know about bittersweet decisions, about regret. Now all she wanted was to trust her instincts, to act on them no matter how afraid she was, to not waste time second-guessing them.

'Do people still believe in marriage?' she asked her mother, seriously.

Joanna laughed and frowned at the same time. 'Of course they do, sweetheart, otherwise they wouldn't do it, would they?'

Would they? It was true that Holly's female school and college friends had been desperate for marriage, but it didn't take much to see that what they wanted most of all was the party, the dress, the spotlight. They wanted those things very badly, almost as if marrying was the only way to achieve them.

'Nor would they *stay* married,' Joanna added. 'Marriage

means you have to think a lot harder about moving on. Couples who don't get married are far more likely to break up. They feel like they've got less to lose, even with children.' Holly didn't know who her mother was thinking of when she said this: Adrian, maybe, who had wanted to marry her, at least for a while; or Sean, perhaps, who most certainly had not wanted to marry Holly, not for a moment.

At least the focus had shifted from James Maitland and *his* marriage, she thought, watching a wistful expression take hold of her mother's face. It was a mood Joanna allowed herself only occasionally.

Holly had worked in catering before as part of her course, including a spell in the kitchen of a pub, and so she knew that it was a noisy and physically tiring environment. It was not, however, the cause of panic that it seemed to be for the other new girl at Butler's, Mina, who was a few years older than Holly but in greater need of carrying. By the time their first shift had drawn to a close, she had burst into tears twice.

'I can't handle this,' she said, as they collected their jackets and bags from the tiny staff room.

'What? I thought you did really well,' Holly said. She knew that by simply being present Mina was accomplishing substantially more than she had managed not so long ago.

But it seemed that Mina was the kind of person who was only satisfied with a fellow sufferer. 'You mean *you* did,' she snapped, startling Holly with her hostility. She had smooth, gentle features and it was a surprise to see them sharpen. 'Everyone loves you. You're totally showing me up.'

'I'm just trying to do my best.' She felt sorry for Mina; it was not at all hard to identify with the sheer misery of defeat, helplessness. 'If we look like we know what we're doing, then people might think we do – that's my strategy, anyway!'

Mina didn't smile. 'Yeah, right.'

Holly wondered if she would even turn up for her next shift. Maybe it was her new way of thinking, but it seemed to her that if you did something wrong the best thing you could do was to put it right as quickly as possible and remember not to do it again – it only made things worse if you pointed out to the world that you weren't on top of things, it made the world alert to weaknesses it might previously have overlooked. Mistakes were a part of living; they had to happen for you to learn.

With this in mind, she settled in quickly. The night James came in, her third, she'd spilled fewer drinks, broken nothing and made just one error with her orders: not bad at all. Her coolness earned her praise from the manager, Marcus, though she wished he hadn't chosen to give it in front of Mina, who had scurried up at exactly that moment to tell Holly she had a visitor.

'I put him in the bar,' she said, as if this had been a terrible imposition on her time.

Holly felt a quivering sensation on her skin, Marcus's kind words already forgotten. 'Is he called James?'

Mina shrugged. 'Might've been what he said. Anyway, he's waiting for you.'

'Boyfriend?' Marcus asked. 'Has he come to walk you home?' The restaurant didn't pay for taxis, but Marcus was nice enough to care about his staff travelling safely.

'Friend,' Holly said. But the word had never tasted so sweet on her tongue, like it meant the same as love or bliss or heaven.

Mina gave Holly a look that said, 'It's not fair, you get everything,' and Holly wished she could say to her, 'This hasn't been happening all my life, I'm nothing special.'

'I'll let him know I'm not finished yet,' she told Marcus, conscientiously, but one look at James and her boss let her finish ten minutes early and join him at the bar. It wasn't just her, then; her colleagues' reactions confirmed what she'd thought: this *had* been happening all his life, he *was* special. Or maybe it was just because he was so expensively dressed for down here: he looked so effortlessly well-bred.

'Hello,' she said, sliding between the two empty bar stools next to his.

He looked up at once, pleasure curling the corners of his mouth. His eyes were darker than she'd remembered and as he turned they reflected the light of the yellow lamps hanging over the bar, giving the effect of switching his face on. In this context, alone and at night, he was a different person entirely from the one she'd met before.

'Hello,' he said, echoing her intonation precisely. They did not kiss cheeks or shake hands or touch at all but just those two syllables caused a physical reaction in her, not a quiver this time but a wobble, a loss of faith in her own sense of balance.

'Sit down,' he said, and his fingertips grazed the seat of the stool beside his. 'You must be tired if you've been working all night.'

He ordered them both a glass of the most expensive wine on the list. She fingered the twenty-pound note in her pocket and tried to catch the eye of Jake, the bartender on duty. It felt surreal to have switched from providing service to receiving it: she almost expected someone to rush up and protest (Mina, most likely).

As they drank, there were a couple of minutes of quick glances and small talk about the restaurant, her new duties and hours, the buzzy location. Then James caught her eye and held it, asking her, in a lower, more confidential voice, 'So why did you invite me here?'

She swallowed. 'Like I said, I wanted to buy you a drink. I owe you one.' She paused, placing her money on the bar in front of her as if in evidence.

'You don't owe me,' he said, elongating the 'owe'. 'I told you that before. It makes me feel bad that you think you're in my debt in some way.' He smiled and edged a little closer to her;

instinctively she did the same. At precisely that moment Jake noticed the twenty-pound note and gestured his refusal to take any payment from her, causing James to say, 'I see you have another fan.'

Another fan. There was a pitching sensation in her stomach. 'So what made you decide to come?' she asked. She knew intuitively that the way to proceed with this conversation was to follow his lead, to ask him the very questions he asked her. 'You didn't have to. Or you could have come with Alexa.'

His gaze met hers with greater insistence and this time she held her own. Neither blinked, until at last James said, 'You know why I came, *without* her.'

'Do I?' Her breath caught in her chest.

'Because I couldn't stop thinking about you.'

'Oh. You mean, after . . .'

'Last time, yes. And the time before. And Paris.' His face was coming closer to hers – or was it hers to his? – and when he spoke she could feel his breath on her face.

'Even Paris?'

'Even Paris, though I don't think I was aware of it at first.'

'I wasn't sure,' she said. 'You didn't text me back straight away . . .'

'That's because I thought I ought to make myself think about it.' He chuckled, a dry, slightly tortured sound. 'I thought I should give myself a cooling-off period.'

'Cooling off?' The mesmerising inference was that there had been heat, a heat so powerful it needed fighting.

'But I knew the moment I read your message what I was going to do. I kept thinking, What just happened? I had to see you again to find out.' The closer he got to her, the more of a murmur his voice became, until his lips were as near to her skin as it was possible to get without actually making contact.

'So you didn't . . . cool off?'

'No. The opposite, in fact.' Hearing his words was the best

161

feeling in the world, like a drug injected into her navel, spreading through her from the inside out.

After that, communication became even more direct.

'I need to kiss you,' he said. 'Can I?'

'Yes, but not here.'

'Somewhere else, then. When can you leave?'

'Now. Give me one minute.' She slid from the seat and through the staff door, collected her bag, called goodbye to her colleagues, the whole time feeling the soaring, swooping sensations of first flight. In the street, James took her hand in the same commanding way she did Mikey's on a busy roadside, as if it went without saying he would keep her safely by him and there'd be no use her trying to wriggle away. A little way down the next side street there was a recessed doorway and he pulled her into it, into him, against his body, to kiss her mouth. He was much taller than she was in her flat work shoes and she had to stretch her throat to meet his downturned face. He steadied her head in his hands as if he feared she would at any second twist away.

'I'm assuming you have to go home tonight?' he said, after a while. He was breathing hard into her hair.

'Yes.' Not having known what to expect, or even to hope, she'd told her mother that there was a staff drink planned for after closing and she might be a little later home than usual. 'Don't you, as well?'

'Yes.'

'Where are you supposed to be?'

'Out with a client.' He sighed as he took her hand, drawing her back into the street. 'I drove down, so I'll drop you home before I go.'

She did not think of Alexa as she followed him to his car and took the passenger seat. She wished she lived fifty miles away so they could drive together on the night roads. Instead, even with the mercy of a red light, they were outside her building within five minutes. In the darkened car, they kissed again and she pressed herself tightly against him. Only now did his hands touch other parts of her, her thighs and breasts and shoulders and hips, making her groan and squirm.

'Do you know how much I want you?' he said.

'No. Tell me.'

'A lot. An obscene amount.'

'That's good.'

'Is it?'

'Yes,' Holly said. 'Of course it is.' She pulled back from him slightly so she could see his face. 'Don't you think?'

He looked back at her, assessing. 'I don't know, not yet. I just know that it *is* and there's nothing we can do about it.' He sounded almost melancholic, as if he knew the battle for his sanity had already been lost and was nostalgic for a time when he'd been in possession of rational thought. She didn't dare dream that their attraction meant as much to him as it did to her. That wouldn't be possible, she decided. But if it meant a hundredth as much to him then that would be enough. And if he decides he never wants to see me again, I won't let myself be sad about it, she thought, because I'll know that this is how it can feel, this is how it *should* feel.

'Can I tell you something?' she whispered, seeing the time glowing red on the dashboard. She knew Joanna might still be up, waiting to hear the key in the door before she allowed herself to rest, but still she wanted very badly to prolong this.

'What?'

'You know when we saw each other in Chiswick?'

'Yes?'

'I wasn't meeting a friend. I went there because I hoped I might find you.'

She saw the twitch of a half-smile on his lips as he said, 'I see.'

'You mean you guessed?'

'Hoped rather than guessed.' His mouth claimed hers again, his hand on her waist, curving over her hip. 'How long had you been waiting when I found you?'

'Hours, probably. I lost track. And there were so many different train stations! I chose that one because it was on the tube.'

'You chose correctly.'

'Yes, I was lucky.'

'No, *I* was lucky.' He kissed her again very hard and then broke away, gazing at her and groaning, 'Oh, Holly, Holly, Holly. Holly.'

Her eyes widened in alarm. 'Why are you saying my name like that?'

'In case I never get to say it again like this. In case you decide you never want to see me again after tonight.'

It couldn't be true: he was saying the actual words she had thought herself.

'That would never happen,' she said, catching his mood and thinking she understood how it was possible to feel joy and sorrow simultaneously. 'It's more likely to be the other way around. I won't not want to see you, not ever. Unless you say I can't.'

'I won't, don't worry.' He gave her a look that had a lasting shimmer to it before he finally let her go.

Inside the flat she turned on the living room light and went straight to the window, saw that he'd waited until he was sure she was safely indoors before starting the engine and pulling off.

Already the bit she loved most about their encounter was when he'd asked, 'How long had you been waiting when I found you?'

Already she knew that after tonight things would move very, very fast.

Chapter 12

Having learned the hard way not to pick at the past, Joanna had mixed feelings when Adrian Hutchins came into the shop on Saturday morning. It was possible – if slightly shameful – that Suze had been quick off the mark to send word that Holly, and therefore Joanna, were back in the land of the living (as if he'd simply been waiting crouched in a hole until the summons came), but just as likely he had come in because he needed to buy a present for someone and had either forgotten she ran the place or hoped she might, by now, have moved on.

Living just a few neighbourhoods apart, it was a miracle they hadn't bumped into each other before now – either that or there'd been a carefully sustained programme of avoidance.

'Jo.'

'Ade?' The old abbreviation came naturally, though she mercifully managed to suppress the flush that had given her away when he'd first suggested they got together, or every time they'd made love, or the last time he'd said goodbye. Often people remarked on how once you knew someone intimately it didn't matter if you didn't then see that person for twenty years, you only had to be together for two minutes and it was as if you'd never been parted; and yet weren't there also old partners who you could see again and not believe you'd ever been as close to as you once were, ever lain in bed together and said things to each other you wouldn't dream of saying to anyone else?

This, she told herself, was how *they* were, Adrian and she. The problem was he looked exactly the same: not enough time had passed for there to be any physical differences or even an update of his wardrobe. She recognised the shirt, she recognised the haircut (about two-thirds between having had one and needing the next), she recognised the easy body language he used to belie feelings of uncertainty, she recognised the bright black eyes and hopeful curve of the lips, both attributes that could be mistaken for a womaniser's when they were, in fact, the charms of a faithful man.

'I was wondering if you were still here,' he said.

'Oh yes.' She tried to collect herself, but she'd gone missing, or at least her voice had, coming out musical and girlish. 'I shall still be here when the building collapses around me, I expect.'

'Is it likely to? I suppose subsidence is a problem in this area.'

'So they say. Are you still working up in Marble Arch? How's it going?' Having worked in a succession of sales jobs while they were together, he had last been based at the West End showroom of a German car manufacturer.

'It's all right, I suppose. We've got redundancies coming up.'

'People aren't buying cars?' she asked. Her voice had recovered and she felt her lungs relax.

He glanced about him. 'Are people buying candles?'

'Yes, actually, but candles are a lot cheaper.'

'Sometimes I wonder.' He grinned. 'We're practically giving stock away at the moment.'

'But you'll be OK?'

He shrugged; he was one of the few people Joanna had known who used the shrug as an optimistic gesture. 'There's always work if you don't mind what you do.'

Joanna thought at once of Holly and her new waitressing position. She hadn't answered a job ad, she had just walked in off the street and enquired. Sean would never do that; the idea that he was now a role model to a young son would not have troubled him to seek work. When they were together, Joanna and Adrian had struggled to suppress their laughter when Holly insisted Sean wasn't prepared to 'sell out'. 'There's nothing to sell,' Adrian said.

'How's Holly?' he asked now, as if tracking her thoughts.

'She's very well.' Joanna decided to leave it there. It was either that or detain him for three hours while she explained how things had got much, much worse before they'd got better; somehow, with Holly, with Adrian, there was no in-between. And he understood that too, of course, could undoubtedly draw instead on any of the countless conversations they'd had in the past about Holly and Sean, about the baby.

'She's not still with that loser?'

'No, she's not with anyone.' It was an unexpected joy to report this. 'I think it's probably better that way for now.'

'Does he see much of Mikey, though?'

'He *sees* him. He puts in an appearance.'

Adrian, who she knew would have liked a family of his own (and presumably still did, he was a man in his forties and had plenty of time; he could start in his old age if he so chose), did not say as he used to that he would like to wring Sean's neck for not understanding what it meant to be a father.

'It probably is better. A lot less complicated, anyway.' And Joanna's ears flared at the inference that the same could be said for them, for *their* relationship.

He turned to look at the picture frames and candles displayed to his right, seemed to reach for something at random – a set of frangipani tealights – and brought his unlikely purchase to the counter. They were closer now, separated at waist height but within breathing distance and unable now to avoid holding each other's eye for a decent length of time.

Joanna became aware of the first prickles of a flush. Oh,

God, they were in the first category after all, the one where it felt just like yesterday – not even as long ago as yesterday, but that morning, as if he'd got out of her bed an hour after she had and followed her into work. He used to say to her, 'I'm yours, you're mine'; most of the time, it was what he said instead of, 'I love you.' She wondered how he would react if she said it back to him right now, over the counter, across the twenty-month void.

She rang the price into the till. 'Is this a gift? Would you like me to wrap it in tissue for you?'

He looked at her as if she'd suggested she roll it in space dust and send it into the sky in a hot air balloon. 'No, you're all right.'

When he'd paid, taken the bag from her and opened the door to leave, when he'd vanished from her view and not come back into it, she felt herself knifed from behind with grief. She was surprised by the furtive violence of it.

A little under an hour later, the shop was full of more personal visitors. Holly and Mikey came first, arriving a couple of minutes before Suze, who often helped out with an afternoon shift on Saturdays.

'Did you have a good time at the drinks thing last night?' Joanna asked her daughter. She'd been too tired to wait up and there'd been no time to catch up that morning before she had to leave to open the shop.

'It was brilliant, yes.' If the new Holly was cheerful, today's version was euphoric, higher than Joanna could ever remember having seen her, even before the postnatal depression. She was exactly what was meant by walking on air. How important it was to earn your own money, Joanna thought, and to earn the respect that came with it. A new job meant new purpose and new colleagues soon turned into new friends: no wonder Sean had been left in her wake.

The joy of it was she was taking Mikey along for the ride. And here he was, shrieking, straining to escape the straps of his buggy and start breaking things. Before Joanna could find something to distract him – a reel of Sellotape, no, too much of a weapon; a piece of ribbon, then – Holly had fished in her bag for a rice cake and slipped it into his hand. She imagined Adrian saying, 'A *rice cake*?' and she replying, 'Oh, the Pushy Mamas introduced her to them,' and Adrian saying, 'Pushy Mamas?' . . .

Suze, arriving in the middle of this private dialogue, was less discreet in her assessment of Holly's enhanced happiness, doing an exaggerated double take at the sight of her and exclaiming: 'My God, you look amazing, girl! Have you been on one of those makeover programmes on TV?'

Holly laughed. 'I *feel* amazing.'

'You're not too hungover then?' Joanna teased.

'No, I just had one glass of wine.'

'I thought you liked those alcopops?' Suze said. 'The vodka things with silly names?'

'They're for schoolkids,' Holly told her.

'Well, that's a reassuring thought.'

'Want out! Want out!' Mikey screeched. Having munched the rice cake, he was agitating again, his cheeks red and sticky. Joanna recognised the mood: centrifugal, unstoppable. He was a cyclone in need of a coastal village to devastate.

'I'd better take him out,' Holly said, on cue. 'We'll go to the soft play in the leisure centre.' This was one of many places she had found insufferable in the past: it was too hot, too noisy, too exhausting. Even Joanna admitted the place gave her a headache, especially on a Saturday.

'It's like she's been born again,' Suze marvelled after the buggy had rolled from sight. 'She hasn't found God, has she, Jo?'

'I don't think so, but I don't mind if she has if He makes her this happy.' Joanna grew serious. 'It does worry me, though, her going from one extreme to the other like this.'

'I must admit I've never seen anything like it before,' Suze said, 'not *this* dramatic. I suppose all you can do is keep an eye on it, just in case.'

Just in case. Just in case this was not a new dawn at all but only an interval before dusk, before nightfall . . . Joanna couldn't dismiss the thought from her mind, but she could prevent it from being voiced. 'You won't believe who else just came in?'

'What, talking of God?' Suze chuckled.

'No!'

'Someone for you?'

Someone for you: there was a sweetness to hearing those words that gave Joanna the same melting feeling in her oesophagus as if she'd swallowed syrup. 'Adrian.'

Suze failed to look as surprised as she might have. 'And?'

'And . . . oh, Suze, I think if I ever do get together with someone, it won't be anyone from before.' And so, in ten seconds, Adrian had been reduced to 'anyone from before': it was a woeful description for him, he deserved much, much better. Better than me, she thought.

'I can understand that.' Suze's expression suggested otherwise. 'But, Jo, you do know it's not if, it's when. Holly's not the only one who's looking good. This new leaf of hers, it's taken a load off your shoulders. I bet you're sleeping better, are you?'

'For now. It makes a big difference to be able to sleep through the night again. If Mikey wakes now, she takes care of him.'

'Which is exactly as it should be.'

'I know. But I miss it, in a way. I can't help it.' She was sensible enough to know that her own dispensability was the inevitable bitter to the sweet of Holly's recovery, but, still, it had occurred so abruptly her reason couldn't quite keep pace with her emotions. Just as the accident had ignited Holly's true maternal instincts, so it had reinforced Joanna's: she felt more protective of Mikey than ever, just as she was being asked to relinquish him.

A cluster of new customers, young women, saved Joanna from any further internal dilemma. One approached the counter with a determined air, dressed in what looked like a bra and a pair of denim knickers but which Joanna assumed had been designed as a top and shorts. 'Can I help?'

'Do you do cards for celebrating your divorce?' She couldn't have been older than twenty-five. 'It's for my best mate. The decree whatsit just came through today.'

'No, I'm afraid we don't,' Joanna said. Many years ago she had perfected the retail face, the one that filtered astonishment or amusement or distaste and communicated instead the re-assurance that she was asked that question every day and it was only a matter of time before she passed the tip on to the manu-facturers. 'But let me show you the cards I have that might work. They're left blank for your own message.'

She and Suze exchanged a look.

'Congratulations, that's what I'm going to write,' the girl told them. 'Congratulations, babe. You're well shot of the bastard.'

'Quite right,' Suze said, and Joanna could tell she was only half joking. 'We were just saying, weren't we, Jo? You girls are better off with God.'

There was a sharp, surprised silence and then all at once the shop was filled with the sound of women laughing.

As sure as night followed day, Dan Payne proposed to Melissa Walsh. As with all Melissa's coups, it was breathtakingly fast, an assassination of the other's will, a decision made by a man who had not the advantage of options. A date was set for early September, allowing time for a honeymoon before Melissa returned to university. Joanna was to be one of five bridesmaids sufficiently white-skinned and plump to emphasise the bride's

171

wasp-waisted superiority, and just in case there was any lingering doubt as to who was the fairest of them all they were to be dressed in floor-skimming coral-pink.

In early July, eight weeks before the wedding, when Melissa had arranged holiday work locally and Dan found himself between bar jobs (Joanna had yet to determine his intended profession, and in fact never did), the couple came to live with the Walshes for the summer in order to save money. It seemed to Joanna that Dan made a point of paying special attention to her, and not always in an attempt to include her in the main conversation, but sometimes to draw her from it.

'Red suits you, Jo,' he'd say, or, 'Cool haircut,' and, best of all, 'You're funny. I like your sense of humour. You're the smart one, I don't care what they say.' ('They', always in these conversations, were Melissa and her parents.) None of his little compliments had anything manipulative about them, for he was quite a simple soul, she was learning – 'Guileless,' their father had said, before it was understood that he was to join the family, and then afterwards, 'Direct, straight. You know where you are with Dan.'

Joanna knew only where she would *like* to be with him: under him, against him, in bed with him.

Any guilt for such thoughts was instantly extinguished by the memory of any one of a thousand childhood episodes in which Melissa had demeaned her. Where was *her* guilt?

As the weeks passed and July gave way to August, she became aware of an acceleration in her desire, an acute appreciation that time was running out. And so it was: Dan and Melissa would move back to Manchester after the wedding and an increased study load in Melissa's final year would mean far fewer visits home than in her first two. Joanna would never again have an opportunity like this summer – like Dan Payne.

Coming downstairs one cool Saturday morning, she found that Melissa and her mother had gone to London for the day for a dress fitting, while her father was out playing golf. Dan had been invited, he told her at the kitchen table, where he sat fingering an empty bone-china coffee cup, but had cried off at the last minute with a headache. For the first time that Joanna noticed (and she *had* been noticing) she and Dan were alone in the house with a substantial length of time stretched ahead of them.

'Are you really ill?' she asked, popping her two slices from the toaster and reaching for the butter, 'or did you just not want to play golf with a bunch of fifty-year-olds?'

'I just didn't want to play golf with a bunch of fifty-year-olds,' he agreed. He fixed her with a look that was brazen enough to make her pause in her spreading, adding: 'Also, I wanted to stay here and fuck you.'

Joanna gasped. The gale-force assault of shock was followed by a feeling of electrification that was unavoidably, shamefully, sexual. 'What?' she managed to say, squeaking.

'You heard me.' He continued to stare at her, his eyes moving down the pyjama buttons, one by one. 'Come here, little sis.'

'Come where?' She was virtually stammering. Any notion that *she* might have engineered a seduction of *him* was laughable in the face of his insolent determination.

'Here, on my lap.' And he reached for her and pulled her from her seat and around the table to him, her left hip brushing the curve of the plate of toast, and then she was on his lap, her bottom crushed against his erection, her upper body heaving as his fingers unbuttoned her top.

'Do I *look* ill?' Dan said, his breath very humid on her face.

'No, you don't.' Joanna had a sudden vision of her own appearance, just out of bed, face unwashed, breath stale, and mustered the dignity to say, 'I have to clean my teeth.'

He released her. 'Go on, then. Meet me in your room in two minutes.'

Never before had she brushed her teeth in a state of such

hormonal disturbance. It was as if she'd just been told she was about to board a spaceship and zoom to the moon. When she reached her bedroom it was just as she'd left it fifteen minutes ago, except he was in her bed waiting for her, naked under the narrow duvet.

She closed the door behind her, though the house was empty, and scurried across the carpet and into the bed beside him, meeting his mouth with hers as though by electromagnetism. 'Dan, we shouldn't . . .'

'Of course we shouldn't,' he murmured. 'Isn't that exactly why we want to?'

'Well, partly . . .' For in that moment she didn't want him *only* because he was Melissa's, she wanted him for himself, the simple, overpowering maleness of him. In that moment, she was doomed to follow him wherever he led: he could have been about to marry the Queen of England and she'd still have been unable to stop herself. (Actually, in this house, the Queen of England was who he *was* about to marry.)

'So are you saying you *don't* want to?' he teased, sliding her pyjama bottoms over her hips and tugging them downwards, clearly enjoying the idea that any resistance to him was purely intellectual.

'No, I just thought you might be thinking—'

He laughed, interrupting. 'I can't work out who's persuading who here.'

But neither needed persuading, plainly. The pyjamas were off and everywhere their skin rubbed together it burned hot. Feeling the length of him against her made her suddenly frantic, greedy to get the penetration itself underway. It was more hectic, more breathless than any of her trysts with Stephen, a different act altogether, animal and nearly demented, like bolting down food with no thought for the risks of choking. She could hear herself making noises she hadn't ever made before, primitive ones, ones that drew the same from Dan and made him grip her more roughly. The way he handled her hurt her almost as much as it gave her pleasure.

It was like discovering a whole extra sense that she'd had no idea she possessed, and only he could activate it.

'You are *wild*,' Dan said, afterwards, and it was true, though she was as surprised by the wildness as he was.

'Do you not . . . do you not sleep with Melissa any more then?' she asked.

'Of course I do. Do you not sleep with whatshisname, you know, that idiot?'

'Stephen. Yes,' she admitted, 'but it's not like this.'

'I don't suppose it is. He'd never be able to handle *this*.' He grinned at her. 'What *is* it like, tell me?'

She'd had occasion to consider Stephen's shortcomings before and had a description ready: 'It's a bit like being stabbed with a foam dagger while trying not to suffocate.'

That made him laugh again. He laughed easily; even Melissa, whose sense of humour could be mean-spirited, made Dan laugh. 'You'll have to tell him what you want, how he needs to do it. He obviously doesn't know.'

'I suppose I haven't known either, really.'

'You seemed to know all right just now.' He paused, enjoying the amusement of it all. 'You know *they* don't know? They think you're still a virgin.'

'Do they really?'

'You're good at keeping under the radar, aren't you? Let's keep this that way as well.'

'Definitely.' She pressed against him, a cat confident of the favours ahead. 'I want to do it again, do you?'

'Certainly do.' He caught her hands in one of his and used the other to remind himself of the shape of her bottom and thighs. 'How long does it take to play golf and sort out a wedding dress?' He spoke of the two activities with the same casual dismissal, neither more or less relevant to him than the other.

'Hours, I should think, unless something goes wrong.'

'I think we're the bit that's gone wrong.' He kissed her very hard, making her gasp for breath when the suction was removed. 'It's a laugh, isn't it? Doing something she doesn't know about?'

It was 'a laugh' to demote 'her' to a pronoun, too, but when she was clear of the first fug of lust, Joanna would remind herself that it was something far more significant: as a first act of rebellion, of betrayal, it had life-changing import; it put a match to her confidence when all she'd ever known was how it felt to have it dampened; it put a voice to that avenging spirit she'd for years been too fearful to avow. It was *everything*. Nonetheless, even before this first illicit liaison had been concluded, she was as sure as Dan was that Melissa must never find out about it. The mere idea of that was extremely frightening, crystallising once and for all the true nature of her sister's dominance. There was no give and take in Melissa's mind, or their parents', no bend; no matter what Joanna chose to believe, for Melissa their roles were fixed for life.

If it came to her attention that the order had been broken, her retaliation would be extreme. It would be permanent.

Chapter 13

Forty-eight hours after they met at the restaurant, James texted Holly with the message: *Spend the night with me.*

It wasn't a question and so she didn't give a yes or no, responding only: *When?*

Friday?

Yes, but I'm working again, finish at eleven.

I'll pick you up at work. Leave the rest to me.

The next day, she said to her mother, 'Some of the guys at work are going clubbing on Friday after we close. I said I might go with them if that's OK with you?'

'Of course it is,' Joanna said. 'It's ages since you had a proper night out.'

'The thing is, we might go to the West End, so I'll probably be back really late, not till the early hours. If I stayed at Mina's, would that be a problem? Could you—?'

'Look after Mikey in the morning as well? That's fine, love, I'm not working this Saturday so the timing's perfect.'

It was exactly what Holly had hoped to hear and she could tell that her mother was pleased too. It had been months since she'd gone out with friends, and they both knew that on the few occasions she had before that it had been purely in the hope that Sean and Letitia might be there, as everyone present must also have known. God, she'd been desperate. *Desperate*. Joanna liked Butler's, thought it a cut above the usual local places, as well as being in a safe and convenient location for night work. That pointed reference to the new job in Sean's presence had not passed Holly by, the unspoken meaning clear to her if not to him: Holly was moving on to a more interesting, dynamic crowd than any he belonged to.

And so she was, in a way.

'I won't be back too late on Saturday morning, I promise. And you could have some time to yourself in the afternoon – I'll take Mikey out, give you some peace.'

She could see from her mother's expression that these were the sort of thoughtful assurances she had not made in the past when enlisting babysitting services. Not for the first time over the last few weeks Joanna looked as though she didn't know what she had done to deserve such privileges.

'Thank you, Mum,' Holly added. 'Not just for Friday, I mean for all the days. For everything.' For supporting her in every conceivable meaning of the word, for being with her when she gave birth, for baking Mikey's first birthday cake, for loving him as if he were her own, for taking them to Paris . . . She didn't think she could say it enough or ever make up for all she'd been given. Her lack of appreciation in the past was shameful, she knew, inexcusable regardless of her state of mind. What had she done to mark this year's Mother's Day, for instance? She'd probably let Joanna cook for her, pamper her on Mikey's behalf; she probably hadn't even changed out of her pyjamas for their celebratory lunch.

Had she even bothered with a card? Even when Joanna worked in a shop that sold them and must have spent hour after hour staring at the messages of appreciation that other daughters would send but her own would not.

'My pleasure,' her mother was saying. 'It'll be a treat to have Mikey to myself.' *Again*, she could easily have added, or *like I always did before*, but she did not.

And so it was that the quick, deflating sense of guilt Holly experienced when she reread James's texts was more for her mother than for any other woman.

Though she had no doubt that he would keep the date, she questioned herself about how she would react if, for some reason, he did not. She'd be OK, she decided. She'd be disappointed – she longed to see him again, a longing that only deepened as their time apart lengthened – but she knew that this had to be his decision, not hers. He was the one who was married. She had suggested the drink, yes, but she could not have suggested the kiss that followed, or this, the next step – not directly, anyhow.

As for Mina, if she'd had the slightest idea she was being used as an alibi in adultery she'd have been straight on the phone to Joanna, to Alexa, to Scotland Yard. Though her dislike of Holly remained within workable limits – they were far too busy to come to proper blows – it had not been helped by Marcus's announcement that he was giving first refusal of an extra shift to Holly.

'Teacher's pet,' Mina muttered under her breath.

'You can take the shift if you want it,' Holly told her, when the manager was out of earshot. 'I'm fine just doing two nights.'

'It's not yours to give,' Mina snapped.

Holly wondered if the other girl knew she had a child or that she'd until recently suffered from postnatal depression. Would the information make her seem more human, more real, because it was obvious that Mina saw her as living some sort of charmed life? It did not distress her as it would once have done, this unwelcome acquisition of an enemy, for it could not impinge on her renewed love for her son and could not blemish the gloriousness of knowing she would soon see James again and they would kiss and touch and spend the whole night together.

It was proof that she had not only returned to what she'd been before but had begun to outstrip it, advance on it.

And of course James kept the date, arriving a little before eleven. There was no drink at the bar this time, for which she was glad, and not because of Mina or any other individual but because of *everyone*: her desire to be alone with him conquered any other thought or impulse. They kissed constantly and openly on the way to the side road where he'd parked; knowing her mother was at home with Mikey, she didn't care who else saw them.

'Hello, you,' he said, as they buckled their seatbelts, as if they had not yet exchanged greetings.

'Hello, you.' Holly giggled.

'You look fantastic.'

'*You* look fantastic.' It was like the game she played with Mikey when she mimicked all his sounds, whether actual words or not, making him laugh and call out, 'Again! Again!'

'You are at some point tonight going to speak to me in words other than my own, aren't you?' James said, amused.

'Yes, definitely. When I've warmed up.'

'I like the sound of that very much.' He grinned at her. 'Let's go.' Pulling into the traffic heading towards central London, he grew more serious, asking her, 'How did you manage this? Is Joanna looking after Mikey?'

'Yes. I said I was going to a club after work and then staying the night with a friend.' She even had with her a change of clothes, something appropriate for dancing, which was absurd as her mother had hardly been going to inspect her bag on departure. 'How can *you* do this? Where is Alexa tonight?'

James's eyes narrowed a little but he kept his gaze on the road ahead. 'She's gone on a hen weekend to Brighton.'

'That's why you suggested it?'

'Yes.'

'Is it true you've been together for ten years?'

'Yup – a long time.' His tone was dismissive, not of the ten years, she realised, but of the subject. She didn't mind; she knew he would tell her his story in his own time.

She hesitated before asking her next question. 'Have you . . . have you done this before?' And she blushed at how impudent it sounded out loud.

James raised his eyebrows as he glanced in the overhead mirror and then cast her a quick look she couldn't decipher. (She'd forgotten how dark his eyes were: in night light, the irises were as black as the pupils.) All too soon, their easy laughter had evaporated and been replaced by something intense and dangerous. She supposed it was impossible, even for them, to ignore the risk of this.

Finally, he answered. 'I don't know what "this" is yet, so it's hard to say.'

'OK.'

It was a close, sticky evening and they had the windows rolled down. The emptying streets had a charred, savoury smell about them, a giant grill that had just been turned off and would take hours to cool. She wished they were sealed in the car instead, disconnected from the real world completely.

'Where are we going? To yours?'

'No, to a hotel.' His left hand reached for her right one and for a while they didn't speak; she quickly came to hate it each time he had to take his hand away again to change gear.

'You are very beautiful,' he told her, turning to look at her at a long red light. 'And don't say the same back. Don't say anything.'

She didn't, but just let him look at her. He seemed to be committing her face to memory, as if he'd been given word of a vanishing. He breathed deeply, audibly, before turning away, and his fingers left hers once more, this time to rub at his temple. The light changed. His hand was back in hers. There were more reds, but he didn't turn to look at her like that again.

The hotel was by Chelsea Harbour and their room high at the top of the building, with one wall formed almost entirely of window. Lights glimmered below in the outline of a bridge, in the rooms of towers across the river, in the waiting taxis. It wasn't any London she had known, winking and provocative in the darkness, more how she imagined Hong Kong or Bangkok.

The room's interior she hardly noticed at first, only gradually becoming aware of the soft blues and beiges of the furnishings, the pale yellow lighting, the low, broad bed.

Breathing heavily into each other's mouths as they kissed, they took their clothes off blindly; Holly was aware of hers falling smoothly away and creating a shiver on her skin. Having felt how different James's lips and his hands were from others she'd known she expected it to be the same when their bare bodies touched for the first time, but even so she was not prepared for the reality, a rush of lust close to nausea.

'I'm going to have to lie down,' she groaned.

He smiled as he pressed closer. 'That's fine with me.' On the bed, he covered her body with his, a hot, moving blend of light and heavy, soft and hard. 'You smell very nice for someone who's been working in a restaurant all night.'

'Really? I feel all sweaty. I should have a shower or something . . .' *First*, she'd been about to say, but it was already too late for that.

'After,' he said, as if agreeing. 'God, you have the most incredible body I've ever seen.'

'Thank you.'

'We have to use something, right?'

'Yes, definitely.'

A few moments later, realising he was already about to slide himself inside her, Holly murmured, 'James . . . James, have you ever . . . ?' She closed her eyes, feeling the beginnings of another blush.

He stopped and she sensed him raising his face from hers. 'Ever what?'

She thought of Alexa's narrow, narrow thighs on the sofa next to her at home; she had judged, without exaggeration, that the other woman's hip span was about two-thirds of hers. 'Have you ever slept with a woman who's had a baby?'

She opened her eyes and found his squinting into them. 'I don't think I have, no. Why? Is there anything I need to know?'

'Just . . . it might feel different, that's all.' In the brief time between his son's birth and his abandonment of her for Letitia, Sean had made a couple of charmless comments after sex, though Holly had not thought them charmless at the time, of course, only truthful, and she had tortured herself with the idea that her body no longer pleased him. I must have been crazy, she thought; not just depressed, crazy.

'I'm just warning you,' she added, mortified now.

'Well, thank you for the warning,' James said. 'Your whole body has gone all hot now.'

'Because I've made a fool of myself. I should have shut up.'

'Never shut up, not with me.'

'OK.'

'Can we carry on now?'

'Yes.'

A little while later he said, 'Actually, I think there *is* a difference.'

'Oh, is there?'

'Yes, it's better.'

Holly laughed. 'Don't lie.'

'I'm not. It's better because it's you, not because of anything to do with Mikey.' He said Mikey's name fondly, familiarly, as if he'd been saying it all his life. It had been that way right from the beginning, perhaps because Mikey *was* their beginning. Holly had always imagined, in those sporadic pinpricks of light through which she'd glimpsed a life after

Sean, that she'd have to keep her child separate from any new boyfriend, to not mention him too much for fear of threatening a fragile ego or of classifying herself as mumsy and past her best, but she knew that in whatever future she and James had it wasn't going to be like that at all. And she realised she would never have let it anyway: Mikey was a part of her, it was impossible now for someone to choose her without choosing him too.

She and James lay stretched out together, facing each other, arms above their heads. Though it was late, she knew they would not sleep for hours.

James asked her, 'So do you love Mikey's father? This Sean character?'

He'd remembered that from Paris; she was sure she hadn't referred to Sean by name since, though perhaps Joanna had mentioned him to Alexa and then Alexa to him. She went very hot again: the idea of James and Alexa discussing her had not occurred to her until then.

'No, not any more. I did, though. I was obsessed with him. But now, if he weren't Mikey's father, I'd probably hate him.' She sighed. 'Oh, maybe not hate, that's wrong. He's not that bad.'

'I'm glad,' James said, drily. 'We wouldn't want Mikey to have an evil dad.'

'I just want him to have Sean in his life, even if he's not perfect. I know how it feels to not have a father. When you're young, I mean, when you care about being the same as everyone else.' Feeling James tense with interest as she spoke, she remembered how little he knew about her, and she him, how completely new they were to each other.

'What d'you mean?' he said. 'You don't see your father? Why not?'

'I don't know where he is, nor does Mum. I haven't met him since I was a baby.'

'He's never tracked you down?'

'I don't want him to track me down,' Holly said.

'No? Why not? Who is he? Do you know anything about him?'

'I know a bit.' She didn't ever want to withhold a personal fact from James, or re-colour a single detail, but this story was not for tonight. 'Can I tell you next time?'

He smiled. '"Next time"?'

Holly realised what she'd said. 'I mean, only if . . .'

'It's OK,' he said, not leaving her hanging. 'Next time, sure.'

There was a silence, then the distant sound of a door clunking shut, perhaps on the floor below. It was a surprise to be reminded that there were other people around them, maybe other couples spending their first night together.

James was studying her with a new tenderness, his fingers smoothing the shape of her skull through her hair, thumbs trailing, caressing. 'I think it's really sad that he's never known his own child,' he said, at last.

Holly blinked. Their faces were so close that her lashes swept over the skin of his cheekbones. 'I suppose.' She nuzzled her head under his ear, into his neck. 'But you can't *make* someone love you who doesn't, can you?'

'Maybe he does love you, in a more abstract way. He probably thinks in another life he'd have liked to know you properly.'

'There's only one life, though,' Holly said.

'There is.' James sighed as Holly raised her lips and kissed his nose, rubbed her cheek against his, an animal bent on sharing its scent.

'I'm not looking to make you into him, you know,' she told him. 'A father figure, I mean.'

James grinned. 'I'm not *that* old.'

'You know what I'm saying: it's not like I'm on some mad quest for the male role model I never had growing up.'

'I'm not sure I know what mad quest you're on, but whatever it is, I like it, so you needn't worry.'

There was another silence, during which Holly traced the conversation back to its beginning. 'What about you,' she whispered, 'do you love Alexa?', knowing that there was no comparison between their situations, knowing she had to accept an answer of 'yes' and would never have the right to expect anything different.

'No,' James said, 'I don't. If she weren't my wife I'd probably hate her. Maybe not hate, she's not that bad.' As Holly gasped, slow to hear the echo of her own phrasing, he smiled. 'I'm joking, I could never hate her. And I *did* love her, I definitely did. But now, oh, you know, since we got married . . .'

Holly didn't answer, not sure exactly what she was supposed to know. She and Sean had never been married, never achieved what James and Alexa had, even having had a child.

'And to answer your question in the car,' he added, 'I haven't done this before, no. There've been times when I could have, but I didn't want to badly enough.'

There was a soaring feeling inside her when she heard this; she knew it was wrong to glory in the betrayal of someone else, but she couldn't stop herself: her body – all of her – was operating outside moral law. Her words came in a rush: 'Why do you stay married, if you think you don't love her? I thought marriage was supposed to make a relationship stronger, not weaker?'

James kissed her on her right eyebrow and chuckled. 'That's a little disingenuous if you don't mind me saying.'

'What does that mean?'

'False. Hypocritical.' He gave her a wicked grin. 'You lure me into bed and then you criticise me for cheating on my wife.'

'I'm not criticising you,' she protested.

'I notice you don't deny the luring.'

'You asked me tonight, remember,' Holly said, with a half-smile. 'I still have your message.' And she intended never to delete it, to keep it for always, like an old-fashioned love letter.

'I remember.' He gripped her hands again, more tightly this time, as if worried she might escape in search of her phone to present him with the evidence. 'But it was what you wanted as well, wasn't it?'

'Of course it was. It is. More than anything.' The fact that she couldn't bear her skin not to be touching his even for a second proved that; the fact that she hated it when his eyes moved from her to something else in the room proved it. Soon he would suggest a drink and get up to find the mini bar or phone for room service, or one of them would need to use the bathroom, and she would hate that too.

'Well, then,' James said, 'who asked who is irrelevant – we're as bad as each other. Though, it's true, I am worse in the eyes of the law. And God. You're young and blameless, you're excused.'

Though Holly laughed with him, she genuinely didn't think they were bad or godless or either one of them worse than the other, she just thought they were perfect, she thought their bodies had been conceived to fit together like this, better than hers would with any other man's, better than his would with any other woman's.

'Seriously, though, why did you marry?'

His black gaze dipped a fraction before refocusing on her. 'She really wanted to, all her friends were doing it, and I didn't have any reason not to. But I think for us it was the beginning of the end, actually, not the beginning. And it's taken us five years to realise it.'

Holly was amazed by this. She wanted to ask him to repeat what he'd said, word for word, so she could understand better. 'You mean *she* thinks that as well?'

'Not exactly. We haven't talked about it, but it's not possible she hasn't had doubts. Buying the new house has brought it all to a head. I just think we're too ashamed to say it, too proud.' He paused. 'But what happened in Paris put things in perspective. It made me think differently about everything, not just Alexa.'

Holly gripped him tighter. 'Really?'

'Yes. I suddenly saw that all the decisions in my life had been made for me, like she's had power of attorney while I've been in a coma or something. And before her, other women or my parents, my older sister. I'd probably have to go all the way back to school to remember a time when I did things because I couldn't live without doing them. Do you know that feeling? It's like I've been asleep.'

Holly nodded in excited recognition. *This* she did not need explaining. 'That's how I felt as well, in Paris. It was like I'd suddenly woken up.'

'That was what you meant in the café that day, wasn't it?'

'Yes.' Remembering that moment in the sunshine, that strange enchanted connection between them, she had a sudden and unstoppable vision of the two of them being together properly, of living together, of closing their eyes together every night and opening them again together every morning. 'But you don't have to do anything, you know,' she blurted, a reaction against her leaping imagination. 'You really don't.'

'Do anything about what?' he asked.

'About Alexa, about being married.'

'You mean *that*'s your mad quest – to have an affair with a married man? The thrill of sneaking about behind someone's back?'

'No!' Though he was smiling again, she couldn't tell if he was teasing or not. 'I suppose I just assumed I would be, you know, overlapping. Men don't leave their wives, everyone knows that.'

'So you *do* want to be a mistress, you're happy with that? Well.' His face had become intensely curious. 'Don't you think you deserve better, Holly?'

'No,' she said, honestly.

'Really?'

'I don't know. And it doesn't matter anyway because I'm happy to be your . . . your anything you like.'

His expression didn't change. 'But why? Why would you be happy with just anything?'

She didn't blink. 'Because I love you.'

James inhaled sharply, but at the same time his gaze softened, became almost merciful, a little like it had been when he was with Mikey in the flat. 'That was very fast,' he said, finally.

'Yes,' she agreed. 'Kind of instant, really.'

'Because I saved Mikey?'

'Because you saved me.' They stared at each other. 'But, like I say, I don't expect anything.' She spoke simply, not wanting to be disingenuous again. 'I don't need you to love me back. I don't mind if you don't think you could ever love me.'

The stunned way he looked at her made her suspect he had never had a conversation like this before. She certainly had not. 'You don't mind *now*,' he said, slowly, 'but I promise you you will in a couple of months' time. At least if you're like any other woman I've ever met, you will.' He began kissing her face again. 'Though maybe you're not like everyone else, maybe you really *do* do things differently . . .'

'I think I do.'

'Anyway,' he said, resurfacing, 'love sounds a bit mild for what I'm feeling. It needs a new word. I feel like I've been possessed or something – no, bewitched. Will that do for a start?'

Holly nodded. 'It's perfect.'

'And you need to know that some men *do* leave their wives. I work with quite a few who have. But their situations, they're not anything like this.'

Holly didn't speak, but only watched in fascination as, once more, James appeared to be realising something in front of her eyes. 'I think the reason this is happening is because I can't live without doing it,' he told her, and he spoke the words with a sense of delighted discovery.

And this time she heard the echo at once. 'Nor can I,' she said.

Chapter 14

Bolts out of the blue were not a concept Alexa gave much credence to, save perhaps in the area of natural disasters and even then she doubted there was little that could not be sensibly predicted by scientists. As for those of the emotional kind, she thought they only happened to people who weren't paying proper attention to their relationships, not people like her who arranged weekend spectaculars at the first suspicion of trouble, and who continued thereafter to monitor fluctuations extremely closely (if, she had to admit, somewhat ineffectually).

And so it was that she arrived home from her friend's hen weekend in Brighton, hungover and exhausted, but nonetheless confident that the remainder of the day would pass as she expected. It was Sunday at about three o'clock when she walked through the door. Five weeks to the day had gone by since she and James had celebrated their anniversary in Paris, not a fact that occurred to her then and there, but one that would later be calculated with considerable shame and despair.

She'd decided on the train that she wouldn't give him a hard time for any shirking of house duties in her absence – as he had pointed out, they weren't Trojans – but would suggest instead that they spent the evening on the sofa in front of the TV, with a takeaway or something from the freezer.

'James, I'm back!'

'In here.'

It was only when she saw him again that it struck her that the James she'd been picturing, prone and chuckling at her stories of hen antics, was the old one, the one who loved and indulged her, not the new one, the one who'd begun to object to her. It struck her, too, that she'd been using these two nights away to hide from her fear of this ongoing transference, to give him the opportunity to revert to James A, or, even better, to allow some time-slip to return them to where they'd been before without either of them ever having to know about the overthrow by James B. She wondered when 'before' was, exactly: before Paris, of course, before she'd divined the need for Paris. Six months ago, she calculated; about then.

He was waiting for her not on the sofa as she'd envisaged, but in front of the near fireplace, standing with a weekend bag at his feet. A certain humourlessness in his demeanour stopped her from going over and kissing him hello. Instead, she flopped on the arm of the seat opposite.

'I didn't know you were travelling tonight?' He went away occasionally for work, though trips rarely involved a Sunday departure. 'That's a shame, I thought we'd start on a box set of something, maybe get a pizza.' These were the sort of suggestions that would not so long ago have had him rejoicing, but now he scarcely reacted. 'James? Why aren't you speaking?'

He looked towards her, not quite meeting her eye, the set of his mouth determined, even grave. 'I have to go, Alexa.'

'Sure, so I see. Where are you flying to?'

'I'm not flying anywhere. I'm leaving.'

'What do you mean, leaving?' Though she hadn't yet understood, it didn't prevent a damp, dismal feeling from creeping across her skin.

Startling her, James threw up his hands. 'I don't want all this,' he cried, as if in revelation to himself and not to her at all, which only confused her more. 'It's too much!'

Though her brain had been reduced to wire wool by the rare treat of litres of cheap cocktails, Alexa gathered from the glances he flicked through the French doors to the terrace at the rear, and past the shutters to the front garden, that the 'all this' and 'too much' he was talking about was the house. He was freaking out at the responsibility, she guessed, the sheer hard graft of it. And it *was* overwhelming; hadn't she just been thinking that herself? Her own time away had felt surprisingly freeing. Tiredness as much as agreement made her reply, recklessly, 'Well, we can move! When we've done it up, we'll sell it and move somewhere smaller. Or we'll move out while we do it up and then move back in again when it's finished?'

Two perfectly decent options off the top of her addled head, but there appeared across James's face a flicker of pity as he hoisted his bag over his arm, the strap pressing into his shoulder. Though he surely didn't mean it consciously, it seemed symbolic, that bag, as if all he *did* want could be contained within it.

'It's not just the house,' he said, at last. 'Actually, it's not the house at all, not really. It's us.'

'Us?' There was a strange lurching moment in which she had to swallow something sour that had risen in her throat. She looked down at her hands, afraid.

'The thing is, I want to be with someone else.'

'What?' Alexa looked sharply up again, but found she was too late to meet his eye. *I want to be with someone else.* Had he really said that? Her first instinct was to distrust her stupid head; she'd misheard and what he'd actually said was he wanted to 'be' someone else, someone different, someone who lived in a house with fewer rooms, presumably. But no, she had heard the 'with' and knew already it was the worst word in the world.

'Did you just say you want to be with another woman?'

'Yes.' His tone was quiet but unequivocal.

The lurching had become nausea, making her think she might actually vomit. She couldn't handle this, there had to be a magical escape. What if . . . what if she pretended she hadn't heard it, would he be willing to pretend he hadn't said it?

Another woman. 'Who?' she demanded.

'Someone . . . someone I've met.'

Alexa felt her face twist into something ugly. 'I can work that much out on my own! Who? Who is she? Tell me!' And she heard that she was shrieking, *sounding* ugly, too. Even without her pounding head, she would have been at a loss as to the identity of the culprit. As random names and faces began to pulse and blend in her mind, that holdall continued to hang heavily from her husband's shoulder, his eyes seeking the door with intent, telling her this was not a discussion that would be going on for much longer.

'Someone from work?' she guessed, wildly. 'You've slept with someone from work? That new assistant you told me about? When did it happen? I want to know, James, I have a right to know.'

He sighed. 'I think it's probably best if I don't tell you who she is, not straight away.'

'Oh, really?' Resisting the urge to step forward and shove him against the mantelpiece, she cried, 'Well, I think it would be best if you did, if that's all right with you. It's fairly crucial intelligence, wouldn't you say?'

But he wasn't going to capitulate, having become now very calm, sorrowful for her hysterical display rather than remorseful, as if he were the witness and not the executioner. Like every other detail in this scene, this confused her, ran counter to her instincts of how a situation like this should be played out.

'When did it start, at least tell me that?'

There was a silence. She thought about Paris, the 'make or

break' conversations with Lucie and Shona that had inspired her planning of the trip. She'd not pre-empted trouble, she realised; she'd been too late.

'Was it before Paris?'

'No, after,' he muttered.

'Honestly?'

'Honestly.'

She exhaled, her breath heavy with relief as she seized on his answer as a lifeline. Since they'd been back only a matter of weeks, it made this dalliance brand new; it was possibly still at the infatuation stage, which was nothing, or at least not everything. It could be managed, it could be survived.

'How can you have an affair when we've just celebrated our anniversary, just bought this house? It's the lowest of the low, James. Why are you even confessing to it?'

He frowned as he decoded the subtle inference of this: that she considered this a self-contained problem, one that may have been more acceptable to her at a later, less crowded date in their marriage. 'No,' he said, quietly, 'it's not an "affair", Alexa, it's a permanent thing. It's what I want instead of us.'

Instead of us. Her stomach somersaulted in shock. '*Marriage* is the permanent thing,' she said, hissing the words. 'Buying a house together is the permanent thing. What did you think we were doing here, eh? Signing up for a summer rental?'

'We shouldn't have bought it,' he said, baldly. 'You know that as well as I do.'

She stared at him, appalled. 'I do *not* know that. No. I don't know what you're talking about. I don't accept this at all.' The despair she was feeling was bodily, increasing her mass; she wanted to wind herself of it by slamming against a wall or rushing headlong into freezing water. 'Is this some kind of joke, James? What the *fuck* is going on here?'

'Of course it's not a joke, I'm trying to explain that I'm leaving, I'm leaving *now*.' The frown deepened with frustration, pity. A flustered sigh followed. 'Oh, I don't want to hurt you, Al, I honestly don't.'

'You don't want to hurt me? Don't say these things, then!' she wailed. 'It's easily solved.'

'I have to.'

'Why?' She put her hands to her head. 'Why do you have to? I don't understand this! Why are you being so cruel?'

Though his mouth gaped, no defence emerged. Of all the adjectives she – and others – had used to describe him over the last decade, 'cruel' was not one of them. Never. And even now the look on his face was not that; on the contrary, it was the tormented look of a victim. That was when she reached for her second lifeline: he was exaggerating, acting! He wasn't planning to leave her at all, it was just a strategy: what this was, really, was a confession of a one-night stand for which he knew he had a better chance of forgiveness if he scared her with the thought of losing him. This other girl was a whim, a moment of madness borne of a stressful year. Her claim on him had no roots, not like her own, his wife's.

'Stay,' she said, shaking now. 'This is silly. Put the bag down and let's have a proper talk.'

'There's no point,' he said. 'It would just be pretending.'

'Pretending what?'

'Pretending we still love each other.'

The lifeline began to slip from her grasp. 'But we do love each other! I love you, anyway.'

He looked doubtful. 'Do you?'

'Yes, of course I do! Don't you love me?'

There was another silence then, a reluctant glance just beyond her, more painful than any spoken disavowal. 'You told me you did, when . . . A couple of weeks ago . . . no, in Paris, definitely in Paris. Did you not mean it then?'

In reply, new James pulled the old James's face he used when called upon for professional levels of factual accuracy. 'I probably thought I did, but I don't think I knew what it meant, not then. Everything's different now.' He sounded so sad, so profound, and he never sounded sad, he never sounded profound. He bantered, he teased, he made light of things. He'd jumped in the Seine to rescue a child and made it sound like he'd fished a shoe out of a pond.

The confusion was such that this last thought did not provoke any suspicion. She had made no connections yet.

'Nothing's different,' she lied. 'Nothing's changed. You're imagining it. I haven't noticed anything wrong.'

'Yes, you have.'

'I haven't!' She could feel her insides sucking and folding, her brain no longer in control of their motions.

'I'm going to go,' he said, with finality. 'We'll talk again tomorrow. I'm sorry, Alexa.'

She followed him out of the house and to the car, still pleading with him to reconsider. It was hideous watching him drive away, hideous. The only thing worse was turning up the path and going back into their house alone.

Having no idea if he would ever set foot in it again.

The next day was the hardest, and not in spite of her having been denied the full facts of the crisis but because of it. For a personality like hers, a state of psychological suspension was no different from actually swinging by the neck. She felt as if she were choking, getting just enough oxygen to stave off unconsciousness. What in God's name was James doing? What was he thinking? If she didn't set this right immediately then she would burst out of her own head.

She couldn't face work: Monday mornings were all about status updates and her status was indescribable. She imagined herself announcing to her team: 'My life is over. I couldn't care less if you poured every smoothie in the land down the toilet.' Unfortunately, her call into the office was picked up by her director, Paul, who she knew would read her absence as having been caused by the excesses of the hen weekend. She and Lucie had been vocal in their anticipation of it.

'Well, Lucie's managed to make it in,' he said, a grade between unimpressed and frigid.

'I'm really sorry,' was all Alexa could say.

She phoned James at his office twice an hour, but a series of unreturned messages and his absence for an off-site meeting for much of the afternoon meant she was unable to get through to him until close to six o' clock. In the meantime she veered between outbursts of hysterical despair and periods of self-imposed restraint, in which she sat in one of a pair of new reading chairs in the designated 'library' area on the first floor, formulating her questions for him on paper: she'd need a written list in case emotions got the better of her.

Lucie phoned to commiserate, happily swallowing what must have been a common assumption in the office: this was a case of hen-induced alcohol poisoning.

'You do sound bad,' she remarked, when Alexa agreed she'd rarely felt worse, 'full-fat Coke, you need,' and her encouragement of unrefined sugar was a sign of how seriously she was taking this lapse in health. Her kindness almost made Alexa cave.

But she would not tell Lucie – or anyone else – about James's walking out, would not dream of doing so while there remained the possibility that it was all some horrible misunderstanding. It wasn't that she doubted he'd slept with someone else – what man would confess this to his wife if he had not? – but his claim that he was leaving for good had not stood the test of a night's sleep (the hangover had, at least, killed the adrenalin fever and facilitated what little of that she got). It explained a few things, however: why he had begun to be impatient with her, argumentative; why his need for her in bed seemed to come and go; why he was suddenly so interested in getting into shape after a decade of indifference. But, equally, the notion of James as an adulterer seemed impossible: infidelity was a question of self-ishness, of risk, it was not the choice of a decent, loyal man like him.

As the day wore on and her list of questions took shape, so the theory solidified that this was a mistake, not exactly a simple one but a mistake all the same. Dialling his number for at least the twentieth time that day, she anticipated how sheep-ish he would be feeling as he answered the phone. He'd beg her to forget the whole thing before she'd had a chance to speak; he'd be back that evening with apologies and flowers. She visu-alised the bouquet, something like the one she had chosen for the Walsh family.

It was a prediction that lasted less than ten seconds.

'Alexa, I'm sorry I couldn't get back to you, I meant to, but it's been a crazy day. I haven't had a second to myself.' She heard him groan, but not the groan of a man driven demented with remorse, more . . . more of one who would rather put this call off till a later date and head to the pub.

'Well, can you talk now?'

'Yes. Shoot.'

Shoot? Who did he think he was talking to?

'I want to know who she is,' she said, already struggling to steady her voice. 'And don't say it doesn't matter because it's obviously the only thing that *does* matter.'

'OK.' He paused. To block out other sounds, she poked her free index finger into her left ear until she felt pain. She didn't think she had ever concentrated so intently in her life. 'It's Holly,' he said. 'Holly Walsh.'

In the seconds that followed, astonishment collided with dread and was instantly eclipsed by it. Somehow, if only by sheer gut instinct, Alexa knew that he could have spoken no more dangerous a name.

'Like I said, I want to be with her,' James said, as if suspect-ing – correctly – that she might not previously have grasped this message in its entirety. Hearing it a second time released a trickle of what was to come afterwards in crushing torrents: shame, humiliation, fury; the prospect of letting the world know that this was what her husband wanted. He had not been acting, he had not been joking: he wanted to be with Holly Walsh. *Instead of us.*

Thank God this was just a phone call: she could control the muscles in her throat better than she could the ones in her face, which were already in spasm.

She managed to say, 'You mean the girl in Crystal Palace?'

'Where she lives isn't really relevant,' James said.

'But that's the Holly Walsh you mean? Just to be clear. The girl from Paris?'

'I don't know two, Alexa.'

'You hardly know one!'

But he knew this one better than she'd realised, obviously.

Though seated, propped upright by the stiffly upholstered chair, she was reeling. Holly Walsh. Physical details returned from their meeting, just over three weeks ago now: the tight, tarty clothes, the unwise streaks in the hair, the south London accent; but also the smooth milky skin, the heavy breasts, the eyes that followed James around the room and couldn't be torn from him. 'Isn't she about eighteen?'

'She's twenty-two.'

'Oh, well, there you go, she's *way* too young,' she said, with disdain, as though youth alone was enough to eliminate the girl from serious consideration. She reminded herself that what she was after in this conversation was answers, information, facts. 'And does she feel the same as you do?'

It was, she knew, about as stupid a question as she could have asked. Who, in that girl's position, wouldn't want a wealthy, good-looking, generous man like James, the kind of man who risked his own life to save your son's? With this thought the dread expanded, squeezing hope to the outer limits of her imagination, for she was starting to see how this might be working, starting to get a sense of the enormity of what she faced.

'I think she does feel the same, yes,' James said, and there was a catch in his voice, a tenderness he couldn't quite conceal. Alexa felt the cold, metallic taste of panic.

'We need to meet,' she said, urgently, her list of questions already abandoned. 'As soon as possible. You've obviously gone crazy or something.'

'I haven't, I promise you. The opposite, if anything.'

What did *that* mean? That he'd been crazy to be with her – and was only now regaining his sanity?

'You must be. No one walks out on their marriage for some moron who can't even look after her own child without him almost drowning.'

'You're right,' he said, reasonably, 'we should meet.' Clearly he'd chosen to ignore her last remark, for her sake if not for his. 'There's a lot to discuss.'

There was a pause in which Alexa tried to compose her next remark, but it was James who spoke first, his voice determinedly sympathetic: 'Look, Alexa, I realise this is a complete shock and I'm really sorry. I just want you to know there's no hurry, I'll carry on paying my way until we can sort things out.' He made this offer in a final, 'I owe you that much, at least' sort of way, which made Alexa see that he was in a different place in this conversation from her, close to the end of it, already looking for a point of withdrawal.

'What do you mean?' She knew she was floundering, could think of no way to save herself. 'What "things"?'

'I'm just saying I'll cover things as usual, until we decide what to do with the house. The mortgage payments, utility bills and stuff. You can't pay all that on your own.'

And before she could respond he was saying he had to go, starting to suggest days and times when he was free to meet her. He might have been talking to a client who he didn't see frequently but who he nonetheless enjoyed getting together with for dinner every so often.

Wednesday lunchtime seemed to be his earliest window.

'No, I want to see you now, this evening,' she insisted. Wednesday might as well have been the next century as far as she was concerned. 'I'll get a cab down to your office, I'll be with you in half an hour, forty-five minutes.'

'I'm sorry, it's just not physically possible.' James spoke kindly but firmly. 'I've got an appointment at seven and I'm already going to be late for it.'

'With the slut?' she spat, losing control once and for all. 'Cancel it. This is more important.'

'With a rental agent,' he said, an edge entering his voice. 'And since I've never met her before I'm afraid I can't tell you if she's a slut or not.'

A rental agent? Alexa was flooded with the heat of rage. 'Well, if you're not meeting *her*, then you won't mind if I go round to her flat and get a few things straightened out.'

The edge sharpened. 'I wouldn't do that. There's no point, anyway, because there won't be anyone at home.'

Because Holly was going to be with him and the rental agent, presumably. What about the mother, Joanna, the one who had written them the sweet thank you note, what was her role in this? 'Tomorrow, then,' she conceded, using the very last of her strength to stop herself from sobbing hysterically. 'I'll come to your office at lunchtime.'

There was another sigh. 'Seriously, I can't. I'm not trying to be difficult, I just can't cancel stuff that's been in the diary for weeks. It will have to be Wednesday. And maybe it's a good thing that we'll both have time to calm down before we meet.'

He meant her, since he sounded perfectly composed. 'James—'

But there was no point pleading because he was saying good-bye over the top of her and then he was hanging up on her. When she redialled, she was diverted straight to his voicemail.

I'm in a nightmare, she thought. This isn't my real life, it can't be. Tomorrow morning when I wake up it won't have happened. Everything will be as it should be.

She sat for a while, motionless, waiting for the dizziness to pass but soon understanding it was not going to any time soon and might never. Reaching for her laptop on the desk, she began to compose an email to her team explaining that she was feeling much better and would be returning tomorrow, but later than usual because there was a problem with her new bathroom and a plumber was coming.

She was startled by an immediate response from Paul. One line: *We need you first thing, Alexa. Can't James handle it?*

No, she replied, grimly. *He's away at the moment, I'm afraid.*

And she logged out before he could come back to her, staring at the screen without actually seeing it, shaking and strung out with the misery of it all.

Chapter 15

By mutual consent, 'once more' was never enough that summer for Joanna and her sister's fiancé. The two continued to sleep together whenever they had the chance, and with Melissa working part-time and otherwise distracted by wedding preparations, and with her parents away on holiday for ten days in August, there *were* chances.

It was a finite arrangement, Joanna knew and accepted that: she *wanted* it that way. When the summer was over and the newlyweds moved back to Manchester, when she started her foundation course at the local college, it *would* end. For his part, Dan had set himself the deadline of the wedding day itself; that was when he would put an end to 'this game', he said, and 'toe the line', but for Joanna the affair represented much more than sport. It seemed to her that in taking from Melissa (or borrowing, perhaps, sharing), she was releasing herself from eighteen years of subjugation; hers was the single enormous wrong that righted all those smaller wrongs she'd suffered.

Dan had become the embodiment of what Melissa owed her and once the debt was paid she had no intention of taking more, however she continued to crave him.

And what cravings! Sometimes she thought what she was experiencing was a malfunction of human impulse; it was too obsessive to be normal, too consuming, too exhausting. She must be what the magazines called a nymphomaniac. Sometimes she feared she would expose her desire for him in front of Melissa and their parents, but, in fact, it was most dangerous when she allowed herself to relax: there were times when she was only a single vibration away from reaching for him across the dinner table – across Melissa! – and, aborting the act, would realise with a damp chill on her skin just how close to catastrophe she'd come.

He was so powerfully, irresistibly beautiful, that was the problem, that was what marked out her immaturity, and Melissa's, for that matter, for whatever their individual agendas they were both seduced by the physicality of him. His muscular strength and movie-star bone structure, *the eyes*: these were why Melissa had wanted to pin him down before someone else did, why all her friends, and Joanna's, envied her so. What a catch, they exclaimed, as if it were Melissa's fishing skills that warranted celebration, not the marriage itself, as if the relationship had nothing to do with the accidental nature of falling in love.

Recognising this – if not the larger issue of his infidelity – Melissa came to the decision that matrimony was not going to be in itself a strong enough adhesive.

'I need to seal the deal,' she told Joanna, as they shopped in town together one day for an outfit for her hen night. Though Joanna generally avoided being alone with her, as a bridesmaid she could not shirk all responsibility and, besides, to behave too evasively might arouse suspicion.

'What do you mean?'

'Get myself pregnant, of course.'

Joanna was aghast. 'Pregnant? Why? You're only twenty!'

Melissa favoured her with the look of smug superiority Joanna had grown to find unbearable but which, on this occasion, she accepted with docility. 'Like I say, to seal the deal. I don't want someone else coming along and nicking him, do I?'

Joanna gulped. 'But how could they? You'll be married in a few weeks . . .'

'I know, but that doesn't stop some men – or women. Come on, you know how gorgeous he is.' Her expression became combative then, menacing, as if she were ready to join battle with any rival who might declare herself right there in the middle of Miss Selfridge. Duly, Joanna's heartbeat stuttered in fright, though it was clear that Melissa could not possibly know of the atrocities going on under her nose. She simply wouldn't be saying these things if she did. The sisters wouldn't *be* here together. No, Joanna would be outside, under a bus, and Dan would soon come tumbling after.

It was hard to explain why she associated Melissa with the threat of physical attack when she had never hurt her bodily, but she did; not only that, but the threat also felt cumulative, as if Joanna had coming to her eighteen years' worth of violence.

'I'll wait a year,' Melissa mused. 'I thought straight after finals, maybe. Until then we'll just keep on practising.'

One night the previous week Joanna had woken in the early hours to the sound of her sister and Dan making love. She could easily tell their groans apart, they were distinct, two individual instruments working on the same piece, whereas she felt sure *hers* merged with his, that they melded into one. She had lain in restless frustration, wondering if Dan remembered she was at home too and not out at a friend's, hoping that when he had finished he would wait for Melissa to fall asleep and then visit her, put her out of her misery.

He had not, of course. There were risks and then there were suicide bids.

'What will Mum and Dad say about a baby?' she asked Melissa.

'Who cares? I'll be a married woman soon. This is what married people do: have kids. Anyway, they'll be happy. They always support me.'

In fact, Joanna knew that their parents had been caught unawares by the speed with which Melissa was approaching marriage and had voiced rare doubt as to the golden girl's decision-making.

'She's in such a hurry,' their mother complained to their father, not knowing Joanna was in earshot. 'I have no idea why.'

'She'll regret it later if she gives up her education now,' their father agreed.

They needn't have worried: Melissa was not going to leave the professional accolades up for grabs. She finished her degree and began her accountancy training as planned, and, despite everything that would happen, she completed that too. Of the career that followed Joanna knew little, but she supposed it did not involve standing in a shop six days a week selling good luck cards.

'I don't think Joanna will be in such a rush,' her mother said.

'Let's hope not if Stephen is the calibre of son-in-law we can expect!' And they laughed together, as if sharing a guilty truth, one that was nonetheless entirely beyond dispute.

The shock of it brought a rush of blood to Joanna's face.

And so, as Dan continued his betrayal of Melissa with increasing gusto, Joanna did the honourable thing and ended her relationship with Stephen.

Even in the context of the last two years' tribulations, when Joanna let herself into the flat at six o'clock on Monday evening it was with a feeling of unprecedented apprehension. How happy she'd be if this were simply a matter of surviving Mikey's witching hour – the overtiredness, the wailing, the mysteriously reinvigorating power of a sleep-promoting bath – or of keeping her patience one more evening in the face of Holly's helplessness.

But all of that paled into insignificance next to what she had ahead of her. For, according to Holly, in two hours' time the

Walshes would be visited once more by James Maitland. This, however, was not to be a social call with flowers or toys or, most crucially, wife; no, according to Holly, the purpose of the visit was to explain to Joanna that her daughter and he intended to move in together.

Move in together! It was preposterous, it was farcical, it was out of the question. It was, she suspected, all in Holly's mind.

Already it seemed inconceivable that it had been only that morning that Holly had said, 'Mum, I've got some news. Have you got five minutes before work?' *Five minutes*? Had she really imagined that would be long enough for the absorption of a bombshell like this? Settling Mikey in front of the TV next door, she had rejoined Joanna at the kitchen table and said, as cool as you like, 'I'm going to be moving out soon. Next week, maybe.'

'*What*?' The bewilderment Joanna felt had barely surfaced, much less fully registered, before Holly added:

'I'm going to live with James Maitland.'

'What on earth do you mean? The Maitlands? Aren't they out in Chiswick?' Hosed suddenly with adrenalin, Joanna's mind began to gyrate, and its first – and, it turned out, insane – thought was that Holly must have won some kind of live-in role with the couple, a domestic help of some sort, her waitressing credentials having been exaggerated somewhat ambitiously in securing the position. As always, Joanna's immediate concern was for Mikey: had a nursery or other childcare been arranged? Would Joanna need to adjust her own working hours to help look after him?

But Holly's next words wrenched her back from *that* side-track: 'No, not the Maitlands, not Alexa. Just James.'

'Just James? What are you talking about, Holly?'

She looked closely at her daughter's face for signs of lunacy, but all she saw was the same euphoric purity she and Suze had noticed in the shop the day they'd joked about her having found

God. Not God, then, nor pride in being employed, as Joanna had naïvely assumed, but something far, far more dangerous: infatuation with a married man. *Belief* in him.

'We're a couple, Mum,' Holly beamed. 'We've decided we want to live together.'

'You and James? Don't be ridiculous!'

Holly smiled, clearly impervious to any slight. 'Is it so unbelievable?'

'Yes!' Joanna cried. 'It *is* unbelievable! Of course it is, listen to yourself!'

'Well, it's true,' Holly said, simply.

It felt stupid but necessary to point out the obvious: 'He's married to Alexa, Holly. They were here together three weeks ago. He lives with *her*, not anybody else.'

'He's left her,' Holly said, the faintest dash of defiance colouring her attitude of extreme patience. 'He moved out yesterday. It's over between them.'

Yesterday! And yet she made it sound like ancient history, something irreversible. Oh, what have you done, Holly, Joanna thought, what have you done? But instinct told her not to accuse, not to waste more time in disputing Holly's claims, but before all else to establish the facts.

'Where is James now?'

'He's moved into a hotel,' Holly said, 'but he's going to start looking for somewhere for us to rent as soon as he finishes work today. We thought somewhere near here. Clapham, maybe, or Dulwich.'

While these were indeed neighbourhoods close to theirs, they were so far beyond the Walshes' budget as to be comparable with Las Vegas or Sydney.

'Somewhere to rent? But doesn't he have a house he's just bought? With Alexa?'

'Yes, but he doesn't want to live there, he doesn't want to live with her, he doesn't want any of that life any more.' As she made these negative statements, Holly looked lustrously happy, all the surfaces of her shining.

Joanna stared. 'This doesn't make sense, explain this to me, please.'

Holly nodded obligingly. 'He wants to live with me and I want to live with him, because we love each other. I don't know how else to say it, Mum.'

It was the word 'love' that really frightened Joanna, prompted her to apply the brakes to her racing thoughts. 'Hold it there. He's told you he loves you, has he?' The question was so familiar it brought a twinge of additional pain, making her think it was something her mother must once have said to *her*, but then she realised it was simply a cliché of the well-worn young girl/married man narrative. Not receiving an answer, she asked her next, most critical question: 'Suppose you *were* to move out of here, what about Mikey? Where does he fit into all of this?'

'He'll come with me, of course.' Holly glanced at the kitchen clock. 'Mum, don't you need to open up the shop?'

'The shop can wait. This is more imp—' But Holly had risen from her seat and was drifting from the room, as if everything that needed explaining had been explained. 'Holly, wait!'

Joanna followed her into her bedroom in time to see her pulling down a holdall from the top of the wardrobe – she was intending to start packing! Attracted by the activity, Mikey got up from the TV and came padding in after them. ''Oliday! 'Oliday!' he cried, seeing the bag.

Joanna pulled him to her for a cuddle. 'Not a holiday, sweetie, no. Hang on a minute, Holly, we need to talk about this properly.'

'OK.' Holly turned, her expression willing.

'Mikey, look, why don't you play with this music box? Over here?' It was one of his favourite toys and he was instantly absorbed. Joanna turned back to Holly, disguising her alarm for

210

Mikey's benefit. 'This is crazy, Holly, you can't move in with him just like that. For one thing, you hardly know him.'

'I know everything I need to know,' Holly said.

'How can you possibly say that?'

'I just can.'

'No, you can't. You think you do, but you don't, trust me. People get to know each other for months, maybe years, before they take a step like living together. *Especially* when one of the couple is already married to someone else.' She was aware, of course, that such basic advice about relationship 'steps' was irrelevant to a girl who'd dropped out of college at nineteen to have a baby on her own, but, still, it had to be said.

'And even if he wasn't married, he's so much older than you – how old is he?'

'Thirty-two,' Holly said.

'That's ten years older!'

'I wouldn't care if it were a hundred and ten.'

'Well, you *should* care!'

'We don't expect people to get it,' Holly replied, 'not straight away. But you'll see we're right. We know how we feel.'

Joanna wanted to ask, again, 'What about Mikey?', to say to the girl, 'Think about your son! You say you'll take him with you but how will this affect him?' First, though, there was still missing evidence to locate.

'OK, let me try to understand this: you've obviously seen James since he came here with Alexa that time?'

'Yes.'

'So you hadn't made this plan at that point?'

'Oh no, nothing had happened then.' Again Holly spoke as if of the distant past, not of an occasion only a matter of three weeks ago.

'When, then? You were attracted to each other when he came here that time, was that it? Then what?'

Holly's expression became evangelical as she remembered. 'We met for a drink first, one night after work.'

A short drink, then, since Joanna could vouch for the fact that Holly had returned promptly after most of her shifts. She supposed it was possible Holly might have misled her about when her shifts began and ended. 'And then?' Hope flickered momentarily that the 'and then' might not yet have taken place.

'And then we were together on Friday night, the one just gone.'

'Ah.' It had, then. That had been the night Holly had gone out with workmates, when she'd said she was staying over with another waitress. The lie depressed Joanna almost as much as the information that her daughter was basing this fantasy about being in love with James on just one night. One night! And that made her wonder something worse, worst of all: was this the explanation of what had happened to her since Paris, the sudden, miraculous lifting of her depression? Had it been not only Mikey's rescue that had given her a 'second chance', as she put it, but also his rescuer?

'I'm just so happy, Mum,' Holly said, her cheeks split by the broadest of beams. 'I can't believe I'm so lucky!'

Joanna couldn't believe it either, but for the sake of fairness forced herself to try. *Could* what Holly was saying be true? *Had* James left Alexa and moved into a hotel? Was he *really* going to begin flat-hunting for them that evening? Or wasn't he actually going to be going home to his new house and his pretty, clever wife? Of course he was, and when Holly realised that this glorious new happiness of hers was going to be extinguished as quickly as it had been ignited . . .

Oh God. Joanna felt such a surge of anguish on her daughter's behalf she thought her legs might buckle. She lowered herself on to the room's only chair, feeling layers of folded laundry compress beneath her. She knew she needed to take the utmost care in her handling of this situation and that buying time was her first concern. 'Holly, I—'

'Gama?' Mikey's box needed winding up and as she took care of it for him Joanna spoke over his head: 'Look, there's no point thinking about packing until you've got somewhere definite to go to. For the time being, you've got a home here.'

Obediently, Holly returned the bag to the top of the wardrobe.

'Listen to me: whatever happens I want you to keep me completely in the picture. It's really important that I know where you and Mikey are, that you're safe and have a proper roof over your heads.' Once more her mind was galloping forwards, the thoughts passing at speed: when Holly realised this was no more than a delusion she might move out just to save face. Then where would she go, where would she take Mikey? Would they be homeless? How would Joanna find them?

'Whatever you do, I will be on your side, even if it's not what I *think* you should do. You will always have a home here, do you understand? No matter what happens. You mustn't just disappear without telling me.'

'Of course not,' Holly said, surprised. 'And of course I want you to know where we are. We're hoping you'll visit us – every day, if you like. We'll find somewhere big enough for guests.'

We're hoping, *we'll* find: Joanna's heart squeezed at the trust Holly was already placing in James. There was no doubt in her mind that it was a trust that was going to be broken.

'Now, when are you seeing him again?'

'This evening,' Holly said. 'He wants to come over and talk to you about everything.'

'Talk to me?' That was something, at least. Joanna's pulse calmed a fraction at the thought that this might all be resolved by the end of the day.

'Yes. He wants to explain. He knows you'll be worried by how sudden it all seems.'

'It doesn't *seem* sudden,' Joanna said, 'it *is* sudden.'

Holly conceded what was plainly a minor point to her. 'He said he'll be here about eight, after Mikey's gone to bed. Is that OK? You don't have plans?'

'No, I don't have plans!' Joanna looked at her watch: the shop should already be open for business by now and Monday mornings were busy for deliveries.

'Great. It will all make more sense later. I promise,' Holly added, with utter conviction, as if she were the mother reassuring the child.

'I *have* to go to work. Don't do anything today without telling me, OK?'

'OK. Don't worry, Mum.'

Don't worry? It would be a day of sporadic fretfulness at best, constant debilitating cold sweats at worst, she knew: she'd need a week's worth of customers to keep her mind off this extraordinary new development.

She could only pray that the pair had remembered birth control.

As the day went on and her anxiety only grew, Joanna found herself returning to her first theory, certain her instinct would not betray her. Holly was deluding herself, if not about her feelings for James then certainly about his for her. Sensible men did not leave their wives on the strength of one night and James was a sensible man. A sensible man who had made a mistake and had surely understood that by now.

By the time he was due to arrive, she had fleshed out the chronology of their affair for herself and was satisfied with it: Holly had become fixated on James after his heroics in Paris – understandably so, especially for someone who was already suffering with mental health problems – and it was from this time that her magical transformation dated. After seeing him again, first in Chiswick, an accidental meeting that Joanna now suspected her daughter of having engineered, and then at home, she had shown her gratitude by sleeping with him. Afterwards, she'd misinterpreted a casual comment or small kindness on his part as a promise of commitment. He would not be coming to conduct some strange dysfunctional version of asking Joanna for Holly's hand; if he came at all it would be to settle any misunderstanding before he went back to his wife and asked her forgiveness, as married men always did. Alexa would overlook the skirmish and normal life would resume – for them, at least.

The real issue here was, how would life resume for Holly? Would it be the old one or the new one? Or something else entirely? Somehow, from somewhere, Joanna was going to have to find the strength to cope with this new disaster – and just as she'd begun reflecting on the bittersweet freedoms of no longer being needed!

But once again her instinct failed her, for James arrived at the flat a little before eight, wearing on his face the same zealous look she recognised from Holly's that morning, and the very first thing he said to her after settling on the sofa was, 'I want you to know this is serious: I've fallen in love with Holly.' With which he reached for Holly's hand and held it between both of his as if that were that. 'I want to be with her and look after her and I hope I can do that with your blessing. I know it must look crazy and wrong and all those things, but this is how we feel.' His tone was as formal and factual as the words were emotional, fanciful, and Joanna, seated opposite and slightly raised above them on a chair brought in from the kitchen, was quite unable to respond.

James went on: 'Yes, I'm married, I can hardly deny that, you've met Alexa, but I want you to know I will be arranging a divorce as soon as I can.'

He wanted her to know much more besides and, seeing his and Holly's twin ardent faces, Joanna decided not to interrupt his flow. There was nothing to be gained from rejecting this proposal of theirs out of hand, however strongly she doubted it would come to fruition; better for the moment to play along, to explore its possibilities more fully.

James spent some time speaking of practical matters, of Mikey and the arrangements that might best suit him. 'We thought if he splits his time between here and the new place at first, there won't be as much of a feeling of upheaval for him. We thought he could be with Holly in the week while you're working and then stay with you the two nights she's at the restaurant – only if you'd like that, of course.'

Here, Holly elaborated: 'We'll handle Saturday daytimes week by week, according to whether you're in the shop or not and whether Sean wants to be involved.'

'You're keeping your job at Butler's?' Joanna queried. One theory that had occurred during the day was that Holly's job might not actually exist but had been a cover for her meetings with James. They *must* have seen each other alone more than twice to have cooked this up in so little time; it was too thoroughly considered, too reasonable.

'Of course I am,' Holly said, puzzled.

'And I'll be at work all day,' James said, 'so the structure of Mikey's day would be the same as it is now. I won't be in his face, taking all Holly's attention, he'll get to know me quite gradually.'

'With all due respect,' Joanna said, for she found James as immensely appealing as she had on their previous meeting and it was impossible to *be* disrespectful to him, 'it might be better if he gets to know you *before* he moves in with you. And I would say that to any new boyfriend of a woman who already has a child with someone else.' Quite apart from the possibility of him bolting back to Alexa, James had no known experience with small children.

'I think he's already proved he cares about Mikey,' Holly reminded her, quietly.

'What you did in Paris was wonderful,' Joanna agreed, addressing James directly, 'but the spur-of-the-moment rescue of a child you've never met before is quite different from sharing his upbringing. Children are a lifelong commitment.'

'Oh, yes.' He and Holly nodded in unison, eager to agree.

'Mikey obviously really likes him as well,' Holly said. 'If we handle it right, I don't think it will be a problem.'

You don't think! Only if James ups and leaves, Joanna thought. Then Mikey will do what thousands of small children did: ask where the nice man has gone and why Mummy is so sad.

'If he has any problems settling in, he can spend extra nights here and I'll come with him,' Holly said, decisively. She and James were switching roles, seeming naturally to know that it was she who ought to speak on Mikey's behalf and not the newcomer. 'And we'll only take a flat that's got an extra bedroom for you, so you can stay over whenever you like.'

James said the place he'd just seen that evening had three good-sized bedrooms and would be ideal.

Ideal!

'If there's any sign that Mikey's upset by anything, we'll rethink,' Holly promised, and James squeezed her hand again, gazing adoringly at her before turning once more to face Joanna. The two of them struck her as a pair of missionaries she'd let in for a cup of tea, clear in her position that she could never be persuaded, only to find herself weakening.

She could not weaken, though: someone had to be realistic here.

'There are other people who are going to be upset, though, aren't there?' Again she looked directly, challengingly, at James. In any other context, she would have felt embarrassed to presume to give personal advice to a man like him, but this was an emergency that threatened the people she loved most in the world. 'Alexa isn't going to let you just walk away to start a

217

new life with someone else – she's your wife, your family, not someone you've just been casually seeing for a couple of months. How does she feel about all this?'

'She's shocked,' James admitted. 'I spoke to her before I left the office. I don't think it's sunk in yet.'

At that moment Joanna was visited by an unwelcome image of another wronged woman, her face at the very moment of discovery, when disbelief was assailed by anguish, an attack so rapid and lacerating that within a second only the anguish was visible.

She forced herself back to James and Holly, allowing a necessary sternness to enter her tone. 'I'm assuming she didn't want you to move out? She must be absolutely devastated.'

The pair of them looked saddened by her words, as if they'd do anything to solve this one drawback to their visionary plan, if only they could think how.

Joanna supplied one possibility: 'Don't you think you owe it to her and to yourselves to wait a little while and think this through a bit more?'

'I suppose it will take a week or so to sort out the new flat,' James said, as if agreeing to a refinement that only made the original plan better, 'so if any doubts do crop up . . .' He let the idea dangle; it was clear that neither he nor Holly anticipated any doubts of their own, but only to have to field those of others.

'I'll stay here until then,' Holly said. 'You're right, there's a lot to organise.' Finally looking at her, Joanna was met with an implacable gaze, a determination that patience would be kept no matter what, and couldn't help feeling that she was being played at her own game. The problem was, this was not a game, not with a young child involved.

'So where exactly do you plan on living?' she asked James. 'You said you've already seen a place?'

'I had a look at it on my way here,' he said. 'The agent said it had just come on the market today so we're lucky with the timing. It's near West Dulwich station, just down the road. There's lots of space, three bedrooms, a shared garden.' Despite being in a highly complicated situation he gave the impression of navigating it all with superhuman ease. Joanna had no doubt he really had stumbled upon the perfect apartment 'on his way', shoehorning its examination between his difficult conversation with Alexa and his interview with his lover's mother, scheduling all appointments so as not to disrupt Mikey's bedtime. 'It's not free until the end of next week, but it's a great place and not far from here. I want Holly to see it tomorrow lunchtime, so if you want to come and have a look at it too, maybe?'

'I'll take you,' Holly told her. Clearly, she already knew the details. 'It's only fifteen minutes on the bus.'

Joanna could hardly take this in: the affability of their invitation, their faith that she'd share their joy. Did neither of them understand how absurd this discussion was? Absurd and potentially catastrophic? James had saved Mikey's life but surely he was now about to destroy Holly's?

She refused to get on their runaway train with them, not yet. 'I can't take time off work at such short notice,' she said. 'I'm in the shop all day tomorrow and the girl I use for temporary cover is sick with a tooth infection.'

'Can't Suze do it?' Holly asked. 'You're always standing in for her?'

'She just covered three days for me when we went to Paris,' Joanna pointed out, and the mention of that city prompted Holly and James to exchange a thrilled look, marvelling perhaps at the recentness of their entry into one another's life.

'Wednesday, then, after work?' James suggested. 'Whatever time suits you, Joanna. I could come and pick you up? Mikey, too, of course.'

Mikey. There was no disputing the emphasis on his happiness in this conversation. In different circumstances (ones less obviously doomed, ones less devastating to third parties such as wives), she could not have argued with James's and Holly's transition plan for the boy. She might have drawn it up herself. No one wanted him to be torn from the only home he'd known, or undervalue his attachment to his grandmother, and so it made perfect sense that he should come to his old room for Fridays and Saturdays, keeping enough of his possessions there for it to be a proper home from home. In different circumstances it would be ideal.

To James and Holly it *was* ideal. They thought they'd thought of everything. They must have thought of nothing else. But how was that possible, so quickly?

Well, the answer was, it wasn't.

Chapter 16

'Did you know Melissa wants to have a baby as soon as she finishes university?'

'Does she? Fuck.' Dan used a tone of mock despair and, by simple association, placed his right palm flat on Joanna's bare stomach. 'I'd better learn how to change a nappy, huh?'

'You make it sound like you don't have any say in it,' she remarked.

'I just do what I'm told.' The hand pressed and she could feel the individual bones of his knuckles on her flesh. 'Same as you.'

She pushed him away and wriggled back into her jeans, no mean feat in the confined space of Melissa's car. The car had been a gift to Melissa from their father when she'd started university, and, since Joanna was not deluded enough to imagine that *she* would be given one when she left home, she'd been making use of it in her own way. Refastening her bra and pulling down her top, she said, 'I do what I'm told because I live with them and I have no choice, not until I can escape their clutches. But as soon as I do, it will be different.'

'Will it?'

'Yes, it will. But you, you're *choosing* to join this clan. You must be mad.'

He grinned. 'I like this clan, in case you hadn't noticed.'

'She's a psychopath, Dan.'

'Maybe I'm attracted to that in a woman.' He gave her a long, appreciative look before turning away to button his own clothing. They were in town on the pretext that he was giving her a lift to the main art suppliers, though she could easily have caught the bus. Finding a deserted corner of the multi-storey, they'd unsnapped their seatbelts and fallen on each other, pulling off their clothes even as they agreed it was too public, too risky.

'Seriously, though,' Joanna said, 'you could call off the wedding and be a free agent.'

He pulled a face in objection to this idea. Even in post-coital discussions like these, he gave every appearance of being genuinely fond of the fiancée he was so blithely betraying and he complained of her very little; only that she'd been on his case about drinking too much or not looking with sufficient commitment for a proper job. It had begun to dawn on Joanna that Dan was not ambitious. In spite of those outstanding looks and the insatiable sexual appetite, his aspirations were ordinary, even lazy. Marrying the prettiest girl in town, living easily thanks to her parents' generosity and/or her career, never having to make a decision in his life: it was as good as it got as far as he saw it.

'Are you going to her hen night?' he asked, turning on the engine for their delayed trip to the art suppliers.

'Of course,' Joanna said. In the mirror her eyes looked smudged, not just her make-up but the irises themselves. 'I'm a bridesmaid, remember? She couldn't *not* invite me.'

'Shame. It would have been the perfect chance, she'll be at the hotel, Gordon and Lynn'll be on holiday. We'd have the place to ourselves . . .' Steering into the open air, his hand was squeezing her thigh, as if daylight made him restless again. 'Hey, I know, come home after everyone's gone to bed. All you have to do is get back to the hotel in time for breakfast and we'd have the whole night together.'

'Don't be crazy, it's miles away, Dan, and I don't drive.' There was silence for a while as he negotiated the town centre traffic and Joanna mulled their lost opportunity. Could she cry off sick from the hen night? Would Melissa even care?

It was then that she had the idea, one that even at its conception struck her as wholly perfect: both the formal completion of full and proper recompense for all she'd suffered and the *symbol* of it. 'But you could . . .' she began. 'No, forget it.'

'Could what?' He glanced across at her, intrigued.

She was so close to freedom from psychological torment she could anticipate it with all her senses, experience already how life as a free woman was going to be.

'You could come to the hotel as well. Stay the night there. I'll have a room to myself. I'll let you in, go to the bar with everyone, then come to bed as soon as I can get away. We just have to make sure you're gone before anyone gets up in the morning.'

The more she thought about it the more predetermined it felt. The hen night, which was to be held in a country house hotel, involved just Melissa and her five bridesmaids. The four others would be staying in two twin rooms, but Melissa had not wanted to share her four-poster with her sister and had talked their father into stretching the budget to an extra room. Joanna had already been told this would be in the cheaper modern wing, some distance from the older part where Melissa would be staying. Safely out of sight.

'It's an idea,' Dan said. Even in profile, the gleam was evident in his eyes, the gleam of the boy who never turned down a dare.

'It's definitely an idea,' he said.

Tuesday morning in late July was not the busiest day of the year at the shop, but even at the height of a pre-Christmas Saturday afternoon rush Joanna could not have failed to notice the whirlwind that was the arrival of James's wife Alexa.

She burst through the door at such speed it was surprising she didn't overbalance as she drew up, or that her feet didn't spark with the friction. Her chest rose and fell frantically beneath an austerely cut white shirt, the sleeves long over her wrists, while tightly belted grey trousers hung over her high heels, almost to the ground. She looked fragile, even frail, a sick child too small for her clothes.

'Where is she?' she demanded, in the gruff voice of someone whose nose and throat were swollen from sobbing.

'Alexa, hello.' It was silly to say it was nice to see her again when it was in fact frightening and complicating, but Alexa was not interested in pleasantries in any case.

'Where is she?' she repeated. 'I've tried the flat, but she's not there. In hiding, I assume?'

Joanna, who had not anticipated this visit, now wondered how she could possibly have failed to. Had she really thought that last night's meeting with James was the end of her involvement in his marriage and not the beginning? She felt at once extremely fearful of and supremely sorry for her visitor – as well as grateful that the shop was empty. In spite of her slightness, there was a dangerous charge to Alexa, a sense that the smallest false move on someone else's part might provoke full-scale violence.

And who could blame her? Not Joanna, that was for sure.

She considered her best move. First and foremost, she needed to get the bull out of the china shop: the owner was her friend, yes, but even Suze would not take kindly to the sight of trashed stock thanks to a domestic dispute to do with Holly. There were too many candles in glass casings, too many novelty mugs and mirrored photo frames.

'Why don't you come out the back, eh?' she suggested, mildly. There was a small courtyard behind the stock room where she took a break sometimes when it was quiet. 'I'll make us a cup of tea and we can talk.'

'I don't want tea,' Alexa said. 'Just tell me where she is and I'll go.'

'Come and sit down, at least. Let me just grab you another stool . . .'

At this, Alexa emitted a curiously juvenile-sounding noise, like the yelp of a trapped puppy. 'I haven't got time to sit down! Why don't you just tell me what I need to know and I'll be on my way!'

She did, however, inch forwards a step or two, which meant Joanna was able to get a proper look at her face. She appeared no less immaculate than the last time they'd met, her face beautifully made-up and her hair sleek. The difference was in her eyes: previously sharp and clear, they now resembled those of someone who'd been left to spin on a waltzer for twenty-four hours. She was still in shock, Joanna thought, and felt her own initial guard flattened by a rush of fellow feeling.

'Look, I obviously know what this is about and I want you to know I don't understand any of it. I'm as appalled as you are.'

Alexa scowled, which triggered a slight tremor in her right cheek muscles. 'I'm more than appalled, I want to kill her! What kind of a person sleeps with a man who she met when he *rescued her child*? When he was with his wife on their *anniversary*?' The menace in her voice was pitifully undermined by the rising distress. Anger was all that was keeping the despair from erupting. 'How long did she give it before she got in there? Two weeks? Three? It's obscene, she's a disgusting slut!'

'Please don't say that,' Joanna protested. 'I know you're upset, but it's my daughter you're talking about and I won't have it.'

Alexa folded her arms, used her fingers to squeeze the upper parts, as if reassuring herself that she was still in one piece. 'It doesn't matter what I call her, we both know what she is.'

Was this true? Joanna had never viewed her daughter as promiscuous or as any kind of seductress; more an innocent at the mercy of her own unfortunate taste in boys – that at least had been her view of the Sean situation. But this, this had no precedent because James was a man and not a boy, a person of intelligence and not a fool, and there was no doubt that Holly's liaison with him had catapulted her into an entirely more adult arena.

Breaking up a marriage: the one thing she had prayed her daughter would never grow up to do.

'What if we'd had kids?' Alexa said. Her nose was starting to run and Joanna plucked a tissue from her box by the till and placed it on the counter between them. Then she positioned the spare stool in front of Alexa before returning behind the counter and settling on to hers. 'Or if I was pregnant? She'd still have done it, wouldn't she? Nothing would have stopped her.'

'*He* might not have done it, though,' Joanna said, taking the question at face value. She'd considered this aspect of the drama last night as she'd lain in bed, sleepless, and had come to the conclusion that none of this would have happened had James had children of his own. He wouldn't have jumped into the Seine to save a stranger, because no one would be so reckless when he had a responsibility to dependents, and if he hadn't jumped into the Seine this bizarre affair with Holly would never have begun.

And Mikey would be dead. She swallowed. Whatever this was, it was not that.

'Please sit,' she said.

At last Alexa lowered herself on to the stool and took the tissue from the counter to mop her nose. 'I hope you're ashamed of her,' she growled.

'I'm certainly not proud, you can be sure of that.' Joanna chose her next words with particular care, even as she sensed that none could possibly suffice. 'Alexa, I know you must see it as a straightforward case of adultery, she's the bad guy and you're the victim, but you have to realise that *they* don't see it

226

that way. I think they really believe they have a special connection that overrides everything else, *everyone* else, including us.'

Alexa scoffed. 'Is that what she's told you? What "special connection"? You mean they really, really want to fuck each other?'

Joanna blinked. It was a long time since she'd been spoken to in such a confrontational way. 'No, that's not what I mean.'

'You can't think they're not sleeping together?'

'No, I'm sure they are. I just mean the thing they think connects them is not that.'

As the blaze of Alexa's hostility was blotted suddenly with curiosity, it struck Joanna that the other woman might know substantially less than she did about the break-up of her own marriage. How could James be so cruel? 'I think it's to do with him saving Mikey,' she continued. 'It's bonded them in an unusual way.'

Alexa threw up her hands. 'Kids' lives are saved all the time, they're always getting into trouble, aren't they? The mother doesn't then go and seduce the rescuer, she concentrates on looking after her child a bit better the next time!'

'The thing is, people *don't* save children's lives all the time. It's a very rare and special event.' And it might be worth investigating, Joanna thought, whether the mother of the rescued child *did* sometimes seduce the rescuer. It might be some sort of known condition, not dissimilar to falling in love with your doctor or psychiatrist. But it didn't seem like the moment to suggest this to Alexa, who was showing no signs of being pacified, the twitch in her cheek growing more pronounced. She was glad now that her guest had refused the tea – it might have ended up being hurled through the window.

'I honestly don't think Holly would have done something like this if she didn't believe it was extraordinary, even meant to be in some way.' Though quite certain this was indeed

Holly's position, Joanna could hear how adolescent it sounded when spoken aloud, deserving of Alexa's scornful reaction.

'For Christ's sake, of course it's not meant to be! She must be some sort of moron if she believes that!'

Joanna drew a deliberately long breath, knowing it was crucial she keep her own pride and indignation at bay. Alexa was the wronged party here. 'Of course it's not meant to be. Saying something is fate is usually just a convenient way of dodging blame when you've hurt other people. Anyone with any experience knows this lightning bolt stuff is just a fantasy. But it's obvious they *do* think it's real.' She paused. 'It's out of character for James, too, is it?'

'What do you think?' Alexa cried, furiously. 'Of course it is! There's no way I'd be with him if it was in his character to sleep with the first girl who made herself available to him. He met her on our *anniversary*. The actual day!' This was the second time she'd mentioned this detail and although it made the betrayal unsavoury, Joanna did not think it was particularly relevant. What had Holly said, in Paris, when Joanna was innocent of what was about to begin that very day? *It's not like it's his honeymoon*, that was what she'd said. And, later: *Do people still believe in marriage?* Well, the poor woman in front of Joanna now certainly did.

'He's never been unfaithful before,' Alexa said. 'She's done something to him, I don't know what.'

In all of this neither of them questioned the assumption that it was Holly who had seduced James: *she* had hunted him down both in Paris and at home and had caused him to behave unconscionably badly. And yet, the truth was Joanna blamed James, she blamed him wholly. Holly was the young and vulnerable one, the one who had been suffering from a recognised illness when the accident had taken place. James was fit and well, a man in his thirties who had, by Alexa's account, resisted temptation before. He was the one with the power and he had chosen to abuse it. Such a conclusion would do nothing to appease Alexa, however, and so Joanna decided not to share it.

'I'm sorry,' she said. 'I really am. If I thought I had any influence over them I would use it.'

It was hard to argue with someone who was agreeing whole-heartedly with you and Alexa's hostility began at last to waver. 'Where is she now? Please, Joanna, I know this isn't your fault. Just tell me where I can find her and I'll get out of your way.'

Joanna looked at her watch. She knew better than to mention the scheduled flat viewings, one that lunchtime for Holly and one the following evening for herself. 'Holly and Mikey are at a drop-in playgroup this morning, I think. That was their plan, anyway.'

'Playgroup? Which playgroup? Somewhere around here?'

Joanna didn't answer. She wondered if Alexa knew that Holly had a job now; she sincerely hoped not, for Holly would surely lose it again before long if Alexa began turning up and shouting about her sexual crimes.

'So you're going to pretend you don't know, are you?' Alexa said, glowering.

'Not at all, I do know, but I'm not going to tell you.' Joanna leaned towards her visitor, speaking more urgently: 'Alexa, I think your anger is completely justified, I really do, but I don't want Mikey to be exposed to it. He's only a child and he's been through enough as it is. Don't forget he almost drowned in Paris.'

'Well, whose fault was that?' Alexa demanded.

'It was no one's fault!' Joanna's gaze slid to the open door. She wished a customer would come in and approach the counter with an enquiry, anything to break this relentless intensity. Then she changed her mind and prayed for the opposite, for any bystander would be sickened by the nerve gas of fresh grief like Alexa's. She could withstand it only because she had been exposed to it before.

'And James, is he with them at this playgroup?'

Joanna was taken aback by the question. 'I'm guessing he's at work, isn't he?' She wondered if Alexa might have lost sense that this was a working day for the rest of the world; she probably imagined everything had entered her vortex with her. 'Wouldn't you be better off talking to him rather than her?' she suggested, gently.

Pure shame passed across Alexa's eyes. 'I can't see him at work, he's making it impossible. He won't see me till tomorrow. And I don't know where he's staying. Is he staying with you?'

Again, Joanna was surprised by the question. 'No, he's not. I wouldn't allow that. He told me he was in a hotel near his office.'

She saw her mistake too late – and just as she was hoping to bring the conversation to a close.

'You've seen him then?' Alexa pounced. 'This week?'

'Yes, last night. He came over to see me. I'm sorry, Alexa. I didn't invite him, the two of them insisted.'

There was a moan then, a pooling of pale misery in the other woman's eyes. 'Tell me the truth, Joanna, did he seem . . . did he seem confused?'

She couldn't lie; she couldn't subject this desperate creature to false hope. 'He didn't seem confused, no. He said that he wants to live with her. They were both totally serious and convinced. That's why I know I can't talk them into calling it off – they'll have to come to that conclusion themselves.'

There was a pause, the silence before an explosion, but when Alexa spoke again it was in a whisper, as if the fight had left her: 'Do you think they will?'

'I don't know. I'm hoping one of them will, at least. Look, leave this for today, please. Wait until you've met James, perhaps things will have changed between now and tomorrow. If they haven't, come over to the flat later this week . . .' *When Mikey's not around*, she finished privately. Perhaps Sean – or more likely Geraldine – might be persuaded to take Mikey out while she staged some sort of intervention. The idea of explaining that to Sean or Geraldine was not attractive, however: she was only beginning to understand the layers of difficulty to follow Holly's and James's reckless behaviour.

Alexa was looking emptily at her, the same kind of expressionless sorrow Joanna had so recently been used to facing in Holly. 'How did you know I worked here?' she asked, the thought only now occurring.

It took Alexa a moment or two to remember. 'When I went to your flat one of your neighbours gave me directions.'

'You were lucky to find someone in. They're normally all at work this time on a Tuesday.'

This prompted Alexa to look at her watch, as if entirely clueless as to what type of information she might find there. 'I have to go to work,' she murmured. 'I have to go now.'

'Well, let me give you my mobile number,' Joanna offered. 'You can phone me whenever you like.'

She felt simple relief as Alexa tapped in her number and removed herself from the premises, her withdrawal as docile as her entry had been tumultuous. She couldn't help James's wife, not today, though she very much hoped someone else would.

She did not get a chance to tell Holly about the visit until late that evening, for Holly had taken Mikey to visit James in the City after work and was not back until almost nine. Mikey had slept on the bus home and was easily transferred from buggy to cot.

'Oh,' Holly said, equably, 'yes, we expected that.'

Faster than she'd allowed herself in a very long time, Joanna lost her patience. 'You expected her to come to the shop and cause an almighty scene? With *me*? Well, thank you for that!'

'No, I meant we expected her to try to find me. She must hate me.' Holly said this with ethereal detachment, untouched by

231

earthly troubles, but, seeing Joanna's exasperation, added, 'I'm sorry if you were put in an awkward position, Mum.'

'She'll be back, Holly,' Joanna warned her. 'She wants to tear you from limb to limb!'

But even this didn't appear to ruffle the girl.

'Wouldn't you feel the same in her position?' Joanna was fairly sure that Holly had not thought to put herself in the other woman's shoes (though, to be fair, when Letitia had stolen her place in Sean's affections she had not fought her usurper, she had only crumbled). Nor had she yet considered the obvious implication that if James could do this so easily to Alexa, then he could do it just as easily to her. 'She's in a terrible state, and I don't blame her.'

From the moment Alexa had left that morning Joanna had felt nothing but horrified guilt for her, the same horrified guilt her daughter should have been feeling but evidently was not. Did James feel it? Last night, sitting on the sofa with his hand clutching Holly's, he'd given the impression that his wife was no more than an unfortunate loose end. He hadn't even had the courtesy to tell her where he was staying. How did that tally with the selflessness of his heroism in Paris?

And *how* had Joanna not seen this coming? Why had she accepted Holly's sudden transformation as something entirely free from any male involvement, something triggered by shock and then sustained by pride in new employment? To think, she'd even warned her daughter that James Maitland was married – albeit mildly, for she'd had many months to refine the art of the inoffensive rebuke. As it turned out, she might have screamed it at the top of her voice and shaken Holly by the shoulders and it wouldn't have made any difference.

Well, she would speak plainly now. 'Holly, did you hear what I said? Look at me! If you and James really mean to go through with this then you will have to accept that other people will oppose it. They'll want an explanation. Not just Alexa, but both her and James's families as well. They *will* come knocking. You are not the only ones in this situation.'

'I know, I know.' Holly spoke in the voice that was becoming familiar to Joanna: contrite, even submissive, but for politeness's sake only; she was, in fact, utterly certain of herself. 'James is meeting her tomorrow to talk things through, work out how to tell their families and everything. He knows he has to explain it to them, he's not trying to get out of it.'

This was the same meeting Alexa had referred to; would it also be the one where James came to his senses and decided to return to his rightful home? Joanna heard again that whispered question of Alexa's: *Do you think they will?*

With a persistence that would have been unthinkable a month ago, she pressed on with her lecture, refusing to let Holly evade her responsibilities. 'And there's not just their side to worry about, is there? What about Sean? He has a right to know you plan to live with another man, even if it will just be weekdays for Mikey at first.'

Holly nodded. 'I totally agree, Mum. I've been trying to meet him to tell him what's going on, but he doesn't return my calls. I must have left ten messages.'

That was because he was still sulking about her rejection of him, Joanna thought; he was waiting for the change of mind that would never come. They had seen him just once since the afternoon when Holly had declined his invitation to go to the park together, and on that occasion he'd been better prepared, matching Holly's coolness with a rather staged insouciance of his own. But it was far too late for tactics of that sort. One look at James Maitland would put paid to any last semblance of a campaign. There was, quite simply, no contest.

'Holly, listen to me. I'm worried you're rushing into this, presenting Mikey with a stepfather who's virtually a stranger to him. You should be thinking long and hard about something as serious as that, and believe me I speak from direct experience.'

There was a silence. Holly looked thoughtful. Joanna supposed she was once more going to cite the rescue as all the entitlement James needed to take Mikey into his life, but instead she said, 'I would have been happy to have Adrian as my stepfather.'

Joanna stared, derailed. Her breath was coming hard, her heart straining: it was so long since Holly and she had argued, her body was overreacting on her behalf. 'But you came to know Adrian gradually over quite a few years. You were much older than Mikey is, a teenager, already quite independent. And he never moved in with us, did he? My point is that even then you were my primary concern. When you were Mikey's age a new relationship couldn't have been further from my mind.'

This was getting dangerous: the last thing she wanted was for Holly to think she blamed her for the absence of a fulfilling relationship of her own.

Holly, who seemed to understand this, let the parallel drop. 'I can't help the way it's happened, Mum, it just did. Maybe it will turn out to be a good thing that Mikey is so young? Maybe he won't remember a time before James?'

Joanna wanted to cry out how absurdly ambitious this prognosis was, that the reason he wouldn't remember this 'relationship' was because it was to be so short-lived, but she could see that Holly was thinking something quite different from her: she was thinking that if Mikey were to forget life before James then it followed that he would also forget the accident itself.

'Honestly, Mum, I totally agree with you that Sean should be involved in our plans and see Mikey more, but I can't force him. James says I should write a letter asking for an official meeting. Then we can work out a regular visit, a fixed time, something that becomes part of Mikey's routine. Sunday tea, maybe. What do you think?'

Joanna had to admit this was a sensible suggestion. She had had regular contact with Geraldine while Holly was depressed, more than during their children's earlier relationship, and knew that Sean's brother Kevin had two daughters with a woman he no longer saw and made contact with the girls infrequently. Geraldine was keen to prevent Sean from following in those disappearing footsteps.

At least it wasn't the other way around, Joanna thought, as she often had: a tug of love between the two families, even some kind of court battle. Not that Sean stood a chance of winning that, either. James or no James, he had no rights legally.

And nor, she knew, did she. As Holly ended their discussion to pick up and reply to a phone message, from James, no doubt, it struck Joanna that whatever was going to happen next she could only react to it, she could not forestall it.

Chapter 17

He meant it, he really meant it. It was there in the very first seconds of their meeting – on the Wednesday, after all, and no sooner, for he had not found it in his heart to bring her allocated slot forward – in the remoteness of his gaze, in the brotherly kiss on the corner of her mouth, a downgrading of intimacy as merciless as any legal instruction.

They met near Tate Modern, a spot they'd used a hundred times in the past because it was midway between their two offices, but that day the place felt as unfamiliar to Alexa as if she'd been transplanted to a foreign riverbank she had no hopes of identifying. As she followed him to the low wall where they had often sat with coffees and sandwiches it felt as if she'd never seen it before and must negotiate its dimensions for the first time.

They settled with enough space between them for a third person.

'I hear you saw Joanna yesterday?' he said, and instantly Alexa bristled. *These* were his opening words! Not 'I'm sorry' or even 'How are you?', but 'I hear you saw Joanna yesterday?'

'In lieu of her home-wrecking daughter, yes, I did. In lieu of *you*. And if she didn't work in a shop that anyone can walk into I don't suppose I would have been able to see her either.' She knew she was setting exactly the tone she had told herself to avoid – pointed, bitter, mean-spirited – but it was too hard not to. As far as Holly Walsh was concerned, her spirit could be no meaner.

'I'm sorry I couldn't meet sooner,' he said, as impersonal as she was personal. 'You're obviously very angry. But trying to hunt Holly down won't help. Please can you just deal with me from now on?'

'Deal': he used the word quietly and without implication but it established his position loud and clear – he saw this meeting, and any future ones, as the facilitation of a necessary negotiation, a transaction. Necessary but not welcome: for all his professional politeness, he was radiating unease as visibly as coloured light. If she'd imagined that the fever gripping him would subside at the sight of her, returning him to the real world, *her* real world, then she'd been mistaken. His withdrawal from her was unambiguous.

But it was a withdrawal she would not accept.

'Where are you staying?' she asked. 'Joanna said you're in a hotel?'

'I am. One near work.'

'That's crazy, James. Come home.' Lest he think she had plunged straight into begging him back, she added, 'There's so much room in the house, why waste money on a hotel? Come back, sleep in another bedroom while we sort things out. We've got six of them!'

'No,' he answered, flatly. 'It's only for a few nights, anyway. I've been looking for a flat to rent, as you know, and I think I might have found one already. We're hoping to sign the lease by the end of this week.' As Alexa gasped, deeply pained by this development, he added that he had not yet told his parents or colleagues of their split because he wanted to know what Alexa thought would be the best way to break the news. 'Split': it had to be one of the cruellest words in the English language. A break could be healed, but a split sounded beyond suture. She thought of the change of address cards she'd sent out so recently, the time she'd spent selecting them and then writing them at the little walnut desk she'd owned since she'd rented her first flat in London.

'So . . . what timing would suit you?' he repeated.

Infuriated and humiliated in equal measure, Alexa turned on him, hissing, 'No timing would suit me! How can you be so cold about this? Don't you see I don't want this to happen? And I don't think you do either, that's the terrible thing. I think you've lost your mind!'

She was the one who'd lost her mind, judging by the interested glances being cast her way. It was another warm, buoyant day, and they were surrounded by people whose lives were not in crisis but were ticking along nicely, people who still had enough faith in human endeavour to stop and admire the view of St Paul's.

James said, 'It is happening, Al, it just is. And I'm sorry if I sound cold, I don't mean to. I find this hard too.' He'd adjusted his tone, though: it was more human, more his own. 'I know it's out of the blue, I know it's not the normal way to do it, but I think delaying would make it worse for all of us because it's absolutely what I want.'

'But that's what makes it wrong,' Alexa exclaimed. 'You can't possibly be so definite so quickly, no one can.'

They certainly hadn't been about their relationship, she thought. Five years it had taken them to feel definite enough to get married. And how much time had passed between their meeting and moving in together? She cast her mind back: two and a half years, something like that, and even then she'd found it necessary to keep her own flat on until she was sure he was sure.

'James, listen to me . . .' She shifted closer to him, still making no physical contact. He did not, at least, recoil. 'What you think you're feeling isn't real, it's some kind of aberration.'

'No, it's not.'

'It is, it is!' She moaned with frustration. 'You know what it felt like when I woke up this morning? Like I'm in one of those movies where everyone's suddenly behaving completely out of character but no one is admitting they're doing it, or that they've even *noticed* they're doing it.'

'Everyone?' he asked. 'I thought you hadn't told anyone?'

He wasn't following; he wasn't understanding. 'You, then,' she said, miserably. 'Just you.'

'Well, I'm not everyone. And of course I've noticed what I'm doing. Look, believe it or not, I'm trying to be as honest as I can here.'

'But it doesn't sound honest. It sounds like you've been brain-washed, you're not who you really are.'

For the first time he reacted with eagerness to something she'd said, as if she'd at last hit on something he could connect with. 'But that's just it! This *is* who I really am. If there was any brainwashing going on then it was before.'

Shocked hurt brought tears to Alexa's eyes. 'You mean you felt brainwashed by *me*?'

'Not necessarily you, or anyone else in particular . . .' He paused to reconsider his phrasing, but the droplet of tact in an ocean of insensitivity only upset her more. 'I just mean I feel for the first time that I'm in the place *I*'ve decided to be.'

'A Holiday Inn down the road from your office?' She gave a bitter little laugh.

'Not literally. Spiritually, I suppose.'

She had never heard him speak like this before – nor any man in their circle, for that matter. The old James, the real James, would have scoffed at this sort of talk, he would have said the right place was where the beer was. He really had lost his reason: how was he even holding down his job in this state of mind? It was beyond belief that he should have spent the morning in his office passing himself off as his old self, wearing a shirt and suit trousers she recognised from dozens of workdays before, that he should still have the faint stain of something inky on the inner edge of his left thumb that she'd noticed last week. He *looked* the same. If his face had broken into a grin, if he admitted he'd been teasing her all along, scaring her for fun, she'd have found that more credible than what he was saying to her now.

'When did it start?' she asked in a low voice. She had no interest in discussing his spirituality, but she craved physical details of the material crime. 'With her.' She couldn't trust herself to say Holly's name without snarling.

He sighed, looked out to the cranes at Blackfriars. 'Very recently.'

'I know *that*. You already told me it was after Paris. Is that even true?' In her few days of crazed imaginings she'd touched on the notion that Holly had been in Paris, on the same boat as them, not by serendipity but by prearrangement with James; he'd been conducting some kind of parallel seduction, which had gone horribly wrong when the child had fallen overboard. But she had quickly dismissed the idea when she remembered her carefully plotted itinerary; it had made no allowances for separate activities. Until the accident they had been together every moment of the day.

'Yes,' he said, 'of course it's true. You know how we met.'

She believed him. It had begun in Paris – and to think she'd taken him there because she'd thought something was wrong between them; she had *led him* to another woman. She could have chosen any other city in the world and whatever had gone awry, however it had come to be awry, it would have been put right again – because Holly Walsh had been in Paris, only Paris.

'When did you start sleeping together?' she said, for that was what she had actually wanted to know. Seeing his reluctance, she snapped, 'You just said you were being honest, well, *be* honest.'

240

'It was when you were away,' he admitted.

'But I haven't been anywhere since then . . .' She faltered, grimacing as she worked it out. 'You don't mean when I was in Brighton? *Last* weekend?'

'Yes.'

'You only slept with her then? When? Which night?'

'Friday.'

She could feel the lines of her frown getting deeper and deeper, being stamped into her face by the sun, ageing her. 'And you decided to go off with her just like that? Before I'd even got home?'

'Yes.'

'Forty-eight hours, not even that? You didn't think you might need a week or two to mull it over?'

'I'd been thinking about it before . . .' Again he stopped himself, evidently observing some distinction between telling the bare truth and sharing unnecessarily hurtful details. As if the bare truth weren't hurtful enough!

'Carry on,' Alexa insisted, 'you're saying you'd been thinking about leaving me before that, before you met her? Just spit it out, please!'

'I meant since I met her.' James looked away for a moment, a romantic misty-eyed pastiche of his former self; if the sight of it didn't signify the end of her world, it would be laughable. 'From the first moment, I just had a feeling.'

Alexa stared. 'So you suddenly believe in love at first sight, do you? That is *insane*, James.' She was transfixed by his ability to be so certain about something that anyone else would know at once to be utter derangement. 'Was she *that* good in bed?' she asked, and then, inevitably, 'Was I that bad?'

His gaze returned to her, clearer now, and corrective. 'It's not about good or bad, it's about what was always going to happen.'

Always going to happen, a variation of the phrase Joanna

had used. Then she was right: this was to do with the rescue, the bond that event had forged between them.

'You saved her child, James, that doesn't mean you have to move in with her. Just walk away. Your good deed is done.'

He looked at her, uncomprehending.

Alexa swallowed. 'What happened last weekend . . . we'll get over it. It won't be easy, but we'll get there, I promise.'

He shook his head. 'No, Alexa, I can't help how I feel, it can't be "got over".'

'Yes, it can. You're an adult, you have self-control, a sense of duty. Only children can't help how they feel.'

James regarded her wonderingly. 'We're all children in a way, aren't we?'

At this, Alexa laughed out loud, hearing her own contempt and watching its lack of effect on him as if from a great height. She'd had enough of this. She had a sudden violent urge to throw her bag into the river, and then herself after it. Would he jump in and rescue her? she thought, grimly.

She leaned towards him, insisting on eye contact before she spoke again. 'Look, since you're in some kind of hypnotic trance and can't seem to work it out for yourself, I'll tell you what this is all about: it's about someone with absolutely no morals or scruples going out and *taking* another woman's husband. And it's about him being stupid enough to let it happen. And regretting it later, because you will, James, anyone can tell you that.'

'And I'm sure they will, when we get around to telling them the news.' He'd reverted to his opening tone, that of the brisk co-worker with an agenda to tackle. 'Which brings us back to the original point: when is the best time to make this public? Do we make an announcement of some kind or do we let people find out on the grapevine? Do we do it now, while everyone's away on holiday, or do we wait till September?'

She felt herself begin to tremble as she understood that he

242

wanted to tell people. He wasn't ashamed, he was proud. He wanted to shout his good tidings from the rooftops, he wanted to introduce their friends to his new love, he wanted to share his madness with anyone who'd listen. This was the twilight zone, she thought, looking about her for salvation. The river wasn't really there at their feet. The tourists were holograms. St Paul's was a mirage.

'She's taking you for a ride, James. Is it money? Is that what she wants? Then let's give her a cheque and get her out of our lives.' This was the third time in the conversation that she had indicated her willingness to take him back and she knew a fourth would be beyond her.

'For your information, Holly works part-time and earns money of her own,' James said, for the first time visibly nettled.

'Works as what?' Alexa snapped. 'Not a childminder, clearly?'

'A waitress.'

'Wow, that'll keep you in the style you're accustomed to.'

'It doesn't need to: I have enough for both of us. Besides, there are some waitresses who earn more than marketing executives.'

'Yes, the ones who offer sexual services. I assume that's what *she* does.' She only half regretted the slur. In critical moments of self-defence she could become nasty, but James knew she didn't mean the nastiness, he knew she was not a bad person. Or did he – did the brainwashed model have access to old knowledge? Or was he seeing her as if for the first time, like someone emerging from a coma, amnesia making a stranger of the spouse at the bedside?

James's sigh suggested *some* residual memory: he was clearly cross with himself for having entered into this bickering. With strained kindness, he said, 'OK, I'll keep it to myself a bit longer if that's what you want. I'll wait for you to say when you're ready to start telling people. But sooner or later I'm going to have to let them know my change of address. It just won't be practical otherwise.'

Change of address, change of bedmate, change of heart.

It won't be practical!

She was glad he didn't ask to come and collect his possessions from the house. If he had she'd have told him she'd already tossed it all in a skip and left it to rot.

On the Thursday, she took another day off work. One more day, that was all. It would not go unnoticed by Paul, however, especially with the launch only weeks away and with her having rolled in at eleven o'clock on Tuesday, but she had no choice: the shock was lifting and the desolation that replaced it was absolute. She could no longer make it through the day without crying; she could not make it through twenty minutes without crying.

Her sense of everything material had been halved in one stroke. And yet, even as the nightmare was unfolding, intensifying, symbols of her and James's togetherness remained on their original schedule: furniture was arriving at the house, sofas and wardrobes they'd chosen together, sold-out kitchen items now back in stock and on her doorstep, a runner they'd wanted for the stairs, packaged in a neat brown cylinder she couldn't imagine unrolling. How much money had they spent on all this stuff? Tens of thousands of pounds, that was for sure, some of it from her individual account. Not to mention the three thousand-plus euros spent on the Paris hotel and the two thousand she'd paid for the photograph she'd given him for their anniversary. The picture remained where they'd set it on their return, leaning against the wall to the left of the fireplace, the one he'd stood before when he told her he was going. He probably hadn't looked at it again since they got home from Paris, his head too full of *her*.

The delivery men looked surprised by her lack of excitement as the packaging was torn away from a huge smoke-grey velvet sofa.

'Nice place you've got here,' one of them remarked, casting an eye up to the high ceiling and back down over the ornate double cornicing. 'These houses are massive inside, aren't they?'

Well, the massive place would have to go back on the market, Alexa thought. She'd spent most of the morning, between outbursts of sobbing, calculating the inevitability of that. Her salary, without James's, could not begin to cover the costs of the place and she had more chance of being elected Mayor than she did of raising enough money to buy him out. He could probably buy her out, though, with a little help from his father, who had supplied the substantial six-figure shortfall between the proceeds from their flat and the amount they could sensibly borrow. She already knew that if James tried to suggest this she would burn the place down before she let that happen. She'd rather go to prison for arson than hand over her keys to that slut.

For Holly was surely poised to take her place in the house, as well as in her marriage. She and her son, the boy who had started this, the boy Alexa had begun to wish had never been born.

She wondered, briefly, if she'd had a period since the last time she'd slept with James. That would snap him out of his dream world, wouldn't it, a pregnancy, a baby of his own? But quite apart from the birth control factor, she'd lost so much weight and experienced so much stress lately that even if she did miss a period it wouldn't mean anything more than an erratic cycle. She was not pregnant.

A hundred times that day she almost phoned his mother, certain Julia Maitland would make him see sense where Alexa had failed, but, in the end, it was just too degrading. Nor did she seek out her own family or friends that day, avoiding their calls, sending texts to put them off. For some deep instinct of self-preservation told her she could not let the world know about this, not yet.

In any case, it hardly mattered if she did because the world would only tell her what she knew already, what Joanna Walsh had already said in so many words: she had to sit this out, wait for it to dawn on James that he couldn't meet someone in bizarre circumstances and a month later abandon his life and take on someone else's. He couldn't look his wife in the eye and say that his leaving her was all just a matter of fate. He couldn't abjure adult responsibility and start behaving like a child, a creature of instinct.

He couldn't choose over her a woman unworthy of him in every possible respect.

She kept on saying this to herself, *He couldn't, he couldn't,* until every second thought began with these words. And yet, whether she accepted it or not, he could and he had.

Chapter 18

It was easier than she'd expected to extricate herself from Melissa's hotel room. By the time the hen party had assembled on the bride-to-be's great four-poster bed, with enough alcohol stocks to eliminate the possibility of any need for midnight foraging, all Joanna had to do was feign an intoxication that exceeded everyone else's.

'I feel really sick,' she slurred, slackening her mouth a little.

'Don't vom on the four-poster!' Melissa wailed. 'Get her to the bathroom, someone!'

Joanna climbed down, letting herself stumble. 'No, I'm going back to my room, I need to go to bed.'

'Lightweight! It's only just gone eleven!' Melissa was content to wave Joanna away, but her friend Fiona began insisting someone should go with her.

'What if she gets lost? She's in that stable block bit, isn't she? It's miles from here!'

'I won't get lost,' Joanna said, trying to look like someone trying to look capable. 'I know the way.'

'Have you got your room key? Show me. And ring this extension when you get there so we know you're OK?'

Relatively sober as she was, Joanna was touched by Melissa's friend's concern. Was this how it felt to have a real older sister?

she wondered, as she made her way down the corridor and across the lobby; why did hers hate her so much? Was it simply egomania gone unchecked for too long, she the most convenient victim, or was there also something about Joanna that inspired such rabid sibling rivalry?

Departing the main doors Dan-bound, she winced as the chill night air hit her face, loosening something in her brain that caused her to ask herself another question, one she had never before asked: Could it be possible that it was not Melissa's oppression of her that had led to her present treachery, but her capacity for treachery that had caused Melissa's oppression of her in the first place? Was that the twist in their story? She'd been so busy assuming Melissa was the she-devil that she'd missed what Melissa and their parents had known all along, *that the she-devil was Joanna.*

It was possible, she decided, crunching across the driveway towards the stable wing; it was possible, but it was not true. And after tonight they'd finally be even, Melissa and she; she would never again be made miserable by her sister. Melissa may not know it, but Joanna would be free.

In her room, Dan was waiting, stretched out on the bed in a hotel robe, watching TV and drinking from the bottle of vodka he'd brought along.

'You took your time.'

She sat on the edge of the bed. 'Well, it is a hen night. I had to pretend to get drunk first.'

Already he was sliding her dress over her shoulders and down over her breasts. 'Couldn't you have pretended a bit faster?'

'Wait,' she said, feeling rushed, even though it was true that it felt like days, not hours, since she'd taken the some-what greater risk of sneaking him into her room in the first place, a manoeuvre that had required the evasion not only of the hen party but also the hotel staff. Luckily, the entrance to her room was closer to the car park than it was the main reception and as soon as she saw his taxi pull up she was able to signal to him from the doorway. A 'Do Not Disturb' sign did the rest. 'I have to let them know I got back OK or they might come and check.'

As she spoke into the phone, he pawed restlessly at her underwear. 'I can't believe your dad is paying for all this,' he said, as she hung up. 'It must be costing him a fortune.'

'No expense spared for his golden girl. Anyway, I don't suppose he realises he's paying for quite *this* much.'

'What, for his younger daughter to be screwed by the groom?'

'You're so romantic, Dan. I can't wait to hear you say your wedding vows.'

He laughed. 'What d'you think she'd do if she knew?'

This was a well-worn topic, one they'd refined to the level of a parlour game – if parlour games were played during penetration. 'She'd castrate me,' 'She'd shave off my eyebrows,' 'She'd burn down my bedroom,' and so on.

But tonight the game felt uncomfortable – perhaps because of Fiona's trust in her, perhaps because it was almost certainly the final time it would take place – and Joanna could not bring herself to take part.

More than once that night she checked that the door was locked, the curtains meeting in the middle, the phone securely in its cradle. 'Remember you need to be gone before seven,' she told Dan. 'Don't worry if I'm still asleep.'

'What, I'm not allowed to know how it feels to wake up together?' He was mocking her, mocking *them*, using the saccharine American accent he sometimes adopted to subvert the clichés of their adulterous affair.

'Just concentrate on disappearing from sight,' Joanna said.

She dreamt that Melissa was standing over the bed and shaking them awake, her skin discoloured, as dreadful as a serpent's, a gorgon's; it was a dream so real that, when she was woken by the phone ringing, her chest was wet with sweat and her heart a Catherine wheel firing inside her ribcage. It was Fiona summoning her to breakfast. She turned to the pillow next to hers not even knowing if Dan would still be there or not.

He was not, thank God. He was in a taxi or, worst case, in the nearby village awaiting the morning bus into town.

'On my way,' she said into the phone.

Walking into the breakfast room, it took a moment or two to locate Melissa and her party and when she did she almost suffered a cardiac arrest. For there, right at its centre, surrounded by five flat-haired, hungover girls, was Dan.

External paralysis was belied by internal tumult: bile rose in her oesophagus as if at the full-turn of a tap; blood roared in her ears; her lungs strained, tight and dry. This was it. They'd been discovered. She'd been commanded not to breakfast but to her sentencing (death, presumably). She considered her options, fairly quickly deciding that flight was her only chance if she was to avoid dying a teenager, but before she could think where she might bolt to, she heard her name being called.

'Over here, Jo!'

'*There* she is!'

She approached like Anne Boleyn to the scaffold, half expecting the diners to put down their knives and forks and start murmuring words of prayer.

'Look who couldn't keep away!' Melissa crowed, her fingers coiling around Dan's neck and into the thick hair above his ear, her lips sucking at his cheek.

'Sweet!' 'Bless!' 'Aw, look at him!' the others cooed, backing singers to their star.

'I spotted him sneaking about in the grounds when I was opening the window! At *this* time of the morning!'

In Joanna's brain, doubt began to advance on terror: this wasn't what she had been expecting to hear, it wasn't what she'd been expecting at all. Surely, surely, they couldn't have got away with it again?

More conspicuous fondling; another noisy kiss. 'He just wanted to check everything had gone OK and I survived the night,' Melissa said, mewing.

'Only just,' someone wisecracked, and amid the laughter Joanna managed to add, 'How devoted. That's lovely.'

'Sit down and have some Buck's Fizz, Jo,' Fiona said, pouring from a jug and passing the glass around the table to her.

As she sipped she felt the initial elation of having had her skin saved being systematically ground into wretchedness. No longer did last night represent the necessary finishing touch to a warranted betrayal, the *coup de grâce* that she'd even begun to interpret as poetic; instead it felt like pure malice, the kind of crime punished by higher powers, the point at which Dan and she had tipped from forgivable, at a push, to categorically beyond redemption.

A glance risked in his direction, the unmistakable daze of shock behind his laughing eyes, told her that he understood as well as she did what the occasion represented: the last time.

Sooner than she had hoped (in this curious new state of emergency she had no expectations, only hopes), Alexa was back on her doorstep. This time, however, it was at the flat and this time the blast was not to be intercepted: one look at the shaking, emaciated figure before her and she knew that what had been hermetically sealed during the week was about to find release.

It was Saturday morning and she had a free day ahead of her; she could think of few less appealing ways to start her weekend. 'They're not in, I'm afraid.'

'I'll wait,' Alexa said. 'I'll wait as long as it takes. I'll wait all day and night if I have to.'

Joanna believed her. 'You won't have to. They'll be back soon, all three of them.' James and Holly, with Mikey, were at the rental agent's signing the lease on their new flat and were due home in half an hour or so. 'I'll make us a coffee,' she added. Why people reached for caffeine in times of agitation was a mystery to her: the last thing Alexa needed was a psychoactive stimulant. Personally, she would have welcomed a morphine shot.

Alexa at least agreed to sit, occupying the same side of the sofa she had on her previous visit, her bag clasped between her ankles as if it might at any moment be snatched by the Artful Dodger. On her lap her fingers picked at one another, incapable of stillness. Joanna imagined her thinking that the events that had taken place since last time were so unimaginable as to be some basic error in cognition, a misconstruction that would be rectified the moment James stepped through the door.

If only, Joanna thought.

She set the coffee cup in front of her guest. 'I've been thinking about you,' she said. 'How have you been?'

'Not great, surprise, surprise.' There was something about Alexa's expression that confirmed Joanna's suspicion that she had still not confided her catastrophe in anyone else. You need a friend, she thought. You need your mum. Then she remembered what Alexa had said about her parents and sister, the rivalries and favouritism that Joanna knew only too well could take hold of a family, destabilise it to the point of collapse.

Deciding against taking *her* original seat, she sat instead on the floor, almost at Alexa's feet, an unconscious act of supplication. Alexa's confrontation with the lovers was inevitable, necessary, but it occurred to her that there might just be time for her to influence the way Alexa handled it. In order to gain, Joanna would have to give, however, and she could only pray this was a risk worth taking.

'Alexa, I know you probably don't want to hear this, but I wonder if it might make it easier to hear a bit about what Holly went through before Paris.'

Alexa's eyes narrowed in distrust. 'Before Paris?'

'Yes. Before she met James.'

'Before she *stole* him.'

'Before Mikey's accident.'

'Before she almost let her son drown, you mean?'

This was how she expressed her torment, then, in sullenness and sarcasm, like a teenager. The exchange reminded Joanna of a particularly trying spell when Holly had been about fourteen.

'I just think it might help to have the full background. She'd been suffering quite badly from postnatal depression, you see.'

Indignation suffused Alexa's face as instantly as a jet spray of colour: that Joanna should be trying to gain *sympathy* for the girl!

'I don't know how much you know about it but in some cases it can be very debilitating for a long time and this was the situation with Holly. She was frighteningly low for well over a year, the doctors couldn't ever seem to get the pills right and she wouldn't talk to the counsellors she was referred to. Nothing worked. Obviously I vouched for Mikey's safekeeping . . .' Here, Joanna paused: there were some truths she'd shared only with Suze, but this was not the time to understate the situation. 'Without that, he might have been taken into care. It was a terrible time for us.'

It was odd to invoke those dark days with the confidence of the past tense; in doing so it made Joanna realise how readily she was adapting to the light. Only six days since Holly's announcement and she was already allowing herself to half think the unthinkable: that James's feelings *might* endure, that Holly *may* have a wonderful future ahead of her. They were, after all, at that very moment signing a lease for a home together. But the distance between this and the nadir of misery apparent in poor Alexa, her obvious *lack* of acceptance, brought a tension to the meeting that was almost unendurable. Joanna's disclosures, which she knew

Holly would hate to be shared with this woman, were going to be for nothing.

She swallowed. 'Sometimes I worried she wasn't going to make it.'

'Well, she obviously just needed the love of a rich man,' Alexa said, hatefully. 'It's the ultimate wonder-drug, I hear.'

'Oh, Holly's not interested in money,' Joanna told her with conviction.

'Maybe not in earning it herself. James said she only works part-time, as a waitress?'

At this, Joanna felt her own indignation rise. 'But that's a big step for her, Alexa, seriously. You have to understand that she hardly set foot outside these four walls for months on end, and even then—'

Alexa interrupted, her face hot with outrage. 'Look, Joanna, I know you mean well, but I don't "have to understand" anything. Nothing you say can make me feel sorry for the person who is trying to destroy my marriage, and I think that's fair enough, don't you?'

Joanna looked down, catching sight of her left hand on the floor, bent at the wrist to prop her; she was startled by how *used* it looked. The skin was reddened at the knuckles, the veins knobbly and blue, and there was a slightly inflamed cut from opening a package the previous afternoon. Could these be the same fingers that had stroked Holly's head as a newborn baby, or entwined with Adrian's as recently as two years ago?

'I'm not asking you to feel sorry for her, I just want to try to explain that this isn't a straightforward situation. She's always been quite vulnerable about boys – men. She went completely overboard with her previous boyfriend, Sean, Mikey's dad. She's a person who throws herself into love in an extreme way, I suppose.'

'I would question your use of the word "love",' Alexa said, acidly, 'but she certainly throws herself into it.'

'Whatever it is, maybe not love,' Joanna conceded. 'But from what I've read, this is classic behaviour for a girl who grew up without a father.'

'How convenient. Absolutely not her fault then.'

'Oh, Alexa, listen to me,' Joanna pleaded. 'This is *not* her fault, that's what I'm trying to say. If it's anyone's fault, it's mine. You should blame me.' She felt uneasy; she was straying into territory she'd never intended breaching, and yet there was a momentum to this dialogue, a strange confessional impulse that Alexa was drawing from her and that she did not seem able to arrest. She began answering the very questions she should have rebuffed, allowing Alexa entry where she should automatically have barred her.

'Why would I blame *you*?' Alexa asked.

'Because I didn't try hard enough to keep in touch with her father and that's obviously affected the way she relates to men.'

'Well, where *is* her father?'

'I don't know. Possibly Birmingham, that's where some of his family were at one stage. We were never together properly.'

'She doesn't see him much, then?'

'She hasn't seen him since she was a baby.'

'Why not?' Now Joanna recognised in Alexa's face the sudden buoyancy of optimism. No doubt she hoped to hear that the man was in prison, ideally for something truly horrendous, something she could take to James to prove that Holly was unworthy of him.

'It wasn't easy to keep in touch. The circumstances were complicated.'

'Why?' Alexa asked, eagerly. 'Why were they complicated?'

Unsettled by her vivacity, Joanna drew breath twice, three times, to slow herself down, to prevent herself from revealing to Alexa what she had revealed to so few in her life before. *This*, at least, had to be properly guarded. But conscience or exhaustion or desperation or *something* had enchanted her and, as if from

255

another room, she heard herself say: 'I'm not telling you anything Holly doesn't know herself, but her father was married to my sister.'

There was a silence, the frightening, airless kind. Alexa just stared at her, clearly taken aback. 'Your *sister*?'

'That's right.' Joanna's regret was as instantaneous as the information was irretrievable. Why had she divulged this? *Why*? It was utter lunacy. Only later did she see that a part of it had been the avidity in Alexa's face, that appetite for some unpleasantness: it had made Joanna seek somehow to deflect the disgust from Holly and on to herself.

Certainly, it was with disgust that Alexa reacted: she raised herself up in her seat, leaned towards Joanna, and said, 'Hang on a minute, are you telling me that what she's done with James is the same as you did yourself with *your own sister's husband*? Well, the apple didn't fall very far from the tree, did it?'

Joanna shook her head. It was easy now to guess her visitor's thoughts: that she, Joanna, must have brought Holly up to disrespect other people's marriage vows, to help herself to what wasn't hers, to create this man-eating monster in her own image. 'It's not the same, far from it.' But she could hear for herself how uncertain she sounded: it was decades since she'd faced revulsion as absolute as Alexa's. 'There was no question that he and I could be together. We didn't *want* to be, actually.'

'What happened then? Are he and your sister still together? How does it work?'

'It doesn't.' Joanna shook her head a second time; unable to withdraw the fateful revelation, she could now only resist providing detail. 'It's not helpful to go into it. The point I'm trying to make is Holly's had a tough time, both as a child and an adult, and as I say the whole thing has been complicated by her illness. What's happening with James shouldn't be judged in isolation.'

'Clearly.' Alexa had the look of a woman who'd been given

the second chance of a lifetime. The energy burned from her upright frame; those featherweight bones that had seemed so fragile looked suddenly indestructible.

'Alexa—'

'Please don't say any more, Joanna. You've made it very clear that you find your daughter's behaviour acceptable and now I see why. Well, I *don't* find it acceptable and I'd like the chance to tell her that in person.'

On cue, there came the sound of approaching voices in the corridor outside, of Mikey's voice raised in bossy excitement, of a key turning in the lock. Distraught, Joanna stood to call out to Holly that they had a visitor (a visitor in whom she'd confided their most shameful secret!), but Holly was already entering the room, blinking as if in response to atmospheric change rather than in direct acknowledgement of Alexa. James followed, simple surprise on his face at the sight of his wife. Mikey darted forward between the two of them, stopping when he saw Alexa's forbidding expression.

As Alexa observed Holly with a cold hatred that turned Joanna's stomach, James spoke, his manner perfectly amiable. 'Hello, I didn't know you were coming.' Joanna saw that he was holding Holly's hand and did not let it go in Alexa's presence; instinctively, she prayed he would. 'How long have you been waiting for me? Not too long, I hope.'

There was a tremor in Alexa's body as she transferred her abominable gaze to him. 'What do you care how long I've waited? You're obviously far too busy playing happy families to consider *my* feelings.'

Mikey stood in front of Alexa open-mouthed, having never heard such a hateful tone in his home (despair, yes, but not loathing), and then stepped back to grip his mother's leg for protection. Not altering his voice at all, James said, 'Holly, why don't you take Mikey to play in the bedroom while I talk to Alexa? Or is it better if we go out?'

'I'm not going anywhere,' Alexa said, 'and I want to talk to her as well as you, if you don't mind.'

The glare had returned to Holly, who faced her enemy square-on, exhibiting no fear but rather an emotion that was suspiciously close to blithe innocence. Could she not see that the woman was demented with rage, Joanna thought, exasperated, and that she, Holly, was the cause of that dementia?

'*I'll* take Mikey,' she said to the three of them. 'We'll watch a film in the bedroom.'

'Good plan,' Alexa said, snidely. 'He's better off with you, I would have thought. Less chance of falling out of a window.'

With Holly apparently impervious to insult and in any case mute, it was left to James to pre-empt Joanna's objection to this remark. 'That's enough,' he said, sharply, causing Alexa to jerk her head in his direction and snap, 'I'll be the judge of that, if it's all the same to you.'

'He's a baby, Alexa. Don't scare him.' Self-assured though James was, Joanna could tell from odd flickers in his face that he was finding it both heartbreaking and repellent to watch his wife in this condition.

In the bedroom, she changed Mikey's nappy and settled him on Holly's bed with his favourite DVD on the portable player. Returning silently to the living room doorway, she found all three standing, James and Holly still hand in hand.

'It's not like that, honestly,' Holly was saying, having at last found her voice, presumably in answer to some accusation of devilry; her tone was as unnaturally placid as her expression.

'She's right, it's not,' James agreed, and he gazed in adoration at his new lover as if they were in the room alone.

'You should see yourselves,' Alexa spat, 'for fuck's sake, it's like you're in a cult or something.'

'It's not a cult,' James said, 'it's love.' And he spoke as if this were a state of affairs decreed by the gods and he powerless to protest it.

At the word 'love' Alexa let out an angry, grievous sound, her suffering utterly exposed. It was the moment when James had to choose whether or not to go to her and comfort her, and all at once Joanna hoped he would. If his feelings for Holly were as sure as he said they were, then he could drop her hand for a minute or two and spare a little compassion for his wife. Unable to watch any more, she retreated to the bedroom, where Mikey welcomed her cuddle.

'Lady angry,' he said.

'Yes, lady is angry. Angry and sad.'

'Angry. Sad.' He still spoke mainly in adjectives. He didn't yet ask why.

'Let's watch the movie,' she told him. But the flat was small and it was easy to pick out James's and Alexa's exchange behind the *Aristocats* soundtrack. It did not sound as if he were comforting her, after all, but rather fending off a renewed attack.

'You've both gone crazy,' Alexa fumed, 'because of what happened in Paris. She was a loony to begin with and you've gone the same way. You both need professional help.'

'We are completely sane,' James said. 'And can I just say that you don't know anything about what Holly was like before.'

'I know a lot more than you think. I know she was more interested in finding a married man to seduce than she was in looking after her child.' Her voice had grown so shrill that Joanna was in no doubt that all their neighbours could follow every word of this human drama if they so wished. Only Mikey was absorbed elsewhere, giggling at the scene on screen. 'Well, once you're tired of sleeping with her you'll see what a huge mistake it was. It happens all the time, it's nothing special, believe me.' There was a long silence after this outburst and Joanna was startled to hear Alexa's voice again when she had expected James's; it was lower now, more plaintive: 'Come back, James. It's not too late.'

Breathing hard, Joanna closed her eyes, but Mikey noticed this forbidden act and used his fingers to roughly prise them open again. He wanted her to watch the cat playing piano. He wanted her to join in with the singing.

'Alexa,' James said, sounding more compassionate now, 'listen to me, please. I'm sorry I hurt you, I can see that it was the worst thing I could have done from your point of view. I know you can't forgive me, I don't expect that. But why would you want to be with someone who doesn't want to be with you?'

Joanna thought of Sean then and Holly's prolonged pining for him, and of past needs of her own. You wanted it because desire for the wrong person was an illness, it gripped you and held you captive and the way it worked was you could not free yourself, you could only wait to be freed.

'Don't twist this,' Alexa said. 'You *did* want to be with me, you *married* me. And if you hadn't met her, we'd still be together. You can't deny that.'

'Maybe, but for how much longer?'

'Longer than you'll be with her, I promise you that.'

Whatever was said next was buried by a clamour on screen and a squeal from Mikey. The next voice she heard from the living room was James's. 'Can we stop shouting at each other and arrange the practical stuff through our solicitors?'

'You can arrange it with the Pope for all I care,' Alexa cried. 'Just don't think you will ever, *ever* have my respect again. You may think you're some big hero but you're the opposite of a hero as far as I'm concerned. You're a coward!'

There was a sense of climax to this last insult that deceived Joanna into believing Alexa was ready to flounce out and bring an end to proceedings, but to her horror James's wife spoke again:

'You know her mother did the same, don't you?'

'What?'

'She had an affair with her brother-in-law, that's who *her* father is.'

Joanna stopped breathing. Mikey looked up at her face. 'Clever cats,' he said, demanding she look at the screen and trying to turn her head with his two hands.

'Yes,' she said, weakly, 'clever cats. Very clever.'

Of course, she'd known Alexa would use the information, it had been a foregone conclusion the second it was shared, but she had not expected the other woman's desire to inflict pain by its use to be so potent it radiated through the walls to another room.

'That's right,' Alexa continued, with an unpleasant cackle, 'her own sister's husband. This kind of thing is completely normal to this family, don't you realise? They haven't got a shred of common decency between them.'

James reacted at once, his tone chilling: 'I know all about Holly's father' – that was a surprise to Joanna and she assumed it must have been to Alexa, too; she could only picture the collapse of all that malignant hope – 'and it's hardly the same deal, is it? That was a fling between kids. Holly's in a real relationship with someone whose marriage was already over in all but name.'

'It was *not* over, I can't believe you're rewriting history like this! Why can't you just admit you've done what a million other men have done, you've just done it ten years early: left your wife for a younger model.'

'Fine,' James said, 'if that's how you prefer to define it, it makes no difference to me. I admit it. Now, please, go.'

At last Alexa had had enough. As she left, she called out to Holly in a ghastly, vindictive voice, 'Enjoy it while you can, you stupid whore, because it won't be long before you're out on your ear as well.'

The front door cracked shut. Promising Mikey that she was

just going to the loo, Joanna joined James and Holly in the living room. The lovers stood in downcast silence, their arms gripped around each other's waist.

Unexpectedly, given her previous reticence, it was Holly who took command. She looked across at Joanna, her face flushed with consternation. 'Why did you tell her, Mum? I don't get it.'

At the sight of her daughter's pain, Joanna felt close to tears herself. 'I . . . I got it wrong. I thought it might help her understand everything a bit better, how this could have happened.'

'We love each other: that's all there is to understand.' As she and James sank closer together, their faces turning to one another's, Joanna read the message with trepidation: they hoped for Joanna's approval but they did not *need* it. What they gave each other was strong enough to make up for any doubts or misgivings on the part of others, be it a devastated wife or a sceptical mother.

She caught James's eye. 'Why don't you two go out for a coffee, have a bit of time on your own. I'll stay with Mikey.'

James glanced at Holly, who nodded. 'I'll just say goodbye,' she said, moving past Joanna without meeting her eye.

After they'd gone, Joanna wrapped her arms around Mikey and watched the rest of the film, seeing it through even though the boy drifted off to sleep before the end.

Only as the credits rolled did she allow herself to consider what that last exchange with Holly could mean. In her attack Alexa had mocked Holly's mental illness, she had accused her of being a bad mother and a whore, but the only slur Holly had objected to was the one about her parentage.

Why? Had her union with James brought new sensitivity to bear on the past? Or could it be that, all along, she'd cared more than she'd let her mother believe?

Joanna felt suddenly alone. It was as if that feeling of

optimism she'd experienced earlier was nothing more than a false dawn.

As if the last twenty-two years had been compressed into minutes, the clemency of passing time retracted at a stroke.

Chapter 19

She made the discovery halfway through the autumn term. Obeying the law of television drama that serious news must be broken face to face, she skipped college and took the train to Manchester, arriving at Melissa's and Dan's flat in the mid afternoon. Though she had discovered from her mother that this was the day of the week that Melissa stayed in class till late, she felt the pitching sensation of dread inside her. Having not visited before, she was uncertain which of the unmarked buzzers to try, or whether he would even be at home to answer, but presently Dan's 'Yeah?' emerged and the door gave way even before she could say her name.

He was waiting in the doorway of the first floor flat, neither his stance (arms crossed, one shoulder slumped against the frame) nor expression (doleful, suspicious) in any way welcoming. 'I thought we said . . . ?' He alluded to their agreement after the near-miss of the hen night that they would forget their affair had ever happened.

'I know,' Joanna said. 'It's not that.' She faltered. 'Melissa's not due back?'

'Not for hours. Come on in.'

'Thank you.'

Leaving her to close the flat door, he led the way into the

living room, which had bare windows overlooking the street and was lit only by the smoky remains of the October day. All the possessions stored over the summer in Melissa's bedroom at home had been assigned shelf, wall or floor space here and it was the sight of this, rather than of Dan himself, that brought home her predicament in an entirely more real and adult way. Unsettled and afraid, she focused on the newer details: the empty lager cans arranged on the coffee table like Stonehenge, a television set she hadn't seen before tuned to a cable channel she didn't know, and a tabloid newspaper open on the sofa. Did Dan ever earn any money? she was beginning to wonder. Was he not, in fact, a bit of a waster?

'Grab a chair,' Dan said, 'you look done in.'

'I feel it.' She'd intended to build up to the news in some unspecified way, but the sensation of her swollen stomach nudging the top of her thighs as she settled into the low seat caused her to blurt: 'I'm pregnant, Dan.' Having startled herself, she turned anxiously to catch his reaction.

It was not pretty. She remembered his face when she'd told him of Melissa's plans for a baby – unperturbed, fondly amused – but this was different: he blanched visibly before his features settled into the sickened grimace of someone who had accidentally overheard police details of a grisly killing.

'It's yours,' she added, sensing this might be necessary.

'Jesus,' he muttered. 'You're going to get rid of it, right?'

His presumptuousness hurt her feelings. 'I don't know, am I? I thought we ought to discuss it first.'

'Nothing to discuss, I would've thought. You can't exactly keep it, can you?' He sounded careless enough, but the way he reached for the empties on the table, trying each in turn for dregs, betrayed his agitation. Giving up, he got to his feet and left the room; there was soon the crack of a new can being opened, in the kitchen, she supposed. He had not offered her anything to drink and so she sipped from a bottle of water she'd brought from home.

When he returned he didn't look at her. The 'discussion' had stalled already, it seemed. They sat in silence for several minutes, Joanna wondering how to restart it or whether she shouldn't simply get up and go, for this was the biblical moment, the moment when the scales fell from her eyes. I don't want you, she thought, looking at his face, those seductive eyes now determinedly averted, denying not only her news but her presence, even her existence. I'm glad I haven't got what she's got. It's not good enough for me.

So transfixed was she by this epiphany that the thump of footsteps on the stairs and the scrape of a key in the lock failed to prompt in her either action or word and all at once, before she was prepared for it, Melissa was in the room, snapping on the overhead light and standing in front of her. She wore a long beige coat, her blonde hair tumbling in windswept clouds on to a pale fur collar, the effect as incongruous in these bleak student digs as that of the Snow Queen arriving on stage in the wrong theatre. Instantly Joanna felt herself shrink in stature.

'Joanna, what are you doing up here? You look like you've put on a bit of weight, have you?'

'I have,' Joanna agreed, still blinking from the sudden blaze of light. Only now did her responses stutter to life. *Melissa*, she was here.

Melissa stooped to kiss Dan on the lips, the sound of the contact lingering in the air.

'Last two lectures were cancelled. There is a God after all!'

Joanna saw her notice the beer cans and narrow her eyes in annoyance. 'Have you been drinking?' The accusation included Joanna, who replied, 'I haven't. I haven't had anything since I arrived.'

'You've not even offered her a cup of tea? Oh, Dan, you're *hopeless*.' Melissa began divesting herself of bags and books and scarves before asking Joanna, 'Are you staying for dinner?

There's nothing in the fridge unless *he's* been shopping, which I doubt, so shall we go for a curry?'

To Joanna's great surprise Dan jumped in, saying, 'Actually, babe, it's not a social call. Joanna's got some news for us.'

'Oh?'

'She's just been telling me she's got herself into a bit of trouble.'

He must have given his wife some clue Joanna could not see or hear because Melissa appeared to understand at once, fixing her golden beam on her sister and saying, 'You're *pregnant*? Oh, *not* that dreadful Stephen? I don't know how you could have slept with him in the first place, Jo. Sooner you than me.'

And Dan laughed – he *laughed* – in simple, almost boyish enjoyment. (It reminded her of something: *It's a laugh, isn't it? Doing something she doesn't know about?*) Then Melissa giggled, too, enjoying the amusement her comment had given her husband, happy, always happy, to make her sister the butt of the joke.

The rage that gushed through Joanna's bloodstream at the sight of their mocking smiles had a frighteningly rapid effect, not only scalding her skin a hot crimson but heightening her senses to what felt like almost supernatural levels: she could have lifted a car or felled a tree, halted tides with her roar. In that moment she hated both of them and containing that hatred was an impossibility.

'Not Stephen,' she said, her face clenched. 'Dan.'

Melissa frowned, confident of her own misunderstanding. 'What do—?' she began, just as Dan rose from the sofa in indignation, calling out, 'Fuck off, that's a lie!'

Joanna scrambled up and, ignoring Dan, addressed her sister head-on: 'You heard me. I said Dan. He's the father, I'm having *his* baby. And it was conceived on *your* hen night – that's why you found him skulking round the grounds the next morning, he wasn't there because he was missing you. Sooner you than me, huh?'

Melissa's frown deepened and then contorted; it was like watching a face being turned inside out, all the emotions on the outside, black and lethal. 'My *hen night?*'

'She's lying,' Dan said, but the fear in his voice gave him away.

'No, I'm not. He knows I'm not.'

She took a step aside, intending to sweep past Melissa towards the door, only to be sprung upon, one hand seizing her shoulder as the other was raised to strike; but that superhero strength allowed her to resist the assault with ease, fending off the blows like a bear toying with a squirrel (they were, in any case, the feeble clouts of a child, laughingly unlike the ferocity Joanna had always believed her sister capable of).

'It won't make any difference, Melissa,' she gasped, 'you can't hurt me now.'

At this, Dan intervened and Melissa turned on him instead, the obscenities raining as she struck at him with both fists – leaving Joanna free to get out of the door and run for the street.

She shook badly during the journey home, both in reaction to the scene just gone and in anticipation of the one that awaited her. One of two things would now happen, she knew: either Melissa would phone their parents and tell them the news, causing one or both of them to dash to her, or Melissa would drive herself home, getting there before Joanna, who had two buses and a train to contend with. Either way, by the time Joanna could make her case, Melissa would have, justifiably for once, secured their parents' alliance.

As the train gathered speed she decided the first option was too much to hope for: it didn't fit with her proven bad luck that she should be permitted simply to get herself home and slip into her bed, sleep herself into oblivion. No, Melissa would be racing her home. Of course, in a film, uncontrollable emotion would cause her to crash her car (Joanna did not wish for this; rather she wished that her own train would derail), but it was not a film and when she walked through the door Melissa was there. She was seated on the sofa in her customary position between her parents, sobbing noisily into her father's shirt collar while his hand stroked her hair. He did not raise his head to acknowledge his younger daughter when she entered the room, leaving his wife to state the official position.

'Joanna,' Lynn said, standing. Her face, disfigured with fear and outrage, had transformed since that morning from middle-aged to old. 'What have you done?'

In short order she was thrown out of her home and visited by an immovable resolve to keep her baby. She had no idea if the one followed the other.

'She says if you set foot in the house again she'll kill herself,' her mother reported by phone. In the hours after Joanna's return from Manchester, Melissa had refused even to look at her, commandeering every second of their father's attention and most of their mother's. The next morning, at his command, Joanna moved to a friend's.

'You've given us no choice, Joanna,' he said.

'You still have a choice,' the practice nurse told her, on two separate visits to her GP. 'It's not too late to change your mind.' While there was no direct attempt to persuade her to have a ter-mination, it had been in the news that the Government was horrified with recently published statistics of teenage pregnan-cies in the UK.

'I won't change my mind,' she said.

At first, shocked by her banishment and by the drama of having jeopardised or even destroyed her sister's fledgling mar-riage, and above all consumed by the physical strangeness of pregnancy, she stayed close to home. Believing that her parents could not sustain this extreme act of discrimination, she traipsed from friend's to friend's, eventually sleeping on the sofa of an old classmate who had decided to move out of her parents' house and needed two others to help with bills. But when Joanna shared word that she was keeping her baby, her friend's enthusiasm faded.

'I don't know if you can get a flat with a baby,' she said.

'It's a child, not a snake,' Joanna said.

'I know, but, still, aren't there rules and stuff? We're *students*.'

So, she wasn't as much of a friend as Joanna had hoped: it happened. The week she passed the point of no return with the pregnancy she dropped out of her course and made two day trips to London to scour the listings magazines for rooms and book viewings. Even as she signed a contract for a tiny two-room flat on the South Circular – so far from what she'd seen of London on previous excursions as to be a different city – even then she didn't believe it was any kind of permanent arrangement. *As soon as I've had the baby*, she'd think, letting the second half of the clause evaporate; *as soon as I've had the baby . . .*

She'd been disowned, but she had not been left in total penury. Her mother had given her a cheque to use for a rental deposit and she had inherited a small sum a year ago from the last of her grandparents. It was just possible to pretend that moving to London in the first term of her foundation course had been her intention all along; she had hoped to come the following year, anyhow, for art college. Though she'd never expected to find herself applying for social security benefits, there was a satisfaction in getting it set up: she'd receive statutory maternity benefit and her rent would be paid for her. Soon there would also be family allowance.

It was only short-term. As soon as she could, she'd arrange to resume her course in London or find work.

After Holly's birth she used the payphone on the hospital ward to call her parents with the news. It was not the first time she'd phoned them at home since leaving, but it was the first time one of them agreed to speak to her for any length of time.

'She weighs six pounds twelve ounces and has dark blue eyes, but they're already turning brown, like mine.' It seemed important to state that the child had not inherited her father's fateful blue eyes.

'We're glad you're all right,' her mother said in a low, furtive voice that sounded far from glad. She was, Joanna assumed, concealing the call from her husband, since Melissa would be in Manchester, preparing by now for finals. As for Dan, Joanna still had no idea of his whereabouts, whether or not he was still living with Melissa in the flat with no curtains and a tableful of beers. Since the revelation of the pregnancy she had had no contact with him; nor had she had any adolescent daydreams of him happening from the mists with a plan to divorce Melissa and marry her.

'I have to stay here another two days, then I should be free to go home.'

Home. Did her mother feel it, as she did, the strange charge that word activated? It was a kind of password that gave permission for them both to drop the act and say what they actually wanted.

There was a silence: who would go first?

'Are you still living in the place you told me about?' her mother asked.

'Yes, but I—'

'And is it warm enough for the baby?'

'Yes.'

'Good. That's good. And you have enough money for everything you need?'

'Yes.'

Somehow, already, the opening had closed. Joanna said instead, 'Please will you tell Dan for me.'

There was a pause. 'Yes,' her mother said, finally. 'I can get a message to him.'

'Thank you.'

Replacing the receiver afterwards, Joanna put the lack of any request to visit her in the hospital, or any invitation to bring the new baby to see them, down to pride or shock or . . . or something. Something that was still critical but not yet terminal; something that would surely be righted in time. After all, her parents couldn't possibly have believed Melissa when she'd threatened to end her life at the mere sight of her sister on the doorstep (Joanna imagined Melissa standing at the top of the stairs, a pistol with a mother-of-pearl handle pressed to her own head, like something out of Hitchcock), and even if they had then surely enough months had now passed for the initial risk to have been downgraded.

She pretended not to notice the ward staff's exchange of pitying looks when visiting hours passed without a soul approaching her bedside. Other than the neighbouring new mothers, the only people who peered into Holly's little plastic crib to say hello were those who were paid to do so.

A few weeks after Holly's birth, when she was confident about travelling with her tiny daughter, she took a coach from Victoria Station to Peterborough and waited for the connecting bus to her old neighbourhood. Pushing open the garden gate and walking the curved stone path to the front door, she continued to refine the hypothesis she'd been developing throughout the journey, and since soon after Holly's arrival for that matter: that while the birth itself might not have expunged the shame of the conception, as she'd hoped – it had been too abstract or remote, perhaps – her parents *would* change their minds as soon as they set eyes on Holly. A real baby, a perfect one. And it wasn't as if she'd had a boy, a miniature Dan to remind them of her crime, was it?

'Joanna!' In the open doorway her mother was paralysed by the sight of her, as if she'd come back from the dead, not

London. At last rediscovering bodily motion, she came out on to the doorstep and pulled the door to behind her, causing Joanna to shuffle backwards. Her eyes slid downwards to the baby.

'This is Holly, Mum.'

'Oh.' Lynn regarded Holly with the look of someone sworn to a low-fat diet who'd been presented with a plate of her favourite cakes: it was a question of pure willpower. It was not the look Joanna had dreamt of.

'What are you doing here? You know you can't come in.'

'What? You don't mean that?' Joanna said. There was a slamming feeling in her abdomen, the same spot she'd had the after-cramps, making her buckle suddenly in pain. Her mother reached out to steady her.

'Listen . . .' Her voice grew urgent. 'Melissa is here. You really can't come in.'

Joanna cursed her decision to come on a Monday morning, for Melissa must have been home for the weekend and not yet departed; midweek would have been safer. 'OK, well, shall I come back after she's left? I'll wait in the café by the post office, so maybe you could come and get me when the coast's clear?'

Her mother drew her lips together as she shook her head. 'You don't understand, Jo: she's living here. She moved out of the flat months ago, in fact I don't think she ever went back there after . . .' She stopped just short of naming the crime itself, as one might with murder or the abduction of a child.

'But what about college?' Joanna asked. 'Did she leave?'

'She studies here. She hasn't dropped out.'

Not like me, Joanna thought. Even in a personal crisis, Melissa managed to triumph somehow.

'What about D—'

Her mother hushed her, as if the sound of his name would set off a siren. 'They've split up and they're getting a divorce. You didn't think they could continue after *that*, did you?'

'That' was beginning to feel very heavy in Joanna's arms and she longed to sit, to be able to place her warm charge somewhere safe and stretch her aching arms. 'But she must leave the house at some point? Doesn't she have to go up to Manchester for exams? I could come back then.'

'When she goes I take her, and then I drive her back home again. Don't you see, Jo? She needs twenty-four-hour care. I had to give up my job, everything!' The strain in Lynn's voice gave way to open despair.

Joanna gaped. 'But why? I mean, I know why she's upset, obviously, but why does she need twenty-four-hour care? It's been months since it happened.'

'She's still very unstable, it's a form of trauma, the doctors say.'

'Trauma? After so long? I don't understand.' Joanna had an image of herself pushing her mother aside, storming the house and slapping her sister's face in the way she'd seen done in soap operas when someone was debilitated with shock, screaming for her to be more reasonable, to get herself a sense of perspective.

But she had forgotten who she was dealing with. Months of solitude, weeks of minute absorption in her new baby, had allowed her to forget.

'They say she has the type of personality that doesn't react in a normal way to something humiliating like this. She likes to be in control and when that's taken away, when she's surprised by something bad, she has a more extreme reaction than the rest of us.'

Joanna could not help raising a wry eyebrow at this. I could have told you that any day of these last eighteen years, she thought, but the gleam of tears in her mother's eyes made her straighten her face at once.

'It's as if she just broke down the day it happened, and she's stayed broken ever since. We've had to take the contents of the medicine cabinet and hide them where she can't find them, we've had to put safety locks on all the top windows. Knives, razorblades, everything like that has to be kept out of sight.'

'But if *he*'s out the picture, couldn't I at least *try* to persuade her? Maybe if she meets Holly?'

The shake of the head was instant and unconditional. 'She's not going to forgive you or him, not ever. And Dad and I can't risk her finding out we've seen you and doing something stupid.'

This was, *still* was, even with the arrival of a grandchild, the crux of the matter: they'd risk losing Joanna – and their first grandchild – but they would not risk losing Melissa.

She did not ask her mother the question she'd asked herself a thousand times: if it had been the other way around, Joanna's man, Melissa's mistake, Melissa's baby, would they have chosen Joanna? But it was academic: Joanna would never have required of them what Melissa had.

Just then Holly stirred, made her only sound to date besides crying and variations thereof: a soft kitten's sigh. 'Would you like to hold her?' Joanna whispered to her mother.

'I don't think that would be a good idea.'

'It's 1989, Mum.' It sounded silly, but the date seemed more relevant than anything else she could think of: you didn't get disowned in the late 1980s, not in this country, not in their culture, their family.

As Holly's sleepy eyelids wobbled open and closed again, Joanna could see her mother wavering. 'All right. Go to the café. I'll come when I can, in half an hour or so.'

In the café, she waited. Holly wouldn't feed and soon became red and disgruntled, earning irritated looks from some of the other customers. After almost two hours, Joanna took her to the phone box by the green and called her parents' number. The phone rang on and on.

After several more tries, she walked back to the house. There was no answer to the doorbell and her parents' car was gone from the drive. It made no sense: surely they couldn't have left because of her?

It was then that she granted entry to the knowledge she'd kept at bay since she'd packed her bag that morning, and, pushing an emergency ten-pound note into a zipped inner pocket, had discovered her old house keys.

Could she? Assuming Melissa hadn't insisted they change the locks, of course, could she?

She let herself in, protecting Holly's tiny head with her palm as she used her left shoulder to give the door the push it needed in colder weather, the stiffness familiar from the thousands of times she'd come home before. Inside, in the hallway, there was silence. Unless someone was sleeping, the house was as unoccupied as the unanswered phone calls and rings of the doorbell had promised.

Where was her mother? Where was Melissa?

She crept into the living room with exaggerated stealth. It was just the same as she remembered, heartbreakingly so, for she might have expected *some* change to mark the expulsion of one quarter of the family unit. She checked the photographs on the dresser and was relieved to find that she was still in them: she hadn't been erased from history. But it hardly mattered, for she'd never liked herself in those photos, the ugly sister standing slightly to the side, Melissa's always the smile at the centre.

Upstairs, seeing her old bedroom – similarly untouched and possibly not dusted since her departure – provoked memories not of stolen hours with Dan, their bodies jammed together in the single bed, ears growing ever lazier for the sounds of others' return, but of much earlier times. She remembered the sole occasion in her infanthood when Melissa had wanted to sleep in her bed with her (she'd been spooked by a film), and the day her favourite soft toy – a leopard – went missing, found by Melissa two days later amid great jubilation. She had, Joanna was quite clear afterwards, taken it in the first place and almost certainly tortured it.

Along the landing, Melissa's room bore witness to her return from Manchester: the overflowing wardrobe and drawers, a desk heaped with college work, a printed exam timetable tacked to the wall. On the vast corkboard used to display photographs, Joanna at last spotted evidence of removal: there was not one image of Dan or her among the hundreds of snaps. Lingering as she did in front of them, she allowed a full five minutes to pass before she turned to the bed and saw what she should have seen straight away, the reason for the house's emptiness, for her mother's sudden vanishing: blood. It had soaked the corner of the duvet and made a stain on the carpet, not an enormous amount, but red enough to have been recently shed; it was Melissa's, surely.

She was seized by panic. It was as if the blood had come from Holly and was still coming, spilling from the baby too fast for Joanna to do anything to stop it. Melissa must have seen her, she realised. She must have heard the doorbell or their mother call out Joanna's name. Perhaps she had even come down the stairs and strained to hear their whispered conversation, or looked out of the landing window above and lip-read their words. Running now to that same window, Joanna looked down on the exact spot she'd occupied a few hours ago: the top of her head would have been easily visible, as would the bundle in her arms.

Clutching Holly, she fled the house, her bag bumping painfully against her back as she went, and took the first bus that came, the wrong one, it transpired, which meant a change when she'd calmed down enough to make sense of the driver's advice. At the bus station she phoned the house repeatedly, at last getting an answer just minutes before she was due to board her coach back to London.

It was her father who picked up, and with a distressed urgency that made her heart shrink with terror.

'Dad, it's Joanna.'

'What are *you* doing phoning?' he demanded.

'You sound upset. Is everything all right?'

'No, it is not all right, Joanna. Far from it.'

'Why? What's happened? Please tell me.'

There was a pause. She imagined him deciding he'd get her off the line faster if he just told her. 'Your sister is in hospital. She cut her wrists, tried to kill herself.'

'Is she . . . ?'

'She's alive, yes. Luckily your mother was at home and got to her before she'd lost too much blood. She'd only turned her back for a couple of minutes, just to answer the door.' It was clear he did not know it had been Joanna at the door, or that she was in town at all: her mother had not shared that information, that blame.

'Where's Mum now?'

'She's staying at the hospital. Melissa will be kept under observation until she's strong enough to see the psychiatric consultant. I've come back to pick up night things for them both.'

There was a silence. Joanna didn't know what to say; whatever she tried, however heartfelt, it would be defective.

'This is how it is now, Joanna, do you not understand that? This is *your* fault. None of this would have happened if—' Her father broke off; she could hear the wayward rhythm of his breathing. He'd been going to say, If you hadn't been born, she was certain, but had stopped himself in time. 'If you'd left Dan alone. *He's* just a fool, he'd do what anyone suggested without bothering about the consequences, but you, you must have known what they'd be. You wanted something like this to happen. You've been jealous of her from the moment you were born.'

For all his imperfect parenting over the years, he had never spoken to her this way. Even allowing for the high emotions of today's circumstances, his words beat her black and blue. 'That's not true, *she* was jealous of me! I loved her!'

'You had an affair with the man she was about to marry, Joanna. The man she *did* marry. Is that your idea of love?'

'No, it shouldn't have happened. We . . . we didn't think anyone would find out.'

'Then you were both fools. People *always* find out.'

'I'm sorry, I'm really sorry.'

'Sorry means nothing now. It's far too late for that.'

Even as they argued Joanna was aware of what was wrong about this conversation: the absence of Holly; he had not once mentioned her. Holly had occupied her mind to the exclusion of all else long enough for it to feel unnatural and frightening when she was not cited, even in a context like this. She thought, then, It's Dad: he's the one driving this madness, this idea that Melissa is extraordinary, blessed. Mum could be persuaded to be fair, but he never could.

'What do you want me to do?' she whispered into the phone.

'Just keep out of her way. Keep out of *our* way.'

'I will.'

She had not expected to return to London so soon, to her two tiny rooms near Tulse Hill station, but when she did she felt its consolations like a change in air temperature, an envelopment of warmth. For the first time, the place felt like her home. And Holly, who had cried and fretted the whole coach journey back, fell quickly asleep in her own little cot.

Part Two

'Tout le monde pleure aujourd'hui'

Chapter 20

It was no longer Holly's habit to give thanks to guardian angels and the other heavenly creatures she associated with the early days of her love affair with James, but there were still moments when she could think of no better explanation for the paradise in which she found herself. Lying on a rug next to a giggling Mikey, the evening sun warming her skin, hearing the sound of a key waggle in the lock and the door open, of James's voice calling out, 'Hi, guys, I'm home! Where are you?': this was one such moment.

Their ground-floor flat was not vast and there could be fewer than a half-dozen possible answers to his question, each of which was discoverable in a few steps, but Holly knew how much James enjoyed the ritual and so called back, 'In here, Mikey's room!' She did not get to her feet to meet him because she was engrossed, at Mikey's command, in the organisation into rows of a couple of hundred plastic animals, new toys ordered by James and delivered only that afternoon. The room, much larger than the one they'd shared in Crystal Palace, was at the rear of the flat, overlooking a little holly tree, with a wonky rectangle of frayed garden beyond. A sliding door opened on to a tiled balcony and had proved a source of great fascination to Mikey, who was content to spend an hour at a time opening and closing it – under strict supervision, of course. Because of that door, it had been all James could do to persuade Holly to give Mikey the larger of the three bedrooms and as it was she checked and double-checked the lock obsessively.

'Hello, you two.' James stood in the doorway smiling down at them. 'What's this then? Mass migration across the Serengeti?'

'Mikey's zoo,' Mikey told him with pride. James stooped to smooth the boy's hair in greeting, cupping the back of his head in his palm – Mikey's small, squarish skull fitted his hand perfectly, Holly noticed – before circumnavigating the toys to kiss Holly.

'We've really missed you today,' she said, her face remaining upturned after the kiss. Even after two weeks of living together she felt pure rapture at the sight of him. 'I had to stop myself from phoning you.'

'You can phone me whenever you like,' James said.

'I knew you'd be busy. And I didn't have anything to report, anyway. I just wanted you to know I wanted to.'

'Well, I want you to know I want you to, too.'

Both spoke in besotted tones, childish versions of their ordinary voices. Sometimes when they did this they exchanged a look that meant, No one else must hear how we speak to each other because if they did they would surely vomit. Holly supposed this must be what the magazines called the honeymoon period.

How she wished it could last forever! For constantly James told her wonderful things, things that made her heart swell and her blood rush.

He told her that when he came back from work and closed the door behind him, he already felt more at home here than he had in any place he'd lived with Alexa or the girlfriend he had been with in his early twenties. As it turned out, their building was of a similar period to the house he'd abandoned across town, with the same black double doors opening on to a large square entrance hall. The light fitting differed dramatically, however, theirs a paper lantern of the type that cost a few pounds in IKEA, the Chiswick one an alabaster chandelier Alexa had hung for a thousand times the cost. Holly said she wasn't sure what alabaster even was; James said it didn't matter because he preferred the paper one, anyway.

He told her that his new home consisted of about a quarter of the square footage of the old one and yet somehow it made him appreciate the one room that *did* have stylish proportions and a beautiful window – their living room, at the front of the house – far more than he had the succession of impressive spaces he'd left behind. None of it mattered, in any case, he said; the only thing that mattered was who you were sharing the space with. They'd taken the flat furnished, with the agreement that when James could extract some items from the Chiswick house the rented ones would be moved into storage by the landlord. Who knows, he said, we might be here for years.

He told her that it had taken falling in love with her to make him see his relationship with Alexa had not contained actual love for several years. You get used to dim light, he said, and then one day you get the dazzle of proper sunshine and only then do you see that you'd been straining your eyes before.

He told her that having Mikey in his life made him question how he and Alexa could ever have wanted to delay having children, or even consider not starting a family at all.

He told her it felt exhilarating to have changed everything about his private life, therapeutic. It was a word he would use only with Holly, but he said he felt almost *reborn*.

He told her that sleeping with her gave him more pleasure than anything else had in his entire life.

He told her he couldn't be happier.

He told her *everything*.

As James now sank to his knees on the rug next to them, careful not to dislodge any of the herded animals, Holly pulled herself reluctantly on to her haunches. 'I have to go to work in half an hour. I'd better start getting ready.'

'Is Mikey all packed?'

'Yes. He's very excited. We haven't seen Grandma since Tuesday.'

In keeping with the original plan agreed with Joanna, Mikey would be spending the next two nights in his 'other home', as they called the Crystal Palace flat. The practicalities of Friday were already established: until Holly started her driving lessons and took a test, James would drive them, first dropping Mikey at Joanna's and then Holly at the restaurant. Later, he would return for Holly and bring her home and they'd stay up late, especially late if they didn't have to get up early in the morning for Mikey. On the Saturdays that Joanna didn't work, she kept him all day, taking him to the park or the shops; on those she did, James and Holly took him to Battersea Zoo or another children's attraction. Both Holly's and Joanna's work schedules were marked on a big calendar in the kitchen and Holly checked repeatedly to make sure she was on top of things.

James got to his feet again, catching her on her way to the door to hold her properly.

'No news then?' she asked.

'Nope.'

They both knew what this meant: three weeks after Alexa's dramatic visit to the Crystal Palace flat, she had still not told anyone that James had left her, which meant he was duty-bound to keep his silence too. This was proving particularly tricky at the office, not least for the extra line of communication it provided for Alexa. Though he could screen her calls to his mobile, he could not be so strict about his office line, especially as his assistant Sara was continuing to transfer Alexa's calls automatically as she always had in the past. 'Is it me or does Alexa sound more frazzled than ever?' she'd remarked, on one occasion. James couldn't believe she hadn't guessed the truth for herself.

'I've had an idea how I can get her to tell someone,' he said. 'I'll do it on Monday.' He was steadfast in his view that a clean break was kinder in the long run than a drawn-out process, with mediation, counselling and all the other things people would be sure to suggest once word was out. 'Then the guilt-trip will *really* start,' he added.

Holly's guilt had yet to make itself known. During their confrontation with Alexa, she'd felt only wary, in the way she might if a fox or an unknown cat had got into her house: she knew she was in no bodily danger but she would still have preferred it to go away again. Until that remark about her father, she had not even registered the other woman's insults, for they were only words she could have predicted to the last syllable, not even surface wounds.

She wondered if one day her guilt might come crashing through the walls with the force of a tsunami, tearing the limbs from their bodies, the hair from their heads.

If it did, she'd need to be ready for it.

Conscience troubled her mother more than it did her, Holly knew, and she wondered if this might be why Joanna was taking longer to get used to the new arrangement than she and James had hoped.

'I thought you liked it?' Holly asked, the first time Joanna visited after they'd moved in.

'It's a lovely place, yes. There's so much more space for Mikey, and a garden as well.' But her smile was pale, her eyes bruised with anxiety.

'What is it then? I know you'll miss us, Mum, but we'll be backwards and forwards so often you won't notice.' Having caused her mother anguish for so long, Holly yearned to bring her a measure of security and peace.

'I know. It's not that.'

'What then?'

Joanna turned to her with eyes hardly less fretful than those of the darkest past. 'Do you really have to ask? Of course I think it's wonderful to see you in a nice flat like this, in a regular job, it's all just what a mother would want for her daughter, but I just wish it didn't have to be a married man who's given it to you. I keep thinking about Alexa, how dreadful she looked. All of this is at her expense.'

'I know it must be awful for her,' Holly said, though the liquid joy that washed through her veins every waking moment meant she could not imagine 'awful' if her life depended on it. 'But marriages break up all the time, don't they? Men leave their wives, women leave their husbands.'

'Maybe with celebrities, but real people stick at it a bit longer. They don't meet someone one minute and decide just to end their marriage the next.'

This, Holly was learning, was going to be the hardest part to justify to others, or even to explain: not the union itself but the instantaneousness of it. For this reason she had not told any of her colleagues that James and she were brand new lovers, moving in together only weeks after meeting, but had simply let them assume he'd been her boyfriend since before she'd begun working with them.

'He stuck at it for five years,' she pointed out, 'ten if you include the time they were together but not married. He gave it a proper go.'

They were standing together at the living room window, raised high over the pavement, and watched as a driver struggled to park in a spot across the street. Holly thought of changing the subject by mentioning her driving lessons, but Joanna had never learned or come close to owning a car and she didn't want to sound as if she were flaunting her new advantages.

Joanna sighed. 'Oh, Holly, you know how pleased I am to see you so happy, but—'

'But?' Holly interrupted, half smiling. 'Which one now, Mum? The age gap? James getting too close to Mikey? Sean going AWOL?'

Joanna ignored her suggestions with a flicker of disapproval, making Holly see her own light-hearted response had been misjudged. 'I was going to say that it's almost as if you're *too* happy. It doesn't seem natural, it's like you're in a trance, a kind of dream world.'

'That's exactly what Alexa said about James,' Holly agreed, trying to neutralise the expression of delight she wore as a default these days. 'We know that's how it must look.'

'It does, and it really worries me. Where's the real-world perspective, Holly, where's the balance? All those issues you just mentioned, they *are* important, and there are plenty of others besides. Do you and James even discuss these things?'

'Of course we do. We discuss everything.' Holly wondered what Joanna wanted her to say, what the right explanation was to her ears. Of all people, her mother was the one she wanted to help understand what had occurred; everyone else, well, let them call James and her dreamers if they pleased. 'It's like . . . it's like how it must have felt when you met Adrian, maybe?'

Though she'd been a teenager when Adrian had entered her mother's life, less attuned to a parent's emotions than she might have been at another age, she could still recall the difference in her mother, the optimism that infused her body language as well as her spoken words, the magical sense of lift about the place. It had happened almost overnight.

But Joanna was shaking her head. 'I know how it is at the beginning of a relationship, of course I do, you're wrapped up in each other and that's totally natural. But even though I was happy to have met Adrian I always tried to be realistic. He *joined* my life, he didn't change it.'

Holly considered this. 'I suppose mine needed changing more,' she said.

There was a silence. Beside her, Joanna inhaled audibly, a sign that there was more to come.

'You know I'm sorry for what I said to her, don't you?' Her voice was quite different now, solemn and abashed. 'Alexa, I mean. I really didn't plan to tell her about our history, I was just trying to make her see your life hasn't always been easy.'

'It's OK,' Holly said. 'James knew anyway.'

'But if you hadn't told him yet, it might have been humiliating. I should have thought of that.'

'I didn't feel humiliated.'

'You seemed upset, though, at the time.'

'I was a bit,' Holly admitted. She risked a smile. 'So I'm not *always* in a dream world, then?'

Joanna conceded this with an apologetic nod.

It was true that while Holly had expected the fact of James being married to cause their relationship to come under unusual scrutiny, she had not bargained for a parallel to be drawn with her mother's early private life and for her own paternity to be of wider interest. *They haven't got a shred of common decency between them*, Alexa had said, and Holly had been insulted on Joanna's behalf rather than her own. Of course Alexa would think *she* didn't have a shred of decency, whoever her father was: *that* was fair. But Joanna had made sacrifices for Holly that Alexa could never appreciate; Joanna embodied the word 'decent'.

'I just didn't think it was anything to do with her, that's all. I don't need to know anything about *her* conception.'

She was aware of Joanna undergoing some sort of internal dilemma, choosing her next words with care. The matter of Holly's father was not something mother and daughter tended often to discuss, a state of affairs that owed less to awkwardness than to a sense that he was irrelevant to their day-to-day habits – past, present and future. But that had changed now. Now, whether Holly liked it or not, her history was going to be fair game.

'I know it's not the background you'd wish for for yourself,' Joanna said, at last, 'but I don't regret a single thing about it, I really don't. Otherwise . . .'

'I know,' Holly said, quietly. 'I don't regret any of it either.' She of all people could understand 'otherwise'. No Dan, no Holly; no Sean, no Mikey: that was the real parallel, the only one that mattered.

Guessing the direction of her thoughts, Joanna asked, 'Have you still not heard from Sean?'

'No, not yet.' She knew Sean had been picking up her messages because Geraldine had stopped by the shop to tell Joanna how concerned *she* was at the speed with which Holly had moved out. Meanwhile, he had not seen Mikey for over a month and though neither Holly nor Joanna had said so out loud, they both knew that his silence was a punishment. He would not have considered that Mikey might miss seeing him or be confused by his absence.

'You won't forget him, will you?' Joanna said, anxiously.

Holly couldn't help smiling. 'You used to say the best thing I could do was forget Sean.'

'I used to say all kinds of things,' Joanna said, sighing.

She couldn't remember the exact dialogue of that first disclosure of her paternity, but it must have been at about the time Joanna had explained the facts of life, so perhaps when Holly was about eight years old. Before that she'd thought a father's role was only a practical one, to do with teaching children to ride their first bike or taking them swimming on a rainy Sunday.

Other factors prompted her first more specific questions: the oddness of her relationship with her grandmother, for instance, the only grandparent she ever saw. Her friends at school saw so much of theirs; visits were weekly or monthly, on every birthday and at Christmas. Some even lived with a grandmother or were minded by one after school while their parents were at work. They found it weird that Holly had never been to hers for a sleepover, or to her house at all. When she explained that she only saw her grandmother for a tea party twice a year, a friend asked, 'Is your nan the Queen, then?'

'I need to tell you something about us that's a bit unusual,' her mother said after one such tea with the Queen.

Holly, who had been earning more responsibility lately, felt pleased to be included in something 'unusual'.

'The reason we don't see much of your grandma and grandpa is because your aunty, my sister Melissa, is very angry with me and they agree with her.'

'It's wrong to take sides,' Holly said.

'Yes, but they have a good reason. They can't forgive me for something I did when I was younger. They thought it was a very bad thing to do.'

'What was it?' Holly felt indignation at the very idea that her mother might be accused of any wrongdoing. In her eyes, Joanna was the principal defender against crime of any sort.

'Well, you know I told you a mummy needs a daddy to make a baby?'

'The egg and the seed,' Holly confirmed. 'The egg comes from the mum and the seed comes from the dad.' She had recently adjusted 'mummy' to 'mum' as an expression of her new maturity. Occasionally, for effect, she liked to call her mother by her Christian name.

'Well, the seed that made you came from Melissa's husband.'

Holly frowned, making the connections in her young mind. 'Is he my uncle then?'

'Yes, kind of. He and Melissa stopped being married almost straight away, but the man who would have been your uncle was also your father.'

'That's not possible.' Holly had met friends' uncles and she knew they were always a different man from the father.

But Joanna said it *was* possible. 'You see, a man can be a dad in more than one family.'

'Is he a dad in another family as well?'

'I don't know. Maybe. After us.'

'What's he called?'

'Dan Payne.'

'Where does he live?'

'I don't know, but Grandma might know if you ever decided you wanted to get in touch with him. When you're older, I mean.'

Holly frowned. 'Older' was a thousand years from now and a slightly frightening prospect.

Joanna gave her a little hug. 'I've always thought it would be best if you just have me. Because of all the unhappy people involved. This way we're on our own and it's nice and peaceful.'

'*We're* not unhappy,' Holly agreed.

'No, we're not unhappy.' Joanna smiled and her hug tightened into a squeeze that stole Holly's breath.

Holly called good night to Marcus and followed James into the street, clutching his hand as they hurried to the car. Rain had sweetened the air and cooled its temperature, making it feel as if the city had vaulted to autumn in the time she had worked her shift. She loved James picking her up from work. It reminded her of their first two meetings: the one when they'd kissed for the first time in a dark doorway near the restaurant, the next when they'd driven to the hotel in Chelsea Harbour and, during the course of several hours of conversation and sex, agreed that everything had changed.

'I have to leave her,' James had said, before they parted.

'You don't *have* to,' Holly said. 'I told you I don't mind.'

'I do, though. I'm not going to make this one of those long, drawn-out agonies. I'm going to do it right away and then we can get on with us.'

'OK.'

And from that moment neither questioned the wisdom of this agreement or the equality of their desire. They were as sure of it and as bedazzled by it as they would be the arrival of a space-ship at their feet: it was out of this world, yes, but it was plainly there and to be ignored at their peril. *It* had chosen *them*. And so here they were just a few weeks later, 'getting on with us'. This, so far, had during any time alone involved lying in bed listening to music or watching films, getting distracted by one another during all but the most gripping entertainment. Holly knew that if she *had* allowed herself to dream ahead that first time then this was what she would have dreamt: a prolonging of what they'd had that first night.

This evening was no exception. Though it was past midnight by the time they got home, they had the following morning free and so scrolled through the schedules for a film to watch. James, who liked old comedies and was enjoying introducing Holly to some of his favourite movies, wanted *What's New, Pussycat?* 'Have you seen it before? It's set in Paris. We should go back there together some time,' he added.

'I don't think I could *ever* go back to Paris,' Holly said, and James turned from the screen in surprise at the pale and tremulous sound of her. (She startled herself with it, for it was the voice of her depression, her lost self.)

'Really?'

She nodded, trying not to shudder. Though it was a warm night, she pulled the covers up over her arms and shoulders, pressing herself more closely against him.

'What, darling? I thought you'd come to terms with what happened?'

'Well, yes and no,' Holly admitted.

James looked stunned, as if confronted with a fundamental failure on his own part. 'Does it still worry you, Mikey's accident? I had no idea. I thought you saw Paris as the beginning of something fantastic.'

'I do. It was, it is.' Holly breathed heavily, her eyelids closed. There was a freckle by the lash line on her left one, James had told her. Sean had not noticed it, or, if he had, had not thought it worthy of remark; or maybe it was new, maybe she was growing new freckles because James liked them so much. 'I just don't want to think about what would have happened if you hadn't been there. I know it's pathetic, but seeing pictures of the river, anything to do with Paris, it makes me think those things. I can imagine him drowning like it really happened.'

James did not argue as he had in the past that if he had not saved Mikey someone else would. He knew Holly didn't believe that. Instead he said, 'But if you hadn't gone to Paris when you did and been on that boat, you wouldn't have met me, would you? Think of it that way. The accident was terrifying but our meeting each other was your silver lining.'

Holly said, 'Oh, I know that.'

Under the sheet, James ran a hand along the length of her naked body, slowing at the curve of her hip. 'So would you erase it if you could?'

'How do you mean, erase it?'

His other hand pushed her hair from her ear so he could kiss her lobe. 'If you could go back and wipe out Mikey's fall, even though it means wiping out meeting me?' She knew he enjoyed the neediness she had inspired in him. He said he found himself seeking reassurances from her in a way he never had before with women. He supposed it was because he knew he would get them from her, her devotion was unconditional: there was not the same risk of scorn he'd felt with Alexa.

'Yes,' she said, simply. 'I would, of course I would. I would never put Mikey through that again if I had the choice. Even if it meant not meeting you.' She gazed up at him with a protective concern, hating to hurt his feelings. 'But I would go on to meet you another way, don't worry.'

'Oh, but that's not how it works,' he teased. 'You only get

one chance. None of this would be.' He didn't mean the flat or their growing array of shared possessions, he meant their love: the way his fingers in her hair and his lips on her earlobes meant more than physical need. They had agreed it would be as powerful even if they didn't speak the same language.

Holly thought for a moment. 'It *would* be,' she said. 'We would get a special second go.'

Special: always, they returned to that word. What they had together was exceptional, a gift that was not available to everyone. So convinced were they of its rarity they had decided that when the world discovered them, when people wanted to know what it was all about, they wouldn't try to explain out of sheer kindness. For surely it would only dismay other couples to learn that *they* did not have this miraculous preciousness in *their* relationships.

It would be too cruel.

Holly touched her lips against his right shoulder blade. Though she'd worked a five-hour shift, she was not at all tired. 'Please can we not watch this film, James? Can we watch something else?'

He fumbled with the remote control and threw it out of reach. 'Let's not watch anything at all.'

Chapter 21

Four weeks and one day, Alexa thought.

Approaching the section of the office occupied by the Innovations team, she willed the corners of her mouth outwards and upwards, roughly approximating what her facial muscles remembered to be a smile. If babies could do it at six weeks old, she reasoned, then she could still manage it. After all, one could not innovate without the ability to smile.

'Morning, Alexa, you're looking very cheerful!'

'Morning, Rich, yes, I am.'

'She's only been married for five years,' Lucie drawled. 'Single figures, Rich. It makes all the difference, if you know what I'm saying.'

Taken aback by the comment, Alexa quickly remembered that it had been Rich's wedding anniversary at the weekend. At forty-eight, he was the oldest member of the team, and had been married for exactly nineteen years. Nineteen. That was *fourteen* more than she had managed. To think she had once privately pitied him for having reached his late forties without having risen any higher in the company than their shared current level; now, and forever on, she would only admire him.

'Thank you for reminding me, Luce.' Rich pulled a long-suffering face at Alexa and returned to sucking on the pomegranate and vanilla bean smoothie in his hand. Their new product was available to them in unregulated quantities but neither Alexa nor Lucie partook because of the calorie count. At least that was why Alexa hadn't taken her share in the past, for they looked and smelled delicious: these days she resisted because she had no appetite. Coffee was her only fuel and it might have been made of ground bark for all she cared; she would have smoked it in a pipe if necessary.

'Hi, Alexa, good weekend?'

'Hi, Josh, fine, thanks.' Another smile-shaped grimace; another fooled colleague. Once Alexa had had a soft spot for Josh, who was tall, gym-honed and eager to impress – back when she was a functioning female, back when she did not suffer an internal collapse at the mention of wedding anniversaries or marital sex or buying houses, back when she could look at these people and see colleagues and friends, not a set of strangers.

'Oh, she's totally gone to ground,' Lucie grumbled. 'That bloody house – we never see her any more.'

'Sorry.' Alexa felt her insides clench and release as she anticipated more detailed questioning from her friend. She looks like she's a different species from me, she thought, contemplating Lucie as if for the first time: she was shiny, energised, wanted, *loved*.

Whereas she, Alexa, was tarnished, enervated, unwanted, unloved. (She could no longer remember a time when she did not live with this torturous and damning interior narrative.)

'Ready, everyone?' Josh said. He and Lucie were already gathering iPhones and memo books for their weekly meeting with Paul.

'Let me just get a coffee,' Alexa said.

Four weeks and one day and still she had not told a soul that James had left her. Somehow, her impersonation of herself was succeeding; even Lucie was hoodwinked. She followed Alexa now into the kitchen to ask, 'Are we meeting at the gym at lunch?'

Alexa poured herself a mug of black coffee. 'I thought I might swim.'

'Again? You're really into it, aren't you? Thinking of doing a triathlon or something?'

'Hmm, maybe.' She'd swum most days since it happened. Sometimes, in the pool, she allowed herself to cry. It was inevitable, really, for it was the one public environment in which tears could be easily disguised; all that water loosened the ducts somehow. There was also the natural link with James: James the teenage swim champ, James the Great, whose amphibious talents had helped him conquer the currents of not one but two dangerous rivers!

It was almost funny that it had come to this: crying underwater, crying into a pair of goggles, *that* was the lunchtime treat she looked forward to – and even then she always scanned the water to make sure there was no one she knew among her fellow submerged. Lucie, for one, avoided the pool for the havoc it wrought on her blowdry.

Mostly, though, she waited until she got home before she wept. Then she might spend five hours continuously sobbing, extended episodes that could actually cause her to feel thirsty halfway through. She kept ice packs by her side to reduce the swelling, in the morning sitting with them pressed to her face as she drank her first cup of coffee and afterwards applying a thick moisturiser she'd chilled overnight in the fridge. (Even in her grief she had developed a strict grooming routine.)

Not that the ice packs and cold cream were working as well as she'd hoped. Lucie had not said anything about her appearance since Alexa had made a pre-emptive complaint about an allergic reaction to an expensive new anti-ageing mask, but apparently Becky on reception had told Rich she looked 'pillowy' and had asked Meg in IT if she'd been secretly having Botox 'or something'.

Or something.

*

She did not meet Lucie that lunchtime and she did not swim. She'd intended to, she really had, but somewhere in the street on her way to the pool she found herself scouring the oncoming traffic for yellow lights. Next thing she knew she was in the back of a taxi, instructing the driver: 'Crystal Palace, please.'

Three times over the last two weeks she had done this: trawled the cafés and restaurants of Crystal Palace and its environs to ask if they had a waitress working there called Holly – in the absence of any prospect of a forwarding address for her husband and his lover, it was all she could think of. For she had something she wanted to give to Holly Walsh, something she carried in her bag every day, perpetually aware of the shape and weight of it under her right arm.

She could not leave it at James's office, not trusting him to pass it on to the slut, and nor did she like to involve Joanna, either to plead with her for the new address or to ask her to deliver the package on her behalf. During their conversation at the flat, before the terrible showdown with James, she'd understood that for whatever reason Joanna actually appeared to care about her. She had not confided in Alexa about Holly's background *only* to clear Holly's name, but also to help ease Alexa's confusion, if not the pain. *It might make it easier*, she'd said; she had known without needing to ask that Alexa had isolated herself, and to know this she must once have done the same herself. Against all her desires, Alexa had felt a stirring of camaraderie with the mother of her nemesis.

But, in spite of this, she couldn't depend on Joanna, not on the strength of instinct. She had never trusted instinct and was not about to start now: it stood to reason that a mother's first concern would be for her own daughter. No, Alexa needed to know where to access Holly directly.

Since that meeting at the flat her loathing for the girl had grown to the extent that she now wished appalling, malicious things on her: death, ideally. Not wanting to land herself in

Holloway, however, she could not perpetrate these appalling, malicious things, nor encourage a third party to do so for her. All she could do was try to break the spell that bound the lovers to one another – the spell that she was convinced would be shattered one way or another – and her first attempt was to present them with evidence that the world had *not* begun the moment that stupid child had fallen into the Seine. No, there had been moments before it, moments that had been documented.

Delivered once more to the high street in Crystal Palace, she resumed her manhunt. In only the second place she tried, a brasserie nice enough for her to decide to stop for a coffee, she struck lucky (or whatever adjective applied in this context to the categorically *un*lucky). A morose-looking girl came to take her order and Alexa asked for a black coffee, her fifth of the day.

'Before you go, is there a waitress here called Holly Walsh, do you know?'

'Yeah,' the girl said, 'I *think* that's her second name.'

Taken aback by her success (again, not quite the right word), Alexa managed to gulp a reply. 'Can I see her, please? Is she here?'

'She's not working today. She just does Friday and Saturday nights.'

Just two evenings – she was lazier than Alexa had thought.

It was Monday: unthinkable that she should have to wait till Friday when she was at last so close. In any case, she saw now that she could not confront Holly in a restaurant full of customers who, judging by the feasting mob around her, might prefer her to be doing their bidding rather than engaging in a contretemps with some scorned wife. Coaxing her address out of the girl was a much better idea.

When she returned with the coffee, the miserable girl said, 'Was you looking for Holly for any particular reason?'

Alexa pounced. 'Yes, actually. I have something she needs for her new flat. I would bring it here, but it's too big, she'd only have to lug it home. Could you remind me of her address and I'll have it delivered?'

'Didn't know she'd moved,' the girl said with mild resentment. Alexa was getting the pleasing feeling that this hopeless creature was not an admirer of Holly.

'Would anyone else know, do you think?'

'You a mate of hers?'

'A friend of a friend, but, as I say, I've got this thing.'

Alexa feared her lie was becoming less persuasive, but the waitress didn't seem to mind, volunteering, 'Staff details are on file in the manager's office, so I suppose I could have a quick look.'

Alexa fixed her with her most imploring gaze, hoping her bloodshot eyes were not too dreadful a disincentive. 'It would be *incredibly* useful if you could,' she said, in mimicry of her old charm.

The girl trotted obediently off. If it weren't for the fact of James having left her practically destitute, Alexa would have left her the biggest tip of her working life.

The street was only ten minutes away and she asked the minicab driver to wait while she posted something through the door. It was a busy road and a little rundown, but the bones of the house were attractive enough, the lower windows quite grand, not unlike those of their (*her*) own home. At the door she drew from her bag the fat envelope marked 'Holly Walsh' and began to wedge it through the letterbox. It was only in posting it, in touching a part of the house itself, that the smallness of the act struck her. James and Holly lived together now: the enchantment that held them was powerful, too powerful to be broken by this. She was going to need a strategy much larger and more incendiary.

She cried on the way back to the office. Four weeks and one

day: all at once it was a unit of substantial mass, a number to be reckoned with. This really was happening to her. Maybe, maybe it had even reached the point where it had *already happened*. She was actually in its aftermath.

She wished she could go swimming, after all, before returning to her desk and the charade of a long afternoon devoted to smoothies; she longed for the merciful touch of cool, chlorinated water on her inflamed skin, but she'd been out of the office for almost two hours and any longer than that would be noted. After repairing her face in the bathroom, she somehow managed a meeting with Rich and their external events planner before heading to the kitchen and placing her hot cheek on the cold stainless steel-coated fridge. Her cheek muscles were pulsing under her make-up; she hoped the swelling wouldn't start up again. She needed to find some sort of balm that would suppress the inflammation during the day, when she didn't have her ice packs to hand. She'd look online and see if there was a condition she could pass herself off as having, a virus perhaps – anything but what it was: heartbreak, its potentially fatal form.

'Lex?' In the doorway, Lucie appeared, face sorrowful. She had some bad news, Alexa could tell, but she didn't think she could handle someone else's drama, not right now. The problem was she had neither the energy nor the imagination to make her excuses fast enough to get past her friend and back to her desk.

'Oh, Lex,' Lucie said, 'I've just come off the phone with James.'

'James?' Alexa looked up, wondering if the new tickling sensation on her cheek was an insect. She swiped listlessly at it and felt moisture.

Lucie came towards her and placed gentle arms around her. 'He asked me if you were OK. He couldn't understand when I said you were fine, why wouldn't you be? Oh, Alexa, he told me he's left. He said it was weeks ago!'

'Four weeks. It was four weeks ago.' Four weeks in which

she had felt more misery than she'd imagined a human being could endure in a whole lifetime, and which showed no signs of abating, only intensifying. How long could pain like this last? Was there any point in remaining to find out?

'When were you going to tell us?' Lucie asked, still holding her. It was strange seeing her normally capricious blue eyes filled with pure tenderness.

'When I couldn't pretend any more,' Alexa said, weakly.

'But we could have helped you, darling. Shona and me. All of us.'

'No one can help me, no one,' Alexa replied, and surrendering to the bodily warmth of her closest friend she began once again to sob.

Chapter 22

Holly was almost five months old by the time her father paid her a visit. Had it been a few months later, by which time Joanna had met Suze and one or two other new friends, she might not have been so lonely, so quick to crumble. As it was, visitors were so scarce that she started when the intercom buzzed, its pitch and volume unfamiliar and intrusive. It was six-thirty in the evening: definitely not the postman or anything to do with reading her gas meter.

'Who is it?' She held the plastic intercom instrument gingerly, as if the person downstairs might come through the cable and spring out of it.

'It's Dan.'

In the thirty seconds it took him to reach her door, her heartbeat had become so forceful she feared her ribcage was going to crack open. And then there he was, looking almost the same, just a little more shadowed, the signs of indulgence starting to show in his jaw and waistline. The look in his eyes was sheepish, as if his crimes were only petty, late for dinner, perhaps, or with the return of something borrowed.

'What are you doing here?' she whispered.

'I was down here anyway . . .' It didn't sound as graceless as

305

it might have done; it just sounded like Dan. He had always been a creature of convenience.

She ushered him into the living room. 'You're working in London?'

'No.' Stupid question, Joanna thought. Dan didn't *do* work. 'Sorry just to turn up, but I didn't have a number for you.'

'How did you find out where we're living?'

'Lynn told me.'

'Mum.' There wasn't time to examine her mother's intentions. Perhaps it was a small attempt to make amends for everything else Joanna had been denied or perhaps it was the straightforward belief that every father should have the chance to meet his child, no matter what the circumstances of its conception.

'So this is where you've been hiding,' Dan said. '*London.* Fuck.'

She ignored the remark. *Hiding*? If that was what you called exile, yes. She preferred to call it making a new life. She watched as he glanced about the room, with its outdated galley kitchen and double glazed windows; thanks to these the traffic on the South Circular was a hum rather than a drone and she'd grown to like it, for it was company of sorts. The place was neat enough: she was not naturally tidy but had become so, having found that disorder worsened her spirits. 'Holly's asleep in the bedroom. Would you like to see her?'

He nodded, wordless.

The baby was completely still, as she always was when claimed by sleep, her face dominated by twin feathery crescents of eyelashes. She had a tiny nose, sharp little ears and the softest coating of hair; she looked in the half-light as much a mysterious woodland infant as a human baby.

'Gorgeous, isn't she?' Joanna's voice caught in her throat.

Still Dan didn't speak. He reached a hand into the cot as if to touch Holly's face but halted when his fingers were an inch or two away, as if he'd lost his nerve mid-impulse.

Next door, he recovered a little. 'Have you got anything to drink?'

'Sorry, yes, would you like a cup of tea?'

'Nothing stronger?'

'No, but there's a pub by the station. Go down there if you need alcohol.' She was thrilled by her own rudeness.

'Shall I just nip out and get a bottle of wine? Then we can both have one.'

Joanna frowned at him. 'Dan, where are you staying tonight?'

'I was going to go back on the train.'

'Back where? Where do you live now? I know you left the flat in Manchester.'

'I moved to Birmingham, near my brother's family.'

She was grateful for the lack of detail: a street name, even a neighbourhood, allowed options she did not want access to. 'There's an off-licence on Norwood Road,' she said. 'Turn left out of here and then right at the lights.'

While he was gone she gazed at herself in the bathroom mirror, unable to reconcile the girl she saw in front of her with the one she'd been when Holly was conceived. She was young enough to have avoided most of the ravages of sleeplessness, but there was something tangibly aged in her, nonetheless: she no longer had the face of someone with her life ahead of her; she had the face of someone to whom life was already happening, and with a vengeance.

She must have been staring at the stranger's face for several minutes because she jumped a second time at the sound of the buzzer.

Dan re-entered at speed bearing two bottles of wine and headed straight to the kitchen cupboards to find glasses. 'Mission accomplished.'

It was a long time since she'd had alcohol, over a year, and the sensation of it reaching her bloodstream was shockingly good. It didn't just smooth the edges, it made her forget the edges had ever been there.

It was the same for him, it seemed, for after only a gulp or two he abandoned previous awkwardness and said, 'I was out of order that day at the flat, Jo. I'm sorry.'

'So you should be. And it's taken you long enough to say it.' As with other indignities she'd suffered in her young life, the apology ceased to hold any power the moment it was uttered. There was no satisfaction, nothing to savour. 'How could you say I was lying?'

As Dan's eyes widened she saw in them a bid for some misplaced sense of honour. She remembered how he'd refused to look at her that day; even before Melissa's arrival, his eyes had been sullen and reluctant. 'To avoid this mess, obviously,' he said.

'It's not a mess as far as I'm concerned,' Joanna said.

'You can't believe that.'

'I have to believe it, and I do.'

Dan had already emptied his wine glass and was reaching for the bottle to pour himself another. Joanna saw now why he had bought two.

'I suppose it didn't help that I told her about the hen night,' she said, presently.

Dan gave a mirthless chuckle. 'It didn't make any difference. She would have been just as mental about it if it had happened before she even met me – if I'd met you first.'

'You do see, then,' Joanna said, 'how she was about me? Even before she found out about us?'

'Yeah, I see. It's weird.'

'Weird is the word.'

Dan sighed. She knew he was thinking that there didn't have to be this drama. Why had confessions been made, threats issued, lives disrupted, when it could all have been avoided? So far in this meeting he'd done little but remind her of his fatal, central easiness, his willingness to fall in with whatever others suggested, the riskier, more hare-brained, the better. She supposed that without it she would not have had even the half-chance with him she'd had.

'They shouldn't have thrown you out like that,' he said, 'Lynn and Gordon. I know Melissa's got them thinking she's going to top herself if they have anything to do with you, but it's not right.'

'She's already tried,' Joanna said. 'Did you not know?'

'What?'

'She slit her wrists.' She almost added, *I saw her blood*, but she stopped herself. She'd been a trespasser that afternoon, she'd shared what she shouldn't have. 'She's all right, though,' she told Dan. 'Don't worry, you haven't got a suicide on your conscience on top of everything else.'

He didn't answer, but the blue gaze tapered, his grip on that moral code weakening.

'Anyway, I deserved to be chucked out,' Joanna said, without self-pity. 'I betrayed her, them, everyone.' Herself. She sipped the wine, allowed him to pour her a second glass with his third. 'Dan, do your parents know you have a child?' Sometimes, in her isolation, she forgot how many people there were who might have given her and Holly more than a passing thought. There was a whole extended family out there: she'd met his parents and brother at the wedding and, if she remembered, he still had grandparents living.

'Yep, they know. Mum thinks I should persuade you to let me stand by you.'

'I don't want you to stand by me. I'm happy to be independent. It's the best way.' Pride could get in the way, she knew that from all the plays and novels she'd read at school, but in this situation it was a source of strength. Holly was her family now and she was prepared to accept that their family might never increase beyond the two of them.

Dan looked neither crestfallen nor relieved by her words. 'You know we're getting a divorce, Melissa and me? There's no chance we'll ever get back together.'

However bland and noncommittal his eyes, there was a quality to his voice that made her see an offer was being made, a suggestion, and not the same one championed by his mother. *It doesn't matter what we do now because it could never have the same fallout, the same meaning*, and this she could agree on.

It would have been easy to blame the alcohol, but it was loneliness that exacted the greater force in launching her towards him and inviting him to kiss her. He responded instantly, unmindfully, just as he had every time before. Sleeping with him again was pleasurable in the obvious ways but what she gained most from it was reconnection with her own body, a reminder that it had a heat of its own, for itself, and not only as a giver of life to others.

The next morning, as she made tea after feeding and changing Holly, he said: 'You don't seem as young now.'

'Well, I'm not, am I?'

'No.' He was gathering his things. She'd noticed that he still had not touched his daughter, who lay on her back on the rug, kicking her legs and making those excited cries and exclamations that would soon become first words. 'I have to go back now.'

'Of course. Have you got a job?'

'Yeah, just something in a pub.' He paused. 'I'll come back again when I've got a break, shall I?'

Joanna handed him a page torn from a notepad. 'If you want to see Holly . . . well, here's my phone number. If you could call me first and give me a bit of warning next time.'

And he looked hard at her, understanding.

When her next period came she had never been more grateful in her life for having insisted on contraception; she was more grateful than she would have been if it had come the first time.

It was easy to stop yourself imagining a child who had not yet grown inside you, but it was impossible to wish away one who was already here.

It had jolted Joanna to hear that Holly had told James about Dan. Though Holly had accepted her apology for sharing the facts with Alexa, Joanna couldn't help fearing that her daughter might withdraw a little from her. Or perhaps that was simply the natural fear of her having moved away from home, of falling in love, for this, Joanna at last conceded, was what had happened to Holly: love. *We discuss everything*, Holly had said about James, but the look of romantic intoxication on her face made Joanna doubt her daughter's definition of 'everything'. She wondered if it included the full extent of her depression; after all, she had not yet to Joanna's knowledge been officially signed off her medication by her doctor, and nor had she consulted any professional about the emotional sea change she'd undergone. Would it be meddling to catch James on his own for five minutes and reassure herself that he at least understood that his new lover might still be fragile?

If so, she didn't think she could stop herself, not yet, not while Mikey still looked at her with that heart-breaking expression of unalloyed faith.

Getting James alone was no mean feat, given how inseparable he and Holly were and how rigid Joanna's own working hours. In the end, she had to rely on luck: visiting one evening at about eight o'clock, she found Holly had popped to the supermarket for Calpol because Mikey had a cough that was keeping him awake. Knowing she'd be back at any moment, Joanna cut short James's small talk to seize her opportunity.

'I'm glad I caught you on your own,' she began.

'Oh, yes?' Immediately she had his full attention. It was impossible not to respond with warmth to that directness of his, that readiness. He gave every impression of being able to listen to a problem and to make a decision about it on the spot, and to stand by it as well – not one of Joanna's own strengths, God knew.

'I wanted to ask you if Holly's told you much about how things were before you met?'

James did not blink. 'You mean the whole falling out with your family?'

'No, not that.' Joanna was unprepared for this to be the first possibility that sprang to mind for him. Had Holly told him the whole twenty-plus-year tragedy of it? 'I mean the postnatal depression.'

His eyes softened. 'Oh. Yes, she told me about that the first time we met.'

'Really?'

'Yes, she said you were in Paris to cheer her up.'

'We were.' Joanna was visited then by a powerful compound of emotions from that same weekend: the naïve hope that Holly might improve; the despair when she realised she would not; the stark terror of Mikey's accident and the scarcely less painful exhilaration of his survival; the bewilderment and disquiet of travelling home with a different daughter from the one she'd arrived with.

'It sounds like she had a terrible time with it,' James said.

'She did. It only got better very recently, you see.'

'After the accident.'

'That seems to have been the catalyst, yes, but it can take a long time to get over a condition like the one she had. We shouldn't just assume she's fully recovered.'

'No, but she's weaned herself off the antidepressants,' James said.

That answered one question, at least. 'Against advice, at least as far as I'm aware,' Joanna said, carefully.

He nodded, in acknowledgement of her ignorance, she soon saw, rather than her opinion. 'Actually, we spoke to my doctor and he said the reductions were gradual enough to be safe. He's written to Holly's GP about it. I promise I'll keep an eye on things, though, Joanna, I know you must be worried.'

'Thank you.' She was grateful that James did not cite the magical properties of his and Holly's love as the only medicine Holly should ever need; she was never going to be convinced that this was a miracle healing, but a succession of steps in an unpredictable process.

'She didn't have anything like that before having Mikey, did she?' James asked.

'No, she was a really happy child, quite an easy teenager, actually.' Hard not to underline the fact that Holly was so recently a child, that she had moved from adolescence to motherhood with precious little in between. 'It all happened after the birth, when things went wrong with Sean. Neither of them bonded with Mikey, and Holly had put on a lot of weight, which she was self-conscious about, I think, because Sean was so insensitive about it. It was all connected and became overwhelming for her.'

'What an idiot,' James said. 'She's perfect.'

Joanna agreed on both counts, but before she could reply James had caught her off guard a second time by asking, 'Is her father susceptible to depression, do you know?'

'I don't,' she said, uneasily. 'He certainly wasn't depressed when I knew him. He liked a drink, I suppose.' She hated how tawdry it all must seem to the handsome, well-educated James: a teenage pregnancy from an adulterous affair; a father who'd lost touch the day after he'd made contact in the first place; a sister whose nervous breakdown had never been repaired; parents who'd all but disowned her.

Sure enough, James's mouth was twisting in distaste. 'I see why she wouldn't seek him out, but why wouldn't he want to make contact with her? She's his own flesh and blood? To not even want to see photos! If that were me . . .'

Joanna listened patiently: after all, these were questions anyone would ask, questions that Suze and Adrian had asked long before James had. What she had not told the others, what she did not tell James now, was how often she'd thought of that last goodbye between Dan and her, of how one small alteration then might have made vast differences to Holly's childhood. If they hadn't fallen into bed together, if their shared need had been reconfigured as something other than a repeat of past crimes, *would* he have visited again, as he'd said he would? If, in the morning, she'd agreed a second date then and there, written the details down for him alongside the number? If she'd made him pick Holly up, stroke her little head, if that last physical touch had been with his daughter, not with her?

'It's not you, though,' she told James, 'it's him. There are plenty of men out there who lose all contact with their children, more than you'd imagine. And remember, it was a different era.'

'Not that different,' James said.

'I think it's hard to be sure what you'd do in the same situation,' she said, not knowing if she was defending Dan or herself. 'If you're not there at the beginning of a child's life, maybe there's just not the same pull later.'

James gave this only a moment's consideration before asking, 'What's Sean's excuse?'

But to this Joanna had no reply.

314

Chapter 23

'Very nice to meet you . . .' Andrew Connelly's eyes grazed Holly's figure in exactly the way many of her male customers did at the restaurant by the time a second bottle of wine had been served: as if she herself were edible. She knew he'd forgotten her name already.

She smiled with as much composure as she could muster. This was it: her first exposure to the outside world, to James's world, and she knew that it was as safe an introduction as he'd been able to arrange, for Andrew was a friend who neither lived in London nor knew Alexa especially well.

'Think of it as our soft launch,' James had told her. 'Not family, not someone we'll see all the time, but someone from *before*.'

Inevitably, this made Holly think of another phrase: *He* was *happy before* . . . Perhaps James was even subconsciously echoing it. After all, of the many 'someone's it could have been, Andrew was the only one who'd been in Paris.

Earlier in the week, on Monday afternoon, she had returned from the park with Mikey to discover that a package of photographs had been delivered to their flat by Alexa. Hand-delivered: that in itself was unsettling. Holly supposed it had been naïve to think that in concealing their new address from her they would also prevent her from discovering it of her own accord. All the pictures were from the Paris weekend, the portion of the weekend before James's and Alexa's path had crossed that of the Walshes, and had been piled in chronological order. The first was a shot of the couple standing beside a sculpture of a man and woman kissing (Rodin, James said when he saw it, admiring the art as if he and his wife were not in the picture with it), and was followed by a dozen or so taken at other museums, parks or cafés. In the café shots, both wore designer sunglasses, held flutes of champagne or tiny espresso cups, and smiled wide white smiles. In these images they looked handsome, well-heeled and pleased with themselves – it seemed to Holly they were like advertisements for money – and they caused no particular anxiety in her.

That had set in only when she reached the last handful, the ones that had been taken on the Saturday boat trip. There were two of James and Alexa sitting side by side in their wooden recliners, her slender legs crossed daintily at the knee and her hands on her lap, his limbs stretched haphazardly out of frame as if making himself comfortable for a snooze; and two more of him alone in close-up, his expression content and indulgent, half a smile for the camera, for his wife. Background figures holding phones and cameras to the riverbank suggested the tour was underway, which meant the pictures must have been taken just minutes before Mikey fell, before James jumped. The realisation of this as she contemplated his sleepy, unconcerned expression awakened something dark and private in Holly, an emotion she had not felt before and could not identify: it was not terror or guilt, though it held intimations of both, but something very specific, a knowledge of some sort, a secret from herself. If you laid her mind flat, all thoughts linear, it would be there in plain sight, but coiled and folded as minds were it was out of reach.

Alexa's accompanying note did nothing to subdue the sensation:

316

To Holly,
He was happy before and one day he'll wake up and remember.
Just you wait.
Your lover's wife, Alexa.

'What's she trying to do?' she asked James when she showed him the photos that evening. 'Is it some sort of threat?'

But he dismissed the despatch at face value. 'She's trying to make me admit that she and I were happy, as happy as you and I are now. She thinks this proves her theory that I've lost my mind. The way she sees it, if I don't love her it must be because I'm insane. Next time it will be wedding photos or presents I've given her, probably destroyed. This is standard stuff, Holls. It's quite civilised compared to some of the stuff I've heard about.'

'Why send them to me, then? Why not to you?'

'Because she's guessing it will be easier to get under your skin than mine. Don't let her.' And he had removed the photos, urging her to do as he intended and cast them from her mind. Nevertheless, it was the next day that he proposed their meeting with Andrew, who had phoned to say he'd be near James's office for a meeting on Thursday afternoon and did James fancy a quick beer after work?

'I told him I'm bringing someone,' James said.

'You didn't want to warn him on the phone?' Holly asked.

'No. The whole point is to see what the reaction is. In the raw.'

'He might already have heard. Now you've told Alexa's friend, they might all know. Maybe that's why he phoned you?'

'No, it's a coincidence. He wouldn't have called if he'd already heard,' James said. 'He wouldn't have been allowed.'

Meeting James in a bar full of rich men in suits, Holly felt a momentary loss of confidence, a fear that he would be a different person here than at home, that he might disguise or deny his new feelings in an environment where the old had reigned for so long. But he did not. He kissed her openly and sat touching distance from her while they waited.

When he arrived, Andrew was not what Holly had imagined: short and round-bellied, with thinning fair hair, like a middle-aged infant. James shook his hand with enthusiasm. 'Andrew, I want to introduce you to Holly Walsh.'

And so the eyes grazed, the name went in one ear and out the other; she could see he assumed she was a young associate of James's brought along for decoration, no one of significance. Already she had decided to be a spectator rather than a participant in this conversation. She felt as if she were passing herself off as a duchess, knowing it was only a matter of time before she made the fateful gaffe.

'How's Frances?' James asked when they'd all settled with their drinks. How Holly admired his affability. He seemed utterly nerveless. She didn't think there could be a man or woman alive who he could not relax with and start a conversation.

'She's well. Actually, she's been trying to get in touch with your other half but I don't think she's had much luck yet.'

Holly held her breath, as if not exhaling would render her invisible. Not knowing Andrew, there was a disembodied fascination in having the power to surprise him like this.

'How is the lovely Alexa?' he continued, and Holly sensed James reminding himself of the purpose of this meeting (how could he be so relaxed that he was able to *forget* it?).

'Actually, to tell you the truth, Andrew, we're not together any more. We split up a few weeks ago.'

'What?' Andrew spluttered into his pint and flushed in shock. He stared at James as if he'd told him the Thames had drained overnight. 'What the hell happened? Weren't you just celebrating your anniversary?'

'Yes, we were.' James's composure did not waver. 'But I met someone else. I'm with Holly now.'

'Holly? Who's Holly?' Andrew began, before following James's easy gesture her way and recovering himself. 'Of course, I didn't take in the name. Well. OK. Fucking hell, mate.'

James laughed good-naturedly at this.

'You know each other from work then?' Andrew's eyes swivelled between them, his expression resetting itself. It was peculiar to Holly to see her own value increase before her eyes in another human face.

'No, nothing like that. You remember the little boy who fell in the river?'

'The one you saved? Who could forget? You're famous in Henley, you may like to know. Frances has practically been taking bookings for you.'

James looked amused. 'Well, that's how I met Holly.'

'I'm Mikey's mother,' Holly said, speaking for the first time.

Andrew frowned afresh as he struggled to bring to mind the details of the drama. Watching him, Holly experienced a brief, bemusing glimpse of consciousness outside herself, of life being lived at an ordinary pace and without miracles. 'Right, sorry, Mikey was the little boy. Jesus, this isn't what I was expecting *at all*.'

'It isn't what we were expecting either,' James agreed.

'I'm going to get a glass of water,' Holly said. Nerves had caused her to drink her wine too quickly and she didn't think she ought to have another.

At the bar, unable to attract the staff's attention, she realised she could still hear the conversation at their table and could apparently do nothing to stop herself from listening.

'Early twenties,' she heard James say, having obviously been asked his new lover's age.

'Bit of a difference, then.' Andrew inhaled so rapidly he almost whistled. 'So how did it happen?'

'I don't know, to be honest. It was like an act of God or something.'

'She's not . . . ?'

'No, she's not.'

'Right. Just thought I'd ask. No offence.'

'Sure.'

There was a pause, then: 'How has Alexa been about it?'

'She's very upset,' James said. 'I'm the bad guy. But I expected that because I *am* the bad guy.'

'You can say that again.'

This was how it was going to be from now on, Holly thought. They'd had their calm, their lovely calm, during which they'd built their nest and made love in it and kept the outside world at bay, and now they had to face the elements. From now on, they were going to have to submit themselves to invasive questioning, not just by James's family and close friends, but by old acquaintances like Andrew, by anyone who fancied asking. James seemed to know naturally how to form the answers, but she felt clumsy, at a loss for the right words. If it was down to her it would just be James and Mikey and her alone forever – and Joanna, of course. Joanna's questions, she knew, were asked for no other reason than motherly – and grandmotherly – protection.

In the taxi going home, James said, 'Well, that was OK, I thought. It could have been a lot worse.'

'Yes, that's true.' There was a pause. 'I heard him ask you my age?'

'They all will,' James said. 'We don't care about that, though, do we? It's not like it's *that* unusual. Half the men in my office are with younger women.'

'*I* don't care about it,' Holly agreed. Mismatched though they were in material wealth, the age gap was of little concern to her. She'd meant what she'd said to her mother about not minding if the difference were a hundred and ten years, just as she'd meant it when she told James she felt closer to ancient than to young. She was a parent, she was the survivor of a disabling illness, she'd experienced the darkest despair and the brightest joy: calculating her life in calendar years was of no relevance to anything.

'You know he also asked me if you were pregnant?' James said.

She nodded. 'I don't suppose he'll be the only one to do that either. It would explain the suddenness, wouldn't it? Everyone will think the same.' She remembered those comments of Alexa's – *You know her mother did the same, don't you? . . . That's who* her *father is* – and wished she could dismiss them as easily as could James.

'Let them think it,' James said, on cue. 'It's none of their business.'

Holly closed her eyes, enjoying the particular peacefulness of it being just the two of them, to be at James's side and speeding towards Mikey and their beautiful new flat with the holly tree outside Mikey's bedroom window. There would always be people who *didn't* want to make it their business, she thought, like the people at Mikey's swimming class. Having listened to Holly's stories of her difficulties in booking lessons at her local leisure centre, James had found a private sports club with a teaching pool and signed Mikey up. In the first session Mikey behaved exactly the same way as the others: the same shrieking excitement, the same wriggling lack of cooperation, the same exaggerated shivering the moment he was set on the side of the pool in a hall centrally heated even in summer. Twelve normal toddlers, twelve smiling parents. In the stands, James chatted with the other men, just like any father.

It was fun that no one knew, Holly thought. They didn't know a single thing about the accident in Paris or about her and James's short scandalous history.

To her right, James began murmuring, 'It made me realise, though . . .' and then he stopped.

'What?' She could hear him breathing close to her ear, a little more rapidly than usual.

'I *want* you to be pregnant.'

'*What*?' Holly opened her eyes again. Beyond him, through the window, an ugly housing estate reared into sight, a grey concrete tidal wave solidified just as it crested. It was a drearier backdrop than that of her own upbringing but, still, the two resembled one another better than either did her new home with James, her new life.

'In the future, I mean,' he continued. 'When the time's right. I want you to have my child and for us to be parents together.'

Holly met his gaze. His face held the same certainty she was used to seeing in it, a reinforced, super-strength certainty, a belief that it was all pre-destined. 'You're very impulsive,' she said, finally.

'Not impulsive, instinctive. That's the best way to live. I thought we agreed on that?'

'Not with babies,' she said firmly. 'I already have one and I need to concentrate on giving him what he missed when I was ill.'

'So you're against the idea long-term?' This was new: until now they'd thought their desires were interchangeable, perfectly meshed both in essence and detail.

'It's not that. It's the depression, James. What if it happened again? I don't think I could live through that a second time.'

'We'd get advice about that,' James said. 'We'll take you to the best specialists.'

'I've seen specialists,' Holly said, though she supposed the ones in her local health centre were different from the ones James had access to, like the doctor they'd consulted about her withdrawal from her prescription drugs. It had been the only time in Holly's life that a meeting with a doctor had taken place at precisely the appointed time.

James bowed his face to kiss her. 'Listen, if there's a strong chance it will happen again then we won't do it. But if we were given the all-clear . . . ?'

Holly didn't know what to say. With her magical new out-look, the one that reflected James's so exactly, everything was possible, life had a permanent 'all-clear'. As their taxi left the down-at-heel neighbourhood for one of more affluent Victorian streets, she remembered what Andrew had been saying just before she returned to their table. He'd turned to James and shaken his head and said, 'Frances won't like this. You were her big hero.'

And Holly had divined more in his words than he had likely intended: that he spoke for all women, not just his wife. She was not the only one for whom James was a hero. The enormity of what he'd sacrificed for her was humbling; she couldn't expect him to give up any expectation of children of his own. She remembered her vow in the hotel in Paris: *I'll do anything*.

She faced him, gripped his hand. 'If there's not a huge risk of PND, then I'm not against the idea of a baby, not if you're for it. But I think you need . . . what did you call it, that time before you got in touch with me, when you made yourself wait?'

'A cooling-off period?'

'That's it. You need a cooling-off period. See if you still feel the same way in six months or a year and, if you do, then we can think about trying.'

James was happy enough with that. 'All right,' he said, kiss-ing her two hands in turn. 'It's a deal.'

Holly sank into his shoulder, shuddering to think what Joanna, Alexa and all the other women out there would say to this development.

'Frances won't like this,' Andrew had said. 'Frances won't like this *at all*.'

With James's encouragement, Holly made an appointment to take a tour of the nursery school that had opened recently at the end of their road. It was in a pretty white villa on the corner, with potted flowers in the front garden and a huge play area at the rear, partly shaded, with swings and see-saws and a collection of pedal cars and scooters.

'If you could let me know either way by the end of the week,' the head teacher told her. 'The place is free at the moment, but it won't be for long.'

'Of course,' Holly said. Even within the cosy swaddling of good fortune she was becoming used to, she knew how lucky she was to move to an area with a brand new nursery: all of her and Joanna's previous enquiries had yielded the same reports of year-long waiting lists and Friday-afternoon-only offers.

It was close to collection time when she was leaving and the local mothers were arriving to pick up their charges. Holly knew they must think she was a nanny or an au pair, for she was much too young to be one of them. They would probably be more likely to accept Joanna as Mikey's mother. Still, it was just a question of patience. She was not a bad person, she'd made friends at the restaurant and she hoped she might make one or two here too.

'How did it go?' James asked that evening, after they'd put Mikey to bed and begun on a glass of wine. Sitting at either end of the sofa, they faced each other, legs entwined.

'It was really lovely, especially the play area. They have nice organic lunches and snacks and the staff are so friendly.' Holly savoured her wine, resting her head on a cushion and closing her eyes briefly. After a frenetic twelve hours with Mikey, this was one of her favourite parts of the day. 'It's very expensive, though. The three morning sessions she offered me would be as much as I earn in my two shifts at the restaurant, which seems crazy.'

James looked surprised. 'You know you don't have to worry about money.'

'I do, though.' Holly wrinkled her brow. 'The whole point is that I want to become more independent, not just change the person I'm dependent on.'

This aspect of their union had not been examined before in any detail, partly because everything had happened so quickly. James had paid for the flat and its new contents; when they went out for dinner he settled the bill automatically, usually before she'd even noticed it had arrived; he always had cash for taxis and anything else they needed when they were out as a three: he gave instantly, without discussion – until now.

'There's a difference though,' he told her. 'It's natural to leave home and become independent of your parents, everyone has to do that. But I'm your partner. You share my income and I share yours.'

'But if I take the nursery place there'll be nothing for me to share with you.' Holly prodded him with her bare feet, waggled her toes against his hipbones and James captured her by the ankles. 'Listen, this is the least of our worries, believe me. I inherited quite a bit from my grandfather a few years ago. Most of it's in the house in Chiswick, of course, but we'll get that back at some point.' He and Alexa would have to sell the house, this Holly *did* know; when he'd met with his solicitor a few days earlier it was the first thing she'd advised. Alexa had no hope of buying him out and he would not rub salt in her wounds by trying to acquire her half.

'I still feel bad,' Holly said.

'Do you?' He swung her legs off his lap and coaxed her out of her comfy corner and into his lap. Soon his hands were inside her top. 'Do you feel bad? How bad?'

She giggled. 'A *bit* bad.'

A little later, they continued the conversation. 'Tell me more about the nursery – did Mikey like it as well?'

'Oh, James, he loved it. They just seemed to have ways of getting him interested, he completely forgot I was there. They have so many great toys and they even teach the kids French. When we were there they were saying the different food words, it was so sweet. Mikey can't even speak English yet!' But even as she chuckled she felt a note of unease, a finger plucking at a string in her stomach. The idea of Mikey learning French made her think of phrases like, *Il y a une personne à l'eau en Seine*. 'Actually, I think Spanish would be more useful.'

Given the debate about new activities for Mikey that followed, she thought he'd missed that comment, but James was too attuned to her for that. 'You know what? I think we ought to go back to Paris soon. Get this whole thing out of your system.'

A second pluck of disquiet inside her: this one more forceful. 'What whole thing?'

'This fear you're developing. You should see the expression on your face, you look haunted. And look how rattled you were by those stupid photos.'

'They weren't stupid,' Holly said. She recalled the unnamed agitation that had engulfed her as she'd studied them and supposed it must have been a variation on the one she was experiencing now: residual terror from the moments after Mikey's fall, bodily resistance to the idea of a return to the scene of the accident – in any form. And to think, Joanna was worried she was *too* happy!

'Don't get me wrong,' James told her, 'it's totally understandable that you would associate Paris with the accident, how could you not? But you can't avoid France for the rest of your life. We might want to go on holiday there, or buy a place there some day.'

Holly regarded him with surprised eyes. 'What, when we have the five babies?'

He grinned. 'The *one* baby. Besides, what if Mikey goes on a school trip to Paris?'

'He won't do anything like that for years.'

'Even so, we don't want him picking up on your anxiety. I think we need, you know, an exorcism.'

Holly's heart rate stuttered and then quickened. 'I don't want to take Mikey back there, James. Please don't make me.'

'All right, just us to begin with. We could go the nights he's with Joanna one weekend. One night, or maybe two – we'll make a treat of it, stay somewhere really nice.'

Holly smiled a little grimly. 'Like your anniversary hotel?' She thought often of her first meeting with James, sitting together on that deep velvet sofa, so deep in fact that you sat in it not on it. She remembered the way he had taken her bleeding foot into his lap: was that how this began, that first touch? If she had a photograph of *that*, would it counteract the claim Alexa's pictures had staked?

'No, obviously not there,' James said, taking her seriously.

He was being so sweet and she wanted so badly to please him. 'Not where we stayed either. It would be impossible to relax.'

'And we want to relax. We'll want to relax all weekend. I'll find us an apartment or something. How about the weekend after next? Will you ask Marcus if you can take time off?'

'I could try,' she said. 'And Mum definitely won't mind, so long as she's not working.'

James was pleased. 'Joanna is like a fairy godmother, isn't she? My parents will help, you know, when the dust settles, and my sister. Her kids will be like cousins to Mikey.'

With typical optimism, he had told her that the reaction of his mother and sister to the news of his marital breakdown reminded him of early childhood, of being sent to his room until such a time that he was ready to come down and apologise for his insolence. Both refused to have any part in 'this debacle', as his mother put it. 'We'll see you when you've come to your senses,' they said.

They must have said much more than this, Holly knew, but James was determined to protect her from their insults. 'Believe me, this is the best outcome I could have hoped for. Temporary disgrace followed by full rehabilitation.'

'You don't think they'll refuse to see you for longer because of me?' she asked. Inevitably, her point of reference on scandal like theirs was her mother's. 'I mean permanently?'

'God, no. They'll come around. When they've got over the social embarrassment, when someone else's son announces a promotion or a new baby or a medical scare, their perspective will shift and they'll come around.'

He was so trusting, so sure; the way he saw it, everything would fall into place. Nothing rocked his conviction that in the end they would be treated like any other couple. Holly didn't know what she had done to deserve him, to win this chance at happiness, but she vowed to herself that she would never take him for granted as Alexa had.

'OK, let's go to Paris,' she said, decisively. She would get her own 'happy' photographs, the 'after' set. 'Maybe it would be good for me to get it out of the way before it becomes a mental block or something.'

'Spoken like a true romantic,' James teased, making her smile, as he never failed to do.

Chapter 24

I really am alone, Joanna thought. Sitting in her still, silent living room she suddenly felt as ravaged by the absence of her daughter and grandson as if a cyclone had just ripped away the television or radio, anything to release some energy into the void, but if she took just one step she would fall and fall and fall.

It was no longer possible to deceive herself that this was exactly the same as the two-week summer holidays Holly had sometimes taken with girlfriends over the years, for they were into the fourth week now. No, Holly had left home and taken Mikey with her, and for the first time in her life Joanna was actually living on her own. (She did not count the few months between leaving her parents and the arrival of Holly: when you were pregnant you were not on your own.)

She said the words out loud: *They've moved out.* Then, *Will I, ever? Or will I stay here until I die?*

She'd had a nightmare once, a terror, in which she had gone into hiding or perhaps under house arrest. It was not clear what she was sheltering from or being punished for, but it was an arrangement that was to stand for the rest of her natural life. She still worked: the flat and the shop were linked by a long concrete tunnel, along which she would scuttle back and forth, petrified by the sound of approaching water, fast and cold and deadly. Holly had not been in the dream.

She'd lived in this building almost twenty years, in this flat for eight, having heard about the original vacancy – a one-bedroomed unit high above her head on the eighth floor – from Suze; so much of the life they'd established here was thanks to Suze. It had been the early nineties and the place had been bought from the council by a private landlord asking a decent rent. Holly had been due to start school the following year and the local primary was not especially terrible. Joanna had part-time cleaning work in the neighbourhood and was keen to live nearby, the better to minimise her daughter's time away from her.

The weekend she took possession, she wrote to her mother and invited her to visit, not knowing what it was she expected but certainly knowing what it was she hoped.

'It's probably best if we stick to our usual arrangement,' came the reply.

That was the first Joanna heard of its being 'usual'.

After that disastrous visit home with the newborn Holly, it had become clear to her that Melissa was the one to whom she needed to direct any future appeals. If she could convince her to forgive her, then their mother and father would follow. And so she'd sent letters to her sister in which she tried to explain – and strenuously apologise for – her position, each time writing her own address clearly on the flap of the envelope. She did not allude to the suicide bid, if that was what it had been, unable to guess whether Melissa should want her to know about it or not, and she did not refer to Dan's unscheduled visit, either, of course; over time, when it was not repeated, it came to seem as if it had never happened.

There was no reply to any of her pleas until, close to Holly's first birthday, one of her letters was returned unopened, with the address on the front crossed out and a line added in

Melissa's spiky handwriting: *Return to sender – Melissa Payne not known at this address.*

Joanna knew at once what that meant: the divorce had taken place and her sister had dropped Dan's name. Joanna had no name, either; she was merely 'sender', undeserving even of a covering note.

The next letter, addressed this time to Melissa Walsh, also came back intact, its 'Return to sender' printed instead in her father's hand.

When Holly turned one and no birthday card came from home, Joanna saw that her entreaties for forgiveness were not only being refused now, while the pain was still raw, but were always going to be. And desperately remorseful though she was for having devastated her sister's life, for having confessed as she had, she could not make the one admission that might have tipped the balance: that she regretted falling pregnant, regretted having her baby. For she did not; and she vowed she never would.

And so she and her mother had established their arrangement. Every six months or so they met in a hotel in central London, two of the few times each year that Joanna and Holly took the bus into the West End. However grand the tearoom, however powerful the atmosphere around them of reunion and celebration, it managed each time to feel utterly soulless at their table. Her mother's obvious discomfort in being there at all (presumably these encounters were kept secret from Melissa and perhaps from their father as well) hampered any curiosity she might have in her daughter's new life: it was as if by not asking, by not knowing, she would have fewer guilty secrets to hide when she returned home.

'Grandma, when will you come to *my* house?' Holly would ask. 'You can see my bedroom. I've got love hearts on the wall.'

'Maybe next time,' 'Grandma' said. Joanna thought of her that way, a grandparent in inverted commas.

On one occasion she waited for Holly to be distracted with her colouring book and said to her mother in an undertone, 'If it's just me who's the problem, maybe you would like to take Holly on her own for a weekend some time? Then she can meet Dad and get to know you both properly?'

But her mother's reaction told her that what she had intuited was true: with Melissa living at home and still 'not right', Holly could not be a house guest any more than Joanna could. How could her heart, or pride, heal when the injury Joanna had done her was permanent? It was a living, growing insult sitting between them in a pretty white dress and sparkly pumps.

A hundred times Joanna asked herself if it wouldn't be better for Holly if they cut off contact altogether rather than to persist with this taste-of-honey agony. She had already asked Suze if she would be Holly's guardian if anything were to happen to her; it had been written in an official letter. But it meant something to her mother, she knew; it meant something to both of them. It was as if they accepted their incarceration, but hoped one day to be released on appeal, or simply pardoned. And for all the humiliation and frustration of the situation, Joanna had not once turned down the cheques her mother slipped her (a source of support over which her sister apparently had no control). She tried not to count on the extra money, but the fact was it made those utility bills less daunting, the extra costs in winter, the charges that came out of the blue. When the time came, it had made the move to this larger flat possible.

'I understand the original row,' Suze said, when she first confided in her the details of her family's dysfunction, 'just not the fact that it's still going on.' This was a sentiment she was to repeat over the years. 'We're in a different century now,' she pointed out in time. 'Melissa may never forgive you for what you did, but doesn't she want to have her own life again? A new boyfriend? A home of her own? Why would she sacrifice *herself*?'

'She's in a state of suspension, maybe,' Joanna said. 'I think

332

of her as Miss Havisham, an old woman in a wedding dress, with cobwebs in her hair and spiders crawling out of the cake.' This was not quite true: Joanna thought of Melissa as she had been in the last moments before she knew, with silky hair spilling over her soft fur collar, a long wool coat sweeping to the floor. Having not seen a photograph since, she had no idea how her sister might have aged.

'She'd rather be a sad old spinster than let them have a relationship with you and Holly? It's not much of a victory, is it? She's cutting off her nose to spite her face.'

'To spite me,' Joanna corrected her. 'And it's probably much more complicated than we think, Suze. Maybe she does have a boyfriend, maybe she has moved on. Maybe her threats don't mean anything any more or she doesn't even have to make them now. Maybe my parents are getting older and don't have the strength to think any differently, maybe they're so used to the rules they wouldn't be able to give them up.'

'Are they so old and weak?' Suze asked.

'They're getting older, yes. I don't know much about their health, but Mum doesn't seem particularly good for her age. She always looks *beaten*.' Beaten by the estrangement between her two daughters; yes, Melissa had prolonged it unnaturally, but the fact remained that Joanna had caused it. Another reason to dread those stilted afternoon teas: when she looked at her mother's face, she was confronted with physical evidence of her own criminal damage.

'That's the other side of the coin, isn't it?' Suze said.

'What?'

'You don't have them in your life, no, but you don't have the complications of their getting older either. When they need proper looking after, she'll have to do it, won't she?'

'Melissa?'

'Yes. You'll be free to focus on your grandchildren.' (Little did they know then that her first grandchild would be arriving within a few short years.) 'No one will expect you to contribute any practical help.'

'Well, I'm glad to hear there's a silver lining to it all.' She was joking, but it was true in a sense. That was the thing about Suze, she had a way of finding the bright side. If it wasn't immediately visible to her she adjusted her seat until it was, a holidaymaker chasing the sun around the swimming pool.

Adrian made contact again. This time it was by phone and this time there was no attempt to conceal Suze's agency, for he mentioned their mutual friend at once: 'Suze said there've been a few changes and you might need someone to talk to? I thought I'd volunteer.'

Joanna, who had not recognised his number on her phone display, found the given three seconds to prepare herself insufficient. 'I'm . . . thank you, but I'm—'

'How about a drink?' he interrupted. 'Come on, Jo, one drink and you can tell me the whole saga.'

It was impossible to dispute his choice of word, whether it was Suze's or his own. Into her mind paraded its main characters – Holly, James, Alexa, little Mikey – as well as the faceless, voiceless figures of all those who must also have been affected by it: members of James's and Alexa's families, their friends and colleagues, people who according to Holly had only that week been told of the marital split. Joanna did not envy them the first impact of shock and anxiety.

'OK,' she said to Adrian, 'but one drink might not cover it.'

'Two, then. Three.' He spoke in the private murmur she remembered from their phone conversations of old: he was surprisingly discreet about his personal life and she knew he would have selected a moment at work when no one was in earshot to make this call. You sound like a government agent, she used to tease him; we're only arranging to go to the pub, not sell state secrets.

And so they were once more, it seemed. 'Tomorrow night?' he suggested.

She had no excuse to hand and certainly no actual plans: whatever Holly's urgings, she was not yet ready to visit her daughter every day (apart from anything else, the tangible energy of Holly's and James's desire for one another made her uncomfortable).

'You're busy tomorrow?' Adrian said, misreading her silence.

'No, no, I'm free.'

'Great, I'll meet you at the Gypsy at eight o'clock.'

Hanging up, she decided that this was exactly what she needed, to discuss the situation with an outsider – better still, an outsider who used to be an insider. There'd be no need to explain the background on Holly's state of mind, for instance, how she had come to be so vulnerable to the charge of her knight in shining armour. No one who had seen for himself Holly's obsession with Sean and its subsequent unravelling would need it given in words.

Nor would there be any need to describe her particular horror of history repeating itself, of how she had been overwhelmed these last two weeks by recollections of her own departure from home and the uncertainties of Holly's early life; how her past was all at once a shipwreck being raised to the surface before her eyes, a team of forensic archaeologists standing ready with their tools.

Still, there was plenty else to tell Adrian, if what he said was true and he really did want to hear the full story. The saga.

When she arrived at the pub, spying him at once at their regular table of old, she stood at his side and said what she should have said on the phone, using a tone that could have been mistaken for one of innocuous greeting. 'I need to know: are you with someone? If you are, I don't want to be here even as a friend. I'll go now.'

Adrian turned to her with mild puzzlement and she had the immediate urge to touch his face, the freshly shaven chin and throat, the slender bone of his nose, an urge that only quickened when he parted his lips and spoke, using that murmur he kept just for her (their heads might have been side by side on the pillow): 'What? You don't trust me, Jo?'

I don't trust myself, she thought. I deceived the person closest to me, and so easily I convinced myself it was justice; what protection would a total stranger have? 'It's not that, it just wouldn't be fair on your new girlfriend, because of our history. No one would want her boyfriend being used as a shoulder to cry on by an ex.'

His eyes scanned hers before he gave her a quick downturned smile. 'Well, I'm not with anyone, so you're safe to take a seat if you dare.'

'I dare.' But she took the one opposite rather than ease into the space he'd made available on the banquette. Immediately he closed the distance between them by leaning forward across the table and forcing her to meet his eye. She hadn't forgotten his intensity, only how that intensity magically compelled her to share what was innermost. When they'd first met, she'd told him more in a single week than she'd been able to in several previous relationships over the course of months or years. She bit into her lower lip and decided to let him speak first.

'Since we're on the subject, I *was* seeing someone, a girl from work, but it finished a few months ago.'

She didn't ask why, but he went ahead and told her. 'She said my heart wasn't in it, only other parts of my anatomy.'

Joanna blinked. 'Oh. That's a bit harsh.'

'Contrary to what you seem to think about men, it's not that easy to go straight from one heavy situation to another.'

Joanna knew him well enough to know that the 'you' he meant was the other woman, the one he'd let down, not her. He had a habit of defending himself against accusations to the wrong party. '"Heavy situation"? Was that what it was?'

'Whatever they say now. "Meaningful emotional commitment".'

'Well, that sounds even heavier. I'd stick to the original.'

He chuckled. The immediate intimacy between them both thrilled and worried her – worried *because* it thrilled, perhaps. The pub table didn't seem to be acting as the solid boundary the shop counter had during their last encounter. To compound matters, the thickening sky and lowered lamplight, the warmth of other people's voices, it all made a date of this as if it had been lit and sound-checked by professionals.

'The thing is, I don't want to go backwards either.' She gazed at him, feeling her forehead wrinkle. 'I'm sorry if that sounds rude, I just want to get it straight. I don't want anyone to get hurt.'

Dipping her eyes a fraction, she saw that the skin around his was more deeply lined than she remembered. Men were marked by pain just as women were, she thought. Exposure to the likes of Sean had made her forget this.

'Let me see if I've got this right,' he said. 'You don't want to be mates if I'm seeing someone else because that wouldn't be fair, presumably because of the animal temptation involved, but you don't want to see me as anything more if I'm not. Isn't that having your cake and eating it?'

'I don't think I want any cake,' Joanna said. 'That's what I'm trying to say.'

He waited a beat before laughing. 'You don't think you want any cake. Fine, I get it.' He motioned to the bar. 'Now that's settled, how about a drink? Are you allowing yourself liquids, at least?'

Joanna flushed. 'Of course, yes, I'm sorry. Please could I have a vodka and tonic?'

'You could.' He widened his eyes at her; a comic look that

said, If I'd known it was going to be this difficult, I wouldn't have suggested it.

And what she was thinking while he was at the bar was, how had she ever imagined it *wouldn't* be this difficult? She'd been in love with him and had never stopped wanting him, only to stop falling short, because too much of her childhood had been spent falling short. And yet she had never been as honest with anyone as she had with him. It was that honesty that she craved again now, why she was here at all, and yet she couldn't fathom if it was possible – or fair – to take it without giving anything in return. And she knew it was unforgivably arrogant to assume it was her call in the first place.

He was back at her side with the drinks. The way he placed them on the table, hers first and then his own only after a quick swallow, the way he slid into his seat while already fully focused on her, the whole choreography of having a drink with him was imprinted.

'Tell me what's been going on then? Suze said Holly's bagged herself a married millionaire.'

Joanna took a slurp of cold vodka. 'I have no idea if he's a millionaire but he's certainly married.'

'Where did she find him? Not in Palace?'

That made her laugh, as he'd intended. 'No, not around here. It started in Paris, though I didn't realise it at the time. I didn't know anything about it until they'd decided they were soulmates and he'd left his wife.'

She told the story as directly as she could, beginning with the rescue and finishing, as she had no choice but to, right in the middle, where they were now, with Holly about to return to Paris with James for a romantic weekend. Though delighted by the prospect of having Mikey to herself for a whole weekend, she nonetheless found the lovebirds' choice of destination mystifying, and a second drink was supplied while she explained why, and then a third.

'Well, she's always been a handful,' Adrian said.

'No more than any other kid,' Joanna protested. 'Probably less, actually. I've just known more about what she gets up to because she hasn't had any other family to confide in. Siblings, maybe an aunty or a cousin or a grandparent she's close to. She's missed out.' She hated listing absent relatives like that, not even knowing how many the list numbered.

'She's got friends, though, hasn't she? At her age that's more important.'

'I'm not sure she has, really. She burned her bridges a bit with Sean. She thought he was all she needed.' And now, it seemed, she thought the same about James. 'Anyhow, when it comes to James, she's acting completely without advice.'

'Except his.' At the sound of his phone, Adrian glanced away to silence the call and Joanna resisted asking him who it was. He appeared to be coping well with the onslaught of a Walsh family update. 'It's out of your control now, Jo. All you can do is bide your time. If it works out with this guy, then great. If it doesn't, she can always come back. It's the same when any kid leaves home – it's tough even when it's straightforward. Is this James nice to Mikey?'

'He seems to adore him. He saved his life, remember.'

'Well, then. This could be a *lot* worse.'

'But it's all too fast! She's already treating him as Mikey's stepfather when Sean hasn't even met him. You know how I feel about Sean, but it's not right.' She was aware that she was kicking against Adrian's reasonableness, resisting his soothing in a way she never did Suze's, and she didn't know why. 'I think I'm just worried she'll have another relapse and I won't be there in time to catch her.'

'Why, where are they living?'

'Just in West Dulwich.'

'Then you'll be there. Actually, if they were on the moon you'd get there somehow.'

She pulled a face, a face she had not pulled since she and Adrian were together – wry, flirtatious, mock-offended – and wondered how her facial muscles could possibly remember it. 'Well, maybe not the moon, but anywhere on earth.'

Adrian was observing her in *his* old way: tender and amused. 'You know what I think, what I've always thought?'

'What?'

'You're too good for this. You might not have seen your family properly for all these years, but you've still got that posh upbringing in you.'

'It wasn't posh.'

'It was compared with all this. Come on, working in Suze's shop all these years, living in that flat, meeting blokes like me in pubs like this, it's a bit downmarket for someone like you.'

When they were together, Joanna had confided in him her occasional frustrations with her job, how she had long ago made the decision to prioritise the need for a stable income, neighbourhood workplace and a boss sympathetic to the demands of lone parenting (not to mention her deep loyalty to that boss) over the rearing of old ambitions. She'd wanted to be an illustrator when she was young; this was later downgraded to art teacher, but it hardly mattered since each goal had remained as out of reach as the other. The shop window displays were her outlet, the day of the month she most enjoyed.

'This wasn't supposed to be how your life turned out,' Adrian said, plainly in the mood to turn the screw.

'This wasn't supposed to be how this conversation turned out,' she replied, but as his gaze intensified she no longer dared joke.

'You must think that sometimes?' he insisted. 'Don't you?'

Working in that shop, living in that flat, meeting blokes like me: he's missed out Holly, she thought, Holly and Mikey. 'Well, we all wonder if this is how it was supposed to be, yes. You have such big plans for yourself when you're young, but they

340

don't work out like that for anyone, do they? I've never thought this isn't good enough, never.' She was startled by her own passion. 'I have Holly and Mikey, that's enough. If anything, this is too good for me.'

As he listened to her, the expression on his face reminded her suddenly of James, of the way he looked at Holly with not only a desire to protect and shelter, but also a *need* to. A fierce need. 'You really mean that, don't you?' he asked.

'Yes.'

'Don't you think you've beaten yourself up enough?'

'I'm not beating myself up. I've just said I'm happy.'

'Have you? We'll be dead a long time, you know, Jo. Let yourself live while there's still the opportunity. Otherwise . . .'

Otherwise she'd be no different from Melissa or her parents, existing in a state of paralysis; otherwise she'd come to the end of her life and wonder if Holly and Mikey *had* been enough. The years they had lived with her were one thing, but what about those when they did not, those that had evidently already begun? Was it at last going to be possible to revive old ambitions, to make changes and take risks? To no longer suppress as second nature the passions that seized her body or the ideas that stirred her imagination, as they had that first day in Paris?

She couldn't answer Adrian. They continued to stare at each other until Joanna felt her eyes fill with tears and looked quickly away. She reached for her bag. 'I'm tired. Will you walk me home?' There was a challenge in the way she spoke to him and he answered it at once.

'Don't worry, you'll be safe with me.'

Given her earlier declaration, he probably meant safe from him, but he'd said 'with', and she had to admit she liked that better.

'I haven't even begun to tell you about Alexa,' she sighed.

'Who's Alexa?' His hand cupped her elbow as they tackled

the pub's two sets of doors, which required the same manoeu-
vrings as a kissing gate.

'She's the wife. The wife who didn't want this to happen.'

'We may need another meeting, then,' Adrian said.

Joanna did not agree, but she didn't disagree either.

Chapter 25

Everyone knew of James's betrayal now. Arriving in the office each morning, taking her seat at team meetings, even walking among strangers in the street, Alexa felt as debased as if she'd had her clothes torn from her in the middle of Waterloo Station and been left to squat on the concourse floor. Shocked messages of condolence were streaming in exactly as if James had died. She fantasised sometimes about how it would feel if this *were* a bereavement, if he had drowned in the Seine that day instead of having risen from its waters shoeless and triumphant. All things considered, she decided it would feel the same but without the brutal, crucifying shame.

She'd certainly be being given an easier time of it at work if he were dead: inevitably, her late starts, the extended lunch hours devoted to swimming or to amateur detective work in Crystal Palace, and her general inattention had earned her a formal warning from Paul.

'I'm very sorry to hear of your difficulties at home,' he opened, with the kind of exaggerated sincerity that only portended an unwelcome sting in the tail. A demanding boss, he was known to reserve his gravest disapproval for his former favourites.

'But . . . ?' Alexa pre-empted, gracelessly. She found herself sitting on her hands as if at risk of corporal punishment.

'There is no "but".' Behind his sleek eyewear glinted the wintry energy of ill will. 'I know you'll do everything you can to keep your mind off that and on your work during office hours. If you think that's not going to be possible, however, then let me know right now and I'll see if I can shuffle the team around a bit to accommodate the distraction.'

Accommodate the distraction: how could he be so cold-blooded? And 'however' was the same as 'but', even if it was buried in the middle of the sentence.

'You can't afford to be so erratic a week before the launch,' he reminded her, but the word 'launch' had ceased to hold any urgency for Alexa, or even any contextual significance: it might have been that she was going up in a space shuttle for all it meant to her. 'Alexa,' he added, sharply, 'are you well enough to be here at all?'

'I'm fine,' she said to her lap. She wanted to add, I pity your wife, but there was no point when she was so manifestly the wife around here to be pitied.

That afternoon, she broke down in tears in a meeting with one of her agencies and, ignoring a second summons by Paul, left for home early. There, she could no longer avoid the phone calls from her sister and even after downplaying events to a dishonest degree – 'We're having a little break. We think it will make us stronger in the long run . . .' – she found that Sammy's gasping reaction only made her want to throw herself off the nearest bridge.

'I would *never* have guessed,' Sammy exclaimed. 'You two are the *last* couple I'd have expected to have problems. I suppose . . .' She faltered, evidently changing her mind about sharing her opinions, ones that Alexa felt sure represented their parents' equally.

'You suppose what?'

'Just that it goes to show, you know, that having all that money doesn't protect you from ordinary problems. We're all the same when it comes down to it.'

As someone who wanted nothing less than to be 'ordinary' or 'the same', Alexa took the remark badly. 'I don't know what you mean,' she snapped, 'but you're obviously delighted by my downfall.'

Sammy began protesting but, unable to trust herself to be civil, Alexa hung up. A phone call to her parents would have to wait until she was stronger. They'd left messages of concern, urging her home for the weekend, but if she could not bear to hear the pity in their voices then how could she survive seeing it on their faces? And there'd only be more of those 'When it comes down to it' comments. When it comes down to what? she thought. *Witchcraft?*

Thank goodness she had her friends. Once their indignation at her early secrecy was out of the way, Lucie and Shona had rallied exactly as she'd known they would. They were willing to dissect the James and Holly affair minutely; for them, no remark was too dark, no pronouncement too bitter, no bid for revenge anything but fully justified. Briskly, they listed the things Alexa needed to do, the professionals she needed to consult, including a solicitor friend of Graham's who could make room in his diary to see her the following week.

'Oh, solicitors aren't involved yet,' Alexa protested, her friends' concentration on assets, on material salvage, catching her off guard. She recognised at once the quick look that passed between them: 'Is she still in denial?' (Shona.) 'Yes, tough love is what's needed here.' (Lucie.)

'Well, they need to be,' Lucie said, crisply. 'I bet he's seen his already. Thank God for the equal division of assets, eh? Imagine this situation fifty years ago? You'd have been cast out without a bean, back to your parents, and that's if you were lucky. No job. Probably three kids by now as well.'

'I think this has been bad enough,' Shona said, seeing Alexa's face.

It was surreal to discuss her marriage as an historical event, irrevocably in the past. In contrast, all references to Holly Walsh were in the present tense and had the taste of promise about them, of a story still to be told. During such discussions, always spirited on the part of her friends, she felt herself grow numb, as if there were no longer sufficient propulsion for her blood to move through her veins.

'I can see why *she* wants *him*, obviously,' Lucie said with a sneer that pleased Alexa, 'but why would *he* want *her*?'

'His mother says for the sex,' Alexa said.

Lucie gaped. 'She actually said that to you?'

'Pretty much. We spoke on the phone earlier.'

In fact, of all her sympathisers, James's mother Julia had come closest to penetrating Alexa's misery, her verbatim account of her dressing down of her son bringing Alexa more than a flutter of grim satisfaction. 'I told him, "You're that girl's golden egg, James. She's just looking for a father for her child, someone to pay the bills and give her a lifestyle she doesn't have to work for."'

Alexa could only assume James had chosen not to pass on this view to Holly. 'You really told him that?' she asked her mother-in-law.

'I certainly did. And do you know what he said to me? He said, "Have you considered that maybe she's *my* golden egg?"' She and Alexa both scoffed at that notion. '"I think that's highly unlikely," I told him. "What does she offer you? No, don't answer that, please, James. I think we can all guess. Do I have to remind you you've just bought a family home with Alexa, you've just celebrated your wedding anniversary? Five years, that's hardly anything, you're barely out of the blocks!"'

Hardly anything. And yet she, Alexa, had thought it was something; she'd thought James thought it was something as well.

'What did he say then?' Julia had the capacity for perfect recall when it came to conversations, not a gift that had always

346

been desirable in the past, but now it sated Alexa's hunger better than anything she'd been offered to date.

'He said, "I realise the timing's not ideal." "Not ideal? Not ideal? It's *abominable*. I can't speak to you any more, James, not yet, I just can't. You've hurt us all too much, not just Alexa, all of us. It's better that we all take some time to absorb the shock."'

'Thank you,' Alexa whispered, though they both knew the shock *would* be absorbed, sooner or later, the natural order reinstated. A mother was a mother was a mother: same as James's sister, same as Sammy, same as Joanna and Holly. They all had it in common except for her.

Lucie and Shona, at least, remained outside the club with her – for now. Already the fear was building in her that they would get pregnant at the same time (Shona after much trying, Lucie effortlessly), have their first babies together, leave Alexa behind once and for all.

'You should see the way Holly looks at him,' she told her friends, 'like he's her Lord and Commander or something. She has no idea what a simpleton she looks.' This, she knew, was stretching the truth. In the weeks since their only confrontation, Alexa had been forced to acknowledge a grudging respect for Holly's handling of it. She'd remained cool, almost impersonal, the martyr of the piece in a strange sort of way, even though Alexa was indisputably the one who'd been sacrificed. Had she reacted the same way to the photographs? Alexa supposed she must have, for there had been no retaliation, no reply at all. No, it would take something rather less subtle than holiday photos to bring this sociopath to her knees; so feeble did the challenge seem now, she had not even reported it to the girls.

'Well, it sounds like an extremely unhealthy dynamic to me,' Lucie said.

'I think the hero worship is the main issue,' Shona said. 'Any normal man would just laugh off her adoration, but he hasn't done that. He must *need* it. I wonder if he's got a hero complex. I've been reading all about it.'

'What is it?' Lucie asked, her scepticism plain.

'It's a compulsion to help others. People who have it believe ordinary life is too dull and are always asking themselves, Is my life good enough? How can I make a difference to things?'

'He could just have given a big cheque to charity if he wanted to help people?'

'No, that wouldn't be enough,' Shona said. 'These people have an overriding need to be needed. They do things that are not necessarily the right thing for themselves, only for the person they are helping. It's atoning for a sense of worthlessness.'

'That doesn't sound remotely like James,' Lucie said, chuckling.

'Not as he was when *we* knew him, no. The condition was obviously dormant, but was triggered by seeing the boy in the water.'

Alexa followed this exchange with growing interest. She recalled something Frances had said in Paris, a phrase in French: *le culte des héros*, that was it.

'You know, when we first spoke about it, Holly's mother Joanna said something like that as well. She thought the whole thing was to do with the rescue, that they're both suffering from delusions of their own uniqueness.'

Except neither of them *was* suffering – only she was suffering – and Joanna had probably accepted these delusions as fact by now. It had all become some terrible self-fulfilling prophecy.

'He may have had fantasies about saving you, Lex,' Shona said, 'but you were always so capable there was never any window of opportunity. You never needed rescuing.'

'Come on, Shona, that's just a damsel in distress rehash,' Lucie scoffed, 'it's nothing new. And Lex needs saving now, doesn't she, and I don't see him coming to rescue her, so it can't be that much of a compulsion.'

But Alexa was willing to take Shona's theory more seriously. It was not a million miles from her continued belief that James was acting under some form of hypnosis or temporary mania. 'If it is something like that, almost a proper medical condition, then it will go away again, won't it? He'll go back to normal?'

Shona looked as if she'd give her eye teeth to agree. Alexa was beginning to see that there wasn't much to choose between wholehearted pity like hers and Lucie's and the pitilessness of people like Paul: both separated her absolutely from the experience of her peers, from her own past.

'I don't know,' Shona admitted. 'The article I read didn't really say.'

She didn't agree, then; she thought what everyone else did, that what James and Holly had experienced as individuals had turned them into a pair so strongly bonded that already, a month in, no one was willing to bet against them.

No one except Lucie, who remained unconvinced: 'Well, I think James's mother is closer to the truth. If there's any medical condition involved, it's his libido. When men leave women it's always about sex. And we all know how long *that* lasts.'

To say Alexa had been disappointed by the absence of a response to her little delivery to Holly Walsh was to give only an inkling of her true umbrage. Having the package returned unopened or sent with the photographs defaced would have at least represented an exchange, a dialogue of sorts with her nemesis. But to be disregarded, ignored outright: it was as much a form of disrespect as was being abused to her face.

Her next move fell into her lap (it was about time *something* did), in the form of the one person in her circle who had been able to speed through the condolences phase and seek to make something constructive out of her desolation: Tracey, her journalist friend. No sooner was word out than she was on the phone to Alexa with an urgent proposal. 'We're running a feature next week on disastrous anniversaries and I have space for one more story.'

At first Alexa dismissed this out of hand, laughing in the new sour way she was getting used to tasting in her throat: 'Disastrous anniversaries? Thank you for thinking of me, but no way.'

'We'd change all the names and use an agency photo,' Tracey said at once. 'No one would even know it was you.'

'Forget it.'

But Tracey was not to be put off so easily and would not be in her job if she were. 'At least hear me out before you decide. You wouldn't believe how many people find it useful to tell their story to a wider audience; it can be a really cathartic process. And we're talking over a million readers, Alexa, all of whom will be firmly on your side.'

How many poor saps had she spun that line to over the years? Alexa thought. Nonetheless, the pitch had already lasted long enough for her to begin to wonder, What if *she* saw it? Slut Walsh. What if Alexa *made sure* she saw it? *That* might be a delivery that provoked a reaction: a good old-fashioned tabloid naming and shaming. At the very least it would give Alexa a petty satisfaction, something that had not been achieved when compiling the photographs, a task that had made her only unutterably sad.

'You really think people would be interested?'

'Definitely, they'd love it!' Tracey said this without irony. 'Infidelity is universal. What happened to you feels like it could happen to anyone. Your husband leaves you for a much younger woman: there but for the grace of God go I, you know?'

'I do know, yes,' Alexa said, drily.

'We pay a fee,' Tracey added.

It was not much, but still, 'all that money', as her sister had so crudely put it, would very soon cease to be available to her.

'Why not put it out there?' Tracey persisted, scenting capitulation. 'Get it all on record, eh? Next Friday, it'll be out, *your* story, not theirs.'

'I'll think about it,' Alexa said, already knowing she would do it.

She insisted on a false name for herself but kept James's and Holly's. Since the only audience of interest to her were the two protagonists themselves, she was damned if she was going to allow them the dignification of pseudonyms.

She read the feature on the tube going into work the following Friday morning. As promised, the illustration was from a photo library, a couple on the top deck of a *bateau mouche*, evocative of exactly the quintessential romantic break in Paris she and James were enjoying before his hero complex kicked in. Her piece had been awarded a whole page and was headed 'Betrayal on the Seine':

> Lorna's husband James saved a child's life on their fifth wedding anniversary trip to Paris, but his heroics were the beginning of pure heartbreak for his devoted wife . . .

The rest had been written in the first person, in Alexa's voice, or in a version of her voice that wavered between self-pity and psychotic venom. *Holly has stolen my husband from under my nose. What next? My home? My job? What kind of a monster would do this to another woman? She must be amoral, a sociopath.* And so on. Though she couldn't remember saying half these things, she had no doubt that she *had* said them. Hers was not a fury that had needed journalistic enhancement.

One quote had been pulled out and enlarged, huge across the centre of the page: *I hate her. I will never forgive her.* In the top right-hand corner, a second read: *I won't take revenge. Karma will do that for me.*

All in all, she sounded a little deranged. Well, perhaps it wouldn't do any harm for James and Holly to think she *was* deranged: it was about time they took her psychological health seriously. She intended to hand the newspaper to Holly at her door like the serving of a subpoena; she would not rest until the girl had read this article and had a little think about what karma might bring for her.

Unable to slip out of the office during the day for fear of further castigation by Paul, she had to wait until the end of the working day, catching the train with the City commuters heading home for their weekends (her taxi habit was, like so much, a luxury she could no longer afford). Arriving in West Dulwich, there was no answer at the flat and so she persuaded a neighbour to buzz her into the communal hallway, whereupon she hammered on the flat door until her knuckles burned and the neighbour had come down to ask what all the fuss was about. Only as she rested on the stoop did it occur to her that Friday was one of the evenings Holly worked. By the time she'd taken an overcrowded bus up a steep hill to Crystal Palace and found the right restaurant, it was seven o'clock.

'Oh, she's not on tonight,' said the waitress who greeted her. This was not the useful one who'd served her before but an overfriendly school-leaver type with irritatingly glossy skin.

'Not on?' Alexa cried, overheated in every possible sense of the word. 'I thought she worked every Friday?'

'She does normally, but she's got the night off.'

Neither she nor a nearby colleague knew why this was or where she might be. 'She's a bit of a sphinx, is Holly,' the barman said.

'That's not the word *I'd* use,' Alexa spat, incensed to be cheated in this way. Flouncing out into the street, she rang James's number, only to get the inevitable voicemail. Running out of ideas, she tried the phone number Joanna Walsh had given her, vowing that if *she* didn't answer either, she would go to her flat and demand to know her daughter's whereabouts, by force if necessary.

The phone was answered by a child – Mikey, presumably, palmed off on Grandma while James and Holly went out to an extremely expensive restaurant, somewhere Holly would not have known existed before she met James and somewhere Alexa would soon have to forget did. 'Where's Grandma, Mikey?' she asked, sweetly. 'Can I speak to her, please?'

The reply was unintelligible, just baby nonsense. She remembered seeing the boy hand in hand with James as they came into the room that time, to all the world natural father and son, and then she recalled a laugh she and James had shared in Paris before the accident. They were sitting in the Place des Vosges, listening to the French children playing in the sandpit, and James had said, 'Funny how so much more appealing kids are in someone else's language,' and he'd laughed uproariously at his own remark. She wasn't imagining it; he really had had no interest in children, none whatsoever. And yet here he was living with one, playing his heart out at being Daddy! Or palming him off on his grandmother while he and his sphinx flaunted their 'love' around town.

In the background she caught Joanna's voice asking Mikey to pass her the phone, but the child kept it gripped; Alexa could hear his breathing. 'Where's Mummy, sweetie? Is she there with you?'

This time she managed to catch a sound that made sense: 'Mummy gone.'

'Mummy gone where?'

This exchange was repeated several times before Mikey added a third word: 'Mummy gone Paris.'

Alexa stopped in her tracks, causing a collision with the pedestrians coming up behind her. She ignored their complaints and continued walking. 'Gone *Paris*? Is that what you said, Mikey, Paris?'

353

Joanna came on the line. 'Hello, sorry about that, can I help?'

'Joanna, it's me, Alexa.'

'Oh, hello again.' Joanna sounded pleased to hear from her, making Alexa realise how used she'd become to almost everyone else greeting her with a certain wariness, no doubt anticipating the joyless ordeal ahead of them. 'How are you holding up?'

Alexa had not the patience to reply. 'Did I just hear right?' she demanded. 'Have they gone back to Paris, James and Holly?'

'Oh, Mikey told you, did he?' Joanna sounded rather less pleased now.

'Just answer me, have they gone to Paris?' The words were coming from her in shrill exhalations, drawing looks from passers-by. 'Where are they staying, Joanna? Where?'

'They have gone to Paris for a couple of days, yes . . .' The weariness in the other woman's voice was clear as she once more faced the job of placating a raving Alexa. 'But I honestly can't tell you where because Holly didn't know. It was going to be a surprise.'

A *surprise*? It was all Alexa could do not to smash her phone to the ground. When she thought of the trouble she'd gone to in planning her surprise trip for James and now here he was surprising another woman, as if their weekend had meant nothing, as if she no longer existed. She pictured him taking the slut to the same boutiques she had led *him* to, indulging his ridiculous *Pygmalion* fantasy by treating her to a new wardrobe to go with her new life: shoes and underwear and jewellery – and an engagement ring, she added rather wildly. He was going to ask her to marry him! That was the only reason men arranged surprise weekends to Paris, wasn't it?

On and on her thoughts raced, taking her to the worst places imaginable: Holly would take James's name when they married,

354

which they were definitely going to do, for there'd be no point to prove other than that she loved him. She'll be Holly Maitland, Alexa thought, sickened. I should have been Alexa Maitland when I had the chance and now I never will be, just as I will never be the mother of his child.

Would Holly? Was she already pregnant? It was both the explanation to everything and the one question Alexa could not bring herself to ask, of Joanna, of James, of anyone.

With anger and sorrow throbbing through her, heating her skin and bringing a rash to her chest and throat, she ended the call and stormed to the bus stop, miraculously arriving home an hour or so later without having assaulted anyone or provoked an assault on her. Still raging with destructive energy, she crashed into the kitchen and began hurling items through the door and into the garden: magazines, a tin of tea, a ceramic bowl, anything that came to hand. A wedding photograph was pulled violently from the wall and launched out of the open door, then, noticing the handbag James had bought her in Paris lying abandoned on a chair, she threw that on to the pile as well. The last item she added before snatching up the gas lighter was the newspaper she'd failed to deliver to Holly. This she set alight, though nothing else caught and once the last flickers of paper had turned to black she gave up and stamped on the heap, losing her balance and almost twisting her ankle. She cracked the framed photo and at least succeeded in burning the photograph. Soon James's and her smiles had been cremated.

It was only when she had seized a barbecue utensil hanging from the outdoor grill and flung it in the direction of the house, smashing the upper pane of the kitchen window, that she at last came to her senses and stopped.

She staggered indoors and sat at the kitchen table breathing heavily and crying into her hands. Her sore foot crunched on broken glass and her arms and legs shook badly; she seemed to have no control over the convulsions and could only wait for them to abate. All she could think of was how much she hated James, hated Holly, hated Paris, hated the world. Mostly, especially, she hated herself.

Chapter 26

At first, Holly's return to the city where Mikey had almost died was so entirely unlike the original trip she began to think it absurd that she had ever worried about it – and continued to worry even as she and James took their first-class seats on the Eurostar and ordered a bottle of champagne, the first of countless differences.

'I wonder if we were on the same train last time without knowing it,' James said, as they left their home city behind.

'No, we came the day after you,' Holly told him.

'That's right, you didn't arrive until the Friday, did you?'

He spoke with fond nostalgia, as if of a journey that had taken place ten years ago or more, and normally Holly would have shared – and basked in – that sensation of ancient mutual history that had come quite naturally with their having found each other. Had they been at home, had they been anywhere but on a train hurtling towards Paris, she'd probably have pleaded for him to tell her again about the moment he'd first known they would be together, in the Chiswick café when she'd held up her face to the sunlight, as if she'd never felt anything so miraculous in her life. It was as if you were prescribed for me, he'd told her; prescribed by fate.

But for the first time since meeting James, Holly felt too

nervous to trust to fate. Even as she burrowed into her comfortable seat opposite the man she loved and watched their drinks sparkle between them, she was stricken by that same menacing unease that had invaded her when she'd seen Alexa's photographs of the boat trip.

The Seine: where everything had begun and everything had almost ended.

'It will be OK,' James said, studying her expression across the top of their champagne flutes. 'It's not usually a dangerous city, trust me, for adults *or* children.'

'I know, and Mikey's not here, I know he's safe. I can't explain why I'm scared.' But at the sight of James's intent, doting gaze, Holly decided to offer the one theory that had occurred to her. 'I suppose it's where my life changed, and I don't want it to change back. I don't want to risk going back to who I was before.'

'But you *are* who you were before,' James said.

Holly grimaced. 'I hope not.'

'No, you are. What you're talking about was how your illness affected you, not who you really were. Besides, you're with me this time. We'll do completely different things, we'll make it special.'

It was sweet how he wanted to make a honeymoon of this trip for her. She felt a pang of sorrow at the memory that Joanna had wanted *their* weekend to be special for her, too, in a different way. 'It's a perfect day,' she'd said several times and, when Holly had decided not to go up the Eiffel Tower, 'Oh, but the view is something special, Holls,' her voice fragile with hope. She'd poured her heart and soul into it just as James was doing now and she'd never given up.

'OK?'

'OK.' Holly smiled.

And it was, at first, considerably better than OK. The apartment he had found in the Marais was like something out of a film, with high ceilings, stout old beams and expanses of exposed stone washed a chalk-grey colour and covered in a haphazard jigsaw of framed old photographs. James said the oak floors were reclaimed (some apartments in the city had floors from the Palace of Versailles, he told her), and all the doors too. The high double windows, three sets in the living room, two at the rear overlooking a small courtyard, each had clay flowerboxes filled with geraniums and there was a note from the owner asking guests to water them each day with the long-spouted watering can provided. Holly's first attempt raised indignant cries from the soaked pedestrians at street level and the two of them hid out of sight behind the shutters, snorting like schoolchildren.

'Come on,' James said, 'let's go out and get a coffee some-where before you get us into any more trouble. I know a place.'

She could hardly bring herself to leave the beautiful apart-ment, but the café he'd chosen proved equally as alluring. They sat in a circular booth of studded green leather and she looked at all the vintage signs that decorated the tiled walls, trying not to stare too openly at the chic, well-heeled clientele arranged about the place. It was entirely different from the Paris she'd encountered by the Eiffel Tower with Joanna and Mikey. The sound of the native language spoken in low, almost groaning voices was like music from a gramophone record, something from before modern times. Even the people's faces, straight-browed and brooding, seemed to her to be of an older race. She supposed there was not the mix here that they had in London; there was an air of preservation, protection. She didn't think there was a skin colour in the world that Mikey had not yet seen.

'What are you thinking?' James asked. He regularly asked her this and he had not, to date, been disappointed with any of the answers she'd given, though she reminded herself every so often that she must be the least articulate, least well-educated woman he'd had a relationship with.

'I was just thinking that it's easier in foreign countries to, I don't know, to feel like you deserve the best. Like here, for instance, I assume this is a pretty nice place . . .'

'I think it is, yes,' he smiled.

'Well, in London I would feel like I didn't belong here, like I wasn't good enough, unless I was the one serving, of course. But here, well, it's just easier because you don't know all the rules about class and money and everything.'

Or maybe it was easier because she had a wealthy boyfriend now. Maybe it was as simple as that: if you could pay the bill without worrying, you belonged.

'I think you should ignore the rules,' James said. 'It's a million times more interesting than following them. You taught me that.' This was a lovely compliment – especially as she had not realised she had taught him anything, except perhaps how to change the nappy of a struggling toddler – and Holly felt grateful tears shining in her eyes as she smiled back at him. 'And they're not really rules anyway,' he added, 'they're just little snobberies for people who have nothing better to think about.'

She wondered who he meant by that: Alexa, presumably, or the mother and sister who remained too scandalised to make contact with the adulterers.

Just about everyone in James's and Alexa's families were aware of his desertion now, as well as a select group of close friends. This, Holly understood, included two couples called Lucie and Graham and Shona and Joe, who James knew without needing to ask would be siding with Alexa. And how could they not? He was quite clear that his behaviour looked indefensible and if he was honest he preferred it this way. He had no interest in making a war of their break-up, he said, even if he had the time to butter up allies, which he did not. It was taking up all of his spare attention getting to know Mikey and that was considerably more important.

The arrival of her *chocolat* rescued her from further soul-searching. It came in a pretty white jug with a little glass of water on the side. The pastry, a thick ring of choux filled with sweet hazelnut cream, was perfect enough to be sealed in varnish and sold as a Christmas tree decoration. She breathed a happy sigh and began sipping.

'I think it's maybe the best thing I've ever tasted,' she announced. 'Look how thick it is!' She showed him the contents of her cup, the consistency of heavy pouring cream and, seeing his face flicker with disbelief, added, 'What? What are *you* thinking?'

James grinned. 'I'm thinking that in the whole of my life with Alexa she never once ordered a drink or a cake like that, let alone both at once.'

Holly stabbed the pastry with her fork. 'You've said that before: she thinks food is evil.'

He considered this. 'To be fair, certain foods are acceptable, like blueberries and pomegranates. And chick peas were praised, I seem to remember.'

'Chick peas?' From what Holly had gathered, Alexa had been obsessed with her weight, monitoring herself daily on bathroom scales ordered from Germany especially for their minute accuracy. 'She looked like she hadn't eaten for weeks when we saw her. Have we made her ill, James?'

She thought about what he'd said the day they met about things going her way with the rescue, as if life were a set of scales and every time one person got lucky someone else got unlucky. Just as she had been cured of *her* illness, so Alexa had begun to suffer. And if James's wife was her counterweight, did that then mean that Alexa's previous luck had caused *Holly's* previous misfortune? If so, did that justify her continuing lack of compassion for the woman she'd usurped?

'Is there anything we can do?' she asked.

'I don't think so,' James said. 'In these situations, people don't want to be comforted by the person who hurt them in the first place. All I can do is make things easier for her in terms of a financial offer.'

'Maybe give her the house?'

'I know Alexa. She won't want the house now.'

Not without James in it. Holly wasn't sure she would want her new flat without him in it: it didn't bear thinking about. She took another mouthful of pastry, mopping the cream with her finger, James still watching.

'I love you,' he said across the table. 'And I don't care what anyone in this city says, it sounds better in English.'

'I agree,' Holly said, mouth full, adding, 'thank you.'

He'd told her he liked her answering the words 'I love you' with something other than a dutiful echo: 'Thank you,' or, 'I'm so glad,' or, 'You make me so happy.'

Holly was pleased that this pleased him, because she did feel thanks and she was glad and he did make her so happy, and she felt nothing but relief that she had not had a panic attack the moment the train pulled into Gare du Nord; had not yet reached the count that would bring her out of her blissful hypnotic state.

In the meantime, if it was a revolutionary sight for James to have in front of him a woman who liked eating thousand-calorie cakes, then she was only too happy to oblige.

In their Marais bedroom that night, she lifted her arm and wiggled outstretched fingers in the breeze that streamed in from the street. The shutters and windows were open, but no one could see them as they lay in the dark in bed.

'James?' She stopped touching the breeze and began playing with his fingers. His hands were her favourite part of him, strong and long-boned. 'James,' she said again, in a voice that was not quite hers, 'I have a secret.'

His face was very close to hers, his breath eager. 'Do you now? Something nice and sordid?'

'No, I mean a real one, something big I haven't told you yet.'

'Oh. I thought I knew everything now?'

'Not this.'

She inhaled deeply, drawing into her lungs some of the warmth he was exhaling. She could feel her heart throbbing faster and more noisily, dominating her senses the way it had that day on the river when it had registered that Mikey had gone from reach. 'It's to do with my father.'

His body twitched in surprise. 'Your father?'

Even as her lips formed the first syllable she couldn't be sure she would actually go through with this. 'I *have* met him. Not just when I was a baby, but more recently.'

'I thought you said he'd never made contact with you?' James's body was still now, his attention absolute.

'He never has. But I've made contact with him. Once.'

'When?'

'Years ago, when I was about seventeen. I did exactly what you suggested I should do now: I searched on the internet and found an address that I thought might be his brother's. I knew his brother's name from something my mum said – he's called Barnaby, it's quite unusual – and I knew he'd gone to Birmingham after breaking up with Mum's sister. Obviously it was likely he'd moved on long ago, but I thought it would be a start.'

'So you wrote to him there?'

'No, I went there. I didn't know what to say in a letter. I've never been very good at writing things down. I just pretended to Mum I was going to school as usual and then I went up to Euston and got the train to Birmingham.'

James's chest was hard against her hand, braced for what he was already sensing was the unhappy ending. 'What happened? I take it it wasn't a success if it was only once?'

She shook her head. She'd promised herself she'd never talk about this, not to anyone, and it was not the passage of five

363

years that had made revelation finally possible, it was James himself, that utter faith she had in him; it was the proof this weekend that he hadn't just made things better for her, he had the ability to *keep* them better too.

'James, he was horrible, really horrible.'

Yes, she had been seventeen, but she had not been so naïve as to expect a Hollywood version of events: the handsome and kindly older man who looked just like her, fixing his garden fence and shielding his face from the sun as he watched her walk down the street towards him; the one who had borne her absence with grace and courage while making a decent alternative life for himself and yet never quite giving up hope; the one who embraced her the second she identified herself and accepted her from that moment as his own. Nor had she fantasised about half-siblings who claimed they'd found in her their missing piece, and she hers in them. No, she had not expected any of that – but nor had she expected what she got.

She arrived at the house at ten past twelve after taking the bus to Aston from Birmingham New Street. It was a city terrace, neither rundown nor done up, its blue door opened by a woman in her forties. Though she was dishevelled and not exactly welcoming, the hallway behind her was tidy and painted a lovely rose-pink, which gave Holly a reassuring feeling.

'I'm sorry to bother you, but I'm looking for Dan Payne,' she said.

'Oh yeah?' The lack of surprise or interest on the woman's face implied that such a manhunt was not unusual.

'Does he live here, then?' Holly could not believe this could be so easy; in truth, she had not prepared for actually meeting her father today.

'Not if I have anything to do with it,' the woman replied.

'So he's *not* here?'

'There's only one place you'll find Dan at this time of day: the Plough.'

'The Plough? Is that—?'

'A pub? Yes.'

'He works there?' Holly had just begun a weekend job in the kitchen of a local pub and she considered this coincidence a positive sign.

But the woman was laughing at her as if she'd said something deliberately droll. 'Yeah, right, that's a good one.'

Not sure if it would be rude to ask her to explain, Holly blurted out, 'Are you his wife, then? Ex-wife?'

This, however, was received as a grievous insult. 'Christ, no! I'm his sister-in-law.'

That made Holly think about her mother: she'd been Dan's sister-in-law, too. 'Oh, sorry,' she said.

'You should be. Brother-in-law is bad enough, I can tell you.' With eye-rolling impatience, or perhaps disapproval, she gave Holly basic directions to the Plough, adding, 'Wouldn't touch him with a barge pole if I were you.'

Holly tried not to fret about these unpromising comments as she walked the few streets to the pub, but the moment she laid eyes on her destination she suffered an outbreak of anxiety that meant she had to stand outside in the paved beer garden for several minutes until she had calmed down sufficiently to continue. It was a big, rough pub, borderline dilapidated, the kind of place Joanna wouldn't allow her to set foot in, much less work, and where at night you might not expect to come out in one piece. At last she pushed at the door. Inside, it smelled of something decomposing and the carpet was sticky, with unidentifiable snacks crushed into it. She very much hoped she wouldn't need the loo while she was here.

She approached the bar, doing her best not to look frightened, and asked, 'Is there a customer here called Dan? Dan Payne?'

The barman repeated her question back to her, laughing – she understood from his emphasis – at the word 'customer'. 'Dan's right there, love, behind you. And you're right, he's a pain, a pain in the backside.' There was mockery in his tone and disbelief in his face, as if he was saying: Why anyone would want *him* is a mystery to me.

'Oh, thank you.'

As she turned she felt something she'd never felt before, like stage fright but darker, more a sense of foreboding. There was only one person who could have been construed as being 'behind' her, a middle-aged man sitting alone at a table by the door – she must have walked directly past him when she'd come in. She could see from his slackened posture and fuddled air that he was very drunk, an uncomfortable sight at this time of day, especially without any of the accompaniments you'd expect, like a newspaper, maybe, or a screen showing a football match or the racing. He was just sitting drinking, with no other occupation. His clothes were shambolic, his hair, from a distance, looked dusty and matted.

She came to a halt at his shoulder and summoned fresh courage. 'Excuse me, are you Dan Payne?'

He didn't look up at first; when he did, only briefly, she saw the broken vessels all over his nose and cheeks and raised blotches on his throat and neck. One of his irises – a surprisingly vivid blue – was slightly off-centre and both whites were riddled with red. 'What d'you want him for?'

At this, the barman called out, 'She's not the drugs squad, is she, you fucking wally? Just tell her it's you!', which made Holly jump and earned the speaker the finger from his 'customer'.

'I wanted to . . . I'm . . .' Stammering, still standing, she managed to say, 'I'm Joanna's daughter.'

His face registered nothing.

'Joanna Walsh,' she clarified, more firmly. Uninvited, she slipped into a nearby seat just as he made a clumsy lurching movement to pick up his drink. She recoiled slightly, thinking he was going to knock the glass and spill it, and one side of his face twisted unpleasantly. She couldn't tell if he was irritated by her presence or by his own slowness in gripping the glass.

In his silence, her face had fired, its heat stinging. Since he didn't seem about to say anything, she ventured more, more than she'd intended so soon. 'My name is Holly. I think you met me when I was a baby. I'm Holly Walsh, your daughter.'

He said something she didn't hear; it was enough, however, for her to see he had teeth missing. He looked at her now, too, but not at her face and she couldn't catch his eye.

'Sorry? I didn't hear you.' Her tone sounded so polite in this environment; she felt like visiting aristocracy and yet she was just an ordinary girl, an ordinary girl completely out of her depth.

He spoke again and this time she thought she heard what he said: 'You've got her tits.'

She stared, starkest horror immobilising any immediate response. His eyes were on her chest, the expression on his face still general displeasure rather than anything else. Her face couldn't flush any deeper but her heart could plummet lower and so it did. 'Is that all you've got to say to me?' she said, the words sticking in her throat.

But the question didn't need answering. Of course that was all he'd got to say, because if he had something better, something half decent, something fatherly, he'd have sought her out long before now to say it. It wasn't as if Joanna had snatched her from his grasp and given her a new identity, she'd always been an easy discovery for someone who wanted to make it, just as he had been for her.

She sat there, somehow feeling both outraged and annihilated. She was facing her father for the first time, but she was utterly alone.

He spoke again, the words running together, but plain enough to separate. 'You a dirty slut like her, yeah?'

Holly began to feel nauseous with confusion. Given what

little she'd known about him, and even allowing for her imagination, she could not have been led to this. If anything, she'd imagined he'd be too good for her: hadn't he been the good-looking catch, the boy who had charmed two sisters? She knew as well as any teenager that the beautiful ones were the chosen ones, the lucky ones, the ones who the rest of the world would trade places with in a heartbeat. Not only had he possessed that fundamental advantage, but he'd also had either the luck or the intelligence to marry into a nice family, one that invited him to come and live with them and share their affluent lifestyle. He'd had a home, friends, a future, *everything*, until . . .

No. She couldn't allow herself to feel responsible for this. Even if her arrival had ended his marriage, he'd had nearly two decades to recover from the catastrophe. It was in him already, whatever it was that had brought him to this pub at noon on a Tuesday when the rest of the world was at work. And it was this that scared her more than anything else, because if it was in him then it was in her.

He continued to leer at her, those eyes, the whites flecked, almost obliterated, by red, the irises sick and glazed. The smell was the most sickening aspect, the smell of alcohol and stale breath and unwashed clothes stiffened by weeks' worth of cigarette smoke. He was a proper drunk, almost a tramp. He was the kind of figure she'd cross the road to avoid, and he was her father.

She thought of home, always kept clean and cosy, of every meal her mother had cooked for her, every bed she'd made, every lost schoolbook she'd found and every shoe she'd polished. Every night her mother said good night to her and went to bed peaceful and sober.

Her gaze falling to his hands – filthy and sore-looking – and not returning to his face, she rose from her seat and left. In the street, she vomited into her mouth, managed to keep her lips closed and swallow it again. She got the bus back to New Street and the train to Euston, the tube across town for the overland train to Crystal Palace: an epic series of changes that had daunted her that morning but that she now approached on autopilot. By the time she reached home, school had finished for the day but Joanna was still at the shop and wouldn't be back for an hour or so. Holly walked through the small rooms, touching all the surfaces, loving their cleanness. Even though it was an overcast day the place seemed filled with light.

'I couldn't believe it,' she told James, her throat tightening. 'I just couldn't believe it.'

'Oh, darling,' James said. 'What a disappointment.'

'I know.' The racing heart had settled again and she felt a welcome detachment, a sense of wonderment that it had been she who had faced that awful man in that awful pub. 'Imagine if they'd tried to be together for my sake, got married or something, and he'd become like that. Imagine if that was what I'd grown up with. I feel so terrible for kids who have to live with that. It's much, much better to just have one parent.'

'I agree,' James said, kissing her forehead. 'I think you had a great childhood, from everything you've said. Joanna did more than her best.' He paused. 'You haven't told anyone this? Not even her?'

'Especially not her. She'd be so upset.'

'You think she still has feelings for him?'

'No, I mean she'd be upset for me, that I should have to find out what he'd turned into.'

'And that was, what, five years ago? He could have changed since then, got help and sobered up.'

'He could.'

'You're not intrigued to find out?'

'Intrigued' was a James sort of word, easy and smooth; he didn't seem to suffer from normal human vulnerabilities. 'No,' she said, flatly, 'I'm not intrigued. If anything I'm terrified, terrified he'll turn up and knock me off course again.'

James had become adept at making the connections in Holly's stories. 'You don't mean that seeing him that time led to your depression?'

'No, not directly, but maybe it led to me getting pregnant when I shouldn't have, clinging to Sean when I should have seen that he was the wrong person to cling to. When I was depressed, I used to think about the man I'd met that day, kind of torture myself with how grim he was. It's hard to explain, but when you're really low, you suck up all the worst memories and make them bigger and blacker, as if all there is to think about is bad stuff. That's all you deserve.'

James was pressing her against him, speaking into her hair. 'Well, there's no reason why you should seek him out again, but if you ever decide you want to, I'll come with you.'

'Thank you.'

'Promise you won't do anything secretive, promise you won't try and suffer on your own. I will always be on your side, you know that?'

'Yes.'

'You can cling to me for as long as you like, the rest of your life if you want.'

And he held her in such a sheltering way, a hundred Dans could have rained down on her and she'd have felt safe from harm. She even wished Mikey was here with her in Paris to share his strength.

Chapter 27

On Saturday, when the morning was still blinking into wakefulness and Alexa herself scarcely conscious, her body knew exactly what to do. It dressed, groped in the desk drawer for her passport and locked up the house behind it. It passed through the underground system as noiseless as a ghost and when it arrived at St Pancras it bought a ticket for the next available Eurostar service to Paris.

She was in her seat before she was fully aware of what it was she was doing.

There was no chance of seeing them, she knew that, but to stay here for the whole weekend while they were there was unthinkable. This was how life had become: a series of choices between options barely a grade apart in wretchedness; a permanent no-win situation.

In motion, she succumbed to fantasy. She was deep enough into her grief by now to be able to make the pretend world feel real; she could flesh out the details of a scenario quickly, feverishly; she could bring the characters to life as deftly as a professional animator. Disney should hire me, she thought, if they don't mind the day-long weeping.

One of her favourite daydreams was that she and James were still happily married and James was telling friends funny little stories of how they'd met, trips they'd taken together, idealised, romantic tales that evoked gasps and smiles from their audience. Always she was the star, the one pursued, the most desirable woman in the world – or in James's world, anyhow:

'I had to ask her ten times before she agreed to go out with me . . . I knew right away she was the woman I was going to marry . . . When we went on our first holiday together she got so much attention in her bikini I might as well have gone home early and no one would have noticed . . . The last time we were in Paris I told her if she bought the mirror in that shop by the Pont Louis-Philippe, I'd divorce her!'

This was her oxygen, these compliments and fond complaints that had never been made, a cutely crafted history that sounded so probable but was quite false. It was the only thing that could preserve her; she had nothing left that was real. There were times when she was absolutely convinced that make-believe was the only thing preventing her from trying to kill herself. Did that mean she was mentally ill, or was this what all humans did when the person who loved them withdrew that love and renounced them?

Eyes closed (though this was not essential for her to enter her trance, she nonetheless preferred it), she felt a nudge of her foot under the table, tried to remember who was sitting there – she'd glanced up when her neighbours had taken their seats, but could not picture the face of the passenger opposite. The thought segued into a new fantasy: she'd look up and see an old boyfriend, one who *she* had rejected and who had since been living in hope of reconciliation; or maybe it would be that very muscly man she'd slept with in Mallorca when she was on holiday with Sammy, before either sister had met their husbands; or perhaps a stranger, an attractive one, intrigued by the beautiful daydreamer opposite, coaxing her from her reverie to start a conversation that grew into something special. He would turn out to be exactly what was needed to save her from herself.

372

She blinked her lids open. A sour-eyed woman in a denim jacket glowered at her as if it had been Alexa who had kicked her.

'Do you mind?'

Alexa saw that her magazine had slid across the table between them and was touching the woman's newspaper as she read, a criminal act, evidently. It made her think of the newspaper she had burned, of the latest act of persuasion that had failed to hit its target.

'Sorry.' She moved the magazine back into her half of the table and closed her eyes again. This crone could do nothing for her. She was neither an old lover nor a new one. She was not James.

Alexa was on her way back to Paris but there would be no second rescue.

At Gare du Nord, without any thought to distance or timing, she began walking south in the direction of the Marais, of the Place des Vosges and their anniversary hotel. What she planned to do when she got there she had no idea. She knew James and Holly would not be staying there – not even they could be *that* perverted – and she also knew she would not be able to get a room for herself even if she wanted one because you had to book several weeks in advance.

Not to mention the fact that she could no longer pay for it. She'd got so used to having what James could afford she had forgotten that she earned a mid-level marketing salary and, after her irregular attendance and emotional outbursts of the last few weeks, had as much chance of an increase as she had of turning the next corner and finding her husband on his knees, begging her to take him back.

At the glass doors of the Hôtel des Vosges, she couldn't even bring herself to go in. What if she was recognised by the manager or another member of staff? They'd been famous, after all,

James and she, treated like VIPs; a press conference had been held. She thought about Andrew and Frances, their excitement about James's television interview, and of the messages Frances had left for her in recent days – 'Is this true?'; 'I'm sure Andrew must have made some sort of mistake . . .' – in which her sense of having been let down personally had made Alexa's eyes fill all over again.

And then she remembered something else: a conversation they'd had the night they'd met the Connellys in the bar. Like skiers trading boasts about black runs, they'd begun exchanging shopping stories.

'The last time we came to Paris, he said if I bought that cushion he would divorce me,' Frances smirked.

'No cushion is worth four hundred euros,' Andrew agreed.

'But is a marriage?' Frances retorted.

Andrew and James exchanged a mock-longsuffering look. 'I don't know what it's *worth*,' Andrew said, 'but it certainly *costs* a whole lot more than that.'

'So did you buy the cushion?' Alexa had asked Frances, thrilled. She couldn't remember the answer now – she assumed yes – but the point was that this was a version of her fantasy conversation with James, or rather, the Connellys had supplied the original and she had been their audience. She'd wanted a marriage like theirs, even though she knew nothing about it beyond their entertaining small talk.

Why had she not been satisfied with what she had already? Surely she had been lucky by anyone's standards?

She saw now that she'd been on a mission to remould James that weekend; she'd needed to choreograph everything, even his desire for her. She hadn't considered that there might be a link between her need to choreograph and his lack of desire.

Nothing had been left to chance. She'd had a guidebook called *Bonnes Adresses* or something similarly pretentious, and she'd studied avidly the chapters for honeymooners. She'd taken

James to the Musée Picasso to see *The Kiss*, and then to the Musée Rodin, also to see *The Kiss*. If there had been an exhibit of Doisneau's *Kiss by the Hôtel de Ville* and the opportunity to pose in front of the city's most famous embrace, she would have eagerly signed up for it.

And yet, James and she, they had not wanted to kiss each other that weekend. Not at first.

On she walked, and on and on and on, towards the Eiffel Tower, in Paris the obvious end. Where did the dispossessed head in London, she wondered, all the visiting and lost souls there. Big Ben, perhaps, or the London Eye? Somewhere that lifted you off the ground and bore you upwards, tormented you with the illusion that you might be able to jump and not fall.

She recognised the bridge, Pont d'Iéna, from the photograph she'd given James: the five low arches, the sculptures atop the pylons, the broad run of steps on the bank below. If she were to reconstruct the dive in the photo, with no training or skill, with no care for her safety, would she be guaranteed a suicide? Too tired to take the last steps towards it, she lay herself down on the grass, her slight figure heavy and useless. Her blisters throbbed. She wasn't going to end her own life, of course she wasn't, but for the first time she thought she could understand why people harmed themselves in little ways, just a nick of the skin with a blade or a small deliberate burn: surface pain was sharp, it had immediate impact; it interrupted, however briefly, the annihilation of heartbreak.

Why, James? Why did you have to jump?

Having asked the question, it was inevitable that she should drift to the landing stages and search in particular for the company they had used, the boat they had taken. Life and business went on, with departures every thirty minutes, and it was as easy to buy a ticket as not.

She took a seat on the lower deck, close to where she and

375

James had sat last time, trying to work out where the Walshes must have been; in the end she got up and climbed a couple of steps to the upper deck to get a better sense. They'd been about where that girl in the sun hat sat now, she thought, a still, solitary figure among the animated couples and families.

I'm not the only one here alone, she thought, but it was of no comfort because as soon as she had returned to her seat and the girl was out of sight, she immediately felt like an outcast again, the only person in Paris who'd been forsaken.

The boat departed. Despite it being the same tour operator, the same type of cruiser, and her having found a seat very close to her original one, there was little that was familiar about the trip. Bridges and buildings, bridges and buildings; the Invalides, the Tuileries, the Louvre, Notre-Dame, who cared? Soon she fell into a hypnotic stupor, not one of her daydreams but more a state of complete blankness, which was in some ways preferable, becoming roused from it only when she heard the words '*Pont Louis-Philippe*', 'the Marais', 'the Hôtel de Ville'. They'd come beyond the point at which the captain had previously aborted the trip and allowed her – and the Walshes – to disembark, past the tip of the Ile Saint-Louis and into the return stretch of river. The boat was as close as it would get to the neighbourhood she'd come from, and she had a clear image of herself shuffling on the pavement outside their old hotel an hour or two ago, then another, less distinct one, of herself upstairs in one of its top rooms, in bed with James, their bodies moving together in a way that was both familiar and unversed. Something had been different that day; he'd been combative, forceful, yes, which she had enjoyed, but he'd also been *inspired*.

She recognised then, as they drifted under the Pont Neuf, the connection she should have made weeks ago, she recognised it at last: when James had finally wanted to have sex with her that weekend, the day after the rescue, he'd just gone to meet Holly Walsh in the lobby. They'd been talking about what had happened on the boat, sharing the details from their respective vantage points, filling in each other's gaps. He'd come back upstairs and made love to Alexa, but he'd been thinking about Holly. And Alexa had mocked him about being a hero, she'd pinned him beneath her and she'd said, 'I bet that girl downstairs would love to be in my place right now, wouldn't she?'

And James had said, 'Shut up, Alexa, shut up.'

Shut up.

Chapter 28

Sharing with James the memory of meeting her father seemed to Holly to have made the two of them, if it was possible, even closer. The following day they meandered for hours, hooked at the elbow, falling in and out of conversation as they went. Paris was beautiful, just the way he had promised it would be, the sunlit pavements flecked with shadow, the buildings elegant but not forbidding as the smarter parts of London were; and there were more of those lovely old-fashioned cafés with their buttery pastries and gluey *chocolats*. They browsed the window displays of stationery shops and *boulangeries*, of boutiques selling handbags and shoes for a thousand euros or more. For Holly, who had never had any money, looking was as pleasurable as owning and she resisted most of James's attempts to buy her gifts. What she liked best was not what he could buy but the things he knew, the little facts, like that the Marais had once been a swamp or that the French for window shopping – *faire du lèche-vitrine* – translated into English as 'window licking'.

James said what *he* liked best was to be allowed to stroll into a café for lunch and not have to hare across town in a taxi to somewhere with a Michelin star. 'I'm not interested in stars,' Holly assured him, 'especially not ones I can't pronounce.'

Though it was lovely to be just the two of them, when they

resumed their rambling after lunch and passed a grand old apartment building with a solitary slide at the centre of the courtyard, Holly thought at once of Mikey. After climbing frames, slides were his favourite: he'd go up and down, up and down, over and over before tiring, each time searching for her praise as if he'd done something new.

It made her wish once more he were here with them after all.

Then, breathtakingly quickly, the atmosphere changed. The sense of intimacy was gone, the road was wider, the traffic faster, the horizon lower. The light had sharpened and the smell soured.

'Oh, look, the islands,' James said. 'I hadn't realised we were so close to the river.'

If not having actively avoided the Seine, Holly had nonetheless been pleased that their explorations had not yet taken them to its banks. At street signs that pointed to bridges or left-bank quarters she'd heard of, she had subtly pressed in the opposite direction. But she was not as familiar with the city as James was and had no natural sense of direction, and so she had never been safe from it, she saw, not really.

'Oh!' A movement to her right at ground level startled her enough to trigger the beginnings of panic. There was a sleeping bag, contoured like a human body, but with no visible head to it. At second glance, she saw it was zipped at the top, too, a padded body bag. A homeless person on the roadside; a sleeping sentry to the darker parts of the city.

'I think he's taking a nap,' James said, oblivious to her sudden fear. 'Why don't we cross the river here and have a drink in the Latin Quarter?'

Holly didn't move. 'Will we pass where Mikey fell in? It was right here, wasn't it, but on the other bank?'

'I'm not sure exactly. If you don't want to, though, we can stay on this side and cross further down. Or not cross at all.'

Still she had not actually seen the water.

James was struck with inspiration. 'How about we go up on the roof of Notre-Dame? Did you do that last time? The views are great.'

Holly tried to impersonate her normal self. 'No. We saw it from the boat, but I wasn't really looking . . .' Her effort collapsed before she could finish the sentence, her attention monopolised by a sudden image of herself that day as if through a keyhole: she'd been smoking a cigarette and she remembered exactly how it had felt gripped between index and middle fingers; she'd closed her eyes to the sun, hating its dazzle, feeling persecuted by it, and lowering her head to escape it, wishing she had a hat, wishing she didn't have to be there. She'd been in a cocoon, Mikey and everyone else outside of it.

James glanced at her with the beginnings of concern. 'It was just before the accident, Notre-Dame, wasn't it? I remember everyone standing up and taking photos. Didn't they slow the boat a bit?' Though he spoke in his usual relaxed voice, she knew he was now monitoring her reaction carefully. Had he planned this route deliberately, then, so he could conjure details of the accident while insisting she face the deadly water in which it had happened? Was this the exorcism he'd spoken of? Why would he do this to her? Why would he want her to relive that awful day?

All at once the smell in her nose was overpowering, not the sour smell of a moment ago but something else, the stink of colour rather than any material: a dark, dark clay-brown. She thought she could feel liquid mud coming in through her nostrils, she was inhaling it, her airways coated in it, thickening with every new breath. Soon there would be just two pinpricks for air, and then nothing.

She pulled her hand free of James's.

'What?' he said, at once. 'Are you OK, darling?'

'No, please, I need . . .' She knew she was failing to conceal her rising hysteria, her sudden and irrational suspicion of him. 'I need some time on my own.'

He was instantly solicitous. 'Is it because we're close to where it all happened?'

'No, yes, oh, I don't know! I just want to carry on walking, get some air.' She was breathing through her mouth, but she was worried that her throat would clog with mud, too; she would die if she couldn't breathe and Mikey would be left motherless.

'Fine, but I'll come with you,' James said. 'You shouldn't be on your own.'

'No, please, let me just go on alone. I'll meet you back at the apartment in a little while.'

'I'm staying with you, Holly . . .'

But she persisted and persisted and at last he let her go. He made her repeat aloud the address and entry code for their apartment before he kissed her goodbye. She went through the motions of returning the kiss but had to pull her mouth from his almost at once, her throat contracting as it sucked for air.

She could not bring herself to cross the river straight away, but stayed on the right bank until the islands were safely behind her, crossing at the pedestrian Pont des Arts. Then she continued upstream in the direction of the Eiffel Tower, following in reverse their route of that terrible day. She could not take her eyes off the water, which appeared to change colour and texture from bridge to bridge, sometimes smooth and still, brown as a mouse's back, other times bottle-green and with currents racing across the surface. At one point she started violently at the noise of children screaming – it sounded like a whole playground-full of them – and was bewildered not to see its source, until sliding into view came one of the leviathan *bateaux mouches* she remembered from last time. It was almost the length of a street, low and heavy in the water, the open deck crowded with children calling and waving to the people on the quayside. Holly shrank against the embankment, watching it pass as if it really were headed for hell.

On the lower walkway there was a smell of urine, evidence of makeshift homes under the next bridge, a mattress, a box of food. A couple strolled by with a small child and Holly had to stop herself from crying out a warning, though the boy's hands were held firmly on either side. Even if he tripped on the cobbles he would not be able to fall into the water. On she stumbled, past houseboats, restaurants, car parks, piano bars, expressways and, the cause of her greatest apprehension, embarkation points for the various tours. The *bateaux mouches* departed from the other side; for hers, she needed to stay on the left bank – she couldn't remember exactly where but somewhere near the tower – and if she kept walking she would come to it. It was where she had met Joanna and Mikey after a morning spent lying on her bed in their hotel room, disconnected from the world but unable to disconnect from herself, no matter which pills she took, no matter how hard she tried.

Though it was August, the weather was cooler than in June and the boat not nearly as busy. The music they played – some kind of jazz – as the tour began was not familiar, though the commentary, played through the public address system in English and with earphones you could use for other languages, she did remember. After waking, Mikey had played with the earphones, ramming them against her leg to get her help in trying them on. She had not given it. But first . . . That was right, fairly soon after the boat had set off, Joanna had gone to get them a drink from downstairs and that was when Mikey had woken up and begun wailing to be free of the pushchair straps. Without Joanna's warning eye, Holly hadn't bothered hiding her cigarette, she had just reached with her unoccupied hand to unbuckle him, not meeting the eyes she knew would be searching greedily for hers because they always were. She had thrust the earphones at him, thinking, *Anything to shut him up*. That was how she'd thought of Mikey sometimes, even when it was just the two of them, not 'you', but 'him', as if he were something she'd never invited into her life in the first place, an irritant she'd been saddled with for an unspecified, but certainly finite, period of time. Someone else's problem.

Giving up on the earphones, he'd spotted the railings, the moving world beyond; he'd pointed to the river and said to her, 'Water! Deep!' using the emphatic warning tone he'd learned from Joanna. When she had not replied, he'd put one hand on the second lowest rail and reached with the other into the air above it. She had not called out, as mothers should, 'Careful, darling, stay close to me,' or, 'Come and sit on my lap and let's look together – what can you see?'

She had thought only, *I wish Mum would come back and deal with him.*

Holly saw now all the safety equipment on the boat, the banks of life vests – *gilets de sauvetage* – enough for two hundred passengers, apparently; the fire extinguisher within easy reach; an orange ring like the one the crew had thrown in for James, its rope thin and strong. These were the things mothers took note of: safety equipment, emergency exits, hazards to be blocked off, disasters to be averted. She knew that now.

A long dredger-type vessel passed upstream and that made her remember something else they'd seen that day, one exactly like it transporting the rusting carcass of a car, perhaps just fished out of the water and being taken for scrap. Mikey had pointed and shouted out in excitement, 'Car, car!'

It wouldn't have taken much to have agreed, 'Yes, what a strange thing to see on a boat,' but, again, she had not cared to respond.

There was a shallow metal case that ran under the rails and she lifted its lid to discover more life vests. It was this casing that Mikey had climbed on to first, and she'd half watched him as he did. He had unusual agility and balance, they'd been told.

He could climb like a monkey. Suze used to say to Joanna and her, 'He could join the circus, this one, earn you a fortune!'

They were approaching Notre-Dame, the section of the river where the accident had happened; here, it ceased to be one slow curve of silver-grey, a single whole body, and became something that squirmed with a million different components, each bent on its separate journey. Holly closed her eyes and kept them closed for several minutes. Whatever there was still to see, she could not bring herself to look. It was only as the boat turned at the tip of the Ile Saint-Louis, to begin the second half of the route, the part they had missed that first time, that she opened them again and began crying, saying to herself, 'I'm sorry, Mikey, I'm so sorry.'

Anyone who'd been observing her for any length of time would have thought she was grieving, that the accident that day had ended in tragedy and not in the celebration of miracles.

When she returned to the apartment she found James waiting for her, pallid with worry. Relief brought instant colour to his face and a faint shake to his voice. 'I shouldn't have brought you back here. I got it wrong.' He went on berating himself: 'I must have been mad. It's completely perverse, forcing you back to where your son almost died – it's so callous. You've been crying! Please, tell me you're all right?'

'I think I'm fine,' she said. 'Honestly.' I can breathe, she thought. Her nostrils felt clear and her lungs felt strong. Something had been achieved by her one-woman reconstruction, though she wasn't yet sure what.

They sat on the sofa not touching, both upright, not yet ready to relax. They had never been like this before, tense and uncertain of each other.

'I wanted to rescue you,' James said, at last. 'That's why I made us come back.'

'Rescue me from what?' Holly asked.

'From whatever it was that was still scaring you – the fear that it might happen again, I suppose.'

'But it couldn't happen again, not with Mikey back in London.'

He gave a heavy sigh. 'The fear of some post-traumatic incident, then.'

She didn't say anything.

He leaned towards her and kissed her between the eyebrows, only his lips making contact, and withdrew again. She waited to learn what her reaction would be to his touch and was relieved to find she still liked it very much. She reached out a hand and laid it on top of his.

'I thought I'd lost you,' he said. He didn't explain what he meant by that, whether he had feared she'd decide not to come back, thereby ending their relationship; or that she'd broken the surface of their shared fantasy, just as she had worried she might, just as Alexa had said *he* would (*One day he'll wake up and remember . . .*); or whether he meant she'd be lost properly, having lost her mind and vanished, or even taken her own life.

'I'd never do anything stupid,' she told him. 'I've got Mikey and you. I'm not going anywhere.'

'Except home,' he said. 'We'll get an earlier train back tomorrow if you like, or even try to go tonight?'

'It's OK, let's stay. I really am fine.' The thought crystallising only then, she said, 'It was weird, but I thought I saw Alexa this afternoon. I really thought it was her.'

James's brow creased with fresh apprehension. 'Alexa? Where?'

'On the boat. It can't have been her, I know that. It just looked like her.'

James said at once, 'You've been on a *boat*?'

'Yes. I wanted to take the river trip again, see exactly where it happened.'

'No wonder you were so upset.' He inspected her closely,

eyes narrowed, mouth defenceless. When she hurt, he did too, she saw; it was more than reflection, it was absorption, something she'd only ever been aware of happening before in Joanna, never in a boyfriend. 'Well, that can't have been Alexa, can it? Why would she be in Paris?'

The same reason she was, perhaps, Holly thought, to revisit ghosts; or perhaps to follow *them*. Alexa knew where they lived, after all – it wouldn't have been too difficult to tail them to St Pancras yesterday and board the same train unseen.

'I think guilt made me think it was her,' she said. As she spoke, a look of pure, unguarded sorrow crossed James's face and it struck her, then, with a sudden, violent punch to her abdomen, what should have struck her far sooner: she had destroyed another woman's life.

'I've taken you from her,' she said to James, swallowing the stammer in her voice. 'If you hadn't met me, if Mikey hadn't fallen . . . you'd still be married to her, she'd have the life she wants.'

She remembered their conversation on the train: he and Alexa had arrived on the Thursday, the accident had happened on the Saturday, they'd had just one whole day before their holiday, their marriage, was sabotaged.

'Which day was your anniversary?' she asked James urgently. 'That weekend with her, you were celebrating your wedding anniversary, weren't you? Which was the actual day?'

'It was the Sunday,' he said, frowning.

The very day she'd walked into his hotel and set this in motion. Whatever he said, whatever he'd initiated since, she had done that, not him. She could have sent him a letter or an email or spoken to him on the phone, but instead she had walked for miles to place herself at his feet and tell him she would do anything he wanted.

'Why are you asking that now, when—?' he began, but she startled him with an abrupt outburst of noisy sobs.

'I should have had these thoughts before, shouldn't I?' she cried, as he tried to comfort her. 'Marriage is a *huge* thing. What if you two had children – would I still have done it?' And she knew the answer was yes, for in her quiet, unhurried way she'd been ruthless; she'd have kept coming back, even if it took years. She'd been almost religious in her pursuit of James, like a disciple set a mission by God, and yet marriage was considered the truly sacred thing between men and women, wasn't it?

'We don't have children,' James told her, soothingly, 'so it doesn't matter.'

'But it does! That's just it: I've been behaving as if mine is the only life that counts – mine and Mikey's.'

'And mine,' he said. 'And they *are* the ones that count, to *us*, anyway. Hey . . .' Her eyes and nose were running freely and he began wiping her cheeks with his fingers. 'I'm the one who chose to end my marriage, not you. And it would have happened sooner or later, I promise you.'

'You say that, but *would* it really, if you hadn't met me?'

'I'm sure it would, it was already getting to the point of no return.'

'But what if we hadn't acted on what we felt?' Holly persisted. 'Could you have got back from that point? You weren't actually *there* yet, were you?'

'We talked about this before,' James said. 'We had to act, didn't we? We couldn't *not*. Whether or not Alexa and I could have saved what we had is irrelevant. And she will be fine, I promise you. I know her. This won't kill her.'

'You're absolutely sure?'

'I'm absolutely sure.'

And she believed this, she believed him, she had to. What was coming next when they returned to London, the slow reintegration into his family and social circles that had so far either resisted their union or been kept in ignorance of it, the continuing campaign to convince her mother that she had made the right choice for her son, it wasn't going to be survived without believing in James with all her heart.

James spoke with finality. 'Listen to me, Holly, I wouldn't have been in Paris if it weren't for my wedding anniversary. We wouldn't have met. There is nothing that would make me want to change that, nothing.'

Though this was her first experience of remorse, the conversation itself was familiarly, consolingly circular: whichever way their meeting had occurred it could only have been the right way, because not having met was ultimately unimaginable to them. Now they were together it was the same as having always been together in the past and always going to be in the future.

Holly stopped crying and they sat quietly for a while, listening to the sounds from outside: greetings and farewells at the café across the street, cars and scooters pulling up and accelerating off again.

'You must be hungry?' James asked. 'Do you want something to eat? I could go out and pick something up?'

'No, thank you.' She stretched out on the sofa, spent. 'I'm tired. I've walked so far.'

'Like last time.'

'Like last time.'

He began kneading the sole of her left foot with his thumbs. 'Have you got blisters this time as well?'

'Probably, but not as bad. Ow, that hurts.'

'I'll run you a bath. Then let's have an early night,' James said.

Once in bed, it wasn't clear who was comforting who, but they ended the day as they'd begun it, gripped in each other's arms, not to be separated by anyone.

Chapter 29

The weekend that Holly and James were in Paris was an August bank holiday, the same weekend the fair came to Crystal Palace Park. When Adrian rang to suggest an outing with Mikey, Joanna agreed at once. It was an irresistible day: fresh and clear, with just a light splatter of white on the rollered-yellow-blue sky, and everyone they passed between the park gates and the fair entrance was smiling.

'Mummy gone,' Mikey told Adrian, in the solemn way he had with adults he didn't know. He couldn't know, of course, that even before he was born he'd had more of Adrian's attention than he'd since had from any other man, including his own father. It wouldn't take long before James caught up, too.

Adrian raised a querying eyebrow at Joanna. 'I thought she was just away for the weekend?'

'She is. Two nights in Paris, with James.' Saying the words brought an anxious wrinkle to her forehead.

'I have a suggestion,' he said, out of Mikey's earshot. 'No worrying about Holly today – especially not in front of him.'

'OK.'

It was a relief to have him there to enforce the rule. Joanna didn't want to think of what might be happening in Paris as Holly retraced her steps of that first trip, or how Alexa must be feeling knowing her successor was retracing *hers*. How she wished that information had not been divulged (the perils of speech development!).

Better, perhaps, to pay a little heed to what it was she was doing here, with Adrian. Getting entangled again, acting before thinking or without thinking at all; allowing herself to be stirred by remarks like the one he'd made the last time they met – 'We'll be dead a long time' – remarks with bigger-picture ideas, and just when she'd decided that the best way to handle Holly's and Mikey's departure was to take life by the day, to screen the future from view.

Easier said than done, of course.

'Here we are,' she told Mikey as they reached the entrance booth of the fair, lifting him into her arms for a better view of the rides. They were the old-fashioned steam kind: swingboats, chair-o-planes and dive bombers, and a huge vintage Ferris wheel with its gondolas dangling like charms. By the looks of things, the entire neighbourhood had turned out for it and as she waved to a few familiar faces from the shop she had the rare and very pleasurable sense of true belonging. She even thought for a moment she'd spotted Sean in the throng, but knew she must be mistaken: Sean didn't do activities, Sean just 'hung' indoors. The fact that he had a soon-to-be-two-year-old child did not inspire him to pick up the phone, as Adrian had, and suggest this outing, one that was causing Mikey to squeal with delight and try to swan dive to the ground. *Still* he had not returned Holly's calls or seen Mikey since they had moved in with James, and refrain from interfering though Joanna knew she must, she wasn't sure how much longer she could allow the stalemate to continue. Certainly it needed to be resolved by Mikey's birthday, a month away.

Remembering Adrian's rule, she broke off the thought and let Mikey go, fishing in her bag for her camera. These days, if absent from events like this, Holly loved to look at pictures with

Mikey afterwards and see what he'd been doing, encourage him to tell her what he'd enjoyed the most.

Perhaps she'd forward a few images to Sean, as well.

'What first?' Adrian asked them, as undaunted by the crowds before them as by Mikey's overexcitement. 'Dodgems, hook-a-duck or candy floss?'

'Candy floss!' screamed Mikey and the two of them scampered off in the direction of the stand. Joanna stood smiling for a moment, absorbing the noise and energy of it all, admiring the way the sunlight spangled as it caught each moving surface, and then she followed.

Later, when Mikey was asleep in his room, or 'old room', as she'd reluctantly begun to think of it, she and Adrian dropped wearily on to the sofa with a beer. At first neither of them spoke, knowing perhaps that conversation would only lead them into the unresolved discussions of old or – more likely and not unrelated – towards the subject of Holly, and it felt lovely to just sit there beside him, aware of the rhythm of his breathing, hearing the sounds of the fair just as he heard them, at precisely the same distance.

Then, without warning and still not saying a word, he placed a hand of his on a hip of hers and began to kiss her. Heady with the day's sun and with the beer she'd drunk too quickly, she found she didn't want to stop him; when, soon, his hands began moving over her body, she didn't want to stop him doing that either. In fact, she was awed by her body's defiance of her, the way it plunged ahead, an animal tearing the leash from her hands. It was as if in recognising its old mate it was instantly open to him.

Did other women feel like this? Undermined by themselves? Surely it was a crucial failing, making as it did a serious temptation of any former sexual partner? Who cared, though, on an evening that had about it an atmosphere of something much more innocent, much less troubled; who cared?

'God, I've missed you,' Adrian was murmuring, having made light work of most of her clothing. She didn't dare say anything in reply, knowing that whatever it was it would only be in direct opposition to what her body was doing and therefore useless anyhow.

They moved to her bedroom. Their entire relationship had been conducted with Holly in residence and so the living room represented public space, even with Holly in Paris and Mikey fast asleep two rooms away.

'We need to use a condom,' she said, speaking at last. It seemed absurd to have to worry about protection when she was in her forties and had begun and ended her childbearing over twenty years ago, but stranger things had happened and – in this life of hers – could be counted on to do so.

After all the rolling and groaning and crushing and clinging she knew by heart, they moved apart again and lay on their sides looking at each other. She could not tell what her own expression was, but the one he wore was of discovering the world finally saved after an unwelcome term of alien invasion. She hoped he wouldn't break their lovely silence to ask what this meant, this sudden surrender on her part. Normally, only women did that, didn't they, but theirs had always been an unusual dynamic, he the better communicator, far more capable of recognising, and defining, the truth than she was.

'What are we doing here, Jo?'

She had to smile. 'I hoped you wouldn't ask me that.' And now she hoped he wouldn't be offended by the implication that she'd been lying there dreading the question.

'Why?' he asked. 'Because I won't like the answer?'

'No, because I don't *know* the answer. Do you?'

The fingers of his right hand played with her hair, smoothed a strand behind her ear, then his thumb brushed a fallen eyelash from her cheek. Things like that, she had missed the most, the casual intimacies. 'I waited around once,' he said, 'and I don't know if I want to wait around twice.'

'Waited around for what, though?' she asked with genuine curiosity. They'd just slept together, after all; he knew her well enough to know that for her that was not an incidental, temporary award.

'For you to admit you need somebody.' He corrected himself. 'You know what? You don't even have to admit it, because I'd be able to tell if you did.'

'And you don't think I do now?'

'I know you don't.' The pad of his thumb was now stroking the skin between her eyebrows, and she wondered if he noticed how deep the lines were getting, tramlines, they called them. Not that she minded if he did: trying to stave off the signs of ageing was an effort too far as far as she was concerned and in any case she'd been aware of them from the moment she'd become a mother. 'Marks of experience' was a better term, she thought, and experience could be had at any age. Out of nowhere she remembered a line from a poem Melissa had recited in school assembly one morning: *When you are old and grey and full of sleep* . . . And she'd read it beautifully, making it feel as if she were not only the lover but also the beloved, and Joanna had been proud of her, proud and envious, two emotions that blended so naturally where her sister was concerned.

She'd fantasised about sabotaging Melissa's text the morning of the recital, but it wouldn't have made any difference because her sister had memorised it. Later, Melissa had been awarded the school Prize for English.

'What's that poem?' she asked Adrian. 'The one that starts, *When you are old and grey* . . .'

He chuckled. 'Is that a nice way of saying I'm not the man I used to be? Or is spouting poetry just part of your evasion strategy?'

'It's a famous poem, I think.' Seeing his look of amused

exasperation, she added, 'I don't mean to be evasive, if that's what you think. I'd like not to be, actually. I just . . .'

'You just . . . ?' But she didn't finish her sentence because she didn't know how to and he sighed, his smile fading. 'I assume you don't want me around in the morning? Because of Mikey?'

'Do you mind? It might confuse him if you're still here. Or if he needs to come in in the night and finds you in bed with me . . .'

'Yep, sure.' Reluctantly, Adrian sat up and swung his legs over the side of the bed.

'You don't have to go right this minute,' Joanna protested, sliding her hand over the warm sheet between them. Since the early months of their break-up she'd rarely dwelt on what was missing, and yet knew now she would start noticing it again. 'Stay a bit longer, it's not late.'

'If I stay, I'll just fall asleep.'

'Tired?'

'Yeah. Must've been all that fresh air at the top of the big wheel.'

They'd gone on the ride without her, Mikey kept safe both by the harness supplied and the circle of Adrian's arms. Since Paris, Joanna had been cautious about letting Mikey do anything with the slightest risk attached, but she trusted Adrian. Perhaps he was right and she didn't need him, but she trusted him and to her that was more important.

She watched him dress. 'Let's meet one evening when I don't have Mikey, during the week.' Had he ever spent the night in this flat without someone else being here with them? As a single mother, she had understood, and emphasised, the importance of her constant presence at home, even during the period when a teenage Holly had stayed out late with her friends and not given a thought to where her mother and her mother's boyfriend might be spending the night. Did Adrian feel that their time together had always been compromised in some way? And could only be so again in the future?

When he didn't answer her suggestion she wondered if it would have been better if they'd applied their rule about not speaking of Holly to themselves.

'How are you getting home?' she asked. 'Shall I phone for a taxi?'

'I'll walk.'

'But it's—'

'I know how far it is. Don't worry about me.'

He kissed her. It wasn't an abrupt goodbye, but it wasn't a lingering one either.

She stayed awake a long time thinking about the day, about the night – mostly about the night. It had been blissful sleeping with him again, the sating of a natural craving she had not felt for any other man since Dan, but there was also an unmistakable sense that something had not gone quite right. Already, without knowing how, she was disappointing him again.

Chapter 30

Alexa thought, How the hell did *this* happen?

There was a man on top of her, a big man, partially clothed and fully inside her, and she could not move her body under the weight of him. He had her arms above her head, effortlessly pinning them with one forearm, and his tongue was in her mouth, probing lazily for signs of life, tasting of lager. She couldn't speak, but it hardly mattered as she had nothing much to say. Other than breathlessness, the only sensation she was aware of was an itch in her left armpit.

Had she passed out just now? More likely she'd drifted into one of her trances and, thanks to extreme inebriation, spent longer than usual in it.

She thought she must be naked, but then she registered that she was still wearing her bra and one sandal. The loss of the sandal displeased her: she tried to kick off the other (her feet, at least, she could move), but it was too tightly strapped and she knew she was going to have to live with the anomaly. Don't think about it, she told herself.

She tried to remember if this man mountain was English or French or something else altogether. He was *very* bulky: perhaps he was from a country where the national physique lent itself to heavyweight wrestling or the shot put – one of the former Soviet territories, perhaps? Then he muttered something into her mouth, having withdrawn his tongue briefly, and she caught a few syllables in English, with no detectable accent. So much for thoughts of Lithuania: he probably lived a mile from her, took the same train as her to work. That released the catch in her short-term memory: he lived somewhere north like Leeds; they'd met in the bar of the hotel she'd checked into, a cheap and friendly place near the Eiffel Tower, though not as cheap and friendly as it should have been given its utter ugliness. This man and his mates had teased her for looking so miserable and then, as she'd both intended and dreaded, he had broken from the group to ply a little harder.

She'd been drinking since she'd returned from the river trip. It didn't take Shona or any other amateur psychologist to tell her that she had tortured herself by re-enacting that afternoon in June when a boy was saved and she was doomed. She had been the last to disembark, her tears coming in the now-familiar extravagant torrents, and the hostess's farewell smile had faded in concern at the sight of her. A folded tissue was offered and the small kindness only made Alexa cry harder.

'*Tout le monde pleure aujourd'hui,*' the woman murmured, and Alexa imagined the words on her gravestone, etched in a poetic, cursive font.

It had been a necessary shedding of tears, she thought now, as had the accelerated drinking binge that followed. But this?

The man was grunting something in her ear, she could hear the phlegm in his throat as he did so. His breath was humid and savoury as he raised his face in expectation of a response.

'What?' she managed to ask.

'Happy now, I said?'

'Oh. Yes, happy now.' And she *was* happy, in a grim insensate way, because she had no choice, she had initiated this and now she could only submit, for he was not going to stop, he was a piece of machinery that had been set to the finite programme of fucking her, forceful and rhythmic and reliable.

I am a mammal, she thought, catching sight of her own bent knees, the steady, pumping movement between them. I have no higher feelings, no intellectual thought. It was exactly how Sammy had described childbirth.

After the man had come he rolled on to his back, surprising her by pulling her with him so she lay flat on top of him, her legs still spread apart. This she liked even less than the act itself, because he was looking properly at her face now, but again he gripped her too tightly for her to disentangle herself. He exclaimed at her lightness.

'You're so tiny, I thought for a minute there I was going to break you!'

'Don't worry,' she said, 'I'm already broken.'

He laughed at the line, but there was an absence of respect in his face that reflected her own for him, and for herself.

At last he let her slide away, reaching for the beers they'd brought up from the bar. 'Might need fresh supplies,' he said to her, grinning. He planned to stay, she saw, and wished they were in his hotel and not hers. Perhaps, if he did go down to the bar for 'supplies' (there was no room service here, oh no), she could lock him out – or perhaps it would be easier not to bother. As he swallowed what was left in the bottle, she sensed that he was already anticipating the story he'd tell his friends. There'd be glory in this for him and a residual human part of her felt pleased for him: just because she had been brought low it didn't mean others shouldn't enjoy their triumphs.

It went without saying that in her old life she would have rejected this hotel room, rejected this man. She would have sneered at their ordinariness, their lack of elegance, she would have dismissed them as matches for someone lower down the food chain, someone like Holly Walsh.

But her old life was gone – soon, she knew, she would no

longer be sure that it had ever existed – and what she inhabited in its place could not be defined in English or French or any civilised tongue.

Inevitably, when she woke in the morning the man was already gone, having taken the contents of her handbag with him. There had been nothing in it of value, at least nothing that exceeded the value of the bag itself, but she would not be able to return to London without her train ticket and some form of ID. She pictured herself sleeping rough here in Paris, under one of those bridges she'd passed on the boat yesterday. If she did, would someone come looking for her? Her mother or sister, Lucie or Shona, one of her colleagues? Would Paul view her disappearance as a blessing in disguise and promptly promote the team assistant into her role? Would James grieve for her?

The hotel manager pointed her in the direction of the local police and the British Embassy, which in turn supplied provisional documents to get her through the UK border controls. She at least had her phone, which had been in the pocket of her blazer, and while waiting for the papers to be prepared she called her bank in London to arrange to pick up some cash from a branch nearby. Told that her overdraft was at unauthorised levels and she would be allowed just a hundred euros, she could only hope this would be enough for her replacement ticket. She walked to Gare du Nord just in case, feet bleeding now.

In the Eurostar lounge she rang Shona, who kept spare keys to her house. 'I've lost my keys, could you come over and let me in when I get back?'

'Back from where?' Shona asked, doubtless bracing herself for word of the latest disaster.

'I'm in Paris.'

'Paris? What are you doing there?'

Alexa hesitated. 'I heard they were here.' No need to explain who 'they' were. 'I thought . . . I don't know what I thought.' This was perfectly true. 'I just had to come.'

'Did you see them?' Shona asked.

'No, of course not. They're probably not even here. I probably got that wrong, like everything else. They'll be coming next weekend, or maybe they've gone to Paris, Texas, or something.' There was a faint strain of hysteria in the laugh that followed and Shona was quick to hear it.

'Come straight home, Alexa. Get a taxi at St Pancras.'

'I haven't got any money, I lost my purse as well.'

'I'll pay the fare. Just get in the taxi and come home, I'll be waiting. Alexa? Promise me this is what you're going to do?'

'Yes.'

'You're going to be fine. I know it doesn't feel like that now, but you are.'

On the train she picked up her other messages. There were three from Tracey, telling her that as predicted there'd been eager reaction to her newspaper feature, mostly in the form of sympathetic emails, which she would forward to Alexa to read. 'One woman actually *rang the office*.' Tracey reported this as if it were a highly irregular occurrence that someone should choose to communicate using their vocal folds. 'She says she needs to meet with you in person, it's important. Obviously, it's not our policy to give out numbers of the people we interview, but give me a shout if you want hers. She sounds kosher.'

Alexa hung up and placed the phone in front of her on the table, on top of the papers she'd been issued at the Embassy. As well as the predictable pounding of her hungover head, she was conscious of swelling around her mouth and soreness on the skin of her wrists; she felt bruised and tender between her legs. Even so, speeding through the French countryside with no passport, no possessions, and no money, she thought she might be feeling mildly more optimistic than she had coming the other way.

Mildly.

Returning home and discovering a letter – the first of many, certainly – from James's solicitor about their separation and the need for a swift financial settlement, Alexa accepted on the spot Shona's invitation to stay with her and Joe for a few nights. Her first job the following week would be to arrange for an estate agent to come and value the house – just as soon as she'd replaced the broken kitchen window and cleared away the mess in the garden. She decided she would use a different agent from the one who'd sold them the property. It was not quite four months since they'd completed on the purchase.

'Neither of you are buying each other out, then?' Shona asked, kindly making it sound as if this were a prospect equally viable for both parties.

'I couldn't begin to raise that kind of money, and last time we spoke he said he wanted to stay in Dulwich. He says he's happy there.' Alexa pulled a face. 'He'd be happy anywhere *she* happens to be. They'd live in a tent, probably.'

There was a regretful silence.

'I saw the article,' Shona said.

'I hope nobody else did,' Alexa replied. She was shy of the language she'd used in the interview and not entirely certain now that she had presented herself in the best light.

They looked at each other: a heavy moment passed in which they both made the formal transition from challenging the fact of James and Holly to accepting it. There was no pleasure in the progression, no relief.

'Do you think Lucie's right?' Shona asked. 'Is it the sex?'

Alexa sighed. She thought of the man she'd slept with in Paris; his heavy, pedestrian, unnamed body had been both completely unwanted and utterly necessary. 'It's everything we said.

It's sex with someone who thinks he's a hero. It's being with the child he rescued and seeing that child live the life he almost lost. It's getting away from me and the house and everything that was prescribed for him by his family from the moment he was born. It's a mid-life crisis ten years early. I wouldn't be surprised if he leaves his job next.'

She startled herself with her analysis, and she hadn't used the word 'slut' once.

'But you're not leaving yours?' Shona said. Lucie would undoubtedly have updated her on Alexa's various absences and blunders.

'No. I can't. I have to have a salary. I've had a warning and I might get another one after last week, but if they'll keep me, I'll stay.'

They both drank from their glasses of wine: rosé, everyone was drinking rosé this summer. Alexa appreciated the fact that Shona must have asked Joe to leave them, knowing that even the unremarkable interaction of a couple looked to her like a parade of togetherness, a taunting. Given the way she'd spent the previous evening – being screwed for all she was worth in every sense of the word – it seemed incredible to Alexa that she should be able to sit here twenty-four hours later in a familiar flat, talking with a friend who really cared about her, drinking pink wine.

She was surviving, not with any grace or originality but, still, surviving. And now she had understood that James was gone and would not be coming back, she could only continue to survive until such a time that she could feel something other than sorrow.

Chapter 31

Of all the previous day's dilemmas, one at least was soon answered: twenty hours. Joanna had asked herself how much longer she could permit Sean's estrangement from Mikey to continue and now she had her answer: twenty hours, give or take.

Of course in dealing with this, in doing something constructive about it, she didn't have as much time to think about Adrian and the comments he'd made, a helpful by-product if she was to keep her sanity that day.

Sean lived in his mother's flat on an estate on the other side of Crystal Palace, sharing its limited space with his two sisters and six-year-old niece. He was the only male in the family, the man of the house who had steadfastly remained a boy. The block was not one of those places you read about in reports about escalating gun crime, but nonetheless it was not somewhere Joanna liked to think of Mikey being part-raised.

Not that this had ever been in any danger of happening: even before the current break, Mikey had never stayed overnight with Sean and had spent time in the flat only at Geraldine's invitation. Father/son visits almost always took place at Joanna's flat and, assuming that Holly's having moved in with James was the primary reason for Sean's extended silence, Joanna intended to offer it for any future visits, at least until Sean and Holly could strike an agreement of their own. Since she had Mikey to stay two nights a week, this could easily be accommodated with no further hurt to Sean's delicate pride.

Sean. Before, Joanna had frowned at the thought of his name, had had to consciously stop herself from spitting it. Now she breathed it with a sigh of something close to pity.

For his part, Mikey enjoyed the adventure of the trip, especially the series of stairwells and external walkways that led to his father's front door. He wanted to stop to examine and name every one of the bikes and other items that created obstacles along the way. The brutal concrete lines and general air of disrepair were invisible to two-year-old eyes.

In a cliché, you'd become aware of the sound of arguing as you approached Sean's family's flat, of moods fractured by overcrowding and inactivity (Geraldine was the only one of the household who worked, at least for more than a week at a time), but the reality was that always there was laughter, as if life were permanently a party just starting up or winding down. Today was no exception and since it was a few minutes after noon, Joanna supposed it could be either.

No one answered the door; the buzzer could not be heard through the music. Finally, after persistent tapping on the kitchen window, one of Sean's sisters appeared, her hair dripping and her pale, doughy form oozing at top and bottom from a tightly-bound green towel. She had the kind of face that youth alone could not raise to beauty; in fact, neither sister had had her brother's luck in terms of bone structure. Joanna had wondered more than once but never asked directly whether the siblings had the same father.

'Your mum not in, love?'

'At work. She's doing extra shifts this month. Holiday cover.'

'Ah. Well, it was Sean I wanted. Is he home? I've brought Mikey to say hello.'

The girl reached to ruffle Mikey's hair, but at the sound of a phone ringing in another room snatched back her fingers and scurried away as if in emergency evacuation, leaving Joanna to make her own way into the living room. It was very small, with the design flaw of windows you could see out of only if you were standing on tiptoe (since the view was of an identical grey tower, it was perhaps no error). A group of young men was gathered on and about the two couches; as well as Sean, Joanna recognised one or two faces from the clusters Holly had been attached to over the last few years. Judging by the density of smoke, they'd been there some time. There were cigarettes burning in every other hand, as well as something stronger. Mikey was wrinkling his face at the smell. He was shy, didn't want to go over to Sean.

'Hello, Sean,' Joanna said, loudly.

Something in the way Sean turned his head, with an air that combined both arrogance and vulnerability, gave her a start of recognition that she couldn't immediately place. He was kingpin in this tiny living room, uneasy about the interruption but at the same time prepared to be amused by it.

'Mikey, mate!' He leaned forward in his chair, beckoning the boy to him. Some of the others also called Mikey's name and gave him baby high fives. One adjusted the volume of the music, another lowered the spliff to his side; there were beers and other drinks on every flat surface. Joanna tried not to think of Mikey's cousin, who lived here permanently.

'We were in the area and thought we'd drop by,' she told Sean. 'We haven't seen you in a while.'

'Been busy.'

'Working?'

There was general laughter at this, which Mikey joined in, not knowing what the joke was. When Sean was in a group like this, it was hard not to feel a little intimidated, even though she knew that individually none of the assembled had an opinion of her she cared to take seriously.

'Whatcha got there, Mikes?'

Mikey handed over the plastic dagger he'd brought with him and Sean at once used it to make a slicing motion against the bare neck of the friend nearest him. There was more laughter.

Having thought she might encourage Sean to spend an hour or two alone with his son, Joanna wondered now if this was a sensible idea. He was not sober. She began to speak to him over the tops of other heads: 'Holly said she wanted to set up something a bit more regular with you, perhaps at her new flat, where there's more space, and a garden? Or if it's easier for you at my place . . . ?' But right then, in the middle of her prepared speech, she had a change of heart, understanding that this wasn't the opportunity for such a discussion and, more to the point, it wasn't her errand to run, not any longer. Holly, with James's support, was more than equal to the task of Sean, who was, after all, purely passive in any trouble he caused. This conclusion was borne out by the cursory, 'What? Yeah,' he mouthed in reply, happy to let the subject drop. She saw in that moment that he wouldn't be in the boy's life for much longer, but would drift off however diligently they tried to keep him, and the absences would start to feel so natural to Mikey it would make no difference when they began to last a year or longer.

He didn't object when she said they were on their way to somewhere else and she would need to whisk Mikey straight off again. For once, Mikey, overawed by the numbers present, cooperated with the extraction.

But as they reached the front door, Sean called her name in an uncharacteristic show of enthusiasm. She turned to find that he had actually raised himself from his seat and was walking towards her. Had she been too quick to deny him the benefit of the doubt? Did he want, more privately, to make an arrangement with her after all?

'Yes?'

'Seen this?' He plucked a newspaper from the kitchen work-top and handed it to her.

'What is it?' It was folded back on a feature that ran across both pages and had the headline 'Unhappy Ever After'. There was a picture of a Seine riverboat, a couple kissing on the open deck. As she scanned the main story, the words 'Holly' and 'James' sprang out at her; they were part of a section called 'Betrayal on the Seine'. 'Sean?'

He shrugged. 'Nothing to do with me. Looks like she's pissed someone off, though, huh?'

Joanna sent him the look that meant he should not swear in front of Mikey, but it was rather less penetrating than usual as her eyes were drawn back to the page.

She must be amoral, a sociopath. I hate her. I will never forgive her . . . It was clear that the author was Alexa, though her name had been changed to Lorna.

Leaning against the doorframe – could he not stand unsup-ported? – Sean was grinning idiotically, and she did not know whether it was from the drugs or from the fact of him being an idiot.

She snapped, 'You've read this, obviously?' It was impossible not to take her shock out on him.

'Letitia saw it. Brought it over yesterday. Holls should watch her back, I reckon.'

In spite of Mikey being there, Joanna lost her patience and spoke freely. 'No, Sean, *you* should watch her back, since she's the mother of *your* child. Does that not mean anything to you at all? You're supposed to protect him, care for him, *love* him?'

Sean scowled, sent a half-glance over his shoulder to check if his sad little entourage had heard the telling-off. 'I know that.'

'Well, *do* it then! Or you'll find he's grown up and forgotten all about you.'

Too agitated to wait for his reaction, which was never going to satisfy her anyhow, she pulled Mikey through the open door and swung it shut behind them. She kept the newspaper; she would read it on the bus and then put it in the bin where it belonged.

On the way home, she told her grandson, 'Cigarettes are very bad for you, you know.'

'Naughty 'g'rettes,' Mikey agreed. 'Naughty Daddy.' This was a new adjective he'd learned and an immediate favourite. She was glad he hadn't known it a few months ago when it might have been applicable to his mother.

Naughty Mummy.

Later, after Holly and James had collected Mikey and presented her with an expensive gift set of wine that could only have been chosen by James, Joanna opened one of the bottles and reflected on the weekend, hardly knowing whether to chalk it up as success or failure. It had had a charge about it of events coming to a head; either that or of having moved categorically beyond her control.

Or was that interpretation just an easy way out, another of her 'evasion strategies'?

Her physical attraction to Adrian had never altered, that was clear; it had been summoned as easily as if by a genie. But she'd sealed it out of reach once before and felt sure she could again if she had to.

Holly had returned from Paris apparently undamaged. As well as the gifts, she had stories, smiles, a visible pleasure in being home again, just like any other weekender. Her joy in seeing Mikey – and he her – was enough to bring tears to Joanna's eyes. She mentioned their having called in on Sean, adding only that he had been too busy for any discussion about ongoing contact; Holly said she was going to get in touch with him again herself the following day to try to formalise a visitation plan.

'I've got a lot of things to do this week,' she said, and would not be drawn when Joanna enquired. A look passed between

James and her that told Joanna *he* knew what the 'things' were. It seemed to her that there was a new maturity evident between the two of them; they were not so helplessly love-struck. At this rate, Paris would be in danger of losing its romantic reputation, she thought.

When they left to make the short drive home, she remembered what Adrian had said that night in the pub – 'If they were on the moon you'd get there somehow' – and understood for the first time that Holly would have gone to live in Chiswick if that was what James had wanted. It was he who had kept them local, knowing Mikey needed it, knowing Joanna did. He was a good, caring man. Yes, his arrival had brought complications to their lives, but she recognised now that she need never have worried about him embodying her horror of history repeating itself.

Today, in Sean's living room, when he had peered up at her from the narrow hedonistic little world that he inhabited, self-consciously alluring, oblivious to adult responsibility, the man he'd reminded her of was Dan. There *was* a parallel between Holly's mistakes and her own, but it was not in the form of James Maitland.

Her daughter had in fact made either a very good choice or a very lucky escape, or possibly both.

Chapter 32

Holly had never realised before how wrong it felt to do the right thing. It demanded an unnatural level of bravery and an enhanced appetite for risk, neither of which she believed herself to possess. As for the protection of her guardian angel: that, she accepted, had finally been withdrawn from service on the second visit to Paris.

Perhaps the positive feelings would occur after the deed had been done – in her case, *deeds*.

She had a busy week ahead. James had offered to take time off work to support her, but she had told him she needed to do this by herself. Having said that, she couldn't do any of it without him, she was quite sure of that.

'Friday will be the worst,' she said, as they ate dinner in the kitchen on Monday evening. 'I wish I could get it over and done with but that's the only day the nursery could take Mikey for a full session.'

'If you change your mind, I can come with you? We can drive up and talk it over again on the way?'

'I wish we could, but I really think I have to face my demons alone.'

Yes, she would face her demons and then she would face James's mother. She and James had returned from Paris to the news that Julia and Rupert Maitland had at last agreed to a lunch to meet Holly: it would take place in two weekends' time, not at their home, which James had not set foot in since he'd left Alexa, but in a restaurant a safe distance from any of their local favourites, reducing the likelihood of running into friends who'd been at his wedding.

James reported these details with a fond roll of the eyes. 'I told you it would be just a matter of time,' he said.

'You did seem very confident.'

'Of course I was. No parent would banish his or her child for any serious length of time – oh!' He caught himself, realising what he was saying, who he was saying it to. 'I'm sorry, darling.'

'It's OK,' Holly said, 'I don't mind. I know my family is unusual.'

'Unusually lovable,' James said, his gaze drifting beyond the open kitchen door to Mikey's bedroom across the hall.

'I'm glad somebody thinks so,' Holly said, only half joking.

If not the least of her problems, Sean was certainly the easiest of her tasks that week. The grinding sensation in her stomach was at its faintest when her attention turned to him, perhaps because his allocation of her emotions had already been drained and drained until there was almost nothing left.

She decided on an email, for good measure printing out a copy and sending it to him in the post:

Dear Sean,
I have left you lots of messages in the last few weeks and am disappointed not to have heard from you. I know you are in London because Mum says she saw you at home at the weekend.

(Sean never left London, he never left south London, but James had said to be clear and factual and not make any accusations that might provoke him.)

411

I would really like you to have regular contact with Mikey. He is your son and he will benefit from a relationship with you as he grows up. You live locally and I do not see our address changing again in the near future, so there will be no travel complications.

Please would you come over on Saturday at twelve o'clock to discuss this. If you decide not to come, I will respect your wishes and make no further attempt to involve you.

Holly

Alexa's office was surprisingly unglamorous. Holly had imagined a London version of the hotel in Paris, remembering how she'd stumbled into the hushed velvet interior and searched for the hidden reception desk, not knowing which objects were furniture and which works of art. But this was a 1970s tower with a grime-stained exterior and functional, rundown spaces within; there was a faint smell of cooked fish. If anything, it was more like *her* hotel in Paris.

'I wonder if you could let Alexa Brooks know I'm here,' she asked the receptionist, giving her own name in an undertone.

A defensive shadow passed across the woman's face. 'Is she expecting you?'

'No.'

'Can I ask what it's regarding?' Her attitude was unusually thorough, even protective. Alexa's troubles were public knowledge, Holly gathered, and not thought to be deserved.

'It's personal,' she said. (It certainly was.)

'All right. I'll try her for you.'

As the woman spoke into the phone it was impossible not to think of that other receptionist dialling James and telling him she was in the lobby, thereby facilitating a meeting that would change the course of their lives. 'Holly Walsh . . . yes . . . Well, she *says* that's her name . . .' – as if someone would have reason to turn up and give a false name! – 'OK, I'll tell her you're on your way.'

412

Holly's heart began to hammer as, for the first time, she wondered if Alexa would try to strike her. On the last occasion they'd met she'd been too focused on James, had directed her flow of anger and despair at him, with only a few throwaway comments for Holly, but this time it would be just the two of them.

The lift doors opened and Alexa came pacing towards her. Her shirt hung flat from her shoulders and her trousers were tightly belted, presumably because they would ride down her hips if they weren't, for she was thinner than ever. But there was a different energy about her today: this was her domain and she was determined to be in charge.

She did not greet Holly, but called out coldly, publicly: 'What are *you* doing here?'

Holly took a step towards her, her mouth forming an uncertain smile. 'I . . . I wanted to see you,' she said. She was disappointed but not surprised by the stammer in her own voice; she had not expected to recapture the composure of that previous meeting. Then, her feelings for everyone but James, Joanna and Mikey had been stoppered, quarantined; only since the weekend had she gained access to them.

'You should have made an appointment. I could have been out. I'm very busy.'

'I know, I'm sorry, I would have come at lunchtime, but I had to do it while Mikey's in nursery and he finishes at one.'

'That's of no interest to me,' Alexa said, her frigid tone drawing a surprised look from a waiting visitor seated nearby. 'Why are you here?' she repeated.

'I came . . . I came to explain. I'll only need two minutes.'

Alexa gave a short puff of disdain through her nose, as though Holly were worthy of nothing more than this. 'It can't be much of an explanation then.'

Nonetheless she led her into an empty meeting room just off the reception area and closed the door behind them. Holly could not read any desire for physical violence in her body language, but it was clear that it was going to be impossible for Alexa to be anything other than stony and obstructive – if she was willing to listen to her visitor in the first place.

They sat at the near end of the long board table. Through windows caked with grey Holly could see a slice of sky, enough to remind herself that the outlook was still bright.

'Well?' Alexa demanded, rudely. 'Is it about the article?'

Holly was puzzled. 'What article?'

But Alexa just made a small groaning sound, as if dealing with someone of proven low intelligence. 'You at least got the photos, did you?'

'Yes.' Already Holly felt derailed: she had not intended discussing the photos and still could not define the particular unyielding anxiety they stirred in her. 'I understand why you sent them to me.'

'Do you? How clever of you.' Alexa spoke in curt, mirthless exhalations, her eyes narrowed as if she could not bear the full ghastliness of Holly.

'You wanted to—'

'Don't tell me what I wanted,' Alexa interrupted. 'It's fairly obvious that means nothing to you. Just say what you came to say and then leave.'

Holly nodded once, before raising her chin. 'I know it's wrong what we did,' she began, 'what *I* did. It was very wrong.'

Alexa's manner altered at once. She stared at Holly, astonished, her head tilting quizzically to one side. Plainly the last thing she had been expecting was a voluntary admission of guilt. 'You admit it then? That you took him? You set out to take him?'

Holly did not blink. 'Yes. There was no big plot or anything, but, yes, I wanted him. I thought it was meant to be.'

'Meant to be, according to you, you mean?'

'I didn't respect your marriage.'

'No, you didn't.' In Alexa's face, amazement was already being superseded by suspicion: Holly knew this must seem too easy to her. 'Who actually initiated it, though? Who said, "Let's not just have an affair behind her back, let's really be together"?'

'I don't remember,' Holly said, though of course she did. She knew exactly what she'd said to James the first night they spent together: *I'll be your anything you like* . . . – she would never have demanded exclusive rights. 'Both of us,' she added, and she shifted in her seat.

'Don't lie,' Alexa said. 'I know it must have been him. You would have settled for less, wouldn't you? A couple of nights, anything he was prepared to dish out?'

Holly concurred. 'I wanted whatever he wanted.'

'Jesus,' Alexa said, disgust and pity audible in those two syllables. 'And you've suddenly decided you're sorry, have you? Guilt's kicked in and you don't like how it feels to be a thief? What if he were an object you'd taken from me, would you give it back? If you'd stolen my car, say?'

Since James had taken their car with him when he left, Holly wondered if Alexa considered that it *had* been stolen. 'If I'd stolen your car, I would give it back, yes,' she agreed. 'I don't know how to drive, though.'

Despite herself, Alexa gave a small smile and bit into her lower lip to prevent it from spreading. 'Holly, you are very young,' she said, succeeding in making this sound like a disastrous flaw in a person. 'Do you even know how to have a relationship? I mean with a man, a proper adult man? Probably closer to your father's age than yours?'

With this unexpected comparison Holly was revisited by the burning indignation she'd experienced when Alexa had contemptuously announced to James her discovery of what she deemed Holly's tawdry parentage; it was all she could do to answer the question at face value. 'I don't know if I know. I only know what not to do, I think.'

Seeing the explosion of anger in Alexa's eyes, she realised the other woman had heard this as meaning whatever *she*'d done to lose James, Holly intended to do the opposite to keep him. 'What I mean is I've made a lot of mistakes before, with Mikey's father. When we—'

'Oh, spare me the details of your teenage heartbreak,' Alexa said.

Again Holly assented without protest. 'What I'm trying to say is that I'm sorry, I'm really sorry. I've done you wrong.'

I've done you wrong: it was an old-fashioned turn of phrase, she didn't know where it had come from, but it described the situation precisely.

'You certainly have,' Alexa said. 'You both have.'

'The thing is, I don't think we can put it right for you.' She was beginning to sense that her candour was giving the impression of childishness, which would substantiate Alexa's view that she was out of her depth, either unready for or unworthy of adult passions, but she knew of no other way to express herself. 'We can't change how we feel, it's too late. I know I can't.'

'So I have to change how *I* feel instead, is that it?' Alexa injected extra acerbity into her voice, perhaps to compensate for the slight shake now evident in her hands. 'Well, you may find things change whether you like it or not. Give it a few years and I imagine they will, when another girl just like you comes along. Men who leave their wives tend to leave their lovers, too, you know.' In saying this she either didn't consider or was deliberately ignoring the facts of this case that safeguarded Holly from such a threat: James's previous fidelity to Alexa, their floundering marriage, the transformative element of Mikey's rescue.

The fact of their love being as strong as spider silk.

'So is that it?' Alexa demanded, when Holly did not answer. 'Is that all you've got to say?'

'I think so.' She wished she could explain better, apologise more convincingly, but she understood that she could not. She of all people knew that what Alexa had lost was incalculable, irreplaceable.

Alexa got to her feet. 'Just go,' she said. 'I can't bear to look at you.'

Nonetheless her eyes travelled very deliberately up and down Holly's body before she left the room. Bewildered, Holly glanced down at her dress before she followed, wondering if she had a mark on it or had not zipped it up fully, but it looked fine. Only in the street did she realise that Alexa must have been checking for the first swellings of pregnancy. They all thought it, then; they all willed history to repeat itself, whether they knew what that history was or not. In the sunlight the dress shimmered a beautiful soft red; she wondered if Alexa had thought the colour deliberate.

Not quite scarlet, but near enough.

Chapter 33

The house was large and impressively maintained, with a well-stocked front garden and a stone-flagged pathway bordered with lavender. It was easily the loveliest house on the street: even the bees that populated its shrubs looked pleased with their choice of address.

Holly had known her grandparents had money, of course, for there'd been handouts here and there when she was younger. 'Beggars can't be choosers,' Joanna told her once, as they queued at the bank to pay in a cheque from her grandmother. Not once had Holly regarded her mother as a beggar and she remained confident she never would in the future, either.

She rapped the knocker twice and listened for the approach of footsteps. General apprehension about this visit was squeezed painfully by the more local fear that the door would be answered by the aunt she'd never met and whose life had been destroyed by Holly's conception – the 'infamous madwoman', as Adrian used to call Melissa – and so it was with gratitude that she smiled at the tall, elderly man who appeared in her place: Holly's grandfather, Gordon.

'Yes?' He regarded her with polite distrust and she realised he did not recognise her.

'I'm Joanna's daughter,' she said. And she told herself that whatever happened next it could not be as bad as the last time she'd uttered those words in that order, five years ago, in a pub in Aston. 'We've met in London a couple of times,' she added, in a friendly effort to jog his memory.

He didn't answer, peering at her now in the doubtful way she recognised from the two occasions he'd accompanied her grandmother for meetings with Joanna. Both times she had been uncomfortably aware of his unwillingness to engage with her – or Joanna. Once, afterwards, Joanna had said, 'I don't know why he bothered coming. He obviously didn't want to be there.'

And he didn't want her to be here, either, Holly gathered. 'Yes,' he said, once more, but this time without the note of enquiry. As in those past encounters, she couldn't tell if the lack of willing was owing to awkwardness or indifference. She supposed indifference, or there surely would have been rather more of the encounters.

'Please may I come in?' she asked, at last.

There was no attempt to disguise his indecision before he agreed to permit her entry, commenting, 'Lynn's at the supermarket, she'll be back soon,' and then: 'You look very like Joanna, you know.' Of this sudden rush of detail, what struck Holly most was that he used Christian names, not relationship names, which had the effect of conferring instant demotion (though she could hardly have considered herself part of his inner circle). Before she'd taken a single step off the doormat, she felt herself starting to prickle with dislike and had to remind herself, as James had when they'd parted that morning, that surprise calls always carried the risk that you might not be welcomed. Additionally, her grandparents were close to eighty and therefore unlikely to have the appetite either for confrontation or sentimental reunion.

But it's never too late: James had said that, as well.

Gordon led her down a carpeted passageway to the kitchen and, without pause or explanation, ushered her through open

French doors to a terrace table – there was a sense that he judged it safer to keep her outdoors, like some unproven canine. The transfer was far too fast for Holly to be able to see anything of the house's interior or even get an impression of its atmosphere, which she had always imagined to be peculiarly formal and contained, like a nursing home for rich people. The outside space, however, she was free to survey: it was a wide, sloping cottage garden, crammed with shrubs and flowers, including hollyhocks, one of the few she could identify, by virtue of sharing its name. A weathered sandstone path led to a mulberry tree, gnarled and ancient, beside which there was another seating area, this one cobbled and in partial shade. It was beautiful and tranquil: an apt venue for the peace accord she hoped to broker.

After bringing her a glass of water, Gordon inexplicably vanished indoors. She wondered how long she should wait before going in search of him – fifteen minutes? Twenty? – but the query was answered within ten by the return of her grandmother. Having deduced that Gordon was helping bring shopping bags into the kitchen, she assumed that at some point in the process he would mention the arrival of a guest; sure enough, Lynn presently appeared at the terrace doors, still gripping an orange carrier bag.

'Holly!' She looked much older than Holly remembered, though admittedly she had not seen her since before Mikey's birth, and her face conveyed an emotion far more unnerving than her husband's dispassion: not surprise, but fear, a kind of realised fear, as if she were coming face to face with the police after a long period in hiding. 'We weren't expecting you!' she exclaimed.

'I know that,' Holly said. 'You've never invited me here, so why would you be expecting me?' Hearing the indignation in her own voice and seeing the additional confusion it brought to Lynn's face, she tempered her tone. 'I'm sorry to surprise you like this. I don't have your phone number and I wanted to talk to you in person, anyway.'

'Are you . . . are you well?'

'I'm fine, much better, thank you.' Holly did not know how much Joanna had shared with Lynn about her illness, but she suspected very little. From her own attendance at previous get-togethers she knew that her mother tended to confide only good news (academic progress, sports accolades, the prompt conquest of flu or a sore throat), or to avoid the subject of Holly altogether in favour of observations about current affairs. Never, to her knowledge, had advice on parenting matters been either sought or offered.

'And is everything all right with your mother?' Lynn asked, anxiously, causing Holly to note that her grandfather had not experienced the same concern. There and then she decided: he cares less than she does. He is completely removed, but she has *something* left. This fitted with the arrangements of the last two decades. Joyless though many of the meetings may have been, Lynn had not once cancelled or postponed.

'She's fine,' Holly said, mildly. 'She doesn't know I'm here.'

At this, the couple glanced quickly at each other as if they'd found themselves in some sort of threatening situation, Holly a terrorist sweeping their village and slaying indiscriminately. Gordon reached for the carrier bag hanging at Lynn's side and transferred it to the kitchen counter, presumably with the purpose of freeing all four of their hands in case of a sudden need for self-defence.

'Don't worry,' Holly joked, 'I'm not armed.' She was grateful beyond belief that she had persuaded Mikey's nursery to take him for the whole day, for it was too easy to imagine him here by her side, trampling the flowerbeds, staring at the frowning faces, saying, 'Sad lady' about his great-grandmother or, 'He bad man' of his great-grandfather, who happened to have thick eyebrows and a bulbous nose a little like Captain Hook.

At this juncture Lynn took her life in her hands and joined Holly at the garden table. Gordon did not follow, but remained on guard by the open terrace doors, in earshot but not in comfortable sight. It made no sense to Holly, but then it had never made sense, her grandparents' behaviour.

She took a sip of water and considered how to begin. She had imagined an interlude of small talk, perhaps an enquiry after Mikey or at the very least a comment about the fine weather, but there was only fretful silence, her grandmother clearly wishing to be put out of her misery as quickly as possible.

'I'm sorry to come out of the blue, but I wanted to see if there's a way we can get over what happened in the past and all be in closer touch again. My little boy is growing up and I'd like him to know his family better. I think Mum would like proper contact as well.' Though she tried to speak with adult authority, the words sounded hopelessly naïve, like those of an infant asking a roomful of Middle Eastern leaders why they couldn't all just be friends. 'I thought that if I approached Melissa and found out how she might feel about the idea of a reunion, then it might make it a bit easier for everyone else to get together a bit more . . .'

Having held constant, if fearful, eye contact, her grandmother averted her gaze at the first direct reference to Melissa.

'Where *is* she?' Holly asked. 'Will I be able to see her today or does she work?' Though there'd been no audible clues of a third resident, she couldn't help imagining another Disney villain tucked away somewhere, watching her from a window above, perhaps, or busy in the bathroom injecting poison into the rosy half of an apple.

'Melissa doesn't live here any more,' Lynn said, still not meeting Holly's eye. Her voice held a note of confession that roused unease in Holly.

'She doesn't? I didn't know that.' She did not remember Joanna passing on this news, but then there never *was* news of

Melissa. She'd divorced her husband and had an emotional collapse; she lived with her parents and relied on them for everything she needed; she'd trained as an accountant and managed sporadic part-time work; she could never forgive her sister her betrayal and for this reason was treated as a human time bomb, one that could go on detonating and never be truly spent: this was all Holly knew of her aunt's adult life.

'Is she better, then?' For a moment Holly worried they were going to tell her Melissa had died – it would explain the oddly mournful manner of her grandmother – but, no, Lynn was now nodding in cautious agreement.

'Yes, we hope so.'

'Well, she *must* be if she's able to live on her own?'

There was an exchange of looks over her shoulder, and even without being able to see Gordon properly Holly thought she sensed a vein of disagreement between her grandparents.

Then Lynn said, 'She lives with her new husband, actually.'

'Her new husband?' Well, there was no question that Joanna was in the dark about *this*; she definitely would have reported an item of this significance and, however feeble her mind, Holly would have remembered it. This must be a recent development, perhaps since the last London meeting. 'That sounds like good news. When did this happen?'

A second set of glances betrayed their guilt before the words confirmed it. 'A few years now,' Lynn said, very flustered.

'A few *years*?' Holly looked sharply from her to the slice of Gordon visible at the edge of the open kitchen doors. She wished he would come and sit down at the table with them: there was something both pitiful and sinister about the way he hovered watching and listening, a protector with no cause to protect. 'How many years?'

Lynn at last resumed eye contact with her, her expression as timorous as Holly had faced in another person as long as she could remember. 'It must be coming up to eight.'

Holly stared at her, shocked. '*Eight years?* Why didn't you tell Mum? She doesn't know this, does she?'

'We thought it was better not to tell her, in case anything changed.'

Holly was dumbfounded. 'But everything *has* changed, obviously!'

'No, no . . . with Melissa, anything can happen,' Lynn told her. 'She's never been stable, not since—'

Holly cut in rudely. 'After eight years, I think you can assume she's stable enough!' She thought of her own breakdown, of how already, after only a couple of months, it felt securely in the past. In eight years' time it would be as if it had never happened. 'Does she have children? Have I got cousins?'

'No, they haven't had children.'

'Well, hasn't she ever wanted to get in touch? With her own sister? She *must* have put their old troubles behind her if she's been able to start again like that? Didn't she want to invite Mum to the wedding?'

At first there was no reply to any of these questions, but then her grandfather could be heard to mutter, 'She doesn't have the best memories of your mother at her *first* wedding.' Had Holly been able to catch his eye, she might have conceded the point, but as it was she expressed her scepticism with the sort of petulant huffing she hadn't indulged in since she was about twelve.

'Tell me where they live?' she demanded. 'Is it anywhere near here?'

'Not far, on the other side of Peterborough.' Lynn's tone grew vague. However distressed, she was not going to surrender the address; Holly was not going to meet Melissa today. She understood now that the reason she was sounding naïve was because she *was* naïve, her suggestions based on how she and James imagined normal people to behave, how James's family *did* behave ('I told you they would come around': as if it were all simply a comedy of manners). With his encouragement, she had pictured herself negotiating an historic reconciliation, not leaving without a firm date for when the whole family might meet for the first of countless happy get-togethers. It was going to be the end of their dark ages, a new beginning made possible by the arrival in their lives of a genuine hero.

What she had forgotten – or not fully appreciated – was that she was not dealing with normal people, she was dealing with bizarre, problematic, obdurate people, ones whose family loyalties had been chronically skewed, perhaps even lost altogether. How else could Gordon and Lynn have allowed an estrangement of this magnitude to endure? It had been *their* job to broker the peace treaty, not Holly's; if not in the early years, they could certainly have made overtures once Melissa had married a second time. Instead, they had chosen to eke out the war, even when one side – and perhaps even both – wanted no part in it.

Had she consulted Joanna and not James she would perhaps have adjusted her expectations.

'I need to go,' she said. She no longer trusted herself to continue the conversation or even to bring herself to meet those dejected eyes of her grandmother without sneering. 'Thank you for the water.'

'You're going back to London?' Lynn asked.

'No. I need to go to Birmingham. There's a direct train from here, I think.'

Lynn looked startled. 'To Birmingham? But why? Not—?'

'Not what?' Holly cried. 'To visit my father? Why shouldn't I? You don't decide what *I* do, you know. You don't even care!' In fact, she had not intended to go on to Birmingham, was not sure if she even had enough time before she needed to head back home to collect Mikey, but she felt an overwhelming desire to salvage something of the day. She'd begun it with such hope; she couldn't bear to end it with what she had now.

'But—'

'But what? Is he not there any more? Has he moved?' An

425

idea occurred to her, an outlandish one, admittedly, but nothing was too outlandish for this scene and she voiced it without hesitation. 'Don't tell me, he's reunited with Melissa? *That's* who she's married? *That's* why you're still so worried?' It would explain why the information had been withheld from Joanna, it justified it; even Holly could accept that.

But Lynn was refuting the suggestion. 'No, they haven't spoken to each other since their divorce, before . . . before you were born.'

'What, then?' Holly was bullish, speaking to the elderly woman more unpleasantly than she'd ever expected or wanted to. 'Why did you just react the way you did?'

With another glance towards her husband, Lynn turned more kindly to her, even laying her fingertips lightly on her arm, the closest Holly had known her to be to a demonstrative, loving grandmother. 'Holly, I'm sorry to have to tell you this, but Dan – your father – has died.'

There was a sudden glare to Holly's vision, a lack of distinction to the shapes in front of her, and a dimming of sound, too, even a loss of sensation in her fingers, as if all sensory neurons were being reassigned to the emotion developing inside her. And it was several seconds before that emotion took its full form: not sadness, nor even relief, but a feeling of rightness, that this was how she had known it would end and perhaps even preferred that it might. Oh, she thought to herself, and with that syllable her central nervous system restored itself and her senses returned. It was over very quickly, as had been her living contact with him.

That was going to be it, then: that one meeting between father and daughter, that single annihilating disappointment. Except she had not been annihilated, after all; she was still here, she was a parent herself now, and she had a hundred times more strength and courage than she'd had then.

'When did it happen?' she asked Lynn.

426

'Recently. Earlier this year. I was going to tell Joanna when I see her next.'

Holly looked bleakly at her. 'You didn't think it was worth a phone call at the time, or a letter? You didn't think we might have wanted to go to his funeral?'

'It wasn't our invitation to make,' Lynn protested, gently.

'Yes, it was! If you'd at least let us know, we could have contacted the right person. He has parents, doesn't he, and a brother?' And there was the sister-in-law she had briefly met, hostile, but no monster. 'My mum had a right to know, it's completely wrong that you kept it from her!'

Lynn, visibly shaken by her vehemence, was quick to agree. 'Of course, you're right. We should have told her at the time. It was our mistake.' Her instant capitulation made Holly see that this was how the family dynamic worked: Gordon and Melissa imposed the will, she yielded to it. Only Joanna had ever challenged it.

And now Holly after her. She looked sternly at Lynn, no longer making allowances for age or frailty. 'You need to tell her straight away, before your next trip to London.'

'What do you mean? Surely now that *you* know . . . ?'

'*I'm* not going to tell her.' Holly would protect Joanna from the knowledge that her parents had kept her at arm's length far longer than they'd needed to, but she would not cover this up. 'She needs to hear this first: *she* needs to tell *me*, not me her. It will be important to her that it's that way around.'

This distinction meant nothing to them, she could see, and she was angry enough now to spell out her thoughts more boldly: 'Besides, I'm not going to tell her I came here today at all. Why would I cause her pain by telling her what you've told me? That you've excluded her even when you didn't have to? That you're cruel, horrible people – though she must already know that, mustn't she?'

At last, her grandfather stepped from her peripheral field of vision and into its centre, coming towards her with a commanding air. 'Hang about, you—'

Holly eyed him with contempt, her mouth quite stiff. 'No, you hang about, *Gordon*. I want to know why you've treated your daughter and her family like dirt for so long? OK, you had your reasons in the past when Melissa was still upset about the affair, but what are they now? Is it because you like having the power to stop people living the way they want to? Because you're a bully?'

'Don't talk rubbish!' He'd come to a halt behind his wife, stormy and threatening at full height, in spite of his years.

Holly glared at him. 'It's not rubbish, it's the truth. Do you even know how long it's been? It's been a lifetime, *my* lifetime! I'm twenty-two, do you realise that? I have a baby of my own!' Her scorn and resentment gushed now, impossible to quell. 'And you know what? *You've* missed out on far more than Mum has, not just your grandchild and great-grandchild, but her! And you might like to know that she's fantastic, the complete opposite of you. Everything you haven't done for her, she *has* done for me. Every single decision she's made has been with my happiness at heart – have you *ever* made a decision with hers at heart? I bet you haven't. She's done amazingly well on her own and anyone but a monster would be proud to have her for a daughter. You don't deserve her, you don't.' As Lynn began to whimper at her side, Holly blazed on, her focus still on Gordon, whose face made quite clear his rejection of every accusation she made. 'The joke is she doesn't hate you. She should, but she doesn't. She'd forgive you in a second. But you're so hard-hearted you can't even forgive her after twenty years. Unbelievable! I don't know why I came here today, I must have lost my mind!'

'You don't know what you're talking about,' Gordon spluttered. He was breathing hard, his shoulders juddering, and he placed his hands on his wife's shoulders to steady himself.

'Oh, shut up,' Holly told him, surprising herself. 'I know far more than *you* do.'

'Maybe we've overreacted,' Lynn admitted, and pathetic though it was, her attempt at conciliation still touched Holly.

'It's about time you did something you should,' she told her, more calmly, and what that something was took shape even as she spoke. 'When I leave here I want you to ring Melissa and tell *her* to get in touch with Joanna with the news about Dan.'

'Melissa?' Lynn repeated.

'Yes. I'm sure she's up to the job. It's time they spoke to each other and this is as good a reason as any.'

'I would say that's a singularly foolish idea,' Gordon said.

'I don't care what you would say.' No longer able to look at him, Holly kept her gaze on Lynn. 'If you haven't done it by this time tomorrow I'll track her down myself and take Mum with me. We'll cut you out of the loop completely. Would you prefer that?'

Before they could reply, she was on her feet and hurrying back through the house the way she'd come. She did not look back as she left the premises.

The adrenalin surge lasted well into the train journey home, a more pleasurable high than any drug she'd tried for it gave her superhuman resolve, maybe even the idea that she'd put the world to rights. But when it abated she was beset by the fear that the new life she was returning to would have evaporated, that she'd only imagined it as part of a mental condition so delusional she wasn't aware she was even suffering from it. Emotional instability ran in the family, after all: Melissa had suffered a breakdown, not unlike Holly's own, perhaps, and Gordon and Lynn had both acted irrationally on a long-term basis. Of all the Walshes, only Joanna had possessed the character to remain constant and she had done it, like so much else, for Holly.

As the train lumbered to a halt between stations and delays

429

were announced to general exasperation, she alone welcomed the standstill – the hurtling had made her crazy – and fished for her phone to ring James. She half expected his number to be out of service, or his name not recognised by the person who answered, his existence denied, and so when he spoke, eager to hear how she'd fared and pleased, always pleased, to hear her voice, she impressed herself by not bursting into tears.

Chapter 34

In making a start at absorbing the shock of all shocks, Alexa had trusted there would be no more surprises in this story. (Even now, a small but forceful part of her continued to protest the authenticity of events.) That trust had been broken first on Tuesday, when out of nowhere there had come Holly Walsh herself – and on her own, too, no protector at her shoulder, no child by her side.

Then, three days later, it was broken a second time, in the form of a woman she had never before met, a stranger who brought with her an aftershock that held enough power to dwarf the original earthquake and all its devastation.

Power that she passed directly into Alexa's hands.

Holly was, frankly, enough of a surprise. Having tried without success over the weeks to find her sworn enemy at either her flat or place of work, having even travelled to Paris on her trail, and having fallen equally flat in her efforts to hound her in print, Alexa had come to the conclusion that she might never set eyes on the girl again – and that perhaps it might be better that way for all concerned.

That was a surprising thought.

'I'm not expecting anyone,' she'd said to their receptionist, when told she had a visitor. 'You must have the wrong person.'

And it was a reasonable assumption to make: the previous morning she had been taken off the smoothie project with the express purpose of limiting her professional contact with outside society. (It was ironic, that demotion, for she'd at last taken to drinking the smoothies – and several a day. It was so much easier than chewing solid food, she didn't know why she hadn't thought of it before.)

But the visitor *was* for her.

Approaching the reception area, she saw Holly standing a few paces from the desk, a still, poised figure in a red sundress and wedged sandals. The dress was sleeveless, high-necked, snug over her curves, both chic and expensive: a gift from James in Paris, Alexa supposed.

My wardrobe will have to last now, she thought. I'll never again be able to afford what I had with him. On the other hand, she no longer *cared* what she looked like, not by her previous standards, which dovetailed quite naturally with the new necessity for thrift.

It had pained her to see Holly's face again for countless reasons, one of which was that its youthful translucence reminded her that hers would soon be forty. That skin, pink and fresh enough to produce sap, practically; and those freckles, cartoon-cute, as if they'd been painted on as part of some middle-aged man's schoolgirl fantasy. No, whichever way you looked at it, whichever way you looked at *her*, Holly Walsh had been put on this planet to make Alexa Brooks feel worse.

Well, her mission had been accomplished.

Of course that ridiculous apology of hers was too little too late, prompted if not by the photographs or the newspaper article then by Joanna's report that Alexa knew the lovers had been back to Paris. Joanna understood how it felt to have salt rubbed into your wounded heart in a way that James and Holly evidently did not: *she* had put Holly up to the formal apology.

But even so, the girl's humility, her eerie, childlike candour, had unsettled Alexa enough to know that the gesture counted for *something*.

She was not looking forward to meeting Ellen Rodgers, the reader who Tracey had put her in touch with, and for that reason hoped she might be able to despatch her after one drink. She didn't think she could cope with the commiserations of a stranger, not when those of her closest friends were hard enough to bear; returning home from Shona's on Wednesday evening, there had been unforeseen pleasure in the novelty of solitude. Nor did she relish the probability that Ellen had got in touch with her because she, too, had been betrayed by a partner, and thought losers should stick together – maybe she ran some sort of victim support group? Quite why they were even meeting in person, Alexa didn't know. When she'd rung Ellen the previous evening and discovered she was up in Cambridgeshire, she'd assumed they'd have a quick conversation about love rats and that would be the end of it. Instead Ellen had insisted she needed to see Alexa face to face and had volunteered to travel down the next day in time to meet her after work.

They met in a bar near Liverpool Street Station, where the train from Cambridge had come in. The first surprise was her appearance: if Alexa was honest, she'd been expecting some sort of provincial crank, whatever that looked like, but the woman waiting for her was fashionably dressed and obviously sane, which was more than could be said for Alexa herself on either count. She wore well-cut jeans and a petrol-blue military jacket Alexa had admired in the shops back when she still had the capacity for admiration, hardly like one of Tracey's tabloid readers at all, if you were going to be snobbish about it. This discrepancy was cleared up in the first few minutes, as soon as they'd been served their vodka tonics and begun talking.

'I couldn't believe it when I saw it in the newspaper,' Ellen said. She had a pleasant, low-pitched voice and a confidential manner. 'Someone left it in the reception where I work – and thank God, because otherwise I would never have seen it.'

'It's very nice of you to get in touch and come down to London,' Alexa said, not sure why God needed to be thanked for anything.

Ellen sensed her lack of conviction. 'I was there, you see,' she said, with a sudden touch of theatre. 'When I saw your interview, I thought, it *has* to be the same trip I was on, because how many children fall into the Seine, *English* children?'

Alexa looked at her, startled. 'You mean you were in Paris at the same time as us? On that same river trip?'

'Yes. A little boy fell overboard and someone jumped in and saved him. It was the most dramatic thing that's happened to me all year!'

'You can say that again.' In all her hopes for the impact the newspaper story might have, which consisted chiefly of causing shame to Holly, it had not occurred to Alexa that it might be read by someone who had actually been there. There had only been a hundred and fifty or so passengers that day, after all. 'So, did you see the girl? The one I spoke about in the interview?'

'I certainly did. She was just across the aisle from me on the upper deck. The child was still in the pushchair when they came on board. Actually, I thought the other woman was the mother, she seemed more the right age.'

'I thought the same. She's twenty-two, apparently, but she does look much younger.' Alexa marvelled at her ability to proffer this detail without raising her top lip in a snarl – the road to recovery, indeed. But she was disconcerted by the position she found herself in: having expected simply to trade sob stories of marital crime, she was unprepared to be plunged back into the memory of that horrible day, and not entirely sure she had the will once more to pick over the bones of the accident itself.

For this, plainly, was what Ellen intended to do. 'I noticed

434

her particularly,' she said, sucking her drink, 'even before the boat set off.'

'Why?'

'Because she was so damn miserable. Why come on the trip if you obviously hate it so much? It's not like those tours are cheap, is it? She had a cigarette and it was a non-smoking boat and I remember thinking she'd get into trouble and why wasn't anyone telling her that, why wasn't the mother?'

Alexa felt a quick thrill to hear this, succeeded by a slump as she recalled Holly's face in her office days ago: glowing with the secret of everlasting love, like the bloody *Mona Lisa* or something. Whatever she'd been on that boat in Paris, she was not it now, and there was nothing Ellen could say to change that.

'Anyway, the trip started and the next time I looked the older woman was heading down the steps, to the loo or something, and the girl was still puffing away and I forgot about them for a while because we were coming up to Notre-Dame and I wanted to get some shots. I'm quite a serious photographer.' Ellen had begun speaking as if giving a police statement, in the belief that every detail might make a difference to a criminal investigation, but none of this was anything Alexa didn't know already or could not have guessed for herself. Holly Walsh had been a sullen, irresponsible, downmarket single mother, unremarkable in most ways. The remarkable aspect of her was how she had been transformed so quickly into what Alexa had seen two days ago: a strikingly self-composed young woman with a convincing sense of humility, of *integrity*.

Do *I* have integrity? she thought, her mind wandering from Ellen's account. And if you had to ask, did it automatically mean no?

'So I only noticed her again because she was on the Notre-Dame side of the boat. I had to look right over her head to get my shots.'

Alexa's attention returned as she suddenly saw what the

point of this might be. 'Are you saying you got a picture of the boy falling?' She wasn't sure how this could aid her cause but in some morbid, twisted way she would have liked to have seen the fall captured: the moment that ruined her life. Frame *that* and give it to the lovers on their anniversary, she thought – not quite the purity of motive associated with a woman of integrity.

But Ellen soon disabused her of this latest fantasy. 'No, I didn't get any shots of him because I was trying to get Notre-Dame without any heads in the foreground, which turned out to be impossible, with everyone moving about and craning over the rails.' She gave a mournful little pout and Alexa resisted the urge to look at her watch; she really didn't want to talk about the frustrations of photography. She wanted to go home and be alone, to not have to think about this any longer. 'Anyway, I was looking through the lens the whole time and they were in the corner of the frame and that's when I saw it.' She paused, clearly for effect.

'Saw what?' Alexa began to feel the sliding sensation of anti-climax. She had the suspicion Ellen might be one of those people who brought terrific suspense to a story, only to disappoint with a non-event of a punchline. Beneath this instinct, there continued to be an undertow of disorientation in revisiting the event at all, even with the new details, even having taken the tour a second time last weekend. Just as she was beginning to entertain the idea that she *might* survive all of this, she was being asked to revive it yet again at the very moment of its conception. What would have been more satisfying was if she'd invited Holly to join them, to make *her* squirm at this stranger's resurrection of her misery and hopelessness.

Satisfied that she had Alexa's full concentration, Ellen resumed: 'Well, when the little boy climbed on to the rails, I saw that she had her hand on his leg.'

'To stop him, right?'

'Yes, I assume so. But he was going higher, he got to the second-top rail and she *wasn't* stopping him, not really. Her hand just moved with him, kind of resting on him rather than gripping. She even turned away at one point and began fiddling with the bottom of the pushchair with her other hand, looking for something, maybe.'

'So she wasn't steadying him as she should have been? She wasn't telling him to get down?' That Holly had been an inattentive parent was not news to Alexa – after all, Mikey Walsh *had* fallen overboard – but there was a strange pleasure in hearing her appalling negligence verified by an eye witness. She began to feel that she might be willing to relive the rescue one more time, if she really had to.

'She wasn't steadying him, no, *or* shouting for him to get down, even when she sat up again after doing whatever she was doing in the pushchair. She *must* have seen then that he was right at the top and about to topple over, but she still didn't do anything.'

'How could she have been so slow to react?' Alexa asked, frowning. 'You'd have to have been half asleep to not guess he was going to fall.'

Ellen gave her a meaningful look. 'Half asleep, yes – or maybe something else.'

'What do you mean?'

'I don't know, I really don't know her reason. But I *do* know that after that she moved her hand from his leg and put it on his back, flat on his back.' Again, Ellen paused. Her eyebrows arched high and her cheeks brightened with excitement as she waited for Alexa to follow where she led.

'Flat on his back?' Alexa echoed. Her eyes were utterly fixed on the other woman's as she half dreaded, half longed for what was to come.

Ellen Rodgers nodded. 'That's right. And then she pushed him.'

Chapter 35

It seemed to Joanna that in the few days since she'd last seen Mikey, he had become stronger, more wilful, less easy to dissuade or distract. Or perhaps he was just playing up because he'd had a long day at nursery and had been expecting Mummy to pick him up, only to get Grandma instead. His loyalties had adjusted, as of course she had hoped they would: it was only right. But acclimatisation to change at *her* age was more painful than she had imagined.

At four-thirty Holly had phoned and begged her to close the shop early and collect Mikey for her. 'I'm on a train stuck outside Euston. We think it's a bomb scare or something. If it goes on much longer I'll have to go straight from here to work.' James could not help: he'd left the office to visit his sister, she explained, and wouldn't be back till he met her at the end of her shift.

'I'll be there in half an hour,' Joanna said. 'He's staying with me tonight anyway, so we'll go straight to my place. And you remember I'm not working tomorrow, don't you? So you won't have to collect him early? I'll bring him to you, if you like?'

'That would be wonderful. I'll need him before twelve if that's OK,' Holly said. 'I'll explain when I see you.'

She didn't say where she'd been that day. Trains from Euston went north. It might have been Edinburgh for all Joanna knew.

438

Now, two hours later, she was struggling to get Mikey into his pyjamas after his bath when, in her pocket, her mobile phone rang. She let him from her grasp as she dug for it, watched him plunge across the room towards the basket of toys she'd just tidied away and start flinging items aside to get at what he wanted.

'Mikey! Stop that!' But he didn't falter, a rabbit burrowing, head down, rear end raised high.

She had connected the call but not yet said hello when an unfamiliar female voice demanded, 'Is this Joanna Walsh?'

'It is. Who's calling?' With her free hand she tried to wrestle Mikey away from the toys, but again he gave her the slip. It was standard toddler defiance, but she was weary after a busy day in the shop and the dash to the nursery and felt unusually exasperated. '*Mikey!*'

Ignoring this, the caller said, in the same direct way: 'It's Melissa.' This time, when Joanna did not speak, there *was* a pause, before the voice added, 'Did you hear me? This is Melissa, your sister.'

Your sister. On impact, Joanna's overriding emotional reaction was doubt – doubt that this person could be who she said she was. She did, however, abandon her pursuit of Mikey in order to perch on the arm of the sofa, waiting to see what the voice was going to say next.

'Are you still there?' it asked.

'Yes.' She half swallowed the syllable, telling herself she needed to concentrate, to speak and listen properly, because this might be real.

A moment later, she knew for sure that it was. 'I got your number from Mum. I'm phoning because we thought you ought to know that Dan Payne died.' Melissa used the surname, as if there might be another Dan they both knew, but of course they had no one in common of any name since the man they had shared, not even their parents.

'Oh,' Joanna said. Her voice was working better but her mind lagged, all but ignoring the news as it contended with the logistics. 'Why did *you* phone me? Mum could have told me that.' When they met in however many months' time . . . Christmas, that would be the next pantomime.

'Actually, we weren't sure when or who should, if at all.' This revelation served as well as any other in answering her question – a reminder that news of Dan, even in death, was Melissa's to dispense. 'But after today . . . well, it doesn't matter. We just decided it was time you knew and that I should be the one to tell you.'

Joanna frowned. At the edge of her vision, Mikey was a blur of movement and colour. She caught an expanse of flesh tone: he'd stripped off the pyjama top again, the better to attack his toys. 'When exactly did he die, Melissa?'

'Back in March, I think.'

You *think*? 'What happened to him?'

'All we know is it was an alcohol-related illness. He had a problem with that, apparently. We didn't go to the funeral. Mum sent a card to the family.'

Joanna breathed in and out very deliberately, an attempt to jump-start her emotions as much as her respiratory rhythm. Yes, she could continue to focus on the mechanics of the news, protest that for her family to have withheld it from her was an outrage, but the truth was that not having been told had made no difference to the lives she, Holly and Mikey had led these last months. Had Dan even known, through the same family source that had reported his death to Melissa or their mother, that he'd become a grandfather?

But already such thoughts were being conquered by ones that could not be so easily reasoned or dismissed. The cadences of Melissa's voice had begun to register deep within her, reminding her that human beings were not like wild animals who couldn't recognise their family members after a certain separation: this was her sister, her only sibling. Over twenty years had passed during which she and the person genetically closer to her than any other in the world had been entirely estranged. Unless Melissa had been making trips to London to surveil Joanna from street corners, then the nearest they'd come to each other in all that time had been the day at their parents' house when Joanna had stood on the doorstep petitioning for re-admission, the newborn Holly growing heavy in her arms. Her presence that day had almost caused a tragedy, it was true, but wasn't it also the case that the real tragedy had come in the years that followed? Didn't the denial of contact between siblings oppose human rights as well as emotional instinct? And for that Joanna could not shoulder the blame, not all of it.

She closed her eyes. Even before doing so she had ceased to be conscious of Mikey's continuing carnival a few feet away.

'How old was he?' she asked, quietly.

'I worked it out: he was forty-eight. Quite young.' Melissa's tone was careless, almost cavalier, and hearing it caused an instant haemorrhage in Joanna's memory, a gush of declarations her sister had made in the past on the subject of age: 'Don't the senior girls look really grown-up, Jo?'; 'When the twentieth century turns into the twenty-first I'll be over thirty, a wrinkled old hag!'; and, 'Dan's twenty-four, can you believe it? I *always* knew I'd marry an older man.' They had not shared the ageing process, after all; there had not even been a Millennium Eve phone call. They had parted as young women and were only speaking again as middle-aged ones.

She knew in that moment that every further remark Melissa made in this conversation would discharge additional sets of perfectly formed memories and for that reason alone she had to shut this down. She may not have needed preparation for the news of Dan's death, but she needed it for this.

'Well, thank you for telling me,' she said, more calmly than she had a right to expect. 'I appreciate it.'

Melissa cleared her throat, made a couple of false starts in what she wanted to say next – evidently it was she, now, who was grappling for the right words. 'The other thing is . . . I was wondering . . . now he's gone and I've had a chance to get used to the idea . . . I just wanted to say, it's over now.'

Joanna could have asked to have it spelled out in full, but there was no need: cryptic would do just fine. And she wouldn't need any time to get used to the idea of him being gone, she thought to herself, for he had always been gone, Dan. Even during those short weeks when he'd been hers, there had not existed a single moment when he had not been about to be gone.

'It was over for me a long time ago,' she said.

Melissa said, 'Does that mean . . . do you think we should meet?'

As she heard the words she'd so longed for twenty years ago, Joanna wondered at how they could touch her so little now. 'I don't know. I have other things I'm worrying about at the moment,' she said, 'and I need to concentrate on those for now. But I'll talk to my daughter about it.'

'Dan's daughter,' Melissa said, almost to herself, as if she'd never said the words aloud before.

'My daughter,' Joanna repeated.

There was a silence. 'So it's not a never then?' It made sense that, as a long-termist, Melissa should be unbothered by the prospect of deferral.

'It's not a never, it's just not a now.'

It occurred to Joanna that this was the same message she'd given Adrian. It also occurred to her, not for the first time, that a psychiatrist might have something to say about the way she handled her adult relationships, about the varying degrees of furtiveness and guilt she brought to them.

'I notice you don't apologise,' Melissa said, suddenly, and in an emotionless tone that made it unclear whether she was making an observation or an accusation.

Either way, was there any answer to it? Joanna could argue that she *had* apologised, many times over, or that it was Melissa who should be apologising to her, having robbed her of her parents in the most determined and sustained programme of sibling rivalry since Cain and Abel, and not only in response to her crime, but in all the years of her childhood that prefigured it, or she could say that apologies had a statute of limitations and there was nothing to be gained from asking forgiveness for what a different incarnation of her had done. She could say that the crime itself, in the grand scheme of life, had not been *that* bad.

'Goodbye, Melissa,' she said.

'Goodbye, Joanna,' Melissa replied.

Chapter 36

Saviours came in unexpected, sometimes unlikely, guises and Alexa had already bidden farewell to hers before she could fully appreciate that she had acquired one. From the moment Ellen was swallowed by the platform barriers into the rush-hour throng, Alexa had one purpose and one purpose only: to find James. Without breaking stride on her way to the Underground, she phoned his office and discovered he had left for the day; his mobile service connected her, as usual, to his voicemail. By now she understood that he had set up his phone to automatically reject her calls. And so for the second Friday in a row she bore the airless and crowded conditions of the commuter train to West Dulwich, thinking only of the moment when she would finally have him in front of her and be able to repeat Ellen's extraordinary claim.

Of course, when she reached the flat, there was no answer, just as there had been none the previous week (did they spend *any* time in their love nest?) and she had to assume that Holly *was* working this week, unless she wanted to lose her job. She couldn't see James's car parked anywhere nearby: perhaps he was dropping Holly at her place of work and would be returning, alone, at any moment. It was no bad thing she had to wait, she told herself as she settled on the stoop: it would give her time to rehearse her answers to his inevitable protests.

She had voiced them herself, after all.

And then she pushed him . . .

When this single apocalyptic sentence left Ellen's lips there had been the kind of throttled silence that followed proper shock, when bodily alterations delayed the utterance of words. Alexa felt her stomach pitch and roll, her face and chest flush deeply, her organs swell and shrink. The air around her face fizzed slightly before clearing once more.

She fixed Ellen with a stern eye, sizing her up afresh. 'Let me get this straight: you saw Holly *push* Mikey into the river?'

'Max,' Ellen corrected her, using the changed name of the newspaper piece.

Alexa dismissed this with a quick gesture. 'Max, yes. Are you saying you think she did it *deliberately*?'

'That's what it looked like to me.'

Alexa swallowed hard, an attempt to staunch the commotion of nervous excitement in her stomach. 'Did anyone else see it?'

'They can't have done,' Ellen said. 'I don't know what it was like on your deck but up top everyone was concentrating on getting pictures of Notre-Dame and the island. I just happened to be in the spot where the girl and the little boy blocked my view: as he climbed on to the rail, his head came further into shot, and then as he went higher I saw the rest of him as well.' Anticipating Alexa's next question, she added, 'It didn't occur to me to run over and snatch him back myself because I just assumed the girl would do it. When I saw her hand on his back I thought that was exactly what she was going to do: grab his top and yank him down. But she didn't. She kind of *guided* him over the top.'

Alexa's gaze narrowed as she scanned Ellen's face for signs of irresolution. 'So it *wasn't* a push?'

'It *was* a push. A light one. He was tiny so he didn't need a big shove to overbalance – he was already perched right at the top.'

445

'Seriously?'

Ellen did not blink. 'Seriously.'

'Then this is incredible,' Alexa gasped. '*Incredible.*' Her bid to contain the hubbub inside her had already failed: her heart was a gong, its sound too huge for her body; she was in danger of having a seizure. All this time, *all this time*, she'd had nothing to fight back with, she'd lost her husband, her house, she'd lost her job in all but name, and all along Ellen Rodgers had been sitting at home fifty miles away with this grenade just waiting to be exploded.

'You see why I had to meet you,' Ellen said, and her voice grew gruff with fellow feeling as she added: 'When I read she'd run off with your husband, well, I knew you'd want to know.'

'Yes.' Alexa frowned at her. 'I do want to know. But so do the police, Ellen. Did you not tell them what you saw at the time, in Paris? Well, you obviously *didn't*, otherwise she'd have been arrested.'

'I couldn't tell them.' She responded to Alexa's ferocious gaze with a heightened intensity of her own. 'It was pandemonium on the boat and the police weren't there anyway, not on board. There was just the crew, who were totally mobbed, and then some sort of lifeguard patrol came on and took charge.'

Alexa cast her mind back to the aftermath. It *had* been pandemonium, both inside her head and out (especially in). 'Yes, I remember, the *Brigade Fluviale*, they're called. The police were on the riverbank with the other emergency services. They took the family across the bridge in cars.'

'That's right,' Ellen agreed. 'The officials on the boat were just trying to shepherd us off – they had to cancel the rest of the tour and everyone was talking at once, wanting to know about refunds and how they were supposed to get back to the Eiffel Tower. If they were looking for witness statements then I didn't hear about it. I was still trying to make sense of what I'd seen, anyway. I was on my own, the two friends I was in Paris with had gone off to a market that afternoon, and there just wasn't an obvious person to appeal to. I did walk across the bridge when I saw the police cars, but when I got to the other side I couldn't get near them. It was taped off at the steps going down to the quayside and I couldn't get through.'

'You should have insisted on seeing someone in authority. If what you're saying is true, then it was attempted murder!' Alexa could feel herself becoming enraged with Ellen. If this woman had reported what she'd seen at the time then Holly would have been detained for questioning, she wouldn't have been free to come to their hotel the next day and begin her shameless seduction. Even if she hadn't actually been charged, but released owing to insufficient evidence, the doubt surrounding her detainment would have been enough to put James off agreeing to any but the briefest contact. She, Alexa, would have had no trouble dissuading him from meeting her in person.

She would still have her marriage, her life, her future.

'I know it was chaotic and confusing,' she said, with forced sympathy, 'but you could have reported it later in the day, when everything had calmed down a bit. Didn't you discuss it with your friends?'

Ellen began to look defensive, even a little insulted by this line of questioning. 'Yes, of course I did, I told them as soon as we met back at the hotel, and we all agreed I shouldn't do anything for the moment. To be honest, I started to wonder if I'd imagined the whole thing, maybe the angle I saw it from made it seem like something it wasn't. We checked my camera, but there were no images with the girl *or* the boy in and so I had absolutely no evidence. I can't speak French, neither can my mates – I don't know how we could have explained it.'

Alexa knew that feeling well enough. 'You could have asked for an interpreter,' she persisted. 'Your hotel could have helped you, the next morning if not that evening.'

'Maybe, but by then I'd heard some English people talking

about the accident in the bar, and they told us it had been on the news that the boy had been discharged from hospital without a scratch.'

'But you must have realised that with a mother like that he was going to be in danger in the future?'

'I suppose by then I just thought it wouldn't make any difference and might end up causing me a lot of hassle.' Ellen sighed. 'Once we got home, it just didn't feel real any more. I didn't think about it again properly until I saw your article.'

They looked hard at each other. Alexa wasn't sure that she wouldn't have done exactly the same as Ellen had she been in her position. When you were in the middle of a longed-for holiday, why spend it in miscommunication with a foreign police force? And when something happened in the blink of an eye, you probably *did* doubt your own powers of perception, especially when it was more convenient to do so.

'I thought maybe someone might have got it on video and gone forward with that, with documentary evidence,' Ellen added.

'No one had anything like that,' Alexa told her. 'Not of the fall itself. There was film of them in the water, which they showed on the TV news, but nothing before. As you say, at that point everyone had their cameras trained on the island.'

'What about CCTV film? Was there not a security camera on the upper deck? That might have recorded what she did?'

But Alexa remembered Laurent, the hotel manager, telling James there had been none. He'd said that journalists had been approaching tourists for shots of the rescue, but only a few had reached the scene fast enough to catch the passengers before they dispersed – as Ellen said, they had been hustled off board at the Pont de Sully, the tour abandoned. One or two French-speaking tourists had contacted the news channels with footage, some of which had made it to the evening news, but the story was short-lived; after the Sunday bulletins it had lost currency, there'd been no follow-up development. Might there have been, though, if Ellen had had the courage of her convictions? Might there have been a full criminal investigation?

'What will you do?' Ellen asked. 'Does this help in any way? It's awful what they did to you afterwards. You were right to say she's evil. Who would *do* something like that?' She answered her own question: 'The same kind of person who would push her own child overboard, I suppose.'

'Yes.' Her anger fading, Alexa was already speculating on the consequences of this revelation, straining to get them underway. Would James believe her if she went to him with this story? In all likelihood he'd dismiss it as vengeful poison, just the latest instalment in her hate campaign against Holly, but what if Alexa were to direct him to Ellen and have her recount it to him first-hand? Would he believe it then? Knowing that his new girl-friend had tried to harm her own child, how could that not change everything about this situation?

Might it even have the power to reverse it?

Ellen was draining her drink, checking her watch. 'Look, I just wanted to let you know what I saw. I thought it was the right thing to do. I'll let you decide what should be done next.' Her tone, her whole demeanour, had grown noticeably more subdued; Alexa knew she had disheartened her with her reproaches about the authorities.

'Leave it with me,' she said, warmly. 'I'm really, really grate-ful you got in touch, Ellen, thank you. If I need to phone you again, can I? Would you be willing to tell someone else what you've told me? Nothing formal, just over the phone?'

'Your husband, you mean?' Ellen asked, doubtfully.

'Just him, I promise.'

'Not the police?'

'No, not the police. It's too late for that.'

It was seven-thirty and still James had not come back. She'd watched a succession of returning family men let themselves

449

into their homes or march onwards towards neighbouring streets, but he was not among them. She had replayed her conversation with Ellen twice and was satisfied she'd committed it to memory without allowing herself to embellish or fabricate a single detail.

There was simply no need, it was incendiary enough on its own merits.

How different this felt from last time, just a week ago, when she'd arrived on these steps with the copy of her newspaper interview, bent on thrusting it into Holly's arms and watching her bubble burst right there at Alexa's feet. Her desire for revenge had been so potent it must have oozed from her, emitting its own scent. How refreshing it was, this new blend of emotions that replaced that crude malice: she was appalled, she was jubilant, she was impatient, she was anxious . . .

She was, if she was honest, a little bit hopeful.

She didn't *want* to feel the hope, but if she'd learned anything at all in these weeks of torment it was that you couldn't help how you felt, you could only wait to see where those feelings led you.

In this case, stymied once more by the failure of her husband to be where she needed him, Alexa decided that meant trekking up the hill in search of Joanna Walsh.

Chapter 37

The day was destined to be her longest ever, Joanna thought, longer even than the one in Paris when they'd been at the hospital with Mikey, marshalled in and out of examination rooms and X-ray units and doctor's offices and waiting areas. Hearing French words for dysentery and meningitis, for hepatitis and E coli and salmonella and bacteria she hadn't even heard of in English – and the word miracle, always the word miracle.

When they'd finally reached their hotel room at the end of it, what lay between its four walls had taken on the soothing, almost nostalgic air of a beloved residence, returned to after weeks, maybe months away.

Who needs The Ritz, Holly and she had agreed.

Now, after settling Mikey for the night, she considered turning off her phone and allowing herself the rest of the evening to absorb Melissa's voice, to examine in solitude the words with which her sister had chosen to break her long silence; to try to make sense, once again, of the way her family had behaved towards her, of the punishment they had judged fit for her crime – and unilaterally too, with no sworn body of impartial jurors to help them reach a fair verdict.

To decide whether or not Dan Payne was worthy of her tears.

But she was a mother and mothers always kept their phones

turned on, always feared an emergency, and when it began to ring again, even though it was neither Holly's number nor James's but one she had come faintly to dread, she suppressed a groan and answered it.

'Alexa, hello.'

'Joanna, you're there, I'm so glad!' As usual, Alexa's voice vibrated with that sense of headlong rush, as if its owner wanted nothing more than to sail right over the verge and be done with it. It was something more than a reaction to terrible behaviour on her husband's part, Joanna decided; it was a kind of self-destructiveness. If she couldn't have things her way, nor could anybody else. It was a characteristic that made her think of no one so much as Melissa; that the two women should phone her in rapid succession unnerved her more than she yet knew.

'I'm sorry I sounded so hysterical last time,' Alexa said, which was, at least, a promising start. 'I was upset about James going back to Paris.'

'Don't worry,' Joanna said, mechanically, 'it was completely understandable. I thought it was a strange thing for them to do myself.' Her tone mimicked the one she'd once used routinely with Holly: always bland, always obliging; never critical, never contentious. 'What can I do for you?'

'Can I come and see you? I've had some disturbing news.'

Join the club, Joanna thought. Knowing Alexa to be dogged, her immediate instinct was to bid for a postponement: 'When did you have in mind? I'm not working tomorrow, but you could pop in and see me on Monday? If you come early, it will still be quiet.'

'*Monday*?' Alexa spoke as if she'd been offered a day the following March. 'I was hoping I might be able to come now if that's OK?'

Somehow Joanna had known she was going to say that.

'I'm at the bus stop near James's place. I really need to see him but he's not there and I have no idea what time he's coming back.'

Joanna had a strong conviction that what Alexa wanted to talk about – and quite evidently could not keep to herself very much longer – was not only 'disturbing' but also dangerous, and that James's having not been immediately contactable was a very good thing. She opted not to pass on to Alexa what Holly had told her a couple of hours ago: that James was this evening visiting his sister and her family, whose address Alexa certainly must know, with the purpose of brokering an introduction in the near future for Holly and Mikey.

'Please, Joanna, can I just see you for twenty minutes? It's really important.'

Joanna relented. 'All right, if you're already on your way, but Mikey's here tonight and I don't want any scenes. I've just got him off to sleep and I want it to stay that way.'

She hung up the phone and sat heavily on the sofa. She wasn't sure if it was Melissa or Alexa or just a general intuition, but she already knew that tonight was going to be her undoing. Finally, after everything she'd survived, she was ready to break. Unable to stop herself, not wanting to stop herself, she sent a message to Adrian, asking if he was free to meet later. They had not spoken since they'd spent the night together a week ago and she had no idea how he would react to the invitation, but she said that if he wanted to come over, at any time, however late, she would be there.

When she arrived, Alexa was ablaze with her usual appetite for urgent confrontation. Within seconds, however, Joanna saw that her mood was quite unlike the previous ones; it was more exhilarated, even a little triumphant. There was no longer the underlying despair.

They sat at the kitchen table with glasses of wine poured strategically small on Joanna's part so as to keep this interview short. 'I don't mean to be rude,' she said, 'but can we get straight to the point? I've had a terrible day.' She was going to cry, she decided. If Adrian didn't come, or even if he did, she was going to sob herself to sleep. Some pieces of news, some events, were not only worthy of collapse but also impossible to engage with any other way.

'Oh.' Alexa looked quite affronted by the idea that someone else might have had a rough time of it. She left a polite little beat for Joanna to withdraw her claim, but Joanna had no intention of doing so. Hers *was* a bad day, even by Alexa's standards.

'Is this about Holly coming to see you on Tuesday? She told me about that. She means well, Alexa, she really does. I know it must be cold comfort, but she just wants to say officially that she doesn't believe this destiny business about James and her any more. She knows she has to take responsibility. She knows she's guilty.'

'That's just it, she *is* guilty!' Somehow Alexa managed to make a sharp, pouncing movement while seated at a kitchen table; she was livid with this oddly gleeful new energy. 'I met a woman called Ellen Rodgers this afternoon, someone who was on the boat with us that day in Paris.'

Joanna felt herself stiffen. She had not anticipated a return to the subject of the accident; and she did not like the eagerness with which Alexa had seized upon the word 'guilty'.

Alexa went on: 'She was on the upper deck, just across the aisle from you. She told me she saw the exact moment when Mikey fell overboard.'

'How awful, that must have been upsetting to witness.' Joanna eyed Alexa with growing agitation: that familiar whoosh of unstoppable momentum was cresting now in the other woman – she would not have to wait long for the crash.

'Yes, it *was* upsetting. You see, she says he didn't fall by accident.'

'*What*?' There was a thrashing sensation in Joanna's stomach that was horribly like the death throes of a small animal.

'She says Holly pushed him.'

As the thrashing failed, Joanna's mind turned inward until she was unaware even of her own breathing. Two months and two shattered families it had taken for the unthinkable to have been thought, the unspeakable to have been spoken, and now the moment was here it felt far, far worse than she could ever have feared.

'In other words,' Alexa added, with an expression of righteousness, almost radiance, 'she tried to kill him. *She tried to kill her own son.*'

Still Joanna said nothing. In front of her Alexa had become a phantasm that she herself had spirited from some nightmarish realm. If she could only carry on breathing, keep herself alive, the figure would dissolve and leave her with what she was built for: human pains, human terrors.

'Why aren't you speaking?' Alexa cried. She pushed aside her wine glass as if it were an offensively frivolous distraction. 'Aren't you horrified by this? Totally repulsed?'

Joanna waited for adrenalin to refuel her, but none came: she was depleted. She had a sudden image of a turtle tucking its head and legs inside its shell, removing its soft parts from the outside world and all its hazards. When it had passed, she reached at last for her defences.

'Oh, Alexa, I don't believe for a moment Holly tried to kill Mikey. What nonsense.'

'She did! This woman saw it, she had a clear view. She was taking pictures and had the two of them in her viewfinder. It's a miracle the whole thing wasn't actually photographed, either by her or by someone else.'

Inside Joanna there was the listing sensation of relief. Her voice, however, could still be steadied. 'The reason it wasn't photographed was because it didn't happen.'

'Why would she make it up?' Alexa demanded, hotly. 'She has absolutely no reason to!'

Joanna looked hard at her guest. She had developed a tendency to tell Alexa too much, to share what oughtn't to be shared; she needed to be extremely careful to put out the fire this time and not fan its flames. 'I'm not saying she made it up, just that she obviously misunderstood what she saw.'

'How can you misunderstand a push?' Alexa threw up her hands in a frantic gesture. 'Besides, you weren't actually there, were you, so how would you know?'

Joanna gave a dismissive nod. 'No, but I heard a full account when Holly made her statements afterwards.'

'But if you didn't see it with your own eyes then you've got to admit it's possible things happened differently from the way she said? She could have given the police a completely false statement.'

The word 'police' gave Joanna a fresh injection of fear, bringing a sharpness to her reply that was close to hostility. 'She told them the truth. It's this woman who has given a false report, Alexa.' She paused, easing a fraction. 'At the very most, Holly might not have acted as quickly as you or I would when she realised Mikey was about to fall, but that is absolutely as far as it would have gone.'

Alexa's mouth twisted. 'But that's negligence, isn't it? That's almost as criminal as a deliberate push.'

'I don't agree with that.' Alexa's intensity had begun to feel physically erosive – when there was so little left to erode. Joanna thought of Adrian and wondered if he'd picked up her message yet.

'What exactly *did* she say to the police?' Alexa pressed her.

'It was agreed that the fall happened so quickly no one could be quite sure of the exact sequence of events,' Joanna said, truthfully. 'The police counsellor said that in traumas like that it could be like trying to remember a dream.'

'But you just said you thought she was negligent?'

'I didn't say that at all, that was *your* word. All I'll allow is

456

that her reflexes were probably debilitated by her illness. It may have made her slower to react or less able to make a judgement.' She struggled to contain a groan. 'What you have to realise is that I had watched Holly for almost two years not reacting the way a healthy mother does. Postnatal depression is a terrible, terrible disease: I've tried to explain that to you before.'

Alexa snorted. She did not want to hear this a second time any more than she had wanted to the first. It was clear that this discussion was not going the way she'd imagined. And what she had imagined, presumably, was that she and Joanna would summon the police and stride along to the restaurant together to watch Holly being publicly read her rights.

'But not everyone who gets postnatal depression wants to murder their baby, do they?'

'No, and nor did Holly.' Joanna drew breath; if it was the last thing she did, she needed to shut this line of enquiry down. 'She loves Mikey with all her heart and would never intention-ally do anything to harm him. What happened would probably have happened in exactly the same way if I'd been sitting there myself.' This, Joanna knew to be untrue. Mikey would have been restrained on her lap, whether he'd objected or not, and it was foolish to think that Alexa did not know this too.

'Well, that's not the way Ellen tells it.' Alexa fixed her with a gaze of near-maniacal ferocity. 'You know I have to tell James, don't you?'

Joanna bowed her head. 'I realise why you feel that way, why you want to believe this woman, but—'

'It's not just the obvious reasons!' Alexa cried, interrupting. 'There's also the fact that if it *is* true then Holly might do some-thing like this again to Mikey. And what if they have a baby together and she gets the illness again? He has a right to know that his child wouldn't be safe.'

Joanna did not want to consider this possibility, though it had loomed large on the borders of her consciousness in recent weeks. She squared her shoulders and faced Alexa with renewed resolve. 'You think telling him this story will change how he feels about her, don't you?'

'Of course it will change how he feels! How could it not? The whole reason he thinks he's in love with her is he sees her as some kind of helpless victim he's saved.'

'He *has* saved her,' Joanna pointed out, 'in all sorts of ways. Won't he still see it like that?'

Alexa grimaced. 'No. He'll be appalled by this, just like I am, like Ellen was. He'll want to tell the police and have her questioned properly.'

'No one is going to do that,' Joanna said, coolly. 'You need to realise that even if it were investigated and a charge made on the strength of this one witness of yours, which seems highly unlikely, it would only end up being a case of diminished responsibility. Holly was very ill and on strong medication. There are endless counsellors' assessments that will tell us she was not in control of her actions.'

She regretted that last phrase, which sounded dangerously like a concession that the story might have merit, but it appeared that Alexa had not noticed: for the first time, she was beginning to look discouraged.

'Well, James needs to decide that for himself. If he doesn't want to hear it from me, I'll get Ellen to talk to him.'

'How did you find this woman?' Joanna asked her, seeking a diversion.

'*She* contacted *me*,' Alexa said, offended by the implication. 'She saw an article in the paper about it and got my phone number from the journalist. She thought I had a right to know the truth.'

'I saw the article as well,' Joanna told her, and she judged from Alexa's expression that she was ashamed of the interview and had not expected Joanna to have seen it. 'Do you think *that* stated the truth?'

Alexa held her eye. 'Yes, I do. In a way.'

'Perhaps this Ellen's truth is only the truth "in a way", too. There are lots of versions of it, aren't there? Yours, hers, mine, Holly's, James's, but they won't all be the same, will they?'

Alexa didn't answer. Joanna could see the demoralisation in her face and wished it didn't have to be like this. It was not a good feeling to know that you were trying to break another woman's spirit, especially one that had already been so badly damaged. At last, Alexa pushed back her seat an inch or two, a gesture of no confidence in Joanna.

'I think you know as well as I do whose version is closest to the truth. There's no way you'd be defending Holly like this if you weren't her mother. What if you were mine, eh? You'd be telling me to expose her, to get her put away, get my husband back.'

They stared at each other, Alexa breathing hard, Joanna still – outwardly, at least – unmoved.

'I don't know if I would,' she said. 'I might give you the same advice I'm giving you now.'

'Which is?'

'Don't tell James. Forget you ever heard it. Holly is in the process of recovering from a serious illness and Mikey is not in any danger. I can guarantee that personally.'

Hearing the echo of previous conversations, she felt unutterably weary, as if time were looping, moving away in an illusion of departure only to return with greater menace. It was out of the question that Alexa was going to 'forget' this story.

'You ask what I would say if I were your mother, well, why not ask *your* mother? Or someone in your family whose opinion you trust?'

Her eyes beginning to leak tears, Alexa reached for her wine, belatedly gulping it, a sight that gave Joanna the faint feeling of a reprieve.

She summoned the last of her character, her spirit, to say:

459

'Sleep on it, that's all I ask. Neither James nor Holly will be back home till after midnight, anyway. You can't see them tonight.'

There was an exhausted silence. Greyness had replaced the flush in Alexa's face and there was a woeful sinking of her shoulders. 'OK, I'll sleep on it,' she said.

At the door she turned back to Joanna with a final flare of energy. 'You know when he was in the water, he cried out for you, don't you?'

Joanna was thrown off guard. 'What?'

'James told me. He said that when they were in the river, when he was towing Mikey to the bank, he called out for you, not for her. James said he thought that was odd because in an emergency, a near-death moment, everyone cries for their mother. Even adults do it sometimes, apparently, it's a primal thing.'

'I didn't know that,' Joanna murmured.

She closed the door and stood with her palm flat against it. Of all Alexa's revelations that evening, this last was the one she most fervently hoped the other woman would choose to keep to herself.

Adrian arrived at the flat at close to ten-thirty. 'Is it Holly?' he asked at the door, his feet occupying the same square of hallway that Alexa's had a short time earlier.

'It's everyone,' Joanna said, her voice catching. 'I want to tell you, I will tell you, but I don't think I can speak straight away.'

'You don't have to speak.' He drew her towards him, enfolding her in his arms, his material warmth. She felt her body sink and sink some more as it passed the burden of its weight to him.

Presently, he steered her to the sofa and lowered her on to it. She couldn't be sure how much time passed in utter stillness before she was ready to talk.

'I think Holly might have been responsible for Mikey falling,' she said, and felt the instantaneous arrest in his breathing. 'In Paris, on the boat. It makes sense. It sounds right.'

'What are you talking about? How can it be right?'

She repeated Alexa's claim, recalling with something close to guilt how the other woman had floundered, and finally sobbed, in the face of repeated denials and dismissals. 'If it is true, she doesn't remember anything about it. She isn't hiding anything, I'm sure of it. I don't think she knows she did it.'

Adrian's face had grown dark with concern. 'How can she not know?'

'Because it wasn't her back then, it was someone else, some kind of lost soul. The way she was, Ade, she'd just vanished from her own body. There was nothing left.'

'The Holly I knew wouldn't hurt her worst enemy, let alone her own boy,' Adrian told her, firmly.

'I know. I should never have left them alone.' She'd known that the moment she recognised the screams as her daughter's. And when she'd reached her, Holly had kept saying, *It's too late. It's too late.*

How soon in the weekend had it been before Joanna had realised that Paris was not working as she had hoped? Being in a new and glamorous city had not galvanised Holly, reminded her of life's infinite possibilities, but had confirmed a view already held that even everyday life with its balance of ups and downs, good days and bad days, was far beyond her reach, something only other people could experience.

Not only had a catastrophe been far more likely than a recovery, it had been almost predictable. And a catastrophe was what it would have been without James, for, like Alexa, like Joanna, Alexa's new witness Ellen had not reacted to Mikey's fall in a way that might have prevented his drowning. No one had, not even the crew, for the simple reason that they were only human. James alone had reacted, James alone.

And the idea that he might now be persuaded to leave Holly

was every bit as terrifying as the thought that he might never have saved Mikey in the first place.

'There's other news,' she murmured.

Adrian tightened his grip, his free hand stroking her hair. 'Go on.'

'Holly's father died. I just heard this evening. I have to tell her tomorrow before she finds out some other way.'

'Jesus, you poor, poor thing.'

Joanna closed her eyes. 'Holly's the poor thing, not me.'

'Both of you are. You as much as her. More, maybe.'

At the sound of his tenderness, she began to cry softly. 'Don't go home tonight, please . . .'

'I won't.'

'I need you.'

'I know that.' He spoke gently, as if to a very young child. 'I told you I would know.'

Chapter 38

It had been a long time since Alexa had approached her parents' home and the house she'd been raised in with any thought other than of how unfavourably it compared with that of her parents-in-law. A modest new-build with a double garage in the suburbs of Welwyn versus a listed Georgian manor house with its own woods in Sussex: it was hardly a choice that called for the flipping of a coin. (Sammy alone might vote against the manor house; she couldn't understand the attraction of 'period'. 'It's just another word for falling apart,' she said.) In the past, when visiting her parents or sister, Alexa had taken luxurious bouquets or gifts of overpriced room sprays and candles, anxious to inject metropolitan style into their humble hinterland residences. She'd even remarked out loud of her intentions.

She was beginning to see that this might, on such occasions, have been considered an unattractive way to behave.

Tonight she arrived empty-handed. It was close to eleven o'clock and silent enough to release a memory of an earlier and mercifully less complicated life stage, of coming home late as a teenager to find one or both of her parents waiting up for her, of clattering through the door as the hall light snapped on and brought her to a standstill with its dazzle, denying she'd been drinking while tripping over an umbrella or a boot or the leg of the hall table and laughing uncontrollably at her own clowning. Sometimes Sammy, three years younger, would appear at the top of the stairs, attracted by the excitement. She'd been in awe of Alexa then, thrilled by their parents' accusations of law-breaking.

She couldn't help smiling at the thought as she rang the bell.

The door was opened fractionally at first, with the security chain on, and then fully once Alexa had identified herself. 'Who did you think I was going to be, Al Capone? This is a completely safe area, Mum!'

'Alexa, it's so late!'

'I know. I should have phoned but I didn't want to discover you were out. I just didn't think I could bear it.'

Her mother steered her inside, her face aglow with surprised pleasure. 'We're never out, you know that. Well, your father is over at Sammy and Rob's, but that doesn't count. Have you not got a coat?'

'It's August, I don't need a coat. *You* look nice.' It crossed Alexa's mind that she had somehow been misconceiving her mother lately, picturing her as a broad-set apron-and-slippers stereotype, when in fact she was a slim woman in her early sixties, dressed in good jeans and a well-cut jersey top. It was not beyond the realms of possibility that Alexa might be happy to be in this kind of shape herself at the same age. 'Can I stay here tonight?'

'Of course you can. Come on through and I'll put the kettle on.'

'Could I have alcohol, please?' Alexa said.

A strange and masochistic compulsion overcame her as she followed her mother through the living room and into the kitchen: to reassess positively each detail of the decor in order to compensate for her critical position of the past. The furniture, the carpets, the mirrors, the glassware, even the books on the shelves: had there been anything she'd approved of? She was determined that there should be.

'I like that Moroccan bowl in the window,' she said, as her mother poured them large glasses of white wine.

'Oh, you and James gave us that, don't you remember?'

'Did we?' She vowed to find something else before she left. When she went to bed, she'd have a good look upstairs too. Settling next to her mother on the sofa, she asked, 'So why's Dad at Sammy's on his own?'

'Poker night. It's a new thing: him, Rob and his dad and three of Rob's mates, every Friday. Sammy has a girls' night. They're trying to get out of a rut.'

'What, by doing exactly the same thing every week?'

'I suppose you think that *is* a rut,' her mother said, apologetically, and it took Alexa aback to see her easy humility: what sort of a monster had she allowed herself to become that her mockery was so acceptable? But she couldn't be sidetracked by the rights and wrongs of a poker night; amends would have to wait till next time.

'Mum, I need to ask your advice about something . . .' Straight away, she stumbled: having intended to talk only of Ellen's new evidence, she found that now she was here, with no sister or niece or nephew to clamour for her mother's attention, she had an overpowering desire to return to the beginning, to the moment the earth had collided with the moon and James had said, 'I have to go.' 'Everything's gone totally wrong,' she said, unable to stop her voice from cracking. 'I feel like I'm being punished for something and the punishment never ends.'

Her mother's eyes filled instantly with tenderness. 'Of course you're not being punished, my love, you've done nothing wrong. Tell me what's been happening with you and James? We're so out of touch, we've been really, really worried about you. Have you been able to sort out your differences?'

'They're more than differences, they're diametric opposites.' And Alexa told her everything, from the Sunday afternoon James left to the last few evenings she'd spent on her own,

465

beginning the process of repacking what had scarcely been unpacked.

'I didn't realise it had progressed this far.' Her mother sighed. 'I'm so sorry. You know how much we liked James.'

'You can still like him,' Alexa said. 'I haven't given up on him completely.'

'I don't understand. You said he lives with this girl now?'

'He does. The thing is, something's happened, something I found out today that might help me save our marriage. That's why I came. I know what I need to do but I want to be sure it's the right thing.' She explained what Ellen had witnessed, including, in the interests of impartiality, Joanna's determined refutals, and refraining heroically from using the word 'murder'.

Her mother listened with an attitude of intense circumspection. It was not quite what Alexa had expected, and neither was her opening question:

'Tell me more about what this Joanna said about the girl's depression?'

'That?' Alexa retold the details she could bring to mind. 'She was in a bad way, not leaving the flat, not able to look after the baby. It went on right until the accident, when she met James and was miraculously cured.'

'It sounds as if they've developed something very special in this short time.'

Alexa had no choice but to concede this. 'That will all change, though, when he hears what I've found out.'

'I imagine it will.' There followed a rather doubtful silence. 'Let me ask you this, and don't jump down my throat, OK?'

'OK.'

'If it changes his feelings for her, then that's one thing, but will it change his feelings for you?'

'Maybe it will remind him what those feelings *are*. Anyway, this isn't about me,' Alexa added, a little piously.

'Well, it is as far as I'm concerned,' her mother said with

indignation, and realising she meant that *she* was the one she most cared about, Alexa felt a shiver raise the hairs on her arms.

Her mother reached for her hand. Startled, Alexa saw that it looked exactly like her own: the length of the fingers, the shape of the nails. 'Do you really think he'll want to come back? And if he does, isn't there a chance you'll be disappointed with what you get?'

Alexa frowned. 'Why would I be disappointed?'

'A lot of my friends are divorced, and now some of your sister's friends' marriages are starting to break up now, as well.' Her mother said this perfectly cheerfully, reminding Alexa that she had never been the sentimental type but always clear-eyed; and that in failing to seek her advice over the last fifteen or so years she may have been missing a trick. 'I've noticed that they all go through a phase after they've split up when they want to remember the beginning, the good bit. They wonder if they've made a mistake, they forget that that portion only lasted a short time.'

'All of our marriage was the good bit,' Alexa said. 'Well, until recently, but it was nothing serious. We did lots of exciting and glamorous things together.'

'But from what you've said about James's new family, the little boy, living a quiet life in a small flat, it sounds as if he might not *want* exciting and glamorous things.'

Alexa said nothing. She thought about Shona's hero complex: weren't heroic acts exciting things? What could be more exciting than risking your own life to save someone else's?

'And if he did want to get back together, are you sure you could get over what he's done to you?'

'It's her who's done it, not him,' Alexa insisted.

'It's both of them. He was the one who was married, not her. If you want my opinion, I think you deserve better than a man who would leave his wife at the drop of a hat and refuse to give her the time of day to discuss it.'

'Really?' Alexa was confounded by her mother's line of argument; wasn't her generation supposed to be willing to move heaven and earth in defence of the status quo? 'I thought you said you always liked him?'

'I did, I thought he was wonderful, but I don't like the sound of how he's behaving towards you now. He's so involved in his new start he doesn't seem to have spared much thought for how devastating it's all been for you – and that's not acceptable.'

Alexa digested this, the shiver on her skin quickening. Even Lucie and Shona had not championed her this trenchantly, even they had not declared categorically that she had done nothing wrong, and yet, somehow, it did not seem to be leading her where she'd hoped to be led. 'What am I going to do?' she whispered, no longer certain she could withstand the answer.

Her mother spoke gently but decisively. 'Well, it seems to me that your choice is to move on and leave them to it, or wade in there and destroy what they have so all three of you are in a mess – all four, if you count the child.'

'They deserve to be in a mess,' Alexa said.

'Maybe, but it's not just that, love. You have to ask yourself how you'll feel in the future having been responsible for something like that. It affects them, yes, but they're *your* actions. Just because you think she's ruined your life it doesn't mean you have to ruin hers.'

'Just because *I* think?' Alexa repeated. 'Don't *you* think she's ruined my life?'

Her mother arched her eyebrows the way she used to when Alexa was little, the way that meant, 'You already know the answer to *that*.' 'No,' she said, 'I think she's ruined your marriage. You're a very strong person, you have been since you were young, and I have no doubt you'll survive this and build up your confidence again. It doesn't sound as if she's so strong. Going in there with this story could really be the end of her and then what kind of a life would that little boy have?'

Still Alexa struggled to reconcile her mother's unconditional acclamation for her with advice that unmistakably echoed Joanna's. 'So you don't think James is entitled to the facts?'

'I'm not sure I'm worried about what he's entitled to. I'm worried about what *you're* entitled to.' There was a pause. 'Look at it this way: you have an opportunity to do some good in this situation. In the end, you might feel happier if you say nothing at all.'

Alexa sensed this was a philosophy her mother might have applied to other situations, some of them even perhaps to do with the parenting of her. Suddenly disabled by the thought, she looked into her empty wine glass and tried to stifle a deep yawn.

'I think you need to go to bed,' her mother said, 'you must be sick of thinking about this. Why not spend tomorrow up here with us, take your mind off it?'

Alexa shook her head, the motion inducing an instant ache. 'That's the problem, I don't think my mind *can* be distracted. I can't go on for much longer like this, I need to get it resolved one way or another.' She succumbed to the yawn before adding, 'It's been good to talk it through, though, with you on your own, Sammy not around.'

Her mother looked puzzled. 'Sammy?'

'Yes, she always seems to be here when I'm home.'

'Alexa, you're never home.'

As they stared at each other, Alexa resolved to say no more; she couldn't allow the conversation to degenerate into an adolescent argument about favouritism.

'I'm more useful to Sammy, I suppose,' her mother said, answering the accusation anyhow.

And Alexa heard Shona's words then: *You never needed rescuing.* Her husband, her mother: they'd only gone where they were needed, but was that just? Why did being strong and independent have to end up causing you loss?

'You're useful to me tonight,' she said. 'Thank you, Mum.'

'Don't be silly, darling. Come on, upstairs, get some sleep.'

Alexa did as she was told. 'I'll probably leave early, before you're up, so I'm sorry if I miss Dad. Give him my love.'

'I will. And come back soon. When you've decided what to do, come back and take a proper break from it all.'

In the spare bed, Alexa burrowed into the soft pillows and battled to close her mind to the trio of conferences she'd experienced in the last few hours. Ellen, Joanna, her mother: their voices resounded in her head as she reached for sleep, challenging, commiserating, suggesting, warning, on and on and on until such a point that it felt they had bypassed her altogether and were talking to each other.

Chapter 39

On Saturday morning, at Adrian's suggestion, Joanna decided to walk to Holly's flat instead of taking the bus. The route took about forty minutes by foot and was for the most part downhill, which pleased Mikey enormously: he leaned back in his buggy and cried out with joy as if he were riding a luge down a steep slope of ice. Although it was one of a spell of beautiful August days, with more promised, to Joanna it felt like their last day in paradise – and she the only person who'd had word of her family's imminent expulsion.

'This has got to come to a head now,' Adrian had said, as if that were a good thing. 'It can't go on like this.' He agreed it was inevitable that Alexa would be back, the effects of her radioactivity delayed but not deterred; whether or not James remained long enough to manage the fallout was anyone's guess. 'If he doesn't, I will,' Adrian had also said.

When she answered the door, Holly looked more flustered than laid to waste, by which Joanna gathered that Alexa had not yet called. After hugging and kissing Mikey hello and paying due attention to the new water pistol he thrust at her, she said in an undertone, 'Sean is supposed to be coming in a little while. At least, he said he was.'

'Ah.' This, then, was the cause of her nerves. Faced with this unforeseen variable, Joanna wasn't sure now how to proceed. Then she reminded herself that Sean fell into exactly the same category as Alexa: people in her family's sphere who she could not expect to influence; she needed to put them both from her mind and concentrate on her own task, which was unpleasant enough. 'Well, I was hoping to talk to you on your own, but it can wait till another time.'

Of course it was silly to think even this little hint wouldn't hook Holly's curiosity. 'No, tell me now,' Holly said at once. 'There's time. What is it?'

Joanna suggested that James play with Mikey while she and Holly went into the garden to talk. He had the sensitivity to agree without question, inveigling Mikey with a known favourite activity: smashing plastic fruits extremely hard with a toy hammer. 'I'll give you a shout if you-know-who arrives,' he told Holly.

You-know-who: little did *he* know.

There was no furniture in the garden, so they settled on the grass in a corner of shade. Dense hedging filtered much of the traffic noise from beyond and the spot felt totally private, a safe harbour. She wondered, Will I remember where I was when I broke this news or will it pass into the void like so much else? Still she was not ready to judge the true weight of Dan's passing.

'You got back OK last night, then? What was the problem with the train?'

'Someone on the rails, apparently,' Holly said. 'We were allowed into the station eventually and I had to tear down here to work. Thank you again for saving my skin with the nursery. It would have been awful to be late on Mikey's first full day.'

Again, she did not volunteer anything of where she'd been yesterday or why Mikey should have needed to spend a whole day in nursery, unprecedented as far as Joanna was aware, and Joanna told herself it was none of her business. She had to get used to not being included in everything now: it was natural.

'So what's going on, Mum?' Holly looked at Joanna with such childlike expectancy that she fleetingly considered the option of permanent secrecy (or cowardice, whichever of the two it was).

'Oh, Holly, there's no easy way to say this, but I heard last night that your father has died.'

Holly did not flinch; untraceable emotions crossed her young brow and then vanished. As Joanna worried what the internal response might be, Holly surprised her by saying, 'I thought you were going to say something much worse than that,' and she even gave a small, apologetic smile.

And so I could, Joanna thought; I could tell her that Alexa has discovered the truth about Paris – or what she and her witness think is the truth – and that she is on her way here now to put her case to James, meaning to destroy at last what has come to appear indestructible.

'Well, it's fairly bad,' she said, gently. She told Holly the little she knew about Dan's end, the alcohol-related illness, the fact that it had happened several months ago, the lack of Walsh family representation at the funeral. Again, Holly showed less surprise, certainly less feeling, than she might have, but Joanna reminded herself that she had no basis for any alternative expectation: Dan Payne was a stranger to his daughter, their only meeting having been when Holly was a baby, far too young to have retained any memory of it. Had she even been *awake*? It was hard, now, to recall.

'How do *you* feel?' Holly asked.

The query caught Joanna unawares. The truth was she didn't actually know how she felt, but she wanted to say *something*, if only to keep the subject open and prevent its being closed for good. 'Well, it's very sad, of course. I'm sorry his life worked out that way because it's a terrible waste. He was only a few years older than me and that's too young to die for anyone.'

'How did you find out?'

473

Joanna recollected the moment her sister's voice had registered with her, the animal recognition that was a perception like no other, the frightening way it had released memories secured previously out of range. 'Melissa phoned me.'

Now Holly gaped. 'Melissa, your *sister*? God, I didn't think . . .' The words fell away; this time, the dumbfounded response was no less than Joanna would have expected.

'I know. And she also said she wants to end the vendetta and see us.'

'Wow.'

'Yes, wow.' Joanna paused, trying to read the emotion behind Holly's half-smile. 'Would you like to get to know her, do you think?'

On this question Holly was able or willing to be more forthcoming. 'It would be nice to be closer to our family, for Mikey's sake, and not just your side, the other side as well. But I think we'd have to find out if Melissa's really willing to put the past behind her, don't you think? Maybe you can talk to her again, find out her take on everything that's happened? Then, if you're happy, perhaps we can meet her together.'

It was an exhausting prospect – a whole other side to the story when it was all she could do to keep pace with their own. 'I think we'll discover that it all just got a bit out of hand,' Joanna said, but it was a preposterous understatement that needed redressing with some genuine candour. 'I don't know what to make of it myself, not yet, it's all so totally out of the blue it doesn't feel real: Dan's death, her making contact again . . .' It struck her only then that Melissa had made the phone call herself precisely so that the last part of Dan's life – his death – would be inextricably bound to her offer of reconciliation. She'd allowed Joanna not a single minute to absorb the news of his death in its own right. 'They're two separate things,' she told Holly, firmly, 'and I'm going to think about them separately. There's no hurry. Maybe we'll decide to meet

474

Melissa, maybe not. But if you and I end up feeling differently, then I'll understand. I'll still support you whatever you want to do.'

'And me you,' Holly said. She hesitated. 'What does Adrian think?'

Given that this was breaking news, it was something of an assumption that Adrian had been told before she, Holly, had, but Holly didn't seem to mind.

'I saw him last night. I haven't told him about the Melissa part yet.' In the end, having shared the news of Dan's death, Joanna had cried herself to sleep, not hearing Adrian's response until the morning, in the precious dawn minutes before Mikey awoke and resumed his command. 'He thinks Dan dying might turn out to be a good thing for us all, in the long run. It's a "you-never-know" that we finally *do* know, it's a loose end tied up.'

Another absurd understatement and not the words Adrian had actually used: imagine having your tragically premature death described as a loose end! Joanna sighed, possibly her heaviest, most heartfelt sigh of recent weeks. 'I'm sorry it's been this way, Holly. It's not how I would have planned to be a parent to you.'

Holly's face became animated with protest. 'Don't say that! I think you're a wonderful parent – I've never heard of a better one in my whole life. I don't deserve half of what you've done for me and Mikey.'

'You don't need to "deserve" it.' Joanna smiled. 'That's not how it works. You get it because there's nothing I'd rather do.'

Holding her daughter's gaze, she saw that Holly understood. The word they used for family love was always 'unconditional', but Joanna just called it boundless: the supply never ran out, no matter what happened – no matter what anyone else said had happened.

'You didn't get it from *your* mum, though,' Holly said, sorrowfully. 'Maybe in the future, maybe I can give it instead?'

Joanna thought of her mother, of the years of grudging contact that had left her so anxious to play life safe, to depend on so few others. Would that change, if she and Melissa were reconciled, or was it too late? 'We'll work something out,' she said.

A peaceful expression settled on Holly's face, the sense that the storm cloud had safely passed. If Alexa could just not come today, Joanna thought, then they could begin the process of coming to terms with this in their own time. One day of mourning, that was all she asked. But Alexa would come, she knew that; her own mourning was so dark and acute that it obscured all others, whether she knew of them or not.

'What time is Sean due?' she asked Holly. It did not take a family mediation specialist to see that his witnessing Alexa's explosive new accusations would be extremely undesirable. Naturally, he'd want to go home and pass it straight on to Geraldine: would they then try to take Mikey away from Holly, from her? Sean might be hopeless, but his mother was not.

Holly pulled a face that Joanna recognised as her own former 'Sean' face. 'I said twelve, but I don't suppose he'll be on time. We decided not to mention it to Mikey in case he doesn't turn up.'

'He hasn't met James before, has he?'

'No. It's a big day all round.' Holly rubbed her eyes in the same way Mikey did, which reminded Joanna that her daughter had been at work till late last night, on her feet for at least five hours, and had probably not had much sleep. 'I'll tell James about my father later, when everyone's gone.'

In a small, inscrutable way it pleased Joanna that she'd said 'my father' rather than 'Dan'. 'That's a good idea: one thing at a time. And phone me later if you want to talk about it, all right? Or about anything else – I'll be in all day.'

'With Adrian?' Holly asked, not without a certain mischievous excitement.

Joanna smiled. 'He has to work till four, but he'll be over later.'

They'd been back inside just long enough to pour cups of the coffee James had made when the doorbell rang. It was a single short buzz, not the sound of maniacal revenge, which meant it had to be Sean, in the event arriving early. A new leaf, indeed.

Holly picked up the intercom. 'It's Alexa,' she told James, frowning over her shoulder as she pressed the door release.

'What's she doing here?' James said with irritation.

Joanna's stomach heaved. I should have warned them, she thought. Why on earth hadn't she? It was because she had allowed the last of her hope to paralyse her, the last of her faith in that original affirmative impression of Alexa, thereby squandering the only opportunity they had had to prepare Holly's defence. Then she changed her mind and thought: James will understand; if he believes Alexa at all, he'll understand that the complications of the crime came very close to excusing it.

Oh, she didn't know *what* to think.

Alexa entered the living room bearing a large board or picture of some sort packaged in bubble wrap. She wore smeared jeans, a loose-fitting white top and flip-flops; her face, bare of make-up and cruelly lined with the strain of the last few months, was nonetheless impassive. Considering she had not been in the flat before, she showed curiously little interest in its interior, hardly glancing about her as she bypassed Holly and advanced towards the others.

'You're here?' she said to Joanna, not unpleasantly.

'Yes, I'm just dropping Mikey back. How are you? Did you sleep well?'

'Not really. I got up early.' Her tone imparted even less than her expression, which somehow made her seem more dangerous than ever. She nodded towards the picture, which rested now at her foot. 'I wanted to go back home to pick this up.'

As Joanna wondered where she'd gone back *from*, James and Holly exchanged a significant look: no doubt they'd had discussions about how they might best retrieve some of James's possessions from the marital home. Please don't ask her now, Joanna thought, don't provoke her and make this worse than it is already going to be. Still her instinct vacillated wildly: maybe it's better that she *does* tell him, she thought next; maybe it's better than having this hanging over us for the rest of our lives.

On cue, Alexa said to James, 'Can I have a word with you alone?'

James, plainly finding this surprise visit objectionable, needed a prompting gesture from Holly before he repaired his face to something more accommodating and said, 'Of course. Come into the kitchen and I'll get you a coffee.'

'Thank you.' Alexa picked up the picture and followed.

It would be only a matter of moments, Joanna thought, before they heard James's raised voice – in disbelief? Anger? Confusion? – and of Alexa's emphatic insistence that it *was* true, Holly *was* a murderess, or at least a creature of violent and unpredictable urges, to be avoided as one might a shark or a bear. In the meantime, Holly, alert to local danger but utterly oblivious to the cataclysmic kind that awaited her, played with Mikey's toy picnic set, getting him to cut the plastic cake into slices and offer a piece to Grandma.

'Thank you, Mikey, I'd love some,' Joanna said, falsely cheerful. 'Could I have the yellow plate, please?'

'Yellow mine,' Mikey said.

'All right, the blue one then.'

'Blue mine.' He thrust the pink one at her, the cake sliding into her lap.

'"Mine" is his favourite word, have you noticed?' Holly said, giggling. She spoke to Mikey: 'But when you have your second birthday party next week, maybe you'll learn "yours", eh?'

'Mine,' he repeated.

I have to say something, Joanna thought, I have to warn her somehow, but when she opened her mouth an unplanned sentiment emerged in its place: 'I'm really proud of you,' she said.

Holly's delighted smile blazed from cheek to cheek. 'Really?'

'Yes. Whatever happens after this, well, you've become a wonderful mother to Mikey and that's an achievement you should be really proud of.'

Doubt darkened Holly's eyes. 'I worry he remembers how I was before,' she whispered, 'when I wasn't so good.'

There was a tense silence as Joanna considered the words Alexa might be simultaneously speaking just feet away.

'I was so bad,' she added. 'Shouting at him, never taking him to the park or anything . . .'

'Oh, he won't remember any of that. He was too young. Besides, he had me.'

Holly nodded. 'He still does have you, doesn't he?'

'Of course he does.'

Far, far too soon, they could hear James saying goodbye to Alexa, wordlessly leading her past them to the front door. It was something, Joanna thought, that she did not stop to accuse Holly personally or to cast one of her bitter – and in this case victorious – insults in her direction. As for what had passed between husband and wife, either James had believed her straight away, for there had been no sounds of dispute or protest, or he'd refused to entertain the report at all, suspecting Alexa of manipulation and revenge.

He came to stand in front of them, his expression ambiguous. Holly looked up at him, innocent, enquiring. This is it, Joanna thought, this is the end of James and Holly. I'll take Mikey and her straight home with me. I'll ask Adrian if anyone at his work knows of a lawyer who might be able to advise. She prayed Holly had stockpiled enough strength to get her through the loss, because Joanna honestly wasn't sure she had enough for two. She willed James not to say anything damaging in front of Mikey.

'That was weird,' he said, his expression settling into one of simple bemusement and nothing like the commotion of violent emotions Joanna had anticipated.

'What did she want?' Holly asked.

'She said she was starting to sort out the house and she wanted to give me something before it got packed away . . .' He scooted into the kitchen, returning with the bubble-wrapped picture. 'It was her anniversary present to me in Paris.'

'That's all she said?' Joanna asked. Her disbelief was such that she had to conceal her face, burying it in Mikey's neck. He wriggled away, disobliging.

'I said she should keep it, but she said she wanted me to have it.' James gazed at Holly in confusion. 'It seemed to be very important to her.'

'Does she mean it like the other stuff? To remind you why you were in Paris, that you were happy together?'

Joanna did not know what 'other stuff' Holly meant. If she hadn't seen Alexa herself last night she might have guessed the picture was a framed cutting of the newspaper interview, but knowing that Alexa now had far deadlier ammunition than that, none of this made the slightest sense.

James seemed to be having similar trouble comprehending. 'No, I don't think so. It was completely unbelievable, Holls, she said to me: "You were the one who had the courage to jump, not me. I wish you hadn't, I wish you hadn't with all my heart, but you did."' At the sight of his girlfriend's bewildered expression, he explained, 'The picture's of someone diving into the water. She bought it for me after the accident, a kind of memento.'

'So it *is* like the photos,' Holly said.

'No, I don't think so. Because then she said she wouldn't cause us any trouble from now on or even phone me again if I didn't want her to, and that was a promise. She said she'll ask her solicitor to move forward with the divorce as quickly and amicably as possible.'

'Wow,' Holly said, for the second time that morning, and Joanna could think of no better word in either context. 'That's *very* different from last time.'

'I know. She really seems to be coming to terms with things.' James lowered himself into an armchair, still gripping the picture. 'I *never* expected this. I don't know if I would even have trusted what she was saying if it weren't for the fact that she looked so totally sincere, and I know she's a terrible actress.'

Joanna had recovered enough by now to be able to take a reasonable guess at his thoughts: this act of dignity on Alexa's part, a far, far greater one than either he or Holly could know, had impressed him deeply; it had reminded him perhaps of Alexa's finer qualities, the qualities that had made him fall in love with her and marry her. One of the saddest things about relationships was how easy it was to let those qualities slip from the present and into the past; in doing so, you ignored your own judgement and experience, you insulted your own intelligence. What James was remembering now was that ten years with someone was not nothing simply because it had ended: it was still something and always would be.

'Well,' she said, smiling at them both. 'I think Alexa's a bit of a hero, don't you? Let's have a proper look at the picture, James. It's a photograph, is it?'

'Yes, an old one from the forties.' James pulled off the packaging, popping a few of the bubbles for Mikey's amusement, and they all sat for a few moments assessing the composition of a young man diving from a bridge into the River Seine.

'Man fly,' Mikey said in an awed voice.

'Kind of.' Holly laughed. 'It's called diving, but it's *like* flying. I think it's really nice, James.'

'I like it as well,' Joanna agreed.

'In that case, we'll hang it somewhere here,' James said. 'We haven't got much on the walls yet.'

As they idly debated possible spots for it, all three speculating privately on Alexa's extraordinary, unforeseen actions, the doorbell rang once more. Holly looked first at James and then at Joanna. 'That will be Sean. Are we all set?'

'I think so.' James straightened himself in that deft way he had of summoning readiness irrespective of what was set before him (and of what he'd just left behind). He smiled at Holly. 'You?'

'Yes, I'm set.'

'Daddy!' At the mention of Sean's name, Mikey had staggered to his feet and made a break for the door.

'I'll let him in on my way out,' Joanna said, slipping her bag over her shoulder and kissing Holly and James goodbye. She captured Mikey by the window, laughing as his hot little body squirmed in her arms. 'Want to open the door, Mikey? Be the first one to say hello?'

And she carried him into the hallway to greet his father.

Reading Group Questions

1. Discuss the relevance of the title in relation to the events of the novel. Who do you think is truly 'saved' by James's actions in Paris?

2. What is your opinion of Alexa? Do you sympathise with her?

3. Discuss the contrasting parental relationships in the novel and what impact these have on the characters' lives.

4. What are your thoughts on Holly and James's relationship?

5. Which character changes the most during the course of the novel?

6. What have you taken away from the story? Has it made you think differently about the relationships in your own life?

7. James is believed by some of the other characters to have a 'hero complex'. Is this something he will grow out of or is it to be a lifelong condition?

8. Joanna is keen to avoid thoughts of self-sacrifice, but which is the most powerful motivation for her life choices: the well-being of her daughter or her own need for atonement?

9. Do you like Holly? Is she a loving mother and a dutiful daughter?

10. Is the story too bittersweet to be considered 'romantic'?

The author on *The Day You Saved My Life*

What was your inspiration for the book?

I remember the exact moment I thought of the idea. I was in the Italian Lakes doing some research for *Other People's Secrets* and crossing Lake Como on a ferry, when someone said that we had reached the deepest part of the water. I immediately thought, well, you wouldn't want to fall in now (I'm a terrible catastrophist and this is how my mind works day to day. I'm great to travel with.). Then I had a vision of a small child falling overboard and how it would feel to experience those horrible frozen moments while people worked out what to do. I pictured the child being rescued by a stranger, not a member of the crew, a tourist who afterwards finds himself embroiled in the family's life.

By the time I came to start the book, a year or so later, I had moved the action to Paris and the Seine, but my working title for quite a while was *The Deepest Part* because I was remembering Como. The next title was *The Homebreaker*, which refers to the character of Holly Walsh. But she's quite a sweet, gentle girl and it didn't feel right for her, as if you'd expect her to be some sort of 'Fatal Attraction' psycho. The final title was ─ched quite late in the process and I'm very pleased with it.

─ it a difficult book to write?

It wasn't one of my easiest, I have to say, partly because I had a health scare in the middle of it and had to take a couple of months off. But in the end I think the break helped, because I don't usually have the luxury of time away from a story. You can go back to it a lot clearer-eyed about its flaws.

It's my longest book to date and there are three narrators, each quite a complicated woman, and so it took a bit of effort to get the balance right in terms of tone. Structurally, it was quite hard for me, but the characters and their journeys came more easily.

Which character did you most enjoy writing?

Joanna is the heart and soul of the story and I enjoyed writing her chapters, because I felt warm and compassionate towards her, which is quite a nice mood to be in as you sit for hours alone at your desk. Alexa was fun to write because she is a darker, vainer character, and I looked forward to writing her scenes in a way I didn't so much with the others. Readers who don't like Alexa should congratulate themselves, because it means they must be very nice people. But I love her, because I'm maybe not so nice.

Are you at all like your characters?

Novelists are often asked this question and many deny any personal resemblance to their characters (fair enough, if you're writing about brutal killers!). However, there is a lot of me in my characters and it would be ridiculous to deny it. Obviously, in this case, I can't be exactly like my three narrators, who are quite different from one another, but there are elements of me in each of them, elements I've exaggerated or explored more deeply. So it's quite self-indulgent, really. That's part of what makes wr fiction addictive; it's very like acting in that respect, you get t cover things about yourself through your work.

The bud of each of my books has been the dilemma or crisis or even the setting; the characters get my attention only after that.

That's when I'll ask myself, how would it feel if this happened to me? My characters often feel helpless in a crisis, taking a bit of time to get their act together and that's very much how I operate in real life. I'm very English. It would be a leap for me to write a blazing-eyed, self-possessed, all-conquering adventurous, someone who's never had a moment's anxiety in her life.

What genre does this book belong to?

Like my other recent stories, it's a contemporary emotional drama. But writers don't think so much in terms of genre as the other people in the book trade do. I think of *The Day You Saved My Life* as just a story, really; an interesting one, I hope.

OTHER PEOPLE'S SECRETS

Ginny and Adam Trustlove arrive on holiday in Italy torn apart
by personal tragedy. Two weeks in a boathouse on the edge
of peaceful Lake Orta is exactly what they need
to restore their faith in life – and each other.

Twenty-four hours later, the silence is broken. The Sale family
have arrived at the main villa: wealthy, high-flying Marty, his
beautiful wife Bea, and their privileged, confident offspring.
It doesn't take long for Ginny and Adam to be drawn in, especially
when the teenage Pippi introduces a new friend into the circle.
For there is something about Zach that has everyone instantly
beguiled, something that loosens old secrets –
and creates shocking new ones.

978-0-7515-4354-4